Also by Kate St.Clair

Spelled
Cursed

ShiFt

THE
PTOLEMY
PROJECT

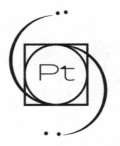

KATE ST.CLAIR

GREENLEAF
BOOK GROUP PRESS

Published by Greenleaf Book Group Press
Austin, Texas
www.gbgpress.com

Distributed by Greenleaf Book Group

For ordering information or special discounts for bulk purchases, please contact Greenleaf Book Group at PO Box 91869, Austin, TX 78709, 512.891.6100.

Design and composition by Kate St. Clair
Cover design by Kate St. Clair
Editing by Wyrd Sisters Editing
www.wyrdsistersediting.com

Publisher's Cataloging-in-Publication data is available.

Print ISBN: 978-1-62634-997-1

eBook ISBN: 978-1-62634-998-8

Part of the Tree Neutral® program, which offsets the number of trees consumed in the production and printing of this book by taking proactive steps, such as planting trees in direct proportion to the number of trees used: www.treeneutral.com

Printed in the United States of America on acid-free paper

22 23 24 25 26 27   10 9 8 7 6 5 4 3 2 1

First Edition

For my sisters.
You keep me Sane and Alive.

"IF A SOUL IS LEFT IN THE DARKNESS,
SINS WILL BE COMMITTED. THE GUILTY
ONE IS NOT HE WHO COMMITS THE SIN,
BUT HE WHO CAUSES THE DARKNESS."

—VICTOR HUGO

LYRA: 1

S omeone is sleeping on her feet.

The pressure is the first thing Lyra's muddled mind slots into place, pulling from a clouded memory of a time it had happened to her before. When a small child had been curled up like a dog at the foot of her bed, pressing her feet into the lumpy gray mattress beneath.

Hoping to displace the pressure, she jerks a knee up toward her stomach and feels the body roll off to the side, freeing one foot. Consciousness hits her all at once, the soft black of sleep dropping out from under her in an instant. She sits up, her elbow popping in protest from being put into motion so quickly.

There is no mattress, only grass beneath her, sharp and cold against her palms. A man lays in a heap on the ground in front of her—a boy, she amends after a second look at his face. His body is wound up in a circle, long legs folded into his chest, and once again the image of her sleeping sister blinks through her mind for an instant before it evaporates.

A sharp kick brings a grunt out of the body, and it starts to unfurl like a flower opening up. The boy squints at her, or maybe it's a scowl. The top half of his face is obscured by dark brown curls that creep down from his scalp. The way they seem to catch every wisp of breeze in the air...they could almost be alive. Snakes in disguise, shielding their master.

"Ouch," he says, accusing her with a glare. His voice is still hazy and rough from being pulled so unceremoniously out of sleep.

"Get off!" she shoots back, barely short of yelling.

The boy takes an age, but slowly he pushes himself up onto his knees and sits back on his heels. He's a lot longer in the torso than he had looked curled up, and fear begins to tingle in her stomach. Lyra scrambles to her feet, hoping the advantage will make her feel a little better, but even at full height she's not that much taller than him sitting.

The boy squints at her, looking somewhere around her elbow, and she crosses her arms against his gaze. As she does it, her right wrist hits her bicep, bulky and unfamiliar.

Someone's put a mobile device cuff on her. It's ugly, blocky and black with a rounded screen like a bulbous eye. Nothing like the slim, gold-faceted cuffs the kids from the wealthier neighborhoods always sported.

"Lyra."

Uneasy hearing her name spoken by a stranger, she looks up.

"Is that your name?" the boy pushes, pointing at her chest.

She uncrosses her arms, the new bracelet scraping against her left forearm and sending a twinge of pain through it. The skin there is warm and reactive, like a healing scab still tender to the air, and she twists to examine it.

Bold, black letters are etched into her forearm.

2

⊚ LYRA F63.1 C

They're so clear and fresh they could have been stamped there, but when she touches them the skin seizes with a dull pain. This has been carved into her, *Tattoos*, her mind reminds her.

"Yeah, that's my name," she says, tracing the letters as her stomach drops. Her mother is going to have a few things to say when she sees that.

The boy scoffs as if annoyed it took her so long to confirm it. He gets to his feet, his legs unraveling underneath him, and looks at his own arm.

"Pollux," he says, and for a moment Lyra thinks he's cursing at her and starts to bristle. "That's me," he adds, meeting her eye.

He blinks, as if seeing her clearly for the first time. "You're very short."

Now bristling properly, Lyra's fingers curl into her palms. She turns sharply, her body itching to put space between herself and the lanky giant, but as soon as she does the world opens up around her and her legs lock.

Underneath them is a lawn of cropped-short grass, spreading out to a tree line that blurs in her vision. They seem to be in a flat clearing; the only buildings are far enough away that they look like smudged white boxes rising over the thick tree tops. If she were any good at guessing distances, she'd say a quarter mile, but fear of being wrong keeps her from stating it aloud.

Lyra looks down at the ground beneath her feet, noticing the white lines painted across the grass. An image of bulky, uniformed kids slamming into each other flits across her mind and the memory of football crystalizes. They're on a football field.

But her memory has bright, near-blinding stadium lights ringing the field, and they are almost completely in the dark. The stands and light poles around them are vacant and lifeless. The only glow comes from the buildings beyond the tree line, which would explain why the night is so dense around them.

"Where are we?" she says aloud, pivoting to scan the space. She tries to make out the closest rooftops, but her vision bleeds everything together into a blurry, watercolor image.

Just the eyesight of an inbred, she thinks sourly to herself, then shakes her head. Wherever the sentiment came from, it doesn't feel like her words.

The memory of her high school floods in, images sloshing against each other. They weren't her words: they were what Homer Oleyedo had said to her when they took their physical evaluations. She'd stood there with one hand over her eye and tried to read the numbers holographed against the far wall while Homer and his group of idiots snickered at her and made jokes about her huge family.

She rounds on the giant, expecting to recognize him now. But his face is still strange, unplaceable.

"Pollux," she echoes, trying not to let herself get distracted by a wayward curl hugging the edge of his eye. "Do you go to C7?"

He stares at her blankly, and she notices for the first time how flat and dark his eyes are. There seems to be no spark behind them, no light of personality.

Eventually he shrugs. "C7?"

"C7 High School? City of Seven Hills?" she presses, willing him to make the connection.

"I don't go to public school," he answers curtly.

"Oh." Lyra deflates, her chin lowering.

She finally catches sight of the clothes she's wearing, charcoal leggings and a coarse gray tee, nothing that came from her closet. Pollux is the mirror image, though his shirt is looser and he has shorts in place of leggings. Both have the letters "Pt" stamped over their hearts, like an unfinished word.

"Why are we dressed the same?"

"Dressed the same, same watches, same tattoos," Pollux pieces together aloud, glancing again at his own name etched into the skin of his forearm. "What are your numbers?"

"F63.1 C," Lyra reads off.

"C is not a number," Pollux quips, tweaking a nerve of annoyance in Lyra's neck. "But mine also says C. F60.2 C. Must be a grouping."

"Of what?"

"Just because I look smart doesn't mean I have every answer," he says, stalking past her toward the edge of the field.

Lyra has to fight the urge to kick him when he passes. She's starting to think they must be part of some kind of prank, since he seems exactly like the kind of person that would be picked to prey upon.

"Well, *forgive me*," Lyra drawls, hearing her mother speaking through her for a moment.

She debates letting him walk off alone, but something about the dark around them unnerves her. It doesn't feel as empty as it should, like someone could be watching them. And if it is Homer she'd rather face him in the company of someone else.

She jogs after Pollux, her shoes strangely tight and stiff on her feet as if they haven't been worn before.

"If we're in the same group, shouldn't we stay together?" she calls as she nears him, hoping it might slow him down.

"I doubt it matters," Pollux answers without looking back at her. "We'll run into each other again eventually."

Lyra blows her hair out of her face, feeling grown-out bangs ticking her lips.

"What makes you so sure?" she grumbles under her breath, positive in the knowledge that once this night is over she will never have to deal with this rude kid again.

Pollux thankfully stops, looking over his shoulder at her with those cold, dull eyes.

"Did you not notice that?" he raises one finger, pointing upward at the sky.

She grudgingly looks up, still waiting for the prank to drop.

All the tension falls out of her muscles and she sways on the spot, afraid for a moment that she might tip over backward. Where there should be space and stars and floating celestials, there is only cold, lifeless metal looking back at her. The sky is a matte gray, convex ceiling too high for her mind to measure. She follows the curve of the walls, noticing how they slope down to form a great bowl around them.

"We're . . .we're in a . . ." Her mind can't filter a single word to name the structure. It's like somehow the world has been shaped into a sphere around them, trapping them inside. Even as expansive as it is, the space closes in around her, stealing the breath from her lungs. She gulps a few times, trying to slow her racing heart.

"I can't tell if that's a window or a screen," Pollux points, almost breezily, and she finally notices the circle of black skylight miles above their heads. "If it's a window, then that's Saturn right there. We're in some kind of space station."

He starts off walking again, and Lyra takes a few wobbling steps after him, sure that at any moment her legs are going to give out from under her.

Cage, she finally lands on, trying to keep one foot following the other. Cage had been the word she was looking for.

AQUILA: 2

W ell, that does it. She has a migraine.
With a crash, the blonde boy tips over the acrylic table in
the room, either looking for something or just to feel powerful, and
walks in a circle around it. Aquila tries not to roll her eyes at how
hard he's trying to not look frightened. It's written in the slackness
of his face, in the bow of his red lips. Aquila had never liked blondes,
but now she knows she's justified in thinking there was something
evil lurking beneath anything that golden.

She casts a wide glance around the room, hoping any recognizable detail will snag in the net of her memory. As rehabilitation
centers go, this is one of the nicest she's been in. The room has the
stark, vacant feel of a place that's had any remnant of the last inhab-
itant scrubbed and sanitized out of it.

Next step on her checklist is examining her body for any damage. She stretches her legs out on the floor, wondering why whoever
brought her and her new roommate in couldn't be bothered to put
them *on* the beds.

She rubs her tense jaw, feeling tiny bumps just beneath her skin.

Not clean shaven, but not too long since the last time. She's so used to telling exactly how much time in between shaves she has before people start to notice that she can almost pinpoint how many hours it's been since her last one. It's the only thing that's kept her from lasering it away. Coming back into her own mind, it's useful to have some way to anchor herself in time immediately.

Her hand drops, slack with relief that it's only been a day she's lost. If only her skin could tell the story of what the last twenty-four hours had held.

There's a clash from the other room, and Aquila forces herself to stand up before the blonde boy breaks everything in the house. When she gets to the doorway, his cheeks are pink and his breath makes tiny whistles in and out of his nose. He looks up from the pile of cushions and the clear acrylic coffee table he's just thrown into the center of the room.

"Is this your house?" he demands.

His eyes are ringed with dark kohl lashes, and for a moment Aquila wonders if he's wearing eyeliner. But it looks more like the markings around a swan's eyes, black bands that are meant to intimidate rather than entice.

"If it were, do you think I'd let you keep breaking things?" she says, tugging on the new black monitor cuff on her wrist. No chance of slipping that over her unapologetically wide hands.

Confusion quirks his brow at hearing her voice, but he doesn't say anything yet. She's used to it taking a while for someone to catch on, if they ever do.

"Nothing in here breaks," the blonde boy says, picking up the coffee table and throwing it over the counter.

The sound of it batters Aquila's ears, and she winces. It's so quiet that drawing attention to themselves seems like a bad idea somehow.

The boy relaxes, satisfied with the mess he's made.

"I'm Cygnus, by the way" he says, bracing his hands on his hips.

Aquila can see the curve of his muscled stomach underneath the fabric of his shirt and hates herself a bit for looking.

She responds with the first name that floats into her mind. "Agatha."

Cygnus cocks his head, pointing to the arm hanging by her side. "Really? That's not what your tattoo says. Mine says my name."

He lifts his arm, flashing her a dark bar of lettering printed across the skin of his forearm. It does say Cygnus, and Aquila presses her own arm against her stomach, hoping he won't push her on it.

Cygnus strides across the room, his fingers wrapping around her wrist and pulling her arm straight. Something about the way he holds her, his dry skin hot against her own, makes Aquila want to twist until his grip breaks.

"Aquila," he reads, his black-lined eyes casting over her accusingly. "Did you just lie?"

"Nice to be accused first thing in the morning," she says, pulling her arm into her chest when he drops it.

"Well, whatever, I guess. Do you know where we are? I must have blacked out."

He thinks we're at a party, she realizes, pressing her lips together to hold in a smile. All the times her father had forced her into rehab when the alter got out of control, it had started the same way. Waking up in a cold, sterile room, no memory of the previous days, already dressed in clothes she didn't recognize with a monitoring device strapped to her wrist. At least this time the hangover is blessedly absent.

In a way, she looks forward to this raging CisHet finally realizing they're trapped in rehab. He certainly seems like the kind of guy who would have problems controlling himself.

"It's still dark," Aquila says evenly, hoping she can get him to at least stop the noise. "We should probably just find our rooms and go to sleep until morning."

"Nah, I need to get home. My parents get mad when I stay out all night."

Cygnus pushes past her, reaching the sliding glass door and yanking the handle. To Aquila's surprise, it opens. Most places keep you on lockdown during the night, in fear of someone escaping or hurting themselves. From the way the door smoothly rolls back, no hitches or bumps on the track made by desperate people behaving sloppily, this facility must be brand new.

Once Cygnus is outside, Aquila takes a steadying breath. She raises her arm, examining the temporary tattoo they've put on her. The edges are so clean and neat, the ink slightly shiny, and she can't resist running her fingertips across it. A flare of pain rises after her touch, and she draws her hand back. That had felt real.

She brings her arm closer to her eyes, squinting in the half-light. The ink she'd thought lay on top of her skin is most definitely beneath it.

A real tattoo, with her real name, for all the world to see. Aquila grinds her teeth, her chin poking forward in anger. How dare they put a *real* tattoo on her? Had her father agreed to this? She remembers how hard he'd fought her when she wanted to get a tiny rainbow behind her ear, where no one could even *see* it.

Rage fueling her steps, she hops over a wayward couch cushion and threads through the open doorway. Cygnus is nowhere to be found, but outside the air is still and undisturbed. It's a very calm night for The Rocks. She can't remember the last time she stepped outside and wasn't met by the harsh wet wind off the water.

There's a row of identical white houses across from her, but their windows are empty. Were they the only patients? It seemed hard to believe, especially in a place that was clearly so upscale. Her shoes squeak against the ground beneath her, and she glances down to see a pristine recycled-plastic tread in place of a street. Obviously only feet are meant to travel in this area, not vehicles.

She walks a few strides, feeling the tread absorb and rebound her energy back into the soles of her feet. It gives her a bounce in her step and a swing in her ponytail that she enjoys for the length of the street. The dark around them seems less heavy than before, and her eyes make out light tubes traveling the edges of the buildings and ground. They're giving off a rosy-toned glow, simulating dawn and the start of a new lighting cycle, which at least means sleeping hours are coming to a close. Though, come to think of it, she hasn't seen light tubes since the Eagle convoys. The thought makes an ache of homesickness clench her stomach, and she reminds herself that the convoy ships haven't been her home for years now.

The road cuts off at a grassy flat, maybe the border of a park, and Cygnus is standing with his back to her in the middle of it.

Aquila takes a few tentative steps toward him, pulled between abandoning him for a few more scraps of sleep and wanting to be the sage rehab mentor who helps him see the error in his ways. When she nears him, she notices the tensed muscles between his shoulders, his head arched back as he looks up at the sky. He seems to be caught in some kind of fit, his breath shaky and unstable, and Aquila moves to touch him before thinking better of it.

Instead, she glances up to see what he might be looking at.

Grass presses into her leggings before she can even process that she's collapsed. The ground seems to be moving just slightly, and her head swims with the same motion as if she's on a convoy again. No wonder it had felt so familiar. Wherever they are, it has the same synthetic lighting and artificial gravity as her beloved Eagle.

Breath fights its way back into her lungs and she realizes how close she had been to fainting. Realization begins to seep into her mind like icy fingers, shocking everything it touches.

They are not in The Rocks. They are not in her city. They are not even on her planet.

ZEKE: 3

He might strangle this girl. He really might do it.

Zeke sucks in his lower lip, trying to keep from interrupting the girl's incessant stream of chatter. In the short time since they'd woken up on the edge of the man-made lake, he'd come to find that trying to break her out of her speech cycle was somehow worse. She seemed to think engaging meant he was actually interested in what she was saying.

While the prattle continues, he takes small sips of breath through his nose, noticing that the processed air inside the structure is somehow softer than on Titan. They must have some kind of conditioning system along with the plants that cover every spare inch of the ground. The air on Titan is still laced with a dry, phosphorescent smell leftover from pre-settlement, only escapable by going inside. But this place is *all* inside.

Best of both worlds, the rumbling voice says, rising above the whispering in his head. It's lucky this is the only voice that's come out since they woke up. The raspy one is much harder to ignore around strangers.

Zeke stoops to test the water in the lake with his fingers. It's cold but not freezing, and slightly slippery with some kind of softener.

You know what else is slippery, the raspy voice guffaws, and annoyance floods Zeke's chest.

"Goddamit," he lets slip, and the blonde girl, Cass (Ew, Cassiopeia is way too long, just call me Cass) halts her monologue.

"What's wrong?" she asks, sitting up in the grass.

Nothing's wrong, other than I'd like to get two handfuls of that backside, the raspy voice goes on, and Zeke forces himself to focus on the splinters of white coming from the light tubes overhead until it fades out. It was those splinters that had told him immediately he was off his meds. His eyes were always the first thing to start unraveling. They took in too much information, ranking everything as equally important and overloading the processing function of his brain. Light became almost unbearable to look at, and every sound was like a speaker in his ear. The humming of anything electric around him translated to a constant whisper in the back of his head, and then the voices started to come out. He'd been through this scenario so many times.

The focus of his eyes shifts, honing in on dark letters stamped across the looming ceiling that arches over them.

CARCER STATION.

Great. At least he'll know the name of the company making auto-drafts out of his bank account for the rest of his life.

"Gawd," the blonde girl says, rubbing the tattoo on her forearm. Everything she says is made worse by the affected accent she's taken on, like she's trying to speak with a marble rolling around in her mouth. The streaming stars his sister used to watch all sounded the same, but it's somehow worse in person.

"This thing better be temporary. Black is the worst color."

Her eyes snap open wide, landing guiltily on Zeke. "Ohmigawd, sorry, I did not mean it that way,"

He lets his lips tug into a smirk at the genuine horror on her soft face. He could let her suffer a little longer just because the stunned silence is better than the constant chatter, but he diffuses her.

"I didn't think you did."

"Good. I'm probably the least racist person I know. People always feel really comfortable around me because I'm so open and accepting. That's just how I've always been."

Jesus, Zeke groans internally, straightening to stand. He grips the hem of the gray shirt he'd been dressed in and starts to tug it over his head. If Cass doesn't like black tattoos, she's about to see way more of them.

The shirt snags on a band around his wrist, and he pauses to examine the mobile device cuff they've attached to him. It's brand new, certainly nothing he could have afforded on his own.

"What are you doing?" Cass calls from the bank.

Zeke checks to make sure they'd given him underwear before tugging off his shorts. The shoes he loses a little more regretfully than the rest. It's been a while since he felt brand-new sock-lining on his feet. Most of the clothes they got were recycles, and that silky, featherweight fabric just couldn't hold up to chemical sanitation.

"I'm getting in," he says, dropping everything into a pile behind him. "I want to see what's at the bottom."

"Oh cool," Cass says, sitting back on her ample backside to pick at her bracelet monitor. "I'll pass. I super don't wanna get wet."

Zeke scoffs, wondering how hard she'd fight if he threw her in first. He turns, dipping one foot into the water. When no bottom meets him, he steadies himself on the edge and takes a shallow dive through the silvery surface.

Instantly, his body sings with happiness at being engulfed in the familiar, comforting weight of water. The constant hum in his head is cut off, and no voices push through the muffled sound of liquid in his ears.

Flashes of water—not this water, but Kraken Mare—jostle in his mind. He misses the waves lifting and dropping his body as they pass, the slight burn across his skin from the leftover ethylene. When was the last time he had swam at home? His mind tries to grip a date, a solid time, but nothing sticks. It's been long enough that he can feel homesick for it, at least.

Zeke forces his eyes open, expecting the prick of pain that usually comes from Kraken Mare's water. But this water is just cool, heavy.

Immediately, Zeke spots the huge silver-blue bodies of fish beneath him. They weave together in slow motion, grazing each other in passing before drifting off in opposite directions. They must be eighty pounds each, almost matching him in length tip-to-tail. They remind him of the tarpon his Mama Beck used to pull out of Kraken Mare, the ones they had to throw back so the species wouldn't grow too sparse. But these are massive, almost too large to move quickly. They're plump from overfeeding and nothing to chase them.

The lake bowl seems to be made of smooth, sloping metal that reaches all the way to the bottom where it disappears under rippled sand.

Zeke pops back up for a breath, spotting movement on the shoreline, but dives again before the voices can start in. He kicks his way over to one of the sides, reaching out to brace his fingers against the slick metal to stop his motion. He lets himself sink a bit, lets his legs drag down until he faces the siding head on. A seam runs through the metal-weave, huge pieces welded together almost perfectly.

His fingers search, feeling for any kind of mark or texture. He can vividly picture the manufacturing plant, the identical sheets of metal they turned out on conveyor belts to be carried off to the loading docks. Each sheet got stamped with the manufacturer's logo.

There it is. He presses his thumb pad into it, marking it until he can drift close enough to make out the symbol. He has to rub away some of the buildup from the water, but he can see the faint half-moon circling a horse head. Gekko. The lunar-based construction company responsible for most of the luxury "floating communities" off-planet. To keep the wealthy away from the factories that made everything they had.

He lets the air in his lungs carry him to the surface, his head breaking through. Back on the bank, Cass stands up suddenly, turning away from the lake, and a pair of figures approach her. They're wearing the same uniform, a boy and girl of roughly the same height with identical black cuffs on their wrists. They talk for a beat, then Cass turns to point at him. Embarrassment warms his cheeks, and he starts to stroke back to the shore before they can discuss the strangeness of what he's doing at length.

He climbs out of the water, dripping all over his pile of clothes as he hurries into them. He dresses quickly, hoping they don't have time to read the slew of ReaperCoin lyrics he has tattooed across his back. Everything about this facility screams upper class, and there are a few lines they would definitely resent.

The two newcomers are like the opposite sides of a coin: the boy is all warm colors, wheat hair, and pink cheeks while the girl is like stark, frigid ice, pale and fair. Her face is scattered with dark freckles that match her hair, and his hazy eyes start to see them as moving constellations.

He looks down, trying to find something less complex to focus on.

"What were you doing?" the guy asks, his eyes lingering on Zeke's chest a little longer than seems necessary.

"I don't answer questions on Mondays, boss," he answers, getting a raised eyebrow in return.

"Okay, well, I'm Cygnus and her name is Aquila, maybe," he says, glancing at the wintery girl. "She might change her mind about that any second."

"Anyone else missing their mode screen?" Cass asks, raising her black banded wrist between them. "And this cuff is definitely not mine. Mine is white with pink gold."

The three of them examine their own, and Zeke glimpses the identical tattoos etched in each of their forearms.

"Pollux says they're like . . . for surveillance," a voice declares from outside their circle.

A small, tan girl has approached with no one noticing, and a longbone boy trails after her a few feet behind.

"That's Pollux," she says, pausing to gesture at him. "Who apparently knows everything while still knowing nothing useful. I'm Lyra," she says, crossing her arms and pivoting back toward them.

"How does he know that?" Zeke asks.

"Does that mean I don't get my own cuff back?" Cass follows on his heels.

A tiny tweak moves across Lyra's eyebrow at hearing Cass's strange way of speaking close up.

"They don't make any outgoing or incoming comms. He says," she adds.

Her partner has taken a seat on the ground just outside the circle and is watching all of them with an irked expression.

"I'm sure we'll get our stuff back when we get out," Aquila says, her gaze traveling over the station ceiling. He can almost see her thinking, piecing information together as her eyes take it in. But for all this girl's internal theorizing, she's still ended up at the wrong answer.

Because now he knows exactly where they are, and he also knows they are not getting out.

POLLUX: 4

Why is no one noticing the birds?

Pollux glances up again, watching the bright sapphire creatures drift over their heads like floating gemstones. They seem completely unperplexed by the presence of humans, which means they've lived with them before. The birds keep going about their business like the rest of the world always does around Pollux. Most people had been trained since birth to follow the loudest sound and the brightest flash of color, which meant being quiet and still made him almost invisible. It's a nice break from the usual. Once he started to talk it was hard to stop himself, and he'd found that talking almost always turned people against him.

One of the herons—he's sure that's what they are—lets out an unattractive honk from its treetop perch nearby and Pollux looks directly at the small girl to see if she reacts.

She doesn't seem to have noticed and shifts uncomfortably when she catches him watching.

"What?" she barks at him after a minute or two.

"Are all of you deaf?" he asks, observing how quickly the mood sours in the circle.

The blonde boy says something aggressive, but Pollux's attention has been snared. He walks through the circle, hearing someone hiss a comment as he goes, and heads toward the middle of the lawn.

A blinking red ring is being holographed across the grass, divided through the center like a pie graph. As he draws closer to it, Pollux makes out eight sections cutting through it, surrounding a ring in the middle with a logo blazed into the center. At the heart of it are the letters "Pt," identical to their shirts.

He stops, lingering just outside the lines of it, and looks up to see if he can spot the source. As if sensing his gaze, the circle widens, making his retinas seize as the light crosses them. He drops his head, massaging his eyelids as annoyance creeps into his stomach.

Access checkpoint to begin program.

Pollux jumps in surprise at the voice reverberating through the air. The small girl appears at his elbow, her eyes round.

"What'd it say?"

Pollux looks at his feet, noticing the sections of the circle have widened and shifted. Eight portions, still equally spaced.

An idea strikes him, and he grabs the small girl at her shoulders, maneuvering her into the outlined space beside him. It's a hard task: she doesn't go willingly, and her shoulders don't provide much of a grip.

"Hey," she growls, angrily blowing stray hair from her face so her fiery eyes can flash at him. "Don't touch me."

It's in that moment that he remembers her name.

"Lyra, stand there," he says, pushing her two more inches into the space.

She crosses her arms and huffs, "Please?"

Something about her stance, her angry little bud of a mouth, strikes him as amusing. He can almost feel the stir of a smile and decides to humor her.

"Please."

The other three have wandered over, and the boy with deep skin and yellow-hazel eyes looks like he wants to say something unpleasant as he watches Pollux's hands drop from Lyra. Pollux always finds it strange, some people's innate drive to protect those they view as weaker. From his experience, it was usually the smaller statured people who proved to be like thorns. Step on them, and they will make their presence known.

He eyes Lyra, trying to see what the boy sees, but there's nothing weak about this girl. In fact, she could be the thorniest of all of them.

"Stand in the octants, *please*," he adds, making sure to look directly at Lyra.

"Oct-what?" the blonde boy chuckles, more to himself than the rest of the group.

"The . . .pieces," Pollux amends, pointing so they get the message.

The attractive blonde girl is the first to oblige, then the two boys follow. Pollux makes a mental note to listen next time they say their names aloud: it'll be easier to get them to do things if he can address them individually.

As soon as the wheaten-haired boy steps into a space, the circle blips blue twice. After a moment, it does it again.

So it won't work without the whole party.

"We're short two people," the deep-skinned boy says, finally getting there.

"What's your name again?" Pollux blurts, forgetting his own rules. People don't trust you when you ask their name too often.

The boy scowls. "Zeke."

"Zeke," he repeats, hoping it etches itself in his memory. "You two were by the lake?"

"Yeah."

"Lyra and I were opposite. You," he gestures to the blonde boy, who asserts "Cygnus."

"You and the trans girl were 45 degrees between us. One pair for every quadrant. The other pair must be toward that far neighborhood."

The energy in the circle suddenly becomes very spiky, and Pollux is aware of everyone's wide eyes holding either shock or anger.

"*Seriously*, Pollux?" Lyra whispers, glaring at him sideways.

"That's a guy?" Cygnus demands, pointing a finger at the transgender girl. "You're a guy? I *knew* there was something weird about you."

"Well, technically she's—" Pollux starts, but Lyra makes a hissing sound to cut him off.

"No more from you," she says, her voice low.

"I've often really wished I was a trans guy," the vapid blonde girl adds dreamily. "I have a lot of masculine characteristics, and I've always been really physically strong. Like, watch, I can prolly pick you up."

She grabs the dark-haired girl around the knees, grunting as she tries to lift her off her feet.

"Please, stop," she states, clearly resisting the urge to elbow the blonde in the face.

There's a piercing screech of metal followed by the ground lurching suddenly sideways. Pollux just has time to see everyone in the circle swept off their feet in unison by the motion before they're plunged into blackness. He can feel the blades of grass under his hands—real, living grass like they had on the Eco-Farm—but every other sense is severed.

There's a scream next to him, short and terrified, but it's the sound that rises out of the dark that makes his skin crawl. A distant roar, or maybe a moan, made up of countless voices blended together climbs through the air. Breath catches in his lungs, and his body flushes cold.

The lights in the distance blink on, followed by their neighbors, chasing away the darkness in a wave across the station. He stares at his own knees, realizing he's on his back, as his heartbeat slowly drains out of his ears.

The sound that had come from the dark haunts him like an echo. The phantoms in the blackness. He wants to ask if the others heard it too, but when he looks at Lyra her skin is gray and drained. She gets shakily to her feet, swallowing noticeably, and Pollux decides against bringing it up.

"What the hell just happened?" Cygnus says roughly, his brow creased.

"Probably just turbulence," the dark-haired girl—Aquila, her tattoo tells him—says from her spot on the ground. "We are in orbit. These big vessels are meant to take a few knocks."

The group tries to shake off the scare, standing and straightening their clothes.

"Let's see if we can find the last pair," Zeke says, scratching the back of his neck. Everyone trails after him, and Pollux sinks back into the shadows to watch.

Lyra is still unhappy with him. Every few steps, she shoots him a narrow-eyed look clearly meant to cow him.

They reach the south quadrant, a few buildings with glass fronts and tables bolted to the ground outside.

"This looks like a shopping strip," Lyra says, slowing to examine a tabletop.

"It probably is," Zeke says. "I used to work at a plant that made carbon tiles and metal-weave for a few projects like this. Luxury housing communities above Titan."

"Why's it empty?" Cygnus asks, pausing to rub his hip. Most likely he took a hard landing on it when the lights went out.

"Most of the time they run out of money," Zeke says. "Investors from Earth trying to make a quick buck out here. None of them understand how much this shit costs." He raps his knuckles against the tabletop.

Pollux scans the street, looking for anything out of place. Something moving on the far right draws his eye. He catches the last glimpse of a face turning away from the top window of one of the vacant storefronts.

He starts off toward it, spotting a stairwell cut in between two of the buildings. The stairs are made of a slippery, bleached polyblend, so he takes them slowly, barely noticing when someone appears on the landing above him.

"Hey, I need help," the figure says, halting Pollux in his ascent. "There's a girl up here, she's hurt." He turns and disappears around the corner.

Pollux hesitates, weighing the situation. *Using your lizard brain,* a voice from his memory says.

Hearing it, it's as if his heart has been trapped in a fist, someone squeezing it inside of his chest. His hands grip the railing, trying to move the pressure anywhere else.

"Pollux, go," Lyra says behind him, giving him a shove and thankfully breaking him out of the trance. Still, he'd never been touched so much by someone he just met.

"You're very aggressive," he says over his shoulder to her.

"Yeah?" she drawls, and shoves him again.

He tops the stairs, spotting the open door in a short hallway. Feet hit the stairs behind him, and he guesses that everyone's followed him again.

The room is empty aside from the figure from the landing, a burly boy with the hood of his jacket pulled over red-tinged hair, and a girl on her back in the center. Her arms are thrown up over her head, as if she hadn't caught herself when she made it to the ground. She wears the same uniform as the rest of them, and he can see strange patterns on the skin of her face and arms. Her peach skin is splotched with white in places, like a calico cat. He'd seen something like that before, back home. A skin condition, something that started with V.

Aquila drops to her knees in front of the girl. Blood coats the left side of the girl's face, and when Aquila lifts her head, Pollux can see a sticky puddle on the floor beneath.

"What happened?" Aquila asks, pressing her fingers to the gash at the girl's brow.

"I found her like this," the stranger says. "The lights went out, I didn't know where to go, so I ran up here, and she was out. I think she must have fallen?"

"You woke up alone?" Pollux asks. Inconsistencies always unnerve him. Though everything about this day is turning out that way.

"Yeah," he answers, looking around. "Didn't all of you?"

Aquila picks up the girl's arm, examining her tattoo, then leans closer to her.

"Lacerta? Can you hear me?" Gently, she taps on the girl's dappled cheek.

"Vitiligo," Pollux says aloud, remembering the word finally. Every single pair of conscious eyes turns to him. "That's what she has," he clarifies, but it only seems to anger the room.

Lyra shakes her head, passing a hand over her eyes like a weary mother, and Pollux wonders what's bothering her now.

On the floor, Lacerta stirs and lets out a soft moan. Aquila bends closer to her, cradling her face.

"Lacerta?"

"Ow," the girl rasps, pressing her palm into her forehead. She looks drowsily up at Aquila.

"Hey," the new boy says, pushing through the others to kneel next to her. "I got help for you."

She blinks slowly a few times, trying to focus. "Who are you?"

"I'm Orion. I found you passed out."

The girl shakes her head, pressing her fingers into her temple. "I can't remember."

Aquila helps her sit up, though it's slow-going and she sways like she might fall over.

"I'm cold," Lacerta says, dragging her fingers over her own arms.

"Where'd you get that hoodie?" Aquila asks the boy, and Pollux blinks in surprise. It's a rare feeling to not be the first to notice something, though he blames it on whatever is causing their memory loss.

"What, this?" the stranger asks, pinching the dark gray fabric. His face is shadowed from the hood, but the chin that juts out from darkness is splattered with freckles. "They're in all the closets. I'll get her one."

"Don't leave," Lacerta groans, leaning back into Aquila's arm.

The stranger, Orion, rests a few fingers on her knee before standing up.

"I'll come right back," he promises, then jogs out of the room.

Aquila readjusts her fingers on the gash. "She needs a phys. Did anyone see a medical center?"

Lyra shakes her head.

"I don't think there's anyone else in here," she says. "Everything has been empty."

"Maybe a few of us should go explore?" the blonde girl pipes up. "I'm a really good team leader. A lot of the comments on my show said I have a commanding presence."

Cygnus spits out a string of curse words then says, "I'm not wandering around when we don't even know where we are."

"You don't know where you are?"

Orion has returned, holding a bundle of soft gray fabric in his arms.

"Do you?" Cygnus asks incredulously.

Orion walks a few halted steps into their midst, dropping the bundle of jackets onto the floor near Lacerta. Pollux swears he sees the slightest hint of a smile, but when Orion straightens again his face is so somber he must have imagined it.

"No," Orion says, taking a knee next to Lacerta. "No idea."

LYRA: 5

Lyra had six sisters. She can see their faces, but she doesn't even need to count them. It's just a kind of deep-seated knowledge. It was a high number for Titan—an unfair draw on the resources, some of her educators at C7 whispered—and the kids at school quickly picked up the opportunity to jab her with it like an instrument of justice.

"The water got shorted last night in Petrum. All the Mullen sisters must have been taking a shower at once."

"They're overhauling the septics again at lunch. The Mullen sisters got their periods at the same time."

"Hey Lyra, do all your sisters have their own mobile devices? Is that why the power has been blacking out?"

She was the oldest, and her mother never stopped telling her what a miracle she was. Even though she'd come out premature, undersized, and malnourished, she was never supposed to happen at all.

"Mother Saturn made my belly into a home," Lyra's mother said once when she was pregnant with Auriga and Lyra was clinging to her knee as Saturn burned red in the sky. It was a trick of the light, the fragile atmosphere upset by a meteor fragment, but it had seemed like the end of the world to Lyra at the time.

"Saturn will never hurt us," her mother had assured her, smoothing her hair out of her face. "She is a mother too. We are all her children now, and she wants us here. I was never supposed to be able to have children, but Mother Saturn looked down and said 'Let me open her belly.'"

Just to prove it, her mother had gotten pregnant ten times. Lyra sometimes felt relieved that not all of them had made it to term, or there really would be nothing to eat and nowhere to sleep in her house. It had been fun having so many siblings when she was younger, in the elementary program where her mother taught, but as soon as she traded the little domed building for the sharp box of C7 Secondary Education Facility it became clear what the rest of City of Seven Hills thought about her family. That her mother was a fantasist who didn't believe in birth control, and her father was a dumb, spineless, chemical worker who couldn't say "no." And after a while, she started to think it too.

For years, her stomach would squirm with shame and annoyance when she thought about her sisters. She felt like they had robbed her of her privacy, the resources she was entitled to as the first generation born on Titan. Even her own identity was taken, as she would never be anything other than a Mullen sister to anyone in C7.

But when she thinks of them now, there is only ache. It's so deep and so cavernous that she feels she might collapse into herself like a dying celestial. Become a black hole that swallows everything around her, even the station itself.

"Lyra!"

She jumps, her heart bobbing into her throat.

Somewhat annoyed, she breathes, "What?"

"Take that spot," Pollux says, pointing to the vacant triangle of light projected onto the ground next to him.

She flicks the bangs, *these freaking bangs*, out of her eyes again and walks over to the group. There's a kid clothed in gray for each section now, and as soon as she steps into place the light changes to a vibrant green. Lyra's wrist vibrates, startling her, and from the way everyone jumps it's happened across all of their cuffs.

A line of text is displayed across the mode face in thin, blocky letters.

Begin Program.

The mode face lights up, a ball rolling across the screen. When she lifts it, it moves, changing positions. She twists her wrist, watching how it always seems to point in the same direction.

Begin Program, the mode urges again, the text blinking and fading. *Begin Program.*

"Jeez," Zeke says, shuffling his wrist to jostle the mode. "They're pushy, aren't they?"

"It's like a compass hand," Aquila says, raising hers to eye level. "Mine's pointing that way."

She nods toward the neighborhood clustered at the edge of the park. A lone building stands in the center, and when Lyra glances at her mode it seems to be drawing the ball to it like a magnet.

"I'm not going," Orion says definitively, shadows pooling beneath his hood like a Rorschach test. "It's probably some kind of experiment."

"What makes you say that?"

Pollux's flat black eyes are watching Orion, unblinking, and the image unnerves Lyra. Everything about Pollux seems to happen under the surface. Even his eyes give nothing away, no hint of emotion, and Lyra gets the feeling he never uses them to express anything. Nothing passes out of them, they only absorb.

"I dunno, the birds?" Orion says, pointing upward. "Doesn't it seem weird to have a bunch of birds inside a space station? Unless you're doing experiments on them."

They all look up, and a collective shock ripples the group. Every so often, a group of birds drifts through the air above them, landing in trees. How had she not noticed them before?

Pollux, on the other hand, seems bored with it all.

"Maybe it's a co-space," he says. "A lot of EPA hubs rent the space out to organizations for money. Animals can't pay you."

"How do you know that?" Lacerta asks. She's been gaining energy ever since they left the abandoned shopping strip, and now she's watching all of them with bright, mistrusting eyes.

"My parents are Eco-Farmers," Pollux says easily. "We used to rent part of the space out to an arborist company. It was half our income."

Zeke scoffs quietly. "Farm boy."

"Who cares?" Cygnus breaks in, growing impatient. "Are we going to the building or not?"

Pollux strides across the circle, heading for the building without a word.

"Guess we are," Cygnus says, following after him.

Lyra trails along too, listening to Lacerta and Cass—though it's mainly Cass—talking behind her. She starts to twist her fingers into her hair, tucking the bangs away from her face, until almost without realizing it she's made a braid.

Aquila's hand appears in front of her, holding out a black hair tie. She'd barely noticed her approach.

"Oh," Lyra says, surprised at the gesture. "That's okay, you keep it."

Aquila smiles gently, and pushes the hair tie into Lyra's open hand.

"It's fine, I like my hair down anyway."

She tousles her long, dark hair with her fingers, and Lyra has to stop herself from reacting when she sees Aquila's joints moving beneath her paper-thin skin. Everything about her is elongated and skeletal. She's beautiful, but in a stark, ethereal way.

While Lyra is watching, Aquila makes a soft scoff. "There they are."

"Who's where?" she asks, glancing around.

Aquila stops, taking Lyra's shoulders in her hands to stall her motion. She bends down, aligning her view with Lyra's, and raises her hand to point to a spot above them.

"Right there," she says. "The people in charge always want the best seats in the house."

At first, Lyra casts around for what she could possibly be looking at, but then her eyes latch onto it. An orb of reflective glass hangs from the topmost part of the station, nearly camouflaging itself by mirroring the same landscape as its surroundings.

"The eye of the giant," Aquila says. The idea reminds Lyra of something her mother would say.

"You think they're up there?" she asks quietly, not wanting to be caught staring. "Watching us?"

"Maybe," Aquila answers, straightening. "Maybe not. Give the appearance that you're always watching and people will police themselves." She looks down at Lyra, arcing her dark, full brows. "Panopticon."

"Right," Lyra answers warily, pulling her eyes from the strange structure. If there are people in there, she certainly doesn't want to be the one gaping.

When the group reaches the building Lyra notices that it doesn't match the rest. Almost like it was constructed at an entirely different time than the neighborhood around it. The doors are perpetually open, but the room past the mouth is dark and vacant except for a bluish electrical glow.

Lyra lingers in the doorway as the others go in, and Aquila props her hollow elbow against the frame. She smirks a bit, looking down at Lyra with her long neck bent.

"Rather them die first?" she asks quietly.

"Something like that."

Homer Oleyedo had taught her well not to trust groups of people. Maybe she should thank him for that.

When no explosions go off, Lyra and Aquila move into the dark with everyone else. There's a table bolted to the floor in the center of the room with a single, intense light bearing down on it. Four clear acrylic containers sit at each corner illuminated by the blue-white glow, but no one seems to be interested in the table.

On the far side, four lines of text are holographed against the light gray wall. The bold cut of the font reminds Lyra of something, and it only takes her a moment to remember the hideous tattoos they all sport. Whoever wrote those used the same style to write the floating text.

Lyra squints, trying to discreetly rise onto her tiptoes to see over everyone.

A - 1 Silver filament

B - 15 mls Fractionated Ethylene

C - 1 oz Copper Concentrate

D - 1 string Hedera Helix

"Is it like a scavenger hunt?" Lacerta says, tucking her arms into the pockets of her jacket. "We all bring one of these items back here?"

"We all have a letter on our tattoos, right?" Cygnus asks, examining his own. "Maybe B is for Team B?"

"Ours say C," Pollux says, looking at Lyra. He has a way of not knowing when to break eye contact, and she can feel him looking at her long past the point of comfort.

"So, everyone finds the item, meet back here?" Cass states, working very hard to adjust her shirt to its most attractive position. She reminds Lyra of one of the girls who got famous on Titan for having their own streams on Vue. The ones who couldn't look ugly even if they'd been dragged through mud. In fact, Lyra is fairly certain she's seen her face on a screen before, on one of the mind-numbing channels her sister Vesta had loved.

"Forget it," Orion says, speaking for the first time in a while. He turns from the circle, stalking back out through the door without another word.

"Hey, boss, hold up," Zeke calls after him, following him into the open.

The rest of them shuffle out, and Lyra is glad to be out of the small room. It gives her the same strange feeling she'd felt on the football field: that there was some kind of unseen presence hanging in the cramped air, not making itself known.

Zeke has caught up to Orion on the lawn, and the two argue at a barely contained pitch. Lyra remembers the way her mother and father had talked like that, when they "weren't fighting" and "nothing was wrong," but their voices were still steeped with tension.

Aquila sits on the grass, running her hands over it like she's petting a dog. Everyone else fans out, waiting for the argument to run its course. Eventually, Orion storms off, and Zeke returns to the group, his brow faintly clouded.

"He doesn't want to do . . . whatever this is," he says, circling his fingers in the air to encompass everything around them. "He just wants to be alone. Wait it out."

"Well, that's dumb," Cygnus says. "Maybe doing it is the only way out. Maybe we're in some kind of test. I heard when you apply for the military, they put you in simulations that are meant to test your skills. Maybe that's what we're doing."

"We're a little young to be enlisting," Lacerta says, then points at Lyra. "That one doesn't look a day over thirteen."

Lyra crosses her arms, her teeth grinding, but it's not the worst insult she's ever been thrown.

"Was everyone born later than T25?" Pollux breaks in. "If not, then we are all between the legal ages of seventeen and twenty-one."

The group falls silent, everyone weighing the information in their minds.

"Because of where Saturn's position is," Pollux goes on when no one prompts him for an explanation. He points to the window where the rings are just visible behind Titan, bands of light in the distance. "It would make me either twenty-one or fifty."

"Maybe you had work done," Cass mutters, unimpressed. "My mom and I basically look the same age now."

"The point being," he sighs, losing patience. "That we are all under twenty-two, at least. Definitely not a military test if we're too young to enlist."

"Let's vote, then," Zeke says. "Who wants to follow the instructions and see what happens?"

Everyone's hands go up, though Pollux takes a good, long minute to consider.

"I don't have a team anymore," Lacerta says tightly, glancing in the direction Orion disappeared.

Cass grabs her arm so emphatically it startles them both.

"Be on my team! You remind me so much of my best friend!"

"If we're switching teams, I don't want to be with . . . whatever that is," Cygnus says, waving his hand over Aquila's spot on the ground.

"You could just call me 'they' if it bothers you so much," Aquila says dryly, tossing a blade of grass in front of her.

"I could just call you 'bitch,' that covers all my bases," Cygnus retorts, his lips twisting into a smirk.

"*Hey!*" It's out of Lyra's mouth before she can stop herself. A hot stab of fury makes her stomach spasm, but she presses her teeth together, swallowing down the stream of words rising in her throat.

She'd like to tell Cygnus exactly what she thinks he should be called, but he looks even ropier than usual.

As if he can sense the battle going on inside her, Cygnus straightens, taking a few lazy steps toward her. His kohl-rimmed eyes cast over her face, and Lyra swears she can feel their touch like a scrape across her skin.

"So cute," he says eventually, extending one index finger to tap the end of her nose. "You're like pocket-sized."

Behind Cygnus, Lyra can see Pollux fighting a smile and she makes a vow to push him off the next roof they come across. Cygnus, growing bored, meanders back over to his spot in the circle.

"I'll be with Aquila," Zeke breaks in. He strides over to her, extending a hand to help her up. Aquila blinks, but lets him pull her to her feet. She's almost taller than him when they're lined up, though she seems to have a perpetual slouch that keeps her from fully stretching out.

"And we're starting right now. Everyone meet back here when they have their item."

Zeke sets off toward the lake, Aquila following at a distance.

"Right-o, Captain," Cygnus says, giving Zeke's back a mock salute.

He steps up to Cass, resting his elbow on her shoulder. "Guess I'm with you ladies."

"Great. We'll handle getting Team A's item too," Pollux says quickly, striding off to the right.

A growl of annoyance burbles in Lyra's throat, but she starts after him. By the time she catches up, she's out of breath and has to keep up an almost-jogging pace to stay with him.

"Why'd you volunteer to pick up the slack?" she huffs. "Do you even know where to find any of that stuff?"

Pollux pulls up suddenly, coming to a dead stop, and turns toward her.

"I do," he says, and lunges for her throat.

AQUILA: 6

Her calves are starting to hurt. Zeke keeps moving farther ahead of her with a determined, storm-off pace, though they'd left everyone behind minutes ago.

Aquila runs her thumb over her tattoo again, the dull pain distracting her from the strain in her stretched-thin muscles. She casts her eyes over Zeke's tight, thick frame enviously. She'd spent her whole childhood with the faint gravity on the convoys, something the on-board physicians would never have allowed if they knew it was happening. As a result, she'd grown up long and stretched like a wisp of vapor being pulled toward a vent. Her muscles never fleshed out, and she's fairly certain her bones are barely-congealed dust, though a phys had never told her that. She wonders if her mother would be upset, seeing her now. If she'd feel like she failed.

"Can you slow down?" she calls after Zeke finally.

He stops, seeming to remember she's there. His fingers unfurl, releasing his clenched fists.

"Sorry," he says when she's caught up. "Something about these people puts me on edge. About this whole thing."

"Is it Cygnus?" she asks, trying not to pant. "He's just a standard issue dick, don't take it personally."

She touches his arm, hoping it'll calm some of the agitation in his stance, but he just shifts uncomfortably. Maybe it's because he doesn't like being touched, or maybe it's because he doesn't like being touched by *her*. The look on his face when Pollux outed her hadn't been overjoyed, but then he'd been so unashamed when he claimed her as a partner that she thought she may have been imagining it.

Aquila drops her hand, slipping it into the pocket of her jacket.

"You seem right at home," Zeke says, examining her like a bolt out of place. "The rest of us are all kinds of scared. But you, you seem like you've done this before."

Aquila shrugs, trying not to fixate on his eyes. They're such a light shade of hazel they almost look golden, shot through with splinters of copper. She's never seen anything quite like them.

"I was older when I came over on the convoy," she hedges. "Being on a floater isn't scary in itself, really."

It isn't totally a lie, but it isn't enough truth for him to sink his teeth into. She'd learned not to give out memorable details, in case they came back to bite her later.

It's true that she'd been older than most on the last convoy trip she made, but it had been her fourth trip, and it had been her father who was flying it. He was a convoy pilot, and after her mother abandoned them Aquila had chosen to stay as he bounced back and forth between Earth and Titan, three years for each trip.

Whatever structure they were on now had the same forced gravity as those convoy ships, and she felt more at home here than she ever had on the solid ground of Titan.

"That guy," Zeke says, setting off at a more relaxed stroll toward the lake. "Orion. He's from my hometown."

"How do you know?"

"We all get these when we turn sixteen," he says, pointing to the right side of his jaw.

A thin line has been etched into the skin just behind his chin, like a notch on a ruler. It must be some kind of chemical burn, but Aquila doesn't want to get close enough to him to see for sure.

"It's a superstition in Huygens Landing. After it flooded, they said the guys who stayed to operate the sea drains were up to here in water," he holds his flattened hand even with the mark. "But they knew they were safe as long as it didn't get any higher. So it's like, a way to measure it, if we ever flood again."

"I like that," Aquila laughs, picturing herself with the same mark. It must have been nice to belong to a community instantly recognizable wherever you go.

"Yeah, but that kid tried to act like he didn't know what I was talking about. He threw me some words, even. And I got this off him."

Zeke fishes in his pocket and pulls out a crude metal spike the size of a finger. It looks like it was made from heated layers folding on top of each other, and the cruel point makes Aquila tense. She's happy when he slips it back into his pocket, out of sight.

Suddenly Zeke makes an angry grunt, shaking his head as if something's flown in his ear. Aquila takes a step away in surprise, but Zeke is already back to normal, dropping to his knees at the edge of the lake. He dips his arm into the water, reaching for something under the surface.

"Let's hope I'm right about this," he says, bracing his other arm on the bank so he doesn't topple in.

His hand emerges covered in a film of opaque gel. He must have scraped it from the side of the lake basin. Zeke brings it to his nose and takes a hearty sniff.

"Oh yeah, that's ethylene, boss."

Aquila smiles slightly at the phrase. "Oh, I'm the boss now?"

"Nah, we Landers people call everyone boss. Don't get a big head."

He gets to his feet, cupping his hand so the gel doesn't escape. "Does that seem like fifteen mills to you? Maybe grab a handful just in case."

Aquila curls her lip slightly, but drops to her knees to scrape her hand along the side of the tank. A huge shadow moves under the water and she jumps back, tripping over her own long legs.

"What the hell is that?" she gasps, scrambling away from the side. "There's a monster in there!"

Zeke snorts. "You say monster, I say . . . probably dinner."

Aquila creeps back to the water's edge, carefully peering into the depths. It's hard to catch at first, but then she starts to see how the shadows separate and drift beneath the surface.

"They're fish," she says slowly.

"Fish, birds, trees, self-recycling air. I think Pollux might be right. We're in some kind of Eco-space."

She steels herself for another try at sweeping up some ethylene, but motion on top of the water catches her eye. A tiny blue fluff is bobbing on the ripples, a chick with little nubs for wings trying to balance on the water's surface. It must have fallen from one of the trees, Aquila realizes, just as a hole opens up beneath it and it's sucked down, pulled in by a giant gaping mouth.

Aquila is on her feet in an instant, heart pounding. After a sickening moment, the chick pops up again, slapping its wings against the water in distress.

"There's a bird out there!" she says, yanking her shoes off with the opposite toes.

Without a hint of a plan she throws her body into the water, hearing Zeke utter a surprised curse behind her. A moment later there's another splash, but Aquila's gaze is fixed on the little bird, willing it to stay afloat.

This water is different from the small pool they'd had on the convoys for recreation. It's heavy and cold, like swimming through glue that's constantly trying to suck you downward. She'd never been in water where you couldn't touch the bottom, and even now her toes reach for it, knowing it's far below her.

She's still so far away, and her body is starting to ache with fatigue. The sound of splashes to her left draws her attention, and Zeke slices through the water next to her. His arms carry him like an arrow, gaining speed with each stroke. He stops just before he reaches the bird, and relief floods Aquila as he scoops it into his hand and holds it aloft.

When he turns back to her, his face is wet and shining, and he's grinning. Everything inside Aquila seems to seize up at once. She can't remember the cold or the fatigue or the monsters beneath her. There's nothing outside of this moment and that smile, and she's as struck by it as if it were a gunshot.

"I see, you're only afraid when it's just *your* life at stake," Zeke laughs.

It's like she's swallowed her own tongue. Aquila opens her mouth, but not a single word comes to her aid. Water sloshes into her stupid gaping maw and she coughs it back out, hating herself for being so thrown.

"Grab my shoulder, boss," Zeke says, passing by her.

Humiliated, she grasps his shoulder and lets him pull her to the bank. The muscle is so dense beneath his skin that she almost loses her grip in the slippery water.

He sets the little bird down first on the grass, then turns to Aquila and grips her waist. For a moment he pulls her closer, and Aquila's heart spasms so violently she almost lets out a gasp. Then he pushes her out of the water, placing her on the lip of the bank before pulling himself out next to her.

The little bird is water-logged and falling over itself. Zeke lets it wander into his hand, then turns to Aquila and passes it into hers.

"Safe and sound," he says, just a hint of that smile lingering in his voice.

The bird huddles against her chest, puffing up after a few shakes. She resists the urge to squeeze it closer, though everything in her wants to cuddle it within an inch of its life. A dry jacket drops across Aquila's shoulders, and she realizes Zeke at least had the sense to take his off before hurling himself into monster-infested waters.

"You look like my cat when we tried to give it a bath," he says, walking back to the water. His arm disappears and re-emerges with a handful of gel once more.

"Now can we get to business? Or is there anything else that needs saving?"

POLLUX: 7

Pollux was not expecting someone so small to have such an impressive kick. He catches himself hard on his knee, one hand wrapping around his stomach. His diaphragm pulses angrily against his lungs, and Lyra pops back up on her feet where he dropped her.

"What the freaking hell are you trying to do?" she fumes, pressing her palm to her neck.

"Calm down," he tries to say, but all that escapes his mouth is, "Fmmtt."

Lyra pulls her hand away, examining it for blood. When she finds none, she turns her blazing eyes back to him.

What a fearsome little creature, Pollux can't help but think to himself.

"Your body-mod," he squeezes out, his voice coarse. "It's made of copper."

Lyra brushes her fingers against the rosy metal bar imbedded above her collarbone, her brows drawing together.

"It is?"

"They only use pure copper," Pollux says, words coming a little easier now. He pushes himself to standing, regaining his dignity slightly. "Because the metal is antimicrobial. It's about the size we need."

For a long moment, Lyra studies him, and he gets the impression she's trying to work out if he's lying or not.

Finally, she grips the bar between her fingers, using her thumbnail to pry it out. She winces, but it comes out fairly easily, leaving a faint pink outline in its place as tiny beads of blood rise to the surface.

"Why didn't you just ask?" she spits, tossing it to him.

"Because you might say no, and I need it."

"Man, you . . ." Lyra shakes her head.

Something tugs at him inside, remembering how someone else had looked at him like that. Like they were disappointed he hadn't done something differently. It's the same nagging he'd felt earlier, like he keeps walking over the same crack and can't remember how it got there, but he forces himself to focus on the present instead. Unanswered questions get tangled up in his mind until the whole process is tripped up. He can't afford for that to happen right now. There is one game: figure out the system, beat it. It's the kind of thing he itches for.

"You can say it," Pollux says, ducking down a bit as he passes Lyra. Some of the longer curls fall across his eyes with the motion and he pushes them back, peeved. "I'm weird."

Lyra takes a moment to follow him.

"That's not what I was going to say."

"What, then?" he says over his shoulder, fairly certain she's bluffing. Most people don't like their behavior predicted, and Pollux has gotten quite good at it.

"I was going to say you should trust people more," she says.

Pollux stops, surprised. He turns back just as she catches up.

"Why?"

"I mean, we're all in this together," Lyra says, touching the red mark on her collarbone. "There must be a reason we all got paired up, right? We're supposed to be on the same team."

"What makes you think that?" Pollux asks, then decides he doesn't care what her answer is. "This may easily be a last person standing situation, we just don't know it yet."

Lyra crosses her arms, her chin lifting. "You sound like you want it to be."

Again, there's that tingle at the edge of his lips, like a smile scratching below the surface. Curious, he lets the muscles in his mouth flex. Lyra screws up her face.

"Why are you smiling like you're going to poison me?"

His eyebrows lift, finding the idea more comical than tempting, but she doesn't need to know that.

"Yikes. That face isn't helping."

"We need to go into one of the structures," Pollux says, getting back on track. "Most light tubes use silver filament to conduct electricity."

They head toward the nearest one, a single story structure with an entrance through the patio. It's identical to the three others clustered around the courtyard, and as they draw closer Pollux notices large, dark letters braced to the corner of each of them. He looks up at the letter "B" as they pass under it, wondering if there's a connection to the letters on their tattoos. Perhaps they've each been assigned living quarters as well.

The door to the patio slides open easily, as everything else has. Everything here has been made to interact with. Even the furniture is made of heavy-duty acrylic, nearly impossible to break without tools. Whoever is in charge doesn't want them smashing anything.

He takes one last look overhead at the control center hovering above them, descending from the structure like a drop of water stretching before it falls. Clearly they're watching, but since no one came to Lyra's aid when he'd grabbed her it makes more sense that it's there for observation more than protection. Someone just wants to watch what they do next.

The house is dim, but when they enter, it senses them and floods with light.

"Turn lights off," Pollux says loudly, and they cut out instantly.

The inside of the house is washed with a gray-blue glow seeping in from the windows. Lyra moves under the closest light fixture, rocking onto her toes to stretch up for it with her fingertips. He lets her try for a few moments before he locks his hand around the glass tube and shakes it loose. It pops out easily from the magnetic socket.

"Watch out," he says, then smashes the tube against the counter.

A shower of shards erupts into the air and Lyra yelps, covering her head with her arms.

"Jesus! You know they unscrew, right?" she demands furiously, stepping out of the circle of fallen glass.

"Yes, I do know that," Pollux says, delicately pulling out the silver filament from the tube. It reminds him of pulling the stamens out of flowers like he used to do at the Eco-Farm, and the thought makes him feel oddly heavy.

He places the filament on the counter, flipping his grip on the remaining piece of tube. It's cracked nicely, leaving a long triangular point intact at the end. He holds out the safe end for Lyra to take.

"But I needed it broken for this."

Lyra eyes it suspiciously, but takes it from him. He strides into the living room, sitting on the couch in the center.

"I need you to cut my hair. It's getting in the way."

Behind him, Lyra snorts.

"I don't know if that's a great idea."

"You said to trust people more," Pollux says over his shoulder.

After a minute or so, he hears her small footsteps cracking across the glass. Her heat presses against his shoulder, and one of her hands grips a handful of curls.

"How short?" she asks.

Pollux swallows, his voice suddenly deserting him. His scalp is singing with sensation at being touched, and the entire network of his mind seems to be glitching. It's like an electrical fire has sparked beneath his skin, and he has no control over where it goes.

"Pollux?" Lyra asks, breaking his haze. He realizes he's caught her hand in his own, keeping her from touching him again and spreading more fire.

Slowly, he peels his fingers away from her skin.

"As short as you can," he says, focusing his gaze on the empty table in front of him to steel himself.

Lyra pulls a clump of hair tight and starts to saw through with the sharp edge. Once it's free, she tosses it to the floor in front of him, and he watches its slow progress through the air. Gravity works differently here, though he's hard-pressed to notice any changes in his body yet. He'd seen it with the birds first, how their dives were halted and sluggish.

"This reminds me," Lyra says, her voice strained with the effort of hacking through his thick hair. "I think I used to do this for my sisters. Not with broken glass, obviously."

"You remember having sisters?" Pollux asks, welcoming the distraction.

"I remember everything," she says, flinging another handful of dark hair. "It's just that it kind of . . . fades out when I think about things that happened recently. The last thing I *know* happened was my Primary Exams. I failed my Primary Exams," she repeats, the motion of her hands slowing.

"That was important to you?"

"Well, yeah," she says brusquely. "I want a coder job. Everyone does. I don't want to work in a plant."

She pauses, her hand resting on his shoulder, and he's acutely aware of the pressure.

"Did you even look for scissors?"

"They wouldn't let us have scissors," he responds, wondering how it isn't obvious to her.

"How do you even know who 'they' are? None of us knows what's happening. Unless you're just not telling us something."

"Clearly," Pollux says, turning over his shoulder. A curl she hasn't gotten to yet flops into his eye. "Clearly, we're in some kind of facility that's meant to hold us. My guess is it's some kind of lottery project where we compete until one is remaining, and the victor goes on to some kind of special program. They wouldn't want us to just kill each other off. That would mean the first person to come across a weapon would be the winner, and that wouldn't prove anything. This is clearly a cerebral game."

Lyra stares at him for a long moment, and he can see thoughts drift through her mind like storm clouds. Then, she grabs the strand of hair in his face and slices through it.

"Some kind of lottery," she echoes, cutting through the few remaining clumps of hair.

When she's satisfied, she turns away and sets the broken tube on the counter next to the silver filament and the copper skinplant.

"That's the best I can do," she says, moving into the kitchen to start lazily searching the cabinets.

Pollux stands, heading to the nearest wall. The screen panel is showing an idyllic lakeside scene with shimmering golden light. After living most of his life on Earth, the light on Titan had been hard to get used to. The atmosphere filtered everything to an orange and yellow glow, trapping Titan in perpetual sunset.

"Mirror view," he says aloud, and the scene shrinks into nothing to be replaced by his own face.

His ribs pull together so tightly and quickly that his breath deserts him. Seeing his face: the black slashes of brows, his sharp nose, and the dark, windowless holes of his eyes, a tremor takes root in his hands as they grip the counter. It isn't like looking at his own face at all. There's no feeling of ownership, more of something being stolen from him and existing outside himself.

This was why he'd grown his hair so long, though he'd remembered it too late. Looking at his face was too close to looking at Castor. And he would never look at Castor again.

"Well, look at that," Lyra crows loudly, sending a splinter of shock into chest. He wheels around, needing to break the spell seeing Castor's face had cast.

She's smirking as she drops something on the kitchen island, sliding it to him so the object comes to rest at the foot of his gaze.

"Scissors. Guess I'm the first one to come across a weapon. How 'bout that."

ZEKE: 8

There's something about this room.

Zeke hovers in the doorway of the strange building that had summoned them, right on the edge of where the light falls on the floor. The collected shadows set his instincts on edge, adrenaline tickling his nerves as if something could jump out from the corners at any second.

As they wait for the others to return with their items, Zeke wraps his hand around his right bicep, trying to seek comfort from his own arms. The fabric of the uniform scratches against his skin, and suddenly the whole shirt feels too tight.

It's too familiar—like the tattoos, like the touches all around the station that are exactly like the hospital. He can't stop recognizing them everywhere. Not in the construction, that's Gekko design through and through, but the medical fingerprints the doctors left all over it. They needed everything sterile, minimal. Nothing to grab or snatch or be out of place. Zeke can only imagine what this place looked like before it'd been stripped of its creature comforts.

The electric hum from the power in the room digs into his

eardrums. He forces his feet to move toward the table in the center. Zeke picks up one of the acrylic containers, seeing no indication that they have to be in any kind of order, and scrapes the slow-moving ethylene gel from his palm.

He places the container back in its original spot. The tabletop pulses green once, lit from underneath its smooth, milky surface. His shoulders drop in relief.

"If I had a superpower, it would be the ability to measure things without a scale," he says to Aquila, who's hovering in the doorway.

She's tucked the chick into her jacket pocket, but she's still cradling it in the crook of her elbow as if afraid to move it. She smiles slightly without looking up.

"That's a great one," she says. "He rushes to the rescue of troubled chefs. He is . . . Measuring Cup Man."

"Don't you make fun of chefs," he says, his mood lightening with every step away from the strange table. "We got precious few in Huygens."

Once he's through the door into the false light, he leans back against the building. Aquila lines up with him but rests just in front of the wall, not quite touching. She never really seems to touch anything, he's realized from watching her. Even when she walks, she somehow manages to keep her feet on the ground for only the barest moment. She's almost liminal, like she doesn't quite exist on the same plane as the rest of them.

The chick has curled up around itself, nearly filling the whole space of her pocket. Its eyes are closed, little spots of dark behind its papery eyelids. Zeke finds himself smiling at the thought of it being so content in Aquila's pocket that it can sleep *that* soundly.

You could crush that thing with one hand, the deep voice grumbles from somewhere behind him.

Crush that girl's throat with one hand, the raspy one seconds.

Zeke shakes his head, feeling them slip back into the fabric of his brain and go silent. How long was it going to take before the doctors finally broke down and medicated him? He'd like to get his hands around the pasty neck of whatever physician thought it was a good idea to experiment with his dosage.

Movement in front of them draws his attention, and he watches Pollux and Lyra crest the hill. With Pollux's height directly next to Lyra's squat body, it feels like he's seeing them through a distorted funhouse lens. He looks away before it stirs up something in his overactive brain.

"We beat you," Aquila calls to them when they're close enough. "Luckily I got paired with the water treatment expert who knows exactly where to find ethylene."

Pollux lets his unimpressed eyes drift over Zeke.

"Oh," he says, his gaze crossing over the mark on his chin. "Water treatment. You're from Huygens Landing. Workers at the water treatment plants get ceremonial scarring to mark—"

"Okay, that's enough," Lyra says, walking right through his cloud of babble. "We're only second because he made me give him a prison haircut with broken glass," she says to Aquila before disappearing into the building.

Pollux hangs lifelessly after Lyra leaves, like he's a coat hung on the rack of his own spine. Zeke resituates against the wall, growing uncomfortable with the long silence.

"What was your item?" he asks Pollux eventually, afraid any more lag time in conversation will leave room for the voices to start.

Pollux seems to remember where he is and perks up.

"Her skinplant was copper, and we got silver filament from the light tubes in one of the residences."

Aquila makes a stifled scoffing noise.

"That's funny. Cygnus told me about twenty times his family owns the biggest tube lighting production company on Earth. Can't believe he didn't think of that before you."

Pollux turns his unblinking stare on her, and Zeke can practically see the gears turning in his head.

"One item of importance for every group."

Aquila straightens slightly. "You think?"

He shrugs. "Clearly they know things about us."

A burble of laughter winds around the corner, followed shortly after by Lacerta, Cygnus and Cass. Their faces are bright and relaxed, as if they could be strolling into a party together rather than trapped in a giant inverted greenhouse.

"Hey, we got it!" Cygnus bellows when he spots them, waving his arm over his head.

His hand is closed around something, and Zeke spots a few tufts of leaves poking through his fingers.

"Hedera Helix is a plant. Who knew?" he says, grinning.

Lacerta makes a ticking sound with her tongue. "I knew. I told you that."

"Yeah, okay, that's fair," he amends, touching her lightly between the shoulder blades. Something about it makes Zeke's skin twitch.

Lacerta pauses in front of Zeke while Cygnus and Cass trot inside, narrowly missing Lyra as she comes out.

"I worked in terrarium back home," Lacerta says, slipping her hands into the pockets of her jacket. "Or . . . maybe I still work there. I can't remember quitting."

A melody issues from inside the room, short and staccato, like the sound of winning a game. It's followed by a deep, bone-shaking grind that makes all of them flinch.

"Guys?" Cygnus's voice barely hides the evident fear, and Zeke pushes off the wall to run inside.

Cygnus and Cass are both cowering near the table as the room vibrates around them. They look desperately to Zeke as if he holds the key to what's happening.

"I put the plant thing in the container thing, and it said stage complete, then this started popping off," Cygnus explains over the sound.

A charged buzz fills the air just as the floor goes still. A breath of wind crosses Zeke's neck and he whips around to face the doorway. A sheet of bright light has filled the space, blocking them in. He can just see the outline of the trees behind it, but warning ripples through him at the idea of trying to pass through.

"What's this?"

Cygnus appears at his shoulder, lifting his hand as if he plans to touch the panel of light. Zeke grabs his wrist just before his fingertips land, making him jump.

"I wouldn't, boss," he cautions.

"That's particle wall," Cass says warily, edging closer. "They had them at my mom's office. The light makes the atoms move faster, it makes a kind of compression barrier."

"What happens if I stick my hand through it?" Cygnus asks, trying to yank out of Zeke's grip.

"Let him do it," Pollux says from the far corner.

Zeke releases him, but Cygnus seems to think better of it once he's free.

"So they closed off the only door," Lacerta grumbles, crossing her arms. "Are we supposed to just wait until they tell us to do something?"

Somehow, Zeke finds himself looking at Pollux. Since this whole thing started, it's felt like Pollux has played this game before. Like he knew the rules when no one else did. If any of them were a plant, an orderly in disguise to make sure no one got out of hand, it would be him.

Pollux doesn't let him down. He's already moving toward the table, his hands hovering over the two closest containers.

"They already told us what to do," he mutters to himself, touching the center of the table. His fingers dip into something, some kind of indent Zeke hadn't noticed before.

"Look for a hole. There will be a hole somewhere in the wall."

It takes a long moment, but everyone eventually spreads out through the space, running their hands over the wall or stooping to examine the floor.

"Hey, look," Cygnus says, his finger on a spot near the floor. "It says Tect right here on the wall."

Cass steps up to it, hands perched on her hips. "You think that's what this place is? Maybe the building is called the Tect?"

Zeke doesn't have the heart to tell them "tect" means "test" in Russian, and the spot they're looking at is nothing more than an electrician's label to signify an outlet lays behind the wall. He'd watched them stamp that very word into paneling at the Gekko plant a hundred times.

Pollux plucks the copper skinplant from its container and places it in the center, his eyes landing on Zeke.

"You. You know about ethylene."

The edge of Zeke's eye twitches, heat boiling in his ribs just like when his manager Caelum would crack an order at him in the plant. The coarse tone of his voice whenever he'd talk to him, like Zeke was always just waiting to be directed, used to grind against his nerves relentlessly. Being around Pollux rubs him that way, how he seems to think they're all his employees.

Huygens Landers will always work for someone, the saying went.

Just never themselves, the deep voice coos in the back of this head. He ignores it, crossing his arms to meander over to Pollux.

"Sure, boss," he says lazily, trying to emphasize how little he cares. "We use it at the plant."

Pollux begins to roll the silver filament between his palms, pressing it together into a wiry ball.

"Can you heat it?"

"It heats naturally in UV light," he says. "There's just not enough on Titan to get it very high."

"What about direct light?"

Zeke shrugs. "Never tried."

Pollux presses his lips together as if he isn't pleased with that answer. Without another word, he drops the silver ball he's made into the container of ethylene.

Zeke is close enough now to see the mold in the center of the table. A small carving in the shape of an "F" has been etched into the opaque surface. Pollux has lined the copper bar with the long side, which is almost perfectly sized to fit.

"That's not going to work," Zeke says, catching on. "It's not going to get hot enough to melt metal."

He plucks the silver from the gel and places it into the mold, wiping his fingers on his shirt.

"But this might do it."

He picks up the container and holds it up to the overhead light. As soon as he does, a ring of marbled white light falls on the table top, shining through the gel. He'd heard this was the reason they never stored ethylene in clear containers: if the light hit it just right, it became a laser burning holes into the ground. But it had always just been a rumor.

Zeke stretches his arms as high as he can, directing the filtered light onto the mold. After only minutes, he swears they're about to fall off. Pollux levels himself with the table, his eyes locked on the mold for any movement.

"Something's missing," he says, then taps the last container which holds a few leaves from Lacerta's plant. "What's this for?"

Zeke lets his arms drop, trying not to sigh with relief as the blood rushes back into them. Hopefully the blank look he gives Pollux is enough to convey he doesn't know without saying it.

Pollux scans the room, everyone's back to them as they look for a keyhole.

"Calico girl," he says, spotting Lacerta.

"Pollux!" Lyra growls from her corner as Lacerta turns away from the wall to face him.

"What did you call me?"

He ignores her and points to the last container. "What is this?"

Her hands perch on her hips, one thin brow arching. "Hedera Helix."

"What's it do?"

"Eat it and find out."

Zeke fights a smirk. When Pollux doesn't react, Lacerta blows out a breath and trudges up to them. The overhead light makes the white patches of her skin even more defined, and Zeke starts to imagine her being two separate people somehow occupying the same space, glimpses of each peeking through. He presses the thought down before it can take hold.

Lacerta bends at the waist to examine the tabletop, trying to piece together what they're doing.

"It's like an old-fashioned key," she says quietly. "We have to use this stuff to make one."

"*Yes,*" Pollux snaps, clearly growing impatient. "So what does this do?"

Lacerta locks him in an icy glare, scooping the leaves from the container and stuffing them into her mouth without a word.

She chews for a few seconds, heaving a sigh as if she couldn't be more bothered. Then she leans over and spits a gelatinous green wad into the ethylene, swirling it triumphantly while Pollux and Zeke gape.

"Now try," she says, plunking the container down in front of them.

The greenery has almost entirely dissolved, only tiny flecks still circling in the thinned liquid. Pollux picks it up gingerly, his lip slightly curled, and holds it aloft until he catches the beam of light. The refraction falls onto the mold, illuminating the metals. After a moment, the silver begins to move just slightly, a pool forming beneath it.

"Don't let the copper start to melt," Pollux instructs, and Zeke moves closer to watch.

As soon as the filament has liquified, he taps Pollux on the hip and he drops his arms.

"Let it cool," Pollux says. He turns to the rest of the room, where the others have started searching the floor on their hands and knees.

"Has anyone found a keyhole? Or anything irregular?"

"There's nothing," Cygnus says, sitting back onto his knees.

"You're not looking hard enough," Pollux barks.

Lyra stands up, her jaw set, and strides toward him. Zeke is sure she's about to unleash a string of pointed insults, but instead, she stoops down at his feet and pushes Pollux until he moves. As soon as his right foot comes up, the hole reveals itself.

The silver has settled into the mold, the copper rod sticking out as the handle, and Zeke is a little taken aback to see it work so well. Using the tips of his fingers, he wedges it out of the indention, feeling the brittle pop as it releases.

It looks almost too sculptural to function, but he kneels down and fits it into the keyhole beside Pollux's shoe.

The floor beneath him starts to vibrate, the tremors shaking his knee caps. The wall to his left undulates, and it takes Zeke a moment to realize he's not hallucinating. The back wall of the room is moving, pulling to one side like a curtain. Light beams through the widening strip of opening, clear and white like the lights in the hospital. Another fingerprint from the doctors.

Once the wall has retracted entirely, the vibrating stops and the room rests. Cass slowly straightens, taking a few steps toward the new space. Zeke can see the dark outlines of two doors cutting through the brightness at the end of the corridor.

"Are we supposed to go through?" Lyra says, hovering behind the edge of the table.

"No, this is bullshit!" Cygnus storms across the room to the exit, stopping just short of the barrier. "We did the game, let us out!"

He kicks the wall so hard it's a wonder his foot doesn't snap in half. A hissing sound creeps in from the edges of the room, and Zeke spots a stream of fog draining from nozzles in the corners.

His skin floods cold. Enforcer proxy drones used gas to knock them out during the ration riots when he was twelve. He can still feel the burn in his throat, the weight in his brain as it filled his lungs and blinded him. Without realizing it, he crouches closer to the floor.

The fog is hovering at the ceiling like clouds, though no one has seemed to notice it yet. Cygnus beats his foot into the wall again, and Lyra rounds on him.

"Will you knock it off?"

He pauses, considering for a long moment. Then his arm snakes out to grab her, hauling her across the floor in a stride. He tosses her sideways into the particle wall.

Zeke had once heard a cable break in the manufacturing plant. It had made a sound almost like music as the metal bowed and snapped. The wall makes a sound exactly like that as it catapults Lyra's body across the room, the rebounding thrum blending with the cry that comes from her mouth. Her hip catches the table, slamming her to a halt before she crumples to a heap on the ground.

Zeke can smell it before he sees it. The jacket at her shoulder has burned away, the seared skin beneath just visible through the hole. She curls around herself, tucking her knees into her stomach, her hand gripping her arm just below the burn.

He blinks, and Cygnus is staring up at him from the floor. He's faintly aware of someone calling his name, but it's almost like a dream fading. Cygnus is breathing hard, blood trickling in a line from his top lip into his mouth, spreading across his teeth. His eyes burn with a cold, constant rage as he stares up, his head resting at an angle against the wall.

Zeke takes a step back, feeling wet across his knuckles, though he's not sure if it's his or Cygnus's blood.

"Freaking psycho," Cygnus spits, using his shirt to catch the stream from his lip. "I said I was sorry."

Lyra is sitting up, Aquila next to her bracing her shoulder. Everyone else is watching him in suspended fear, not sure what to do.

Pollux lets out an agonized yelp, doubling over suddenly. The fog at the top of the room has thickened and lowered, though only Pollux is tall enough to have caught a wisp in the face. He grinds his palms into his eyes, his knees nearly buckling.

"Jeez, what is that?" Lacerta says, finally seeing it.

"Let's just move to the other room," Aquila says, standing to help Lyra get shakily to her feet.

The pair shuffle toward the light, their heads bowed, and Lyra grabs a fistful of Pollux's shirt as they pass to lead him along. Zeke turns to follow, but his head jolts forward with a sudden impact. He stumbles a step, bringing his hand to the ringing at the back of his skull. Cygnus is standing behind him, his fist cocked back like he's about to strike again.

"Don't ever put your hands on me again," he growls, his blonde hair matted against his forehead.

Zeke braces, tensing for the blow to fall. A shape moves on his right side, Aquila materializing out of the air like a specter.

"Awesome," she says, an edge to her voice he hasn't heard before. "Well said. So your manhood has been restored, right? Can we move on to the next challenge, or do we all need to be blinded by gas to prove we're tough?"

The tiniest hint of something moves behind Cygnus's eyes, but he's already running for the next room before Zeke can work out what it is.

The hissing has started again, the nozzles vomiting another layer of gas into the room, and Aquila ducks to avoid the encroaching clouds. He follows her out, running into the next room in a crouch. As soon as his foot crosses the threshold, the walls begin to move again, sealing them in.

Pollux sinks to the floor, kneading his eyelids, and Zeke takes a peek at his right hand. One of his knuckles must have caught a tooth when he hit Cygnus. Shame it didn't shatter every one of those pearly whites.

There's a whisper of sound from the corner, like the pressure released when opening a bottle for the first time, and a drawer pops out of the wall. Everyone goes rigid. When nothing happens, Cass tiptoes closer to peer inside.

Her hand disappears into it and comes out with a tiny white tube. She pops the top and takes a sniff.

"Smells like Lidocream," she says, tossing it to Lyra.

Lyra squeezes the contents into a mound in her hand, slathering it on her shoulder and closing her eyes. Her tan skin has drained to a sweaty gray, but she starts to flush with color after a few seconds.

"So, what?" she says, tucking the tube into her jacket pocket. "We play the game right, we get rewards?"

"No," Pollux says, drawing everyone's gaze to his corner. His eyes are furiously red and streaming tears. "I think it's pretty clear. Play the game, or pay the price."

He looks up, his irises covered in a milky glaze, and he doesn't seem to be able to focus on anyone's face.

"Who wants to go next?"

LYRA: 9

Up until now, the worst burn she'd ever had was when her sister Vesta had flung near-boiling tea on her for shutting off the video streaming.

The noise never ceased in her house. Every room always had someone in it, and they were always making noise. She'd learned to live with a low-level headache just behind her ears all the time, but that day every stray sound was particularly pinchy in her brain.

Vesta was watching a music competition in the living room, her legs crossed and her filthy sneakers on the couch, tears spilling over her round cheeks. The singer was wailing, tapping here and there on her soundboard to create a concussive racket. That was the day Lyra's mother had seen her collarbone skinplant and called her "out of control," and the words were still stinging the inside of her ribs.

When the shrieking, piercing sound reached a peak of terribleness, Lyra stood up and pulled the cord from the projector hub. The world was blessedly silent for all of half a minute before Vesta stood up in a fury.

"What is wrong with you?" she yelled. "It's just music!"

"That's not music," Lyra said flatly.

"How would you know? You never listen to music because you're dead inside! Mom said you were born before you developed a soul."

"Vesta, shut up!" Lyra said, jumping to her feet. She didn't remember throwing her mode screen, but there it went catapulting across the room to smack Vesta in the forehead.

She'd screamed like she'd been stabbed and grabbed her mug off the heater, sloshing an arc of liquid at Lyra that hit her bare thighs.

Pain flashed across her skin, but it was gone in an instant. That was the thing about burns: you thought they were over quickly, but really they were just lurking. They waited until you were in the shower, or getting dressed, or trying to sleep, then they came back for their real assault.

Lyra had stormed up to their room, locking Vesta out, though she probably hadn't tried to follow. She'd gathered a handful of paper from their bathroom and a dry washcloth, tossed them into a pile in the bathtub, and set them on fire.

As the glow surged, she sank down to the floor, resting her chin on the lip of the tub to feel the warmth. She pressed her father's lighter to her heart, still hot from holding the starting flame.

The paper burned first, the rustling like the softest base melody playing in her ears. The cloth came in later, the threads popping and cracking as they burned, staccato and sharp, punctuating the strain. When the whole fire joined together, the high notes blending into the constant melody, it was the most beautiful song that crested and peaked as the flames burned brightest, then faded into a whispering, haunting remnant. Lyra clung to the side of the tub, cold growing inside her as the sound died. Vesta was wrong. Lyra loved music. But she couldn't hear it in the wails or pounding beats of musicians. Fire gave its life to sing to her. Nothing any human did could ever compare.

Her knees knock together, shivers jolting through her even though the burn on her shoulder doesn't hurt anymore. It hadn't behaved the way that heat burns do. The pain hit the moment her skin touched the particle wall, and refused to release its hold on her since.

Aquila pats a little more Lidocream over the raw, crusted skin, using her spindle-like index finger.

"It almost looks like a keyhole," she says. "Maybe the scar will make a nice memento."

"Because I want to remember this so badly," Lyra answers, having to force it through her clenched teeth.

"Memories are the currency of life," Aquila says. "Or something comforting like that."

"If you're not going to help, can you talk quieter?" Lacerta says, aiming a glare at them as she feels along the wall. Cass and Cygnus are doing the same thing on the opposite side, keeping their distance from Lyra.

"We'd be a lot more helpful if we weren't having to watch out for your psycho boyfriend," Aquila snaps back, and a glow of gratitude warms Lyra's stomach. No one at C7 would have ever taken up the mantle for her.

"Look, I didn't know that would happen," Cygnus says, almost convincingly remorseful. Lyra had just heard Homer Oleyedo put on the same act too many times.

"He said he was sorry," Lacerta seconds, turning toward them.

The floor beneath her sneaker lights up when she steps on it, a perfect square of illumination. She jumps back like it might bite her, and the light fades.

"What . . ."

She places her foot down again, and the tile flushes the same bright teal.

Pollux lifts his head from the tent of his arms, his eyes swollen and squeezed shut. "Is it a clue?"

"The floor is lit up," Lacerta answers.

He scrambles to his feet, clumsily knocking an elbow into the wall.

"How?"

"Like, in a square, under my foot."

"This one does it too," Cass says. She tests a spot, making it light and dim with each touch.

"Can someone explain better?" Pollux sniffs, tethering himself to the wall with his hand.

Aquila rolls forward to her knees, reaching out to run her fingers over the floor in front of her.

"The floor is made of tiles," she says, wedging her fingernail into a miniscule crack that runs perpendicular along the floor. "Their weight is triggering some of them to light up."

She stands, slapping her foot down in a circle around Lyra until another tile blinks. Aquila extends a hand to her, wrinkling her nose apologetically.

"Can you stand on this?"

Lyra gets to her feet heavily, but once she's up the trembling in her limbs seems to dissipate. Aquila starts to hunt once more, positioning Pollux onto the next square she finds. Once she moves off, he starts to cast his arms around him tentatively, his fingertips almost reaching Lyra. Taking pity, she catches his hand in hers to steady him.

"I think I like you better blind," she says.

His grip is stiff in hers. "I'm not blind, I'm having a temporary reaction."

"You hope."

Aquila has finished assigning people to tiles, seven bright spots of color reflecting off the polished walls.

"Why isn't anything happening?" she wonders aloud.

"There's supposed to be eight of us," Zeke says quietly from the back of the room. "I knew Orion bailing would come back to bite us."

Aquila wilts a bit. "Can anyone reach two?"

"Pollux might," Lyra says, eyeing his long legs.

She moves his hand to her shoulder, just above the burn, and stoops to grab his shoe.

"Let me have your foot," she says, giving it a tug when he resists.

Finally he lifts it, his weight wobbling a bit as he rebalances himself. His fingers grip her shoulder, and a strange feeling starts to tug at Lyra's heart as she maneuvers his foot onto her tile.

There's something about the way he trusts her, the faith he puts into the hand on her shoulder despite the height difference between them.

It's a stretch, but Pollux spreads evenly between the two trigger tiles, one foot on each. Lyra weaves between the others, tapping each square she passes until, finally, one in the far left corner sparks up.

There's a sound of heavy locks rolling over, and the two doors at the end of the room slide open. Lyra can just glimpse the stretch of a short hallway through each.

"Why is no one moving?" Pollux asks after a long moment. "You saw what happens when we hesitate."

He finds the wall and uses it to guide him, heading for the open door on the left.

"Let's just split up again," Cygnus says, trying to sound casual. "Each team take one room?"

"How about you go alone, and the girls stay with us?" Zeke says, his voice harsh.

"How about you don't tell us what to do?" Lacerta quips back.

"Yeah, guys, stop treating Cygnus like he *intentionally* hurt Lyra," Cass says loftily. "It was an accident."

"You think?" Lyra snarls, her blood igniting. "Can I accidentally throw you off the nearest building?"

"Do whatever you want," Aquila says, striding to Lyra and hooking her arm. "We'll go with Pollux."

Zeke follows after them, and Lyra can't help but feel a small degree of relief when Cass, Cygnus and Lacerta split off to the room on the right. As soon as they're all inside, the door closes behind them.

"Well, this is cozy," Zeke says, shuffling as close as he can to the wall.

This room barely deserves the word. Lyra's initial impression had been right, it's little more than a short hallway braced with doors on either end. The wall to the right is glass, showing the trio in the room next to them.

Cygnus notices them, his eyes widening, and his red lips start to flap.

"Soundproof," Aquila says, tapping the window with one finger. "Well, that's a blessing."

"What's in here?" Pollux asks, feeling the walls blindly.

Lyra turns to the left, noticing rows upon rows of small square boxes built into the wall. Each one is covered with circular buttons. As she moves closer, she can spot faint numbers on each keypad.

"It's a wall of lock boxes," she tells Pollux. "And a two-way window into the other room."

"What else?"

"Why don't you sit this one out?" Zeke says, eyeing Pollux's puffy face.

"You need my help. Why else would you all have followed me in here?"

"Wow, Pollux," Aquila drawls, leaning her back against the glass while Cygnus pounds the other side. "Is our adoration that obvious?"

Lyra punches a few of the keys, noticing the tinny beeps they make. After her finger leaves the last one, a series of red numbers replaces the keys, projecting over them in a sequence.

"Whoops."

The others tense, turning toward her.

"What whoops?" Zeke demands. "What did you do?"

"I think it locks you out for a bit if you enter the wrong code. This one has a timer for sixteen minutes now."

Aquila swallows, her face paling. "Or maybe they gas us at sixteen minutes?"

"No, there's no point to that," Pollux says, running his hands over the glass window. "We can't solve anything if we're all incapacitated. They only gassed the other room because we weren't leaving it."

"You seem to know a lot about what 'they' would and wouldn't do," Zeke says slowly, his tone measured.

Pollux pauses, his arms dropping heavily to his sides.

"Oh okay, that old chestnut. He's smarter than us so he must be a spy, is that what you're implying?"

"I don't think you *are* smarter than us," Zeke shoots back.

There's a long stretch of silence that Pollux finally punctuates with a snort. "Really?"

Zeke chuckles, but it's as threatening a sound as the growl before the bite, and the intent isn't lost on Pollux.

"I wasn't trying to initiate a physical altercation," he says, backing down.

"That's too bad because I *love* physical altercations," Zeke says, but Lyra gets the sense he's just toying with Pollux now.

"Okay, that's enough," Aquila sighs, her eyes on the room next door. "I think they found something over there."

Cass is inches away from the glass, her palm flat and weighed down with a matte black cube about the size of an orange. As she holds it steady, Lyra notices the edges pulse with a glow that seems to move around the cube in a loop. Cass points at it, then exaggerates a shrug.

Pollux has sunk to the floor again, resting his face in his hands as if the pressure on his eyes is comforting.

"What is it?" he asks without lifting his head.

"Cass has a cube that's blinking," Lyra says when the others ignore him.

"Any particular pattern?"

Lyra presses closer, motioning for Cass to raise the cube. She does, but Lyra can see Cygnus roll his eyes behind her and the sentiment stings almost as much as the dull throb in her shoulder.

"It goes around the faces, then the points, then the edges," she relays.

"Maybe it's a code?" Aquila says. "To open their box? Like the blinks add up to something."

Pollux heaves another excessive sigh. "Tell them to try 6, 8, 12. Faces, points, edges."

Lyra points over Cass's shoulder at their wall of lockboxes until she understands. Then she holds up six fingers, then eight, then counts up to twelve. Lacerta punches them in as Cass translates. As soon as she's done, a timer pops up in red across their wall, the same as the one Lyra had triggered.

"I think it was wrong," Aquila says. "They just got a timer too."

Zeke runs his fingers over their own wall, but nothing responds. The timer on the lockbox continues to run down.

"Guess we better get comfy," he says. As soon as the words leave his mouth, he shakes his head as if he's trying to clear water from his ear. Lyra catches Aquila shooting her a concerned look, but she doesn't react. Even with the ticks, Zeke had stood up for her when no one else had. That earned something in Lyra's eyes, even if it was just her silence.

Zeke sinks to the floor as well, kicking his feet out in front of him and leaning against the wall like he's in his own living room.

"Hope no one has to pee. This one is going to take a while."

AQUILA: 10

On the convoys, Aquila had learned to love small spaces. She had her snug little room off the cockpit, meant for on-duty pilots to take a quick nap if they had a long stretch. Her father had commandeered it from the first co-pilot, who liked to make the trip back down through the ship to her family when she was off. He liked to have Aquila close, just in case he needed her to take the helm when his head was too foggy. The other co-pilots who came later didn't have the heart to make her pack up her hanging clothes and collection of Dunie toys that lined every flat surface, so she'd kept it for years.

It was the first space she'd had that was *hers*, not shared with her mother while they waited for her father to get done with his shift. She'd loved crawling into it, bracing her back against the wall to feel the thrum of the engines as she slept.

She would hole up for hours at a time, taking up so little space in her father's mind that he often forgot to check on her for a day.

That was probably why he'd waited so long to send anyone after her when the hull was pricked by a tiny, iced fragment of iron, collapsing the floor above her and crushing her room into a tomb.

Luckily the ship was compartmentalized in case that exact event were to happen, or she would have suffered the same fate as the families who were dragged out to suffocate in space.

She remembered very little from the days she spent immobilized between the walls, other than the sensation of being caught in a perpetual finger trap that was constantly pulling her in two tightening directions. There was no space to kick or twitch, and she remembers feeling like the room in her chest for her lungs to inflate was a luxury. Her elbow had been pinned across her face, but even if she could have seen there would have only been darkness around her. The only thing that truly stuck with her was the smell of her own body, the sweat and blood and filth and burned tips of her hair from the light tube that had been smashed into her skull.

It took them eight hours to clear the debris and get her out, and she only found out later that it took her father a full twenty-seven to remember she was there and in need of rescue. When they had finally started to chip away at the mass of twisted metal that surrounded her, they heard her babbling out a conversation and laughing as if it were the funniest thing that had ever happened to her. The rescue staff said she had spoken more words during her rescue than the whole two years prior to it. But she hadn't been there for any of it. In her panicked state, she had abandoned her own mind and another presence had slipped in.

In this room, with their legs splayed across the floor an inch apart and their collective breath heating the small space, that same presence is trying to push their way in again.

She can only thank her guiding stars that she'd ended up on this side of the glass. Being this close to Cygnus and his posse for any length of time would have resulted in casualties of some kind, though it's hard to say who would have prevailed.

The other room doesn't appear to be having any more luck than they are. Cygnus has finally exhausted himself trying to break the cube open and the girls are gossiping in the corner like the world is their social hour.

The clocks keep ticking down, though she could almost swear they go slower with each minute.

"What else is in the room?" Pollux asks for the fourth time, and a collective sigh rises into the air.

"*Nothing*, we're not blind," Lyra says, picking at the straps on her shoes. "They're probably trying to teach us patience. No better way than a forced time-out."

She pushes her legs out straight, admiring her sneakers.

"Why do you think they dressed us in all new things? These are the nicest shoes I've ever owned."

Zeke lets a breath pass through his nose, the corners of his lips curling up in agreement. "Right?"

"I don't think I've ever had shoes where the sock lining wasn't worn to crap already," she goes on.

"You guys have never had new shoes?" Pollux asks incredulously, directing his voice to the wall. They'd sat him facing a corner, just to minimize the time spent looking at his pitiful face. Or maybe to minimize his interjections in the conversation.

Aquila notes how both Zeke and Lyra stiffen, their foreheads bunching.

"There were nine people in my house, you think we were buying new stuff?" Lyra growls.

"Yeah, they were in a real hurry to bring the good shit out to Huygens Landing," Zeke says stormily.

Pollux rolls his head back.

"Don't give me the 'oppressed by the system' line. Everyone who moved to Titan did it of their own free will."

"Do you know the incentives my family got to do it?" Zeke says, his tone inching toward fury. "They practically gave them a house to move to Huygens. No one told them it's because no one wants to live there."

"My mom used to say one rich person needs six poor ones to run their lives," Lyra adds. "That's why they needed us on Titan."

Aquila laces her fingers together, wilting a bit with relief that she hadn't told the truth about living in The Rocks. What would they think of her, squirreled away in her polished, dustless house that was "too big" to be comfortable. What a spoiled brat she'd turned out to be.

Zeke rubs his thumb over the tattoo on his forearm, stretching out the numbers and letting them snap back into place. The ink looks older almost against his dark skin, somehow less aggressive than the pitch black cutting across her chalky-white starkness.

"Funny how places like these make us all equal," he says quietly. "Doesn't matter where you came from. We all wear crazy the same."

As he's speaking, the room fills with a sharp buzzing sound, and the last few seconds of the time run out. The others get to their feet, but Aquila's brain is still trying to catch up. Her eyes graze over Zeke, trying to pull some meaning from his stone features. Some context or nod for what he'd just said.

Places like these. Had he been to a rehab facility like her? The time to ask is slipping away, circling the drain, and she opens her mouth to seize it.

The room plunges into darkness so quickly that her stomach leaps as if she's just dropped off a ledge. There's a pressing silence, all the ambient sound suddenly amputated. A red light appears over-head, bathing them in a grim, bloody glow. Shadows pool under their eyes, sharp triangles of black under their noses, turning her friends into frightening skulls in the half-light.

Aquila's veins rush with cold panic. She suddenly can't remember how to breathe, and the strange sensation of floating wraps around her.

An electric hum rolls through the floor and a moment later the lights come back on. The blackout had only lasted seconds this time, but she felt it so much deeper than the first. She had spent too much time on these big structures; she knew the gasps of a sick engine.

"Yikes," Lyra says, unable to keep the rattle from her voice. "Is that part of the test?"

"Probably just power cuts," Zeke says. He's just trying to assuage them, obviously, and it's almost heroic.

Next door, the trio is huddling around their first lockbox. After a moment, they break apart, their faces contorted in frustration.

"They did the wrong code again," Aquila says. "They got another timer."

"And there's nothing else in our room?" Pollux says from his spot on the floor.

Lyra lunges to kick him but Zeke snags her around the waist at the last second.

"There's nothing in here, Pollux!" she fumes. "They're the only ones who got something! Maybe you picked the wrong room, genius!"

"What's the pattern again?" he asks, ignoring the hissy fit.

Aquila is trying very hard not to stare at Zeke's arm around Lyra, how his hand falls just above the curve of her hip. The hem of her shirt has ridden up and his thumb dips below it, and a sickly heat starts to cloud around Aquila's body at the thought of him touching Lyra's bare skin.

Embarrassment cuts through the sulking, and she shakes the jealousy off. They're trapped inside a coded cage and she's thinking about a boy, wondering if he might feel something when he looks at her. She'd always prided herself on being too strong-minded to fall for the games the boys on the convoys played, yet here she is, her mind spinning because the tattooed brawler is touching someone else. The banality of it makes her want to slap herself.

Needing distraction, Aquila goes to the window and waves until Cass notices her, then motions her over. She points, and Cass holds the cube up for her.

"It goes faces . . . edges . . . points."

Pollux stands, unwinding his legs from underneath him.

"That's not what you said before," he says.

Lyra stills, her cheeks turning red beneath her tan skin. "I . . . well, I thought . . ."

She shakes Zeke's arm off, grasping her wounded shoulder and pressing herself against the wall. Her eyes attach to the floor, and Aquila can't help but feel slightly sorry for her.

"On ours," Pollux says, turning himself around to face the room. "Try 6-1-2-8."

Since she's closest, Aquila stretches her finger out to punch in the code. The numbers are so faint they almost vanish into the button surrounding them, and each beep makes her heart jump as if she's hit the wrong thing.

As soon as she touches the last one, the square jumps forward, revealing a drawer hidden behind it. A jittery thrill runs through her, though she can't put her finger on why. Nothing they're doing is random or unplanned, which means any victory is tainted. Yet she still can't help the excitement as she pulls open the drawer as far as it will go.

"Did it work?" Pollux asks, the only one not crowding closer to see what's inside.

"It did." Zeke reaches in, coming out with a handful of the brightly colored spheres. "It's full of little balls."

Lyra snorts to herself while Pollux braces his fingers around his left eye, trying to pry the lid open to see.

"Great. So we have their key, they have ours, and we can't talk to each other."

"Teamwork makes the dream work," Aquila drones.

She hazards a glance at the separation window and almost jumps when Cass, Lacerta and Cygnus are all lined up on the other side. An identical expression is spread over their faces: their mouths are wide, their palms pressed against the glass, and their eyes are shining with panic.

Lyra points, unease weighing her features. "What's up with them?"

Aquila turns, giving them a wide-armed shrug. They all start to make the same hand gesture, their hands closing the distance between them and the glass, and realization starts to grow in her mind.

"I think their room just got smaller."

As she says it, her vision fading at the edges, she's only partially aware that the voice speaking does not belong to her anymore.

POLLUX: 11

Someone has put a lot of thought into exactly how to torture him. Meticulous, merciless thought. He tries to slow his breathing, the heat of Zeke's arm seeping into his skin. The room has closed in around them, funneling them together until there was barely enough leeway to move around each other. The more nervous they got, the more the others sweat, and the musty tang has filled what space is left of the room.

With nothing to look at, no sights to decode, his thoughts just keep pinging around inside his brain like flies in a jar. The others are too slow telling him crucial details about the puzzles, sometimes mistaking things altogether, and the lag of information is nearly unbearable.

And he has to pee. Just to tie it up in a bow.

Lyra moves next to him. He can feel the air density change again. They have about three feet left between the window and the wall, which is nothing to be concerned about yet, but Lyra keeps turning back and forth like the room might collapse if she takes her eyes off it.

Pollux tries to focus on the puzzle, to see the pieces in his mind.

"Try 3-1-4."

"Are you just guessing now?" Zeke broods, his shoes squeaking on the floor as he moves.

"No," he answers honestly, perturbed at the idea. "Yellow is third on the color spectrum, red is first, green is fourth."

There's a shared silence, and he imagines they're exchanging some sort of joke about him since he can't witness it. The beeping of the buttons rings out in the small space followed by a musical trill.

"Oh my god," Aquila's voice says, the surprise acutely insulting. "He did it."

There's a suction through the air followed by the hiss of the doors opening. Lyra's hand closes around his wrist. Immediately his muscles clench, retracting under her touch as sparks pulse up his arm. He yanks out of her grasp.

"Don't touch me," he pleads, hoping she can't detect the desperation in his voice.

She's silent for a beat, and he wonders if she's making that same face she did earlier, her mouth pulled in tight and her eyes burning.

"Fine," she scoffs. "Find your own way out."

Once he's sure she's gone, he runs his palm along the wall, following the echo of voices. They're upbeat, repeating each other's names excitedly, which strikes him as strange.

His next step plummets through the air and he stumbles off the step beneath him, nearly hitting the ground before a pair of hands stop him.

"That's a good look," Castor says. "You falling all over yourself."

It's like he's hit a wall he can't see. His whole body seizes at the voice.

Pollux jumps back, his arm pulling out of Castor's grasp, and the wall meets him on the next step.

"Jeez," Cygnus's voice says. "Calm down. I just wanted to say your thing is over there."

It's so clearly Cygnus that he wonders how he could have mistaken it.

"My thing?" he asks, his heartbeat dying down in his throat.

When silence greets him, he swallows, peeling his back away from the wall behind him. He casts his arms around, waiting for them to connect with something, then takes a step forward when they don't.

"Okay," Lyra's voice comes to him, directly to his right. "As much as I'd love to watch this, my conscience won't let me."

He drops his arms, wondering how long she's been watching him. The thought of her witnessing his moment of hysteria is displeasing.

"Don't throw a fit," she says, drawing closer. "I'm going to touch your hand."

Pollux braces, waiting for the spike of nerves up his arm. But when the warmth of her palm envelopes the back of his hand, it doesn't come.

"Did you die?"

He presses his teeth together. "No."

"Great."

There's a sharp tug on his arm, and he's yanked a few steps before she stops again.

"This one's yours."

Pollux uses his fingers to crack open one eye, ignoring the shard of pain it drives into his pupil. The wall is in front of him, but he isn't in any of the rooms from before. A cubby hole sits at shoulder height in front of him. The glare of lights angers his delicate iris, and he looks up to see his own name emblazoned overhead.

Glancing around the room, he confirms that the other's names are displayed as well, each with their own box below. Lacerta is rooting around in the opening beneath Orion's name, and as he watches she pushes something into the pocket of the jacket tied around her waist.

Pollux lets his eyelid close, reaching forward into the mouth of his own. As soon as his fingers touch the strings, he knows exactly what's inside.

Ever so gently, he extracts the violin from the cubby, hearing the boxy sound when it knocks against the side. Disbelief suspends him for a moment as he tries to work out the meaning behind the gift.

"Get anything good?" Lyra asks, her voice coming from his left this time. "Seems like everyone got something that already belonged to them, which seems like a crappy prize."

His fingers tighten around the neck of the instrument, but he doesn't answer. Objects of sentimentality, restored to everyone for completing an assigned task. It's a clue he can't decipher yet, and the lack of knowledge is beyond irritating.

Lyra's touch encircles his wrist again, and he tries not to resist as she pulls him forward.

"The door is over here," she says, leading him a few steps until his feet touch grass.

They start off across the lawn. Pollux tries to picture the layout of the grounds around the main building, the half-moon of houses that surrounded it separated by grass. The weight of the violin against his side is so familiar that it casts a sense of split reality on his surroundings. During their first hour together, Lyra had said this place felt like a dream. But his dreams were technical and bare, reworkings of problems he hadn't solved or things that needed to be finished. There was nothing out of place in his dreams. But this, feeling the same worn patch under his thumb, the indents on the looping keys where he'd pressed too hard, the deep-pulsing knowledge that this is *his* instrument, here, in this place . . . he's starting to understand what she meant.

Lyra leads him firmly, more quickly than he'd like, but soon they even out on flat ground. She stops, and there's the sweeping sound of a door rolling on its track.

"This one says C on it, so I'm guessing it's ours."

Pollux's feet catch on the jamb as they go in, jostling the instrument and causing it to make an upset twang.

"What is that, anyway?" Lyra asks.

He stops himself from claiming it's his outright, in case it might lead to more questions. "A violin."

"Can you play that thing?"

He lifts it even with his face, his chin finding the divot like it had so many times, and pops the bow from its mount on the back. As it slides across the strings, tiny vibrations light up his fingers, and the sound of it climbs through the air around him. The familiarity of it, the feel, the tone, creates a certain ache in his heart he can't explain. He plays an ascending progression, the strings pressing into the pads of his fingers like keys into locks.

"God, okay, enough of that," Lyra orders, cutting through the music and walking past him.

Odd. Pollux lets the violin hang again, missing the sound of it already. Very odd. Most people could only stand him when he was playing the violin. Castor had told him it was because it's the one time when he stops talking.

"Here," Lyra's voice comes back into his earshot. "I knew I saw a first aid kit in the other house."

There's a splash of liquid on the floor and Lyra's hissed curse follows.

"You're going to have to sit down so I can reach," she says.

He lets her guide him into a chair and leans back when she tells him to. A moment later, blessedly cool liquid runs over his swollen eyelids, coursing across his raw cheeks. It's over all too quickly, but his skin begins to relax, the smallest crack of light reaching his corneas. He touches his face, noting the inflammation has already started to recede.

Blinking a few times brings the room into focus. Lyra is sitting cross-legged on the couch, the contents of a first aid kit scattered across the table in front of them. She's rubbing something into her shoulder, and Pollux finally sees the result of the burn Cygnus had inflicted on her. Must have been what he was smelling the whole time they were trapped together in the shrinking room.

Her skin has paled from its usual caramel tone, but the knot in her forehead starts to disappear the longer she rubs the burn. He notices the bottle of Lidocream in her lap, already half gone.

"We might need that later," he warns, but her eyes slice at him.

"Pollux. Shut up."

Rather than push her further, he gathers the contents of the first aid kit back together, closing it and moving it to the kitchen counter out of her reach. She scoffs.

"We're not going to run out, Pollux. They're in every house."

She stands, stomping past him into the kitchen to throw open the cupboards. Rows of brightly colored parcels are stacked inside, food enough for weeks.

"Every house is stocked. We have everything we could possibly need."

Pollux blinks, realizing the overhead lights are on. Behind Lyra, the windows to the courtyard are black and glossy.

"They're simulating night," he points out, though it's more a confirmation to himself.

"Yeah," Lyra says, crossing her arms as she twists to look. "Kind of creepy. Maybe they think it'll make us sleep."

As soon as she says the words, he can put a name to the feeling that's been hanging across his whole body, dragging him down. He's exhausted. Every cell is overworked, and his mind aches from over-use...or maybe the latent swelling.

He glances at the cuff on his wrist, wondering what hour the station is programmed to reflect. But instead of a clock, the mode face shows only a single blue ring. At its center is the same symbol that bullets their tattoos, the Pt amidst a ring with arrows arcing around it. When he holds it closer to his eyes he can see the faint outline of four more unfilled rings rippling out to the border of the frame.

Lyra turns, noticing him puzzling over it.

"Yep, we got a completion ring."

She tugs her braid loose, shaking her hair out with her fingers as she walks past him.

"Happened right after we beat the shrinking room."

She lifts the hem of her ragged shirt to sniff the fabric, flashing him the entirety of her abdomen in the process.

"Do you think we're allowed to shower in here?"

Pollux glues his eyes to the floor at her feet, hoping she can't see the heat rising in his cheeks.

"Please don't undress in front of me," he says, taking note to emphasize that he's saying please again.

Lyra lets her shirt drop. "Calm down, prude."

Pollux walks past her, wanting to escape before she can mock him further. He reaches the first door in the hall, confirming to himself that it's a small, sparsely furnished bedroom. The closet is an open design, rods built directly into the corner, and more versions of the same uniform hang in rows. He pushes them aside, noticing the range of sizes as if the room wasn't meant for anyone in particular. His fingers land at last on the few sweatshirts toward the back.

Orion surfaces in his mind like a cork popping up in water. He'd been wearing the same jacket as they were, grabbed from the nearest closet, yet the hem along his neck had been a distinctly different color. Looking through the selection, Pollux doesn't see a single navy shirt that matches.

There's a puzzle there, waiting to be solved, but the pieces are still nebulous and unshaped. He touches the soft fabric of the shirts again, plucking out a female-sized shirt and setting it aside for a reason he can't articulate.

He goes to the bed, his joints loosening as he sits down. Water rushes through the pipes in the ceiling overhead: Lyra is showering in another part of the house. He checks the mode again, swiping across the screen so it scrolls back to the time. If they're adhering to a standard 9/15 daylight split, there should only be about seven hours left of simulated night. Once he's rested, he'll start on the next puzzle. Orion.

"Lights off," he speaks aloud, and the room plunges into darkness.

ZEKE: 12

Zeke could swear these pristine, polished houses are offended by his presence. After all, they were never meant for someone like him. They expected to be filled with the type of person who glittered in the light, the kind he saw when his sister streamed shows from the big cities. Like Cass with her channel that she can't shut up about. People who wanted a view of Titan from their bedroom but not to dirty their shoes with Titan mud.

The thought makes him smile slightly, imagining how this house would look after he and his family had tracked through it a few times in work boots.

He lets his fingers brush the pill bottle in his pocket, reassuring himself that it's still there. It was almost too surreal, to see it sitting so new and untouched in his box. His own prescription bottles were covered in fingerprints and peeling labels, degrading a little further every time he brought them in for refills. It had felt like a trick, like they were testing him somehow. He's still expecting it to be empty, or full of placebos. That's the kind of trick they would play on a patient, just to see if you would comply.

Aquila rummages through the cabinets, eventually selecting a yellow bag of puffed corn.

"Nothing fresh, though," she says, pursing her lips.

"*Fresh* stuff?" he asks, feigning shock. "You rich girls need a mountain of apples or something, boss?"

Her face pinches a bit, and he regrets teasing her about it. If she was determined to pretend she didn't come from money then he'd let her, though it'd been obvious to him the first time he saw her. She was too clean, her hair too glossy, despite the fact that she looked like she hadn't eaten in weeks. It wasn't a look Zeke preferred. On a good day, when he wasn't trying to keep the voices in check he might have been caught eyeing Cass, with her bump of a backside, or even Lyra had she not reminded him so much of his sister Dione.

Yet he still found his gaze lingering on Aquila's full lips, or her thick eyebrows. Or those haunting eyes. His Mama Rie had eyes like that, ones that you came to resent because every time they pinned you, there was no looking away.

Aquila hops up onto the counter, crossing her legs beneath her. She forces open the bag she's holding, pulling out a kernel of puffed corn between two fingers and poking it into her pocket to feed the chick. The smile spreads across Zeke's lips, and he shakes his head slightly.

"I see where your priorities are," he says, reaching into the cooler box for a bottle of water.

The sound of Lacerta and Cass laughing echoes off the glossy walls, and annoyance bubbles in his stomach. The others seem right at home in these factory-made condos. They don't even question why they have access to them, what purpose the people in charge could have for allowing it.

Only way you're ever going to get inside a house like this is as the cleaning crew, the deep voice warbles. Zeke shakes his head sharply, clearing it out before it can say more. Aquila's chemical-blue eyes watch him curiously.

"I'm going to see if there is a shower in this place," he says, hoping to divert her speculation.

He reaches behind her head, pulling down another package of food and dropping it in her lap.

"You better feed yourself and not just that bird," he adds before turning away.

Cygnus, Cass, and Lacerta are sitting in the living room, their feet all over the couches, and it strikes him that there's no dirt in the entire station that could muddy their shoes. For someone who's been living in a perpetual mudhole his entire life, it's an odd reality. He'd stopped being bothered by the film of caked dirt on their floor, the clumps on the door knobs. The absence of it is somehow worse. It's yet another reminder that nothing in this place belongs to him. He's a guest, a prisoner, a trespasser, only there at the pleasure of the doctors.

He walks by the gaggle without a word, though he can feel their gaze follow him. The room at the end of the hall has light streaming from the doorway, and as he draws nearer he can see the lip of a chrome sink.

As soon as the door slots closed behind him, he claws at the pocket of his shorts. The bottle rattles as it comes out, and when he pops the top he recognizes the flat, bitter smell of Moxifarin. So it is the real stuff.

He tips out the contents into his palm. Only six pills roll out, sticking to his warm skin. Six pills. It's a cruel joke, but better than nothing.

He selects two, tossing them into the deepest part of his throat he can reach. They fight all the way down, but Zeke can already feel relief starting to ease his muscles. As soon as he relaxes a bit, he catches a whiff of himself. It had been meant as a distraction, but getting cleaned off starts to tempt him.

It's a small bathroom, but the half-shower in the corner is still big enough to get the job done. There are clean towels stocked in the clear cabinets, and he wonders how often someone will come by and replace them once they've been here a while. A sweep through the shelves finds him a can of hair-removal gel, and he slathers some on his face before setting it back. His mind floats over Aquila, remembering the way she anxiously rubbed her jaw, and he moves the can to the sink instead.

Zeke strips, kicking the uniform into a damp pile on the floor. He gives the cuff on his wrist another tug, but it seems determined to stay on. As he steps into the stream of water, he thinks back to the last hospital when his roommate had bitten the tip off his tongue while showering alone.

It's strange, the lack of actual physes or orderlies in this place. There's not a hospital in his memory quite like it. He'd always known there were places where rich kids got sent when they became too embarrassing to their families, but it's nothing he ever thought he'd be sent to.

Steam fills the shower, thick and heavy, pressing up into his sinuses. A trace of a scent comes to him, something left over in the tissues of his nose. It's sickly-sweet and plastic, and an image of an oxygen cup flashes through his memory.

They put you out, the raspy voice whispers. *Who knows what they did to you while you were sleeping.*

His coworker Volans had said the same thing to him when he'd gotten back from his first hospital stay. With the fresh diagnosis tattoos, the Gekko manufacturing facility wouldn't take him back, which was the whole point of slapping the codes where anyone could see them and look them up. So any beady-eyed HR rep could steal a look and know exactly what kind of monster hid in your mind. Couldn't have someone like that slipping into your work force. Or maybe, someday, back into the shallow gene pool of Titan.

Zeke had ended up at the water treatment plant just like everyone else in Huygens did at some point. They'd put him in the basement, monitoring fume levels every fifteen minutes. It wasn't a job that required any brain power, but that's what happened when you were diagnosed. People stopped believing you could do anything, like you were at risk of breaking down at any moment and throwing yourself out a window.

"Did they put you under?" Volans asked while Zeke entered the latest reading.

Zeke had chewed the inside of his lip, not wanting to engage in a conversation.

"You can't let 'em do that, boss," he went on, jiggling his foot and sending a shower of dried dirt across the desk. "That's when they start snipping stuff in your brain. One little cut and you're a mushroom."

"Do you mean vegetable?" Zeke had said, annoyance flooding his spine.

"Yeah, you're a vegetable," he amended, his deep rumble of a voice trembling in Zeke's ears. "Fight it, even when they try to put you down. Fight it in your mind, and they'll never be able to get you."

Zeke taps the shower knob, cutting the stream off. The heat is starting to stifle him, and he needs to keep himself from getting worked up. Memory loss was a side effect of anesthesia. It would make sense that he couldn't remember how he'd gotten here, but something tells him there's more to it than that. Instinctively, he touches the corner of his eye, and finds it tender.

Muscles remember being hurt, Mama Beck's voice says, and his heart wrenches a bit at hearing it. *Even when they heal, they remember.*

The door slides open and he whips a clean towel out of the cabinet. Cygnus squeezes himself through the opening, closing the door behind him, and Zeke tenses.

"Hey, don't freak out," Cygnus says, holding up his hands.

Purple bruises have bloomed beneath his thin, pale skin, spreading out across his cheek. There's a clod of dried blood in the center of his top lip, which must hurt when he talks, and that's at least slightly satisfying.

"I think we got off to a bad start," he says, his feet moving him closer slowly. "I'm sorry for what went down with that girl."

"Lyra," Zeke says, the rebound of his own voice startling him for a moment.

"I'm sorry. It wasn't a good look. Are we cool?"

He tightens his grip on the towel at his waist, Cygnus's presence closing in on him. He certainly doesn't seem scared he'll get hurt again, and now Zeke wonders if he had even liked it on some level.

"No, we're not cool, boss," he says, his voice rising. "And can you get out of my space?"

Cygnus keeps coming, one step at a time in that unfazed, slow crawl.

"I just don't want you to see me like that," he goes on, each step falling closer. "We need to stick together, you know?"

One more step, Zeke tells himself. One more step and that lip is getting split open again.

The door slides back, making both of them snap toward it. Aquila leans against the frame, lazily crossing her long right leg in front of her left. She pops a cluster of nuts into her mouth, and Zeke is at least slightly relieved to see her eating.

"What's the party theme, guys?" she asks lightly. "Hetero prison shower?"

Cygnus makes an annoyed gurgling sound in his throat. "Can't you find another house to haunt, ghost of toothpick?"

"Hey Cygnus, there's another bathroom. Right there," Aquila says, pointing behind her where indeed there's a darkened half-bath across the hall. "Or are you scared to go by yourself?"

He strides to the doorway, shoving her backward so hard she stumbles.

"You're the only one who needs to be scared," he murmurs to her, his head bowed close to her ear.

Zeke steps out of the shower, his slick feet sliding a bit, but Aquila just smiles and crunches another nut cluster.

"Noted."

Cygnus snorts, turning sharply and pacing down the corridor. When his footfalls fade, Zeke marches out of the bathroom, slapping water across the floor as he heads for the room at the end of the hall.

"You shouldn't mess with him," he says as he passes Aquila. "That guy is unstable."

"Yeah, I get a real rapey vibe," she agrees, following after him at her own pace.

Zeke turns on the lights in the room, heading for the corner. Orion had said there were uniforms in every closet, and he wasn't wrong.

He fights a shirt off the hanger and wrestles into it, using the towel to block Aquila's view while he pulls on new shorts. Once he's dressed he grabs the blanket off the bed, leaving a mess behind. He likes the idea of someone having to clean up after him, since they seemed so determined to have as little contact with their patients as possible.

"Where are you going?" Aquila asks as he skirts around her.

His blood is still boiling, and being under the same roof as Cygnus is going to set him off sooner or later.

"I'm sleeping outside. Screw these weird houses."

He storms down the hallway, passing the group in the living room that goes silent at the sight of him, and out the patio door. The strangeness of what he's doing starts to dawn on him as he walks barefoot across the grass, but he's committed to the spectacle of rebellion so he walks until he reaches the center of the lawn. He's halfway between the neighborhood and the puzzle room, or the Tect as everyone has started to call it. As he fans out the blanket, it strikes him that it must have been meant as a sort of rec center, the way it's situated in the center of the neighborhood. It's a strange, almost second-hand experience, being in a structure obviously meant to foster a luxury lifestyle but with all the comforts stripped away in order to make it suitable for them.

He sits heavily on the blanket, already regretting his decision as his low back protests the hard ground. The sound of rustling foot-steps behind him grows louder, and his muscles go stiff.

When he turns over his shoulder, it's Aquila padding softly toward him with a pillow under her arm.

"Easy," she chuckles, spotting the agitation on his face. "Just me."

She sits down near him, just off the blanket as if she's afraid to touch it.

"You know, A-House is open," she says, tossing her pillow behind her. "But I've never slept outside before."

Her hand scoops the inside of her pocket and she brings out the chick, placing it on the ground in front of them. It stretches out, shaking until its feathers fluff in all directions then settle back down. It starts to hop over the grass as Aquila watches, her lips pressed together to hide her smile.

"Did you name it yet?" Zeke asks as she tosses a puffed corn kernel into its path.

"Fish Bait."

A snort of laughter escapes him.

"That's cruel."

"You love it," she says, casting a sly smile his way, and he's stuck staring at those tinted red lips again. Something about her is easier, more present than before. She'd been so frantic in the Tect, but not a trace of that energy remains now.

"You seem different," he says aloud.

Her smile spreads, her eyes dancing like hard diamonds.

"Better?"

His stomach clenches. Why is it suddenly so unnerving to talk to her?

"Just different."

He peers at the inside of her arm, trying to make out the numbers on her tattoo. But they're nothing close to his.

"What . . . what does yours mean?" he asks haltingly, pointing to her diagnosis code.

It takes her a moment to realize what he's talking about.

"Oh. I forgot I had this," she says, brushing her fingers over the tattoo. "No idea. I've never been to a rehab that does that."

"A rehab?" he echoes, the idea like a foreign word. "That's what you think this place is?"

A flash of pink rises in her cheeks, and she picks at the grass by her knee.

"Yeah. That's where we are, right? The uniforms, the inability to leave, the constant monitoring?" She nods up to the dark orb that hangs over them.

"Sure, except, I've never had a drug problem in my life."

The meds made him sick at the scent of alcohol, let alone hard drugs. Not to say that there wasn't access to them in Huygens, but it had always seemed like a risk he couldn't take. His brain was volatile on a good day. Drugs would be like dropping a stick of dynamite into it.

"Have you?"

As soon as he asks it he wishes he hadn't. Her eyes widen, though she keeps them glued to the ground, and shame settles across her thin shoulders.

"Is that what this is?" he asks, taking her wrist gently to turn the tattoo upright. "Are you a diagnosed addict?"

She tugs her arm back, tucking it against her stomach.

"I don't know what you're talking about," she says roughly.

"Hey, look, I'll tell you mine," he says, huddling closer to show her his own numbers. "That, F20.9, that . . . that's a diagnosis code. For schizophrenia."

Aquila's dark brows knit together in confusion, and she touches the faded ink.

"I have paranoid schizophrenia," he repeats, softer, as if he can make it sound less threatening. "So whatever yours is, it can't be that bad."

She drops her hand, examining her own tattoo again. "I don't know what mine means. I didn't have it before I got here."

"Aquila," he says, laying his hand over her kneecap. Her skin is so chilled that he almost draws back. "I don't think we're in a rehab. I think we're in a hospital."

She presses her lips into a line, looking down at his hand with a strange expression until he takes it away, afraid he's overstepped a boundary.

"A hospital. So we're all sick somehow?"

He lowers himself backward onto the ground, pinning his hands beneath his head just in case they want to do something stupid again.

"I think mentally, yeah."

"So you hallucinate?" she asks, stretching out a fingertip to stroke the top of Fish Bait's head. "Or hear voices, or what?"

"Both, when I don't medicate. As long as they give me the right dosage the voices just turn into static."

A tiny smile tugs the corner of her lips like a puppet string.

"That's kind of cool. Maybe you should give them names. They could be like your imaginary friends."

A cold cloud of unease drifts into his stomach, and he turns on his side to try to alleviate it.

"If I give them names, I start to think they're real." Even as he speaks, the static buzzes just behind his ears, trying to take form.

"What's wrong with that?" Aquila giggles, but it's less than convincing, as if she knows she's stumbling around something grave.

"If I think they're real, I start to do what they say."

LYRA: 13

Every sound through the night makes Lyra rocket out of the bed. She can't call it *her* bed, *her* room, because the overhanging knowledge that it isn't has her leaping at every sound, as if the person to whom it belongs might come walking through the doorway at any moment.

She rolls on her side, uncurling her fist. Her skin sticks to the smooth surface of her hollow lighter, the one she'd taken from her father's box of things from Earth and used for years. Eventually, Vesta had told on her for scorching the bottom of their tub one too many times, and her father had drained the last of the fluid from it before returning it to her.

He'd thought it was the pictures of planets on the peeling label that she was interested in, though they were almost unrecognizable from her fingertips wearing them off. Neither he nor her mother had ever asked her why she loved it; to Lyra, it seemed like they thought it was an embarrassing side effect of being a teenager. Something that would go away on its own if they just didn't talk about it. Even now, she can't help the simmering residual shame at how comforting the lighter is, empty or not.

After a while, it becomes clear she isn't going to be able to relax enough to sleep in this strange, sterile room.

She tugs on a clean pair of leggings from the closet and slides open the door to the living room, thinking maybe she can get the media streaming to work on the screen she'd seen earlier.

Pollux is perched on the couch, his long legs braced in front him, and she rolls her eyes.

"Can't sleep either?"

He looks up as she meanders past him into the kitchen, but it's the barest of glances.

"I slept a satisfactory amount. I don't like oversleeping because someone tells me to," he mutters, his spine bending as he hunches over the coffee table. The instrument he'd gotten from the game is out in front of him, and he appears to have taken all the strings off it and is now reattaching them so carefully it almost looks like surgery.

Lyra selects a bottle of water from the cooler box and takes a hearty swig.

"So you don't like simulated night?" she asks, thinking about the way her house used to dim and shutter during designated sleeping hours. "Must make it hard to live on Titan."

"Everything is hard on Titan." His answer is so quiet it might not have been intended to reach her at all.

Something about the sudden softness in his demeanor makes her stomach clench. Titan might be one massive compound she could never escape, but it was her home. The thought of being Pollux, years away from the place you grew up, almost makes her pity him. Yet just as soon as the feeling materializes, Pollux bolts upright, startling it out of her.

"I'm going to find Orion," Pollux says, staring her dead in the eye. "I want to ask him some questions."

She swallows, setting her bottle on the counter. After a stretched moment of silence, she crosses her arms.

"Did you want to invite me?"

He blinks slowly. "I thought I just did."

The station outside feels massive after being inside the condo. Lyra feels as if she's expanding in all directions with so much space to fill. It reminds her of the game she and her sisters would play, pressing your arms into a door frame for a minute and stepping away to feel the sensation of floating and spreading.

Titan looms through the expansive window of the station, orange and yellow glowing together like fingers of fire. Her eyes pass over the black mirrored observation center above them and she looks away quickly. It reminds her of the security cameras at school, and something in her doesn't want to be caught looking at it.

No matter how far they walk, they don't seem to get any closer to the window, which makes her feel like they're in a giant hamster ball. Pollux is still not convinced it's a real window, but somehow she can feel the presence of Titan even though it's miles away. There's no way a projection could feel that real.

Pollux walks with his hands hitched up under opposite arms, his legs storking out in front of him every step. Lyra finds herself watching him with a smile tickling the inside of her mouth. He certainly isn't the kind of person she would have chosen to hang out with at C7, but she ping-pongs between wanting to hold his head underwater and actually being happy for his company.

The far cluster of buildings where they'd first run into Orion appears over the tops of the trees, and eventually the grass gives way to paved ground.

The pair of them walk side by side down the deserted strip. Every window they pass looks like a blind eye in the dingy blue glow from the lighting tubes that run like veins through the structures, and she starts to wonder how fruitful this mission will really be.

"Looks pretty deserted to me," Lyra says, her voice rolling off the walls.

Pollux rounds on her, stopping her in her tracks, and bends to press his index finger over her lips. Her first instinct is to shove him as far as he'll go, but the look in his eyes makes her pause. He's focusing, listening to something she can't hear, his face just an inch away from hers. There's a dark freckle on the left side of Pollux's mouth, hovering just above his lip, and she wonders how she hadn't noticed it before. His finger across her mouth is cool and smooth, and an erratic flutter twists the air from her lungs.

He drops his hand, and breath floods back in through her nose. Turning quickly, he takes off down a thin alley between houses to their right, leaving her stunned behind him.

Jeez, Lyra, really? she chastises herself, forcing her feet to move. Pollux is halfway down the corridor, and the sound of soft, garbled voices finally reaches her. Light is bouncing off the smooth walls from a high window on the left, and she grumpily wonders how Orion was able to figure out the media streaming as she follows Pollux around the corner.

He stops dead on the other side and Lyra has to veer off to avoid slamming into him. She glares at the back of his head, but his eyes are glued to the window above.

"Why are we sneaking up on him?" she whispers.

He jumps as if he'd forgotten she was with him. "I want to see what he's doing."

"Okay, well," Lyra squints, trying to focus on the balcony across from them. "Why don't we climb up there and see if we can see what he's doing next door? It's really dumb to sneak around out in the open."

Pollux looks at her sideways, as if trying to puzzle out why she would know the proper way to sneak. Rather than wait for him to decide, she pushes him along the wall until they reach the opposite patio, then ducks around him to tug open the sliding door.

The scene inside freezes her feet in place. While the other houses had been pristine and untouched, this one looks like it'd been robbed. Or at least someone had tried, but she couldn't remember anything of worth in theirs.

The furniture is all overturned, some of it taken apart or shredded into clouds of fiberfill. The cabinets all hang open and the food is strewn across the kitchen counter. Some of it must have started to rot; a dense, moldy smell hangs in the air that Lyra's nose tries to reject with every breath.

Pollux's face mirrors her disgust as he steps inside, though he seems more upset by the general mess of things. Lyra points upstairs, wanting to escape the room and the stench as quickly as possible.

He follows her up the sharp steps, his footsteps louder than she would like, even though luckily Orion seems to have wrecked this house and set up camp next door instead. They reach the landing on the top floor, the sounds of streamed voices growing louder. The balcony door is open, and light from the neighboring house falls across the floor. Lyra is suddenly afraid he might be able to see their shadows moving and heads for the nearest wall. Pollux grabs her wrist, yanking her to a stop, and her foot slips on something beneath her.

She steadies herself on Pollux's forearm, glancing down to see the floor is covered in a slimy, rust-colored film. A trail leads to the nearest bedroom, dark swoops of color as if something had been spilled and unsuccessfully scrubbed.

The smell has thickened, choking down her throat, and a heavy hand starts to close around her heart. Something about this house deeply unsettles her, and her skin starts to crawl with the urge to be anywhere else.

Pollux leaves her, walking softly along the trail until he reaches the door and nudges it open with the toe of his shoe.

"Pollux," Lyra hisses, but he disappears inside.

Grinding her teeth, she follows after him, picking her way carefully over whatever is greasing the floor. She maneuvers through the doorway, afraid to touch anything, and finds Pollux standing in the middle of the room with his back to her.

She isn't aware she's screaming until his hand traps it against her mouth, sending the vibration through her jaw. She reels back, pressing her spine into the wall behind her, unable to tear her eyes from the body across the room.

The floor seems to tilt, rocking from side to side, and she slides to the ground for fear of falling over. Her knees jam into her chest, trying to put something between her and the scene in front of her.

A figure is slumped against the opposite wall, its head propped to one side. Her brain would like to make it into a boy, but anything that might have told her that is gone. His scalp has been removed, leaving a blood-matted gray cap in its place, and the nose has been cut down to a blackened triangle at the center of his face. His skin is so pale he looks like shaped moonlight, cold and silvery.

Pollux moves closer, squatting in front of the body and peering at it as if it's a trick of the light. It's then that Lyra realizes it wears the same clothes as Pollux, the same as the whole group, with a bright Pt embroidered into the dark fabric. Pollux tips his head to the right, studying the body's arm, and she notices with a turn that strips of flesh have been cut out so cleanly it almost appears mechanical. But that isn't what Pollux is looking at.

As he lifts the limp forearm, she finally notices the tattoo, stark across his drained skin. It reads "Orion."

Scrambling to her feet, she runs for the door. She flings herself down the stairs, barely catching herself against the banister on the turn, and slams to a stop four steps from the end.

Orion, or at least the boy who took the name for himself, is standing in the living room, his face turned toward the open patio door. She freezes, debating whether to run back up the stairs before he sees her, but Pollux's footsteps beat the floor above her and Orion turns.

They stare at each other for a long moment, both seeming to be frozen by indecision. Then his eyes raise, watching Pollux settle on the stairs behind her.

"He was dead when I found him," Orion says, his freckled lips barely moving.

"Is that why you felt the need to knock his skull against the wall?" Pollux asks. Not a hint of emotion marks his tone, and Lyra wonders how he can be so unaffected by the panic and revulsion that's burning her alive from the inside.

Orion hangs his head slightly, tugging at the sleeve of the hoodie he still wears as if he can feel Lyra looking for his tattoo.

"I didn't mean for anyone to get hurt. When the station blacked out, the walls came down for a second, and I thought I had a shot at getting out of here. I ran for it. I came across the kid upstairs, and the girl, passed out. He woke up first and got physical with me, I had to knock him out. I didn't mean to hit him so hard, but I was scared. I thought they would blow my cover and I'd have to go back to the other side."

"Other side of what?" Lyra gulps out, her voice betraying her own fear.

"G-Block. With the other young adults."

"What does that mean?" she pushes.

"What, you think you're alone in here?" he snaps. "This is just one block, out of who knows how many. You're not the only group in here."

His eyes have grown wide enough that the whites are flashing in the dimness. Her grip tightens around the stair banister, her palms slick. The thought of others like him lurking in the station all around them makes her skin crawl, but the only thing more unnerving is how much it seems to scare Orion as well.

"Look, I'll leave you guys alone," he says, sincerity weighing down his tone. "I don't want to mess anything up for you. I'll keep to my side, you'll never see me again. I swear. Just, let me stay here."

Pollux brushes past her, drawing even with Orion, and for once Lyra is thankful for his imposing height. To her surprise, Orion retreats a step, closing himself in his own arms and staring at the floor. It's a show of submission she wouldn't expect from a murderer who had done what he'd done to the body upstairs, and watching it makes her gut squirm.

"The game," Pollux says. "What do you know about it?"

Genuine confusion pulls at Orion's brow.

"The game? I . . . I don't know anything about a game. But trust me, I won't get in the way."

"What about the building? The tests they made us do? You said you didn't want to be a part of them."

"I don't know anything you don't know," he insists, his palms opening in surrender. "I just didn't want to get caught and sent back."

Pollux huffs in frustration, turning away from Orion. He's halfway to the open door before Lyra realizes he's leaving her there.

She jumps off the last step, skirting around Orion and hurrying for the patio frantically. She can practically feel him grabbing her the whole way, but she makes it to the door untouched.

"I get it, you think I'm a monster," he says, the sound of his voice jolting her to a stop. She whips around, but he hasn't moved a step. He lifts his head, spearing her to the spot with his gaze.

"But he's who you should be worried about." He nods his head in the direction Pollux left. "He's a sociopath. He's more dangerous than I could ever be."

He starts back up the stairs, turning his back to Lyra, and she bolts while she has the chance.

POLLUX: 14

Lyra is walking erratically, weaving toward him and away from him again, running to catch up, stopping altogether. It's becoming distracting, though he knows where the behavior is stemming from. Many people suffered some sort of dissociation after seeing a dead body. Like somehow their own survival was immediately threatened by it. Even growing up on the Eco-Farm, when death had been a part of almost every day, he noticed how heavy his parents got around it. Occasionally they couldn't even look at it head on, requiring slaughterers to do the work for them.

Death had only ever made Pollux curious. A body that functioned one moment could be rendered useless by severing one tiny connection, and once it was gone it was nearly impossible to restart. Almost nothing else in the world reacted that way. Even plants once cut could be transplanted to grow again, or took days to die. All other forms of energy were transformed rather than vanishing, and yet the energy that filled humans and animals seemed to evaporate at the moment of their death. Perhaps that fact was what everyone was so upset by. That there was a mystery no one could solve. Rather than finding it fascinating, the uncertainty of it unsettled them.

Pollux stops, turning to Lyra, who freezes a few feet behind him. "Are you disturbed?"

Her face, which had been slack in surprise, now gathers together in anger.

"Jesus, Pollux," she fumes. "Yes, I'm fucking disturbed."

"You're not in danger," he tries to assure her, harking back to the shows his mother and Castor used to watch. Some figure in power would always diffuse tension by promising no harm would come to their companions.

"I have to disagree with you there, Pollux," she says wearily, rubbing a spot on her temple. "Do you know that kid? The body hacker?"

"No."

"He sure seemed to know you."

Pollux shrugs, wondering where this tempest of a mood is coming from. Lyra seemed to always be swinging from one extreme emotion to another, which must be exhausting for someone her height. The lack of sleep is also starting to weigh on her; he can tell from the faint crescents under her eyes and lag in her movements.

"I think you should get some sleep," he suggests, thinking maybe it'll soothe her. He'd like to see her back to the wry, slightly irritated Lyra from the day before.

"Can you answer the question?" she says, her hands on her hips. "I did."

She presses her fingers into her eyelids, blowing out a hard breath. "Jeez, why can't you just be . . ."

"What?" Pollux snaps, hearing his mother's voice rolling out of Lyra's mouth. "Cute and cuddly? A normal human being? Why don't I have feelings like everyone else? Why couldn't it be me that's dead instead of Castor?"

There's a hitch in the anger on Lyra's face. "Did someone say that to you?"

He catches himself, wondering how he'd allowed the last statement to leave his lips.

"I told you I don't know anything about this place," he says, trying to tamp down the sparks of anger ricocheting around his ribs. "I told you that within five minutes of meeting you."

Lyra chews on her thumbnail, the tension in her face giving way.

"You did say that," she agrees.

"I won't lie to you," he says, stepping closer to her.

She flinches, going rigid, and he stops. The wariness on her heart-shaped face—the same way his parents had started to look at him after they'd caught Castor and him in the slaughter house—sends a shard through his heart, though he isn't sure why. Nobody is ever completely at ease around him. It shouldn't come as a surprise. But she had seemed to be able to see past that, at least for a time.

He deflates a bit, turning around to continue on his path. The next logical move is to put some space between himself and the fake Orion. It isn't out of the question to think he might seek out some revenge for them disturbing his hiding spot. Pollux had seen the same behavior in the Garter snakes they let loose at home to keep the rodents at bay.

Oftentimes, if he or Castor had disturbed their nests looking for hatchlings, the snakes would follow the boys' scents back to wherever they were hiding.

After a moment, the sound of Lyra's footsteps across the grass catches up to him.

"Who was Castor?" she asks, her voice heavy.

The muscles of his jaw tense. "My twin."

"Did someone really say those things to you?"

He's about to turn to her when a glow up ahead draws his attention. It's different from the constant luminescent web of light tubes that run through the whole station. This is selective, a bright spot just beyond the nearest belt of trees. He holds an arm out, bracing as Lyra steps into it and gives off an annoyed grunt. Just beneath the sound of her breathing is a faint electrical hum.

He heads for the light between the trees, the sound gaining strength the closer he gets. Pollux weaves through the trunks until he gets to the other side. A second later, Lyra joins him, her head tilting back in stricken awe. Rising up in front of them is a glimmering wall, ten feet high at least, just opaque enough to obscure the view beyond it. Lyra touches her shoulder absentmindedly.

"Particle wall," she says, the shine of it reflecting off her irises. "He was telling the truth."

Pollux turns to stare down the length of it, watching as the light turns to a thin thread in the distance.

"It must go all the way to the end," he states aloud, then catches himself. Why had he started making observations out loud?

"But why?" Lyra says, a slight whine coating her voice. "Why are they keeping us in one part?"

Obviously being trapped in the same enclosure with Orion is not ideal, but at least they were separated from the others in the station. Orion is manageable. All in all, he'd struck Pollux as a predator of opportunity, much like a shark. He posed little threat unless you were already bleeding. The real Orion's mistake had been in letting the imposter too close while he was down.

The butchering had of course come later.

"I'm sure the groups were decided for a reason," he answers her eventually. "And they don't want us mixing."

Lyra folds forward, huddling into a ball near the ground, and tucks her head against her knees.

"Nothing makes sense," she says, her voice muffled and quivering. "Why are we here? What are they doing to us?"

Pollux shifts his weight between his feet, debating if he should engage her physically somehow. He stretches out his hand, pausing just above her head. The memory of her hands in his hair, igniting every cell in his body at once, makes him pause. He'd made the mistake of touching her again already, just before they found Orion. The warmth beneath her skin had been enough to derail his mind for almost a full minute, sending it skidding across slick thoughts that had nothing to do with the task at hand. Deciding against it, he lets his hand fall back to his side.

"Let's go back," he says. "I don't think the Orion imposter will come after us. He'll stay in this area, where he can't be detected."

Her head pops up, her warm, brown eyes locking onto his. There's the faintest hint of umber in them, like the last traces of a campfire.

"Why does none of this scare you?" she asks, looking up at him.

A dismissive answer jumps onto his tongue, but he pauses. Fear wasn't something he sat with often, since there were so few legitimate threats, but the truth is that he had been scared. When the station plunged into darkness and he heard them—the voices of the others. The fear that had washed over him in that moment was unlike anything he'd felt before. It was caustic and consuming, devouring him whole in that moment. That kind of terror only came from a deep knowledge of an enemy that had been erased from Pollux's memory. His brain may not be able to place it, but the pathways in his body remembered it as if it were carved into his DNA.

He glances again at the particle wall, and the barrier begins to take on a new significance. If the station were to black out again, how many would come through the next time?

"It does scare me," he says finally, looking down at Lyra. "I am scared."

AQUILA: 15

Her nails are bitten. The newly exposed skin smarts every time she puts pressure on her finger tips, and her cuticles have been gnawed down to jagged spikes. The only remnants of polish are tiny black flecks caught in the cracks.

Bitch, she groans inwardly, stretching her hand out to examine the damage. If only there were someone to punish besides a hidden part of her own brain. She isn't too happy about the fact that she seems to have slept outside either.

She lets her hand fall back to her chest, tilting her head to check on the chick. It's sleeping against Zeke's outstretched hand, its beak tucked into its own feathers. At least the alter took care of it and didn't decide to throw it back in the lake. It was hard to tell what she'd choose to like or dislike; clearly she hadn't been a fan of Aquila's manicure.

She runs through the checklist: no new piercings, no hangover, no evidence of some of the other activities the alter had gotten up to before. She looks at Zeke, reassuring herself that his clothes are still on. Even so, shame begins to creep in from the corners of her mind. What had she said to him?

The station is starting to glow with a blush half-light, the tubes emitting a tone she remembers from dawn on the first day. Her fingers automatically go to her jaw, testing hair growth beneath her skin, but it's nothing more than the last time she checked. One night. That's all she'd lost. It's a relief, and yet part of her wishes it had been longer. At least then maybe they would know more. She could have woken up once it was all over, back at home, promising her father that she was clean and would never touch critch again.

Zeke stirs, taking a long breath in, and the chick gets to its feet to shake out its ragged feathers. Zeke's eyes crack open at the sound.

"Hey, boss," he says, his voice husky with sleep.

"Hi," she says, her throat contracting at the rasp of her voice. She must have been doing a lot of talking.

Zeke turns over, using the back of his hand to gently corral the chick over to her before sitting up.

"You get any sleep?"

"I'm not sure," she answers honestly.

"Yeah, I can't remember the last time I slept rough like this," he says, stretching his arms behind his back. The round muscles of his shoulders move beneath his shirt, and Aquila tries not to stare at them. There's no way to know what kind of a fool she already made of herself last night.

Zeke plucks up an open bag from the ground, giving it a test shake before dumping out the last few puffed corn kernels.

"Don't worry, Fish. We wouldn't think of getting breakfast before you do," he chuckles as the chick throws itself on the food.

"Fish?" Aquila giggles. "Did you name him after his conquered foes?"

Zeke pauses, his face faltering a bit.

"You named him Fish Bait," he says slowly.

"Oh, right," she says breathily, trying to brush it off before he questions her. "Sorry, lack of sleep."

She stands up, her joints popping angrily. A shape moves across the glass door in the house to their right, drawing her eye. A moment later Pollux paces by, his arms crossed and head lowered.

"Do you know where Lyra went?" she asks, remembering the cauterized skin on her shoulder. Somehow she can't picture Pollux tenderly doctoring her wounds. He's about as comforting as an ice bath.

"She left with that jackoff," Zeke says, nodding to the house labeled with a C. "Looks like he's not blind anymore. Pity."

"Speaking of jackoffs, what happened to Cygnus?" she asks, glancing around the half-circle of houses.

"He left us alone after you told him off," Zeke says, stuffing his feet back into his shoes. "You shouldn't mess with him like that."

Great. Yet another thing to worry about piecing together. She bends, scooping up the chick and tucking him into the pocket of her jacket. The longer she keeps talking to Zeke, the higher the chances get that she'll slip and say something else incriminating. Maybe she can shake down Lyra for a few details to help her cope.

Through the patio glass, Aquila can see Pollux walking in circles around the living room, making a ring around the sofa where Lyra is sleeping in a heap. He looks up when Aquila slides open the door, then goes back to pacing without a word.

"Is Lyra okay?" she asks softly, cutting across his path to kneel in front of the couch. Lyra is wearing a new shirt so the burn isn't exposed anymore, but from the way she's passed out she doesn't seem to be feeling it. In fact, if she wasn't rattling in breaths through her mouth Aquila might think she was dead.

"She's having some mental strain," Pollux says, pausing to look at her.

"No kidding. Is she in any pain?"

"I've been reapplying Lidocream while she slept."

"Oh," Aquila says, taken aback. Caring for a sleeping girl is definitely not something she would have assigned to his personality. "That was . . . nice of you, Pollux."

"The painkiller kept her sedated," he says. "She's quieter when sedated."

"Ah." That definitely seemed more like him.

Lyra starts to move, lifting her chin off the cushion to open one eye.

"Hey," she croaks. "Have we been rescued?"

Aquila's gaze flicks up at Pollux, whose dark eyes are watching them with an unblinking stare. "Hardly."

Lyra sits up slowly, her face set in an unhappy pout as she swings her legs around.

"I'm sorry I abandoned you," Aquila says, guilt sitting like a stone in her stomach. Had she been conscious, she would never have left Lyra alone with Pollux. The alter tended to put more precedence on chasing down a hook-up than doing the right thing.

"Yeah, you just dropped out after the Tect," she says, rubbing the dark skin beneath her eyes. "You didn't even say bye. What did you get, anyway?"

"What do you mean?"

"What did you get from your box?"

No trace of a memory comes to her rescue. Usually she at least has a foggy remnant of when the alter takes over, like the scraps of a night after getting too high, but this time . . .

She forces her brain to focus, pulling out the last image she remembers. When the room had started to close in on her.

In her moment of weakness, she'd scrambled for any other reality and opened the door to her mind. Of course the alter had jumped into the pilot's seat. And now she has a vital piece of information that Aquila may never get.

"I can't remember," she finally says.

Lyra narrows her eyes, something turning in her mind. Then she jumps, whipping her arm into her lap just as Aquila's wrist vibrates with a sudden surge from the mode. The screen is glowing with the same vibrant text as the first day.

Begin program.

She locks eyes with Lyra, the same fear mirrored on her face.

"Another one?"

"We don't have to do it though, right?" Lyra half-laughs unconvincingly.

The text on Aquila's mode disappears, replaced with a line of numbers that spins downward. "I would guess the fact that they're giving us a countdown timer says otherwise."

"Yeah, but they can't *make* us."

"I can make you," Pollux says quietly, his hands under his arms as he watches them.

Anger flashes across Lyra's face and she rockets to her feet, standing on the couch with her fists clenched.

"You can try," she snarls at Pollux so ferociously that he cows a bit, taking a step back.

"It requires all of us to get through," he argues, though the hard edge in his voice has dulled considerably. "We're already missing one."

Disbelief stirs in Aquila's chest. "Why would you want to go back into that place?"

Pollux shifts his shoulders. "Why not? I want to beat the game."

"It *hurt* us."

"When?"

"Are you crazy?" Aquila's voice starts to strain. "Lyra burned her arm, they tried to crush us in a shrinking room. You were the one who got a faceful of poison!"

"Cygnus hurt Lyra," he says evenly. "The gas wasn't permanent, and it only happened because we didn't follow the rules. The room wouldn't have crushed us, it was just a way to induce panic. See how we worked under pressure."

Lyra climbs off of the couch, setting foot on the ground. "Says you."

"Don't you want to know what the next reward is?" he presses. "Or what happens when we beat the last level?"

Lyra pauses, her hand lingering over the pocket of her jacket. After a long moment, Aquila scoffs.

"You're kidding, right?"

"What was yours?" Lyra asks, pinning her with her gaze. "What was in your box?"

"Nothing important," Aquila lies, hoping it's at least partially convincing. "Nothing worth risking my life over."

"He has a point," she says reluctantly. "Cygnus was the most dangerous part of being in the Tect. And if there's anything that might get us out of here, I want to try. My parents . . ." She swallows, her face dimming. "My parents must be worried. I can't imagine where they think I am."

"Your parents might have put you here," Pollux says.

Hearing the fear that's been haunting the back of her mind being spoken aloud is like having her stomach plummet through the floor.

From the way Lyra's expression buckles, she's been agonizing over the same thing too.

"Maybe your parents hate you, but mine actually like me," Lyra says roughly, sniffing.

Pollux's face darkens. He lets his arms drop and turns, striding to the door and squeezing through the opening Aquila had left. Lyra presses her palms over her eyes.

"Shit. I think that was too harsh."

"You really care?" Aquila asks wryly. "I'm not even sure that version of android comes with feelings."

"No, he's . . . he isn't . . ." She seems to give up on picking the right word. "I think he's right. I think the only way out is to follow the rules."

The chick rotates in Aquila's pocket, finding a more comfortable spot, and her heart wrenches at the thought of taking it back into that hellmouth. If Cygnus had picked her instead of Lyra to hurl into the particle wall, Fish might not have made it at all.

She straightens, walking into the nearest bedroom and carefully tugging off her jacket. Fish's scruffy head pops out of the hole, wondering about the sudden motion. Aquila sets him on the bed, arranging the jacket in a nest around him.

"At least he'll be safe in there," she says to Lyra, closing the door behind her. Lyra makes a face like she wants to disagree, but says nothing as she follows Aquila out of the house.

Pollux is already most of the way across the lawn, heading for the Tect like he works there. Zeke stares after him, turning around only when she and Lyra reach him.

"He's really doing it," he says to them. "He's really going back in."

There's a burst of voices from the house behind him, and Cygnus, Cass and Lacerta trickle out onto the patio.

"Hey, come on!" Cygnus calls, spotting them. "Round two!"

Cass does a jerky dance in response, and they all burble with laughter.

Zeke winces slightly. "Y'all have fun."

"Lyra wants to go, too," Aquila says, and he ticks his head at her incredulously.

"Yeah, well, Pollux is pretty convincing," she sighs. "Don't you want to see what the next prize is?"

Something passes behind Zeke's eyes, his hard expression shifting. He glances ruefully over his shoulder at the Tect, seeming to relent to the idea. Concern weighs down his features when he finally looks back to Lyra.

"If that blonde bastard comes near you again, I promise he's not getting out of there with all his parts."

Lyra's face drains a bit, but she nods and forces a smile. As she starts the trudge across the lawn, Zeke leans in to Aquila.

"I would say the same goes for you, boss," he murmurs. "But you didn't seem to need any help last night."

"Hmm," she hums, her lips pressed together so she can't give anything away. Cygnus's face floats across her memory, twisted with barely veiled rage, but there's no trace of what she might have said to him. And now she is going to be locked in a building with him for who knows how long.

Aquila forces her legs to move, following Zeke across the lawn. Her feet get heavier with each step toward the building.

Everyone is standing outside the door, evenly spaced apart so that no one touches. As she moves into the gap between Lyra and Pollux, what lies inside starts to sharpen into focus.

The walls are gone, leaving one vast, open space. In their place, the room seems to be filled to the ceiling with angular gray mountains.

It takes her a moment to process the sight. Once she can grip the strangeness of it, her mind begins to dissect it. The floor has risen into solid, ascending structures that jigsaw together, some ridged with steps and others smooth and sloped. An obstacle course. It reminds her of the playscapes they had for children on the convoys, yet somehow more spiky and ominous.

The others start to move into the Tect, and Aquila folds her arms around her stomach as she steps forward. Her thumb hits something hard and metal tucked into the waistband of her leggings. Curious, she pulls out something that glints silver in the light.

It's her asteroid ring, the one her father had given her the day she got her pilot's learning permit. Seeing it, her finger suddenly feels its absence, though she'd forgotten all about it until this moment.

Clearly, she'd gotten it back at the end of the challenge she can't remember. Though, for the life of her, she can't fathom why the alter would have hidden it from her.

ZEKE: 16

Lyra's hand slips further out of his grasp, sweat making their skin slick. His toes dig into the bottom of his shoes, trying to grip the narrow ledge beneath them. Her feet scrabble against the glossy slope that stretches down to the floor fifteen feet below.

A faint static buzzes in the back of his mind, something that without the meds would be manifesting as a voice telling him to drop her, or maybe that he was going to fall. But he hasn't heard a voice or felt like his head was swimming since the dose of Moxifarin. Even in this moment, he has to be grateful for that.

"I'm going to swing you back, then forward," he says.

Lyra nods, looking like a dangling kitten below him.

Ignoring the pain of his joints starting to separate, he swings her back toward the others waiting on the platform behind them. Then he forces her forward, every ounce of strength he can give going into the motion. Her feet beat against the slope, gaining momentum until the last second.

He lets go and she flies the space of the gap, her fingers just grasping the lip of the next ledge.

At first, nothing happens, and Zeke starts to worry she doesn't weigh enough to bring it down. Then, slowly, the ledge starts to lower, evening out until it's level.

Cheers echo through the space, bouncing off the walls so it sounds like there's more of them than there are. Lyra pulls herself up, red-faced but smiling, and extends a hand to Zeke. It's a jump from the perch where he's balancing, but nothing too substantial. He makes it easily, even if he only has one foothold for leverage.

Halfway. They're already halfway through this misery.

His kneecap pulses, reminding him it's not happy about getting knocked around. He's fairly certain Cygnus had a hand in him tripping during the hurdle section, but there's no way to know for sure.

Cass steps off the ledge, bouncing off the foothold on the slope and hoisting herself up onto the platform with Zeke's outstretched arm. Lacerta follows, then Pollux, who looks thoroughly displeased at having to grab his hand. Zeke turns his back when it's Cygnus's turn, and an incredulous scoff comes from his direction. A second later Cygnus barrels into Zeke's back from behind, almost knocking him off the platform. Zeke tries not to glance over the side as he's jostled.

It isn't the kind of drop that would kill you, but with only the hard floor to catch you at the bottom it was sure to hurt.

They line up like kids waiting for primary school, trying to puzzle out the next obstacle in their path. A chasm of space spans between their ledge and the next, much too far for any of them to jump.

"Anyone have any ideas?" Aquila pants, her hands braced against her knees.

This course hasn't been kind to her, and he keeps picturing her plummeting off the raised ledges to land in a heap of broken bones on the floor below. But despite her lack of muscle, she hasn't complained once, or tapped out, or even lagged behind. She'd even been the one to double back on the rope walk to help Lacerta when she was too afraid to cross.

Aquila rubs her fist across her mouth, her eyes like blue ice as she focuses on the next challenge. Something shifts in Zeke's chest as he watches her squeeze to the front, peering at the course laid out before them. A long, upright pole is leaning against their platform, rungs jutting out like petals around the body.

"Are these footholds?" she asks, stretching her shoe out to touch one of the rungs. "Maybe we stand on the pole and it takes us across?"

"It would take momentum to move it," Pollux says, bending to examine where it rests. He snaps upright suddenly, pivoting to look over the length of the platform. "If we take a running start, it should be enough to carry it over."

Cygnus squints dubiously. "So take a freaking flying leap onto it?"

"Yes."

He crosses his arms, his eyebrow quirking. "Feel free to go first."

"How will we get it back once we're on the other side?" Lacerta points out.

Pollux sighs through his nose, walking to the edge and squatting down to point.

"It rests on an incline. When we're on the other side, we just have to push it back this way."

"There are only two spots," Lyra says, dread slowing her words. "We have an uneven number."

"One person just stay behind," Cygnus says. There's something about the way his gaze falls on Aquila that makes Zeke bristle.

"Yeah, nah, we saw what happens when we don't follow the rules," Cass says, looking over Pollux.

He shrugs, his patience clearly draining. "One trip will have three. Lyra will volunteer, she's the smallest."

Lyra points a glare in his direction. "Oh, will she?"

"We'll go with Lyra," Aquila says, reaching out to rest her palm on Zeke's collarbone. "Right?"

Her skin is so soft and light that part of him wonders if she's touching him at all. She's close enough to him that he can see each distinct freckle scattered across her face like spilled salt. The brightness of her skin, the line of black hair against her neck, those ethereal blue eyes, all start to swirl together in a kind of hazy fairytale image in front of his eyes, and he forces himself to look away.

"Mhh hmm," he answers, his heart pulsing between his ribs. The Moxifarin should have numbed him out, yet still his veins are flooding with adrenaline he can't explain.

He presses himself back against the wall with Aquila to one side and Lyra to the other, clearing a runway for Cass and Cygnus. They count each other down, starting from the furthest point on the end of the platform and running toward the pole. At the end, they both grab rungs, their feet catching footholds below them, and the pole tips away from the ledge. Cass is glowing with laughter while Cygnus pokes her between the ribs, jokingly trying to loosen her grip as the pole lazily moves across the space. When it nears the other side, they turn in preparation and leap onto the far platform as soon as it touches.

They jump together, landing bent-kneed and wobbling a bit as they get their footing. Cygnus slings his arm around Cass's shoulders and grins back at them like he's just beaten the whole game himself.

"Push it back to us," Pollux calls after a long moment of watching him gloat.

"Oh, right," he catches himself, using one foot to push the pole off.

It moves glacially slow, but finally it lands back on their side. Pollux moves away from the wall, turning back to Lacerta.

"You can be on the left side of me," he tells her, hesitating at the end as he clearly tries and fails to remember her name.

Lacerta rolls her eyes, getting into position. "Oh joy."

The pair of them make the sprint, launching the pole with their last step and clinging to the rungs. At some point over the middle, Pollux says something that makes Lacerta smack the side of his head with her open palm, and he scowls the whole rest of the way across.

Lyra peers over the edge, judging the distance to the polished floor beneath them.

"I dunno," she says, her eyes wary. "That seems really far."

Something about the expression makes Zeke think again of his sister. Dione was afraid of everything, every person, even the shadowed part of the alley they walked home through. She had the same small build as Lyra, same as his Mama Rie, although Dione was softer. Soft things didn't fare well in Huygens, among the muck and metal. She stood out like a bright flower, drawing far too many eyes.

Thinking about her now, his stomach turns sour. He can see hands covering her face, groping her neck, squeezing the light from her eyes. He blinks a few times, clearing the image until he's looking at Lyra again.

"You just hold on," he assures her. "Aquila and I got the rest."

Far from confident, Lyra climbs onto the rungs, positioning herself on the far side of the pole and locking her arms around it so she doesn't take the spots where their hands will go. Zeke lines up with Aquila at the back of the platform, noting the sheen across her forehead. He nudges her, coaxing out a reluctant smile.

"You gonna catch me if I fall?"

"Don't look at me," she says, but a laugh lurks beneath her words. "My arms are purely decorative."

"On three?"

She nods. "One."

"Two."

"Three!"

They keep pace all down the platform, their feet finding rungs just as the pole lifts off away from the ledge. All three of their heads knock together and their arms become a tangled mess, everyone grabbing onto each other. Zeke's stomach seems to levitate inside him as they swing across the space. The girls' hair is flying into his face, and Lyra makes a sound like a cat being dunked in water as she buries her head into his elbow. Aquila's hand is wrapped around his forearm, and her eyes are scrunched from laughing so hard, and he can't seem to stop watching her face.

Suddenly the pole jolts, and the three of them tumble onto the opposite platform in a pile of knees and elbows. Lyra flops onto her back between them, cackling out the strangest laugh he's ever heard, and Aquila props herself up to wipe tears out of her eyes. Zeke's abs begin to ache and he realizes he's laughing too, his breath wheezing out of him like a steam geyser.

When his muscles fatigue and they've laughed themselves out, they get shakily to their feet. Cygnus is watching them with a look of disdain.

"Wasn't *that* funny," he says broodily, turning away.

The rest of the course is far from easy. It makes them climb to the ceiling, slide down ropes, jump across narrow footholds . . . yet every time Zeke looks at Aquila, the heaviness lifts. He even starts to forget about the distance to the ground below, the ache in his knee.

As they crawl through a narrow tunnel for what seems like ages, he watches Aquila move in front of him. Her breathing is labored, but it's something more than exertion. When she pauses to let Cass gain a little more ground ahead of her, he notices the shaking in her legs.

"You okay, boss?" he asks quietly, hoping Cygnus behind him can't pick it up.

She sniffs, her hair hanging like a curtain over her face.

"I don't like small spaces," she says, her voice jumpy.

"Really? I think it's cozy," he jokes. "Reminds me of the sewer where I grew up."

She snorts, but it's less than convincing. The shivers worsen, racking her body in waves that shake the hanging fabric of her shirt. Her shoes tremble, making a tinny squeaking sound against the glossed surface of the tunnel. He catches one of her ankles in his hand.

"You're fine," he says. "Whatever you're afraid of, it isn't real."

It had never worked when Mama Beck said it to him, but here he is reusing old mantras like a worried parent. Aquila's shaking starts to wane, her muscles relaxing.

"Thanks, boss," she says softly, and he's glad to see a hint of humor returning to her.

When Cass has shinnied far enough down the tunnel, she starts to move again, her breath evening out.

The tunnel takes them over gaps in the flooring, narrowing their path or making them climb over blockages. It seems to go on for ages, built into the very walls of the Tect, and by the end of it sweat is trickling into Zeke's eyes and ears. But then the darkness around them starts to lift, and a pinpoint of light grows into an opening in front of his eyes. Clean, cool air touches his brow as Aquila swings herself around to put her feet on the solid ground at the end of the tunnel.

It's emptied them out in the same room as the last challenge ended in, and everyone else has already gone to their labeled cubby to collect. Zeke recognizes the bottle sitting in his from across the room. His muscles release as he draws nearer, reaching out to grab the Moxifarin. It's the same weight as the first one. He curls his fingers around the bottle, trying not to let anger poison his mood. Three doses per challenge completed. The message was clear: stay in line and we'll *let* you stay sane.

Zeke glances sideways to the space left of him, the one that was meant to be for Orion. He just catches Lacerta's hand dashing into his box, her eyes slicing at him as she stuffs her clenched fist into her jacket pocket. Without a word to him, she turns her back and hustles toward the door.

POLLUX: 17

It's odd to see the amount of comfort the others derive from being together. After witnessing what Orion was capable of, it made much more sense to remain alone. Even Lyra, who had seen the body firsthand, now seems even more determined to stay around the group.

The patio of each house is organized around a center light tube feature that's surrounded by square, decorative stones. The squat, thick tube in the middle is flickering with red and orange pulses, trying to mimic the look of flames. Lyra can't seem to stop glancing at it from her seat on the ground. Her fingers pick at the bracelet she'd gotten from her box, touching each bead individually.

"This is one of my parent's products," Cygnus says, leaning forward to examine the light feature. "That's a Beaumont for sure."

Across the circle, Aquila rolls her eyes.

"I hope tomorrow is another obstacle course," Cass says, licking salt off her fingers from the dehydrated okra she's eating. "My legs are already more toned, lookit."

She hikes up her leggings, flashing them a calf. If modern media is anything to go on, Cass should be the most desirable of the group, with her shimmering skin and long limbs. Yet neither Zeke nor Cygnus seems interested in her performance.

"You sound like you *want* to keep doing this shit," Lacerta says, crossing her feet on the stone ledge.

"I was kinda made for this stuff," Cass shrugs, pursing her lips. "I feel like it really brings out the best in me. My channel back home was all about adventure challenges. I'm pretty sure this is a hidden camera show, I mean my channel just hit 14 mil right before all this. Coincidence?"

"Most likely," Pollux says, drawing everyone's attention to his seat in the shadows.

Silence follows, apart from Lyra's small snort of laughter, and he goes back to testing the strings on his violin. His prize for the obstacle course had been his tuning sensor, the same one he'd kept in his pocket since his and Castor's first lesson. The letters have worn off entirely, but he knows it just by the light triggered when the optimal tightness has been reached. He touches the tine to the last string, a tiny ripple of contentment moving through him when the green light glows.

"Do you actually play that, or just fondle it?" Cass says, watching him with her luminous green eyes.

"Yes," he answers.

After a moment, she follows up with, "Okay, well, play something. My brain is going insane with only three channels to stream in this place."

He lifts the base onto his shoulder, fitting the divot under his chin, and pops the bow from the back in a practiced move. His parents used to trot him and Castor out for their friends, and once Castor had quit, just him. It wasn't something he minded; people liked him when he played. It was maybe the only time he felt people looking on him with something other than thinly veiled dislike. When he played, he became unique. Being a twin afforded him very few opportunities for that.

The memory of Castor beside him, the sound of his violin intertwining with Pollux's makes his skin wash cold. He draws the bow across the strings, the vibrations of sound pushing out any thoughts.

The last thing he'd memorized had been a three violin sonata, and he'd only just mastered looping in the last layer of playback into the first two. The spiccato had given him trouble, and he can vaguely remember Castor teasing him about it on the front lawn of their Titan home.

This time, though, when it comes time to work the last cadenza into the others, his fingers move over the strings like they've done it a thousand times. The reactions around the circle are different. Most are of rapt attention, which is common. There are so few people who could actually play instruments beyond school level. Many have not even seen a violin in real life, more because of their cost than anything else. Zeke looks wary, like he's trying to find the trick of it.

Only Lyra is wincing like the sound is irritating her. The look tweaks her face until the last note dies in the air, then she slumps slightly in relief.

"Wow, Pollux," Aquila says, touching the corner of her eye. "You're so talented."

Lyra scoffs softly, her little fingers moving over the beads. Her eyes snag on her tattoo and she pauses, then lifts it closer to her eyes.

"Did anyone notice the little letters inside the circle?" she says.

Beside her, Cass squints at her own tattoo. "Oh yeah. It says P+ like our shirts."

"I think it's a 't'," Zeke says. "Pt."

"Maybe it's an abbreviation," Aquila lofts. "For like . . . pterodactyl?"

"Ptosis," Pollux says aloud, his own brain cataloging possibilities. "Pterygoid."

"Yikes, what is that?" Lyra says.

He looks up, confused at first by someone responding to him. "It's a bone."

"Ptato," Cygnus says.

Zeke lowers his head into his palms as if he's physically pained. "Po-ta-toe, idiot."

Lacerta stands up, stretching her mottled arms over her head.

"Wow, I am destroyed," she says. "I'm going to shower."

Zeke stands up too, and Aquila follows, lifting the heron chick out of her lap. She wraps one arm around Lyra's shoulders in a good-bye before following Zeke to B-House.

Cygnus, Cass and Lacerta slide open the door to the patio, ducking inside. Pollux watches them until they've gone beyond his sight, wondering how they don't seem to have a shred of survival instinct between them.

When he stands, Lyra is waiting in front of him.

"Should we just take C-House again?" she asks. "Wow. I just realized we have a *house*."

Her face is turned up to him, and he notices the warmth flecked through her irises. An ache starts to bloom in his chest, a strange desire to play for her again. He wants that same look everyone else gave him to claim those soft features. He wants to play something that reaches her the same way it seemed to reach others. But this time, he wants it to be one of *his* compositions.

"There are enough houses for us each to have our own," he points out. With everything that's happened, she must have overlooked that fact the same as everyone else.

She blinks at him, a peculiar expression shifting her brows.

"I don't really want to be in a whole empty house by myself," she says quietly. "I would think you could understand why that is."

She reaches forward, her fingers tightening around his wrist. The spasm of nerves up his arm is less intense than usual, but his jaw still tenses against the feeling of his muscles squirming beneath his skin.

"Come on, just humor me, please," she says, rolling her eyes. "We're supposed to be partnered, after all. Team C for the win."

"I don't believe it's a competition," he starts to say, but halfway through Lyra scoffs and starts to walk, tugging him sharply behind.

Once they're through the patio door of C-House, she releases his hand. He drops it to his side, remarking how quickly it cools once her warmth is gone. Castor used to say he was made of metal. Once, when he'd felt particularly arrogant, he'd told Pollux that he was really just a copy of Castor their parents had made out of robot parts. He might have believed it, if he hadn't just heard them talking about how far behind humanoid robot development was.

"I'm just going to take the couch again," Lyra says, flopping down onto the long cushions. "It's too weird being in those rooms. It feels like they're supposed to belong to someone else."

She buries her head in her arms, settling in for sleep without even sterilizing her mouth. Irked, Pollux goes to the bathroom, grabbing a tooth cleansing pouch from the cabinet. Lyra is somehow already asleep when he returns, but he says her name until she rouses.

"What?" she groans.

Pollux holds the pouch against her mouth until she relents and lets him pop it in. Her bottom lip brushes his finger, and for a moment he's unable to move it away.

After a bit of swishing, she sits up to reach for an empty water bottle on the table and spits her mouthful, then promptly flops back down onto the couch and throws her arm over her face.

"Thank you," she says, her voice drifting.

Pollux curls his fingers into his palm, traces of heat still dancing along his index. "You're welcome."

Her limbs relax, and he moves onto the couch opposite her. His diaphragm has started fluttering in an uncomfortable way, like he can't draw a full breath into his lungs. He leans back, trying to let his mind focus on anything else, but another flash of her warm lip against his skin interrupts his thoughts.

The longer he spent with this group, the more unstable his capacities seemed to get. He'd spent so much time learning how to organize his thoughts like an office, everything perfectly in place. Yet one tiny, ill-tempered girl seems determined to barge in and throw everything onto the floor every chance she gets.

Just focus on the game, he tells himself, attempting to realign his thoughts. The game is the only thing that matters. At least he has that.

The Tect doesn't call them again for three days. No one else seems to be perturbed, other than the confused murmurings the first day after the obstacle course. Pollux, thinking it might be a test, went to the mouth of the building only to find it vacant. The intricate structures that had been there the day before had sunken in the floor, only thin lines demarcating their presence beneath. He couldn't help being impressed. It was a clever design: a room that allowed for whatever the challenge might need.

On the first day, he'd tried to compose, thinking it would only be a matter of time until they were summoned. Without headphones, he had played aloud while Lyra stretched out on the couch in front of the screen, letting out a groan every half hour to signify that her muscles were still sore. She had eventually stood up and stormed over to him, seizing the neck of the violin and insinuating that she would force it up his rectum if he kept playing.

Zeke and Aquila had invaded their house toward the middle of the day, and the three of them splayed out in the living room, discussing their lives outside of the station and trying to piece together the last sound memories they had. They talked into the night, spreading food from the cabinets over every surface and trying to lure him into conversation with pointed questions about his childhood. He started to miss when it was just Lyra always prodding at his shell.

He tried to escape it the second day, walking the entire length of their perimeter wall. It only took ten minutes to travel from one side to the other, but he had busied himself exploring other houses. After a few hours, he returned back only to find that none of the others were even awake yet. At dusk, Zeke impressed everyone by hand fishing a giant tarpon from the lake. Pollux watched its gills gulp in air as it flopped its massive body against the grass. Its eyes were wide and glassy, and his fingers had started to itch to see just what muscles were powering the motion.

By the third day, he's given up hope. He stays quiet and resigned, trying to make peace with his thoughts as the others continue about their new normal. It reminds Pollux of something like a summer camp, the way they've all temporarily forgotten the outside world, content to please themselves in the moment.

Zeke promises to teach everyone how to swim in a pond Pollux had found on the backside of the neighborhood. The other three join in, and he gets the impression Cygnus has been waiting for an opportunity to take his shirt off since they got to Carcer. When the lights start to dim again, they run cords from the trees and throw blankets over them, creating makeshift tents around the water. They seem delighted with their recreation of camping in a closed, synthetic environment, and it strikes him that they probably didn't camp on Titan. Any natural vegetation was restricted to the cities where it could be tended, and the electrical storms formed so quickly that it posed a substantial threat if you were without real shelter.

He and Castor had camped often growing up. Their land reached down to a small creek, and there was always a healthy crop of trees shading it. They used to catch minnows or mudbugs from the water and study the composition of their bodies, taking notes on their mode screens. They would discuss the strange ways their parents behaved, how different their movements and speech patterns were depending on who they were talking to. They tried to outline ways that they could mimic the behavior, how best to impress them. Somewhere along the way Pollux fell behind, and Castor mastered his way into everyone's hearts. After that, Castor stopped wanting to spend time with Pollux, lest he tarnish the perfect mask he had worked so hard to create.

Pollux stands up, his hips slightly sore from sitting in one spot for so long. Lyra is climbing through the opening in her blanket tent, arranging her pillow on the ground, which means she definitely isn't planning to come back to the house with him.

He starts to walk back around the pond, already hearing notes in his head for his next composition, but Cygnus makes him pause. He's been helping the two girls in his group toss their blankets over the cords, but as they giggle he turns over his shoulder to glance at Lyra's lone tent on the edge. His smile loses its warmth, like it's been on cables that are suddenly cut. His eyes harden for just a moment into the predatory eyes of a cat in the grass, surveying its prey.

Just as quickly as the look appeared, it vanishes, and he's back reaching overhead to smooth the blanket out.

Pollux starts to branch away from the water, heading back toward the neighborhood, but his steps falter. Something about Cygnus has left him deeply unnerved. Deja vu is a glitch, he knows that, a mistake in the brain that happens when it confuses new information as memory. But he can't help feeling that he has seen a look like that before, and that he knows exactly what will follow.

Aquila is setting up an extra wide tent with Zeke, while the chick they're fostering runs around their feet attacking their elastic laces. He draws up to her, and she glances at him over her shoulder.

"What's up?" she asks brusquely.

"I want to ask a favor."

Her arms drop and she turns toward him.

"Can you sleep in the same tent as Lyra tonight?"

Aquila chews on her middle fingernail, her full lips ragged as if she's been doing it all day. Something about her expression strikes him as odd. It's almost as if she's holding her facial features differently, the tension in entirely opposite areas than usual.

"She's not my partner," she says, her tone slack. "Why don't you do it?"

For a moment, he just stares at her. The past two days, whenever he caught her eye, Aquila would look away. She seemed uncomfortable being gazed at, almost apologetic that she was taking up space.

Now, she stares squarely back at him without a trace of the demureness she'd had before. A phantom shiver sweeps across his back, an uneasy feeling that he is somehow talking to a stranger.

"Aquila," he says, needing confirmation.

Her vast blue eyes stay fixed on his. "Yes?"

Pollux moves away, stepping over the heron chick as it lunges for his shoe. Lyra is still fussing with her tent, trying to even out the wrinkles on the line by hopping along its length with her arms stretched as far as they will go. He reaches out to adjust the lay of the blanket, feeling her come to rest beside him.

"Thanks," she huffs, winded from the effort. "But you can't have my tent, Pollux."

He toes his shoes off, taking a seat on the grass. "I don't need a tent."

The light tubes have transitioned to their nightlight settings, a dim blue glow filling the station. Pollux glances up, tracing the tracks of light up the curve to the ceiling above them. Who was doing the same up there, looking down at them?

Lyra climbs into her tent, poking her head out the other side to look at him.

"You're going to sleep right there?"

"Yes."

She rolls her eyes, laying her head on her pillow. "Suit yourself."

Lyra falls quiet for a long while, and he finds himself watching the surface of the pond ripple with the vibrations of the station. If he focuses, he can feel the same micromovements shaking in his joints. How long had it been since he'd been on solid ground? Long enough for his legs to ache with desire to experience gravity again. To feel bound to something beyond dispute.

"Will you tell me about Castor?"

The sound of Lyra's voice startles him, but the shock of hearing Castor's name spoken aloud is somehow worse. He tries to think of something he can say to placate her, some benign detail about Castor, but his mind floods with images until he's drowning under them. The day he and Castor had sat on the roof to watch Chinese satellites pass over them, how they'd stayed up all night during a yearly hurricane talking. How well he knew the twitches and movements of Castor's face, and how Castor knew his. The look he would give him when their parents were behaving in the overzealous, bubbly versions of themselves they used when talking to their children. How he'd seen the light leave Castor's eyes, the cord cut and the force of his life passing beyond the point of recall.

Pollux tries to swallow, feeling as though his throat has been crushed. His lungs refuse to inflate, sending panic into the pulmonary muscles in his chest. Silently he begs for the sensation to pass, to be numb until he can stop seeing Castor in front of him.

"I can't," he says finally, barely more than a whisper.

When no answer comes, he looks over to Lyra. Her face is slack, her eyes closed tightly, and her breath comes in a steady rhythm.

They wake the next morning to the sound of their modes.

The low buzz that summoned them before is ringing through each of them, and even Lyra can't sleep through it. Pollux's cuff blinks with the text, *Begin Program,* before flipping over to a timer that counts down the number of minutes they have to report to the Tect. Everyone leaves their tents, their hair matted and eyelids still puffy.

"Well," Zeke says, passing a hand over his face as if to strip away a mask. "Guess it's back to work."

LYRA: 18

Her mother was one of the most superstitious people Lyra had ever known, so much so that often it felt like they didn't live in the same reality. She felt cold spots in their house that she called spirits, she had premonitions in the form of stomach aches, and there were certain areas of City of Seven Hills that she wouldn't even go into because she claimed they had clouds of black around them. It had always seemed like a ridiculous obstacle to self-impose on your life, but Lyra had never questioned that it was just part of her quirky personality.

Until she'd seen the Tect.

A cloud hangs around the building, unseeable but just as frigid and ominous as the last time she'd been walking toward it. It thickens the closer she gets to it, slowing her steps like she's walking through water.

Pollux, on the other hand, marches ahead like he's been waiting the whole three days for this. While his personality is always the same, steady blend of irritating and authoritative, she'd seen firsthand the way his eyes sparked during the challenges, the charge behind his movements while he was in the Tect. He wasn't slowed by some phantom black cloud no one could see.

The group funnels through the door, Lyra bringing up the rear. As soon as her foot crosses the threshold, the particle wall jumps into being behind her, and she curses herself for not paying better attention to the countdown timer. The forceful hum sends a shiver through her shoulder, as if the tissue remembers the sound responsible for its injury.

Lyra sidesteps away from it, just in case Cygnus is feeling psychotic again. The room finally sharpens into view, and her gaze is met with a towering wall.

The Tect has been sliced into a maze. Two entrances stand on opposite sides, giving a glimpse of paths diverging in different directions inside. They remind her of the mazes her sister Ursa would draw. Ursa had a mind like a professor, always wanting to solve a problem or pull some order out of chaos. She went through a phase where she drew version after version of line mazes on her mode screen, trying to design one that no one could solve. Lyra had always been the worst at them, crashing into dead ends over and over until she called Ursa something rude and threw the screen onto the couch.

This is different, she promises herself. This time, she's going to be the one to solve a piece. After her mistake in the shrinking room, she'd felt useless, standing in the corner while everyone else worked. In the obstacle course, she'd barely been able to keep up with the long limbs and athletic bodies of the rest of the group, always needing a hand to get across the jumps or a boost to get onto a platform. If they're being judged, she's behind on all counts.

"Well," Cass says, turning to the group. "Should we just hop right in?"

In lieu of answering, Pollux simply strides right by her and into the maze. Cass scoffs and follows, but as soon as she nears the door a particle wall bands across the opening. She leaps back, a startled squeak ringing out of her. After a moment, the particle wall flicks off. There's no sign of Pollux on the other side, meaning he must have picked a path and started down it.

Cass looks back at them, her eyes wide.

"I think it means one at a time," Lacerta says, walking tentatively toward the entrance. When nothing happens, she sucks in a breath and jumps through. A second later, the particle wall shields her from them.

By the time it disappears again, Cass is ready. She hurries inside, catching herself on the corner of the next wall to stop her motion. They take turns after that, each waiting for their opening and scooting through as fast as they can.

Lyra can't make herself move. She watches the others go through, her heart racing every time the wall beams into place. Her arm aches, the burn stirring beneath the scabs, and her skin starts to prickle with sweat. Aquila touches her hand, giving her a reassuring smile before jumping into the maze herself.

She swallows, the eerie feeling of being alone sweeping over her. As much as she doesn't want to accidentally throw herself into another particle wall, she equally doesn't want to go through this challenge alone. She pushes herself across the threshold, jumping as the wall ignites behind her.

The maze breaks off into three paths in front of her, and she searches for some sign of which the others had picked.

"Aquila?" she calls, stepping toward the far right corridor.

Another particle wall leaps up in front of her, blocking her path.

"Okay," she mutters, trying to catch her breath. "Got it. Not that way."

The middle corridor gives her no argument, so she starts down it. The smooth walls and floors reflect the light tubes overhead, reminding her a bit of her school hallways. Her mind starts to drift back, shuffling through images of the last few days she remembers. Her sister Corva performing her dance recital, the dinner they had the night after Lyra took her Primary Exams, the weekend when Vesta went on her first date. But nothing past that, like it never existed.

She rounds the corner, stopping as her sight falls on the uneven flooring. She stares at it for a moment before it changes right in front of her eyes, tiles dipping into the floor below to create pedestals. They continue to shift, rising and falling, some fast and some slow.

Lyra walks closer, noting the first few tiles take longer to sink into the ground than the rest. She peeks over the edge, expecting to see a plummet like the obstacle course, but the bottom is only a couple of feet down. Not even much of a step.

Briefly, she contemplates just walking straight across, stepping down into the trough if need be. But if this is a test, she's meant to puzzle it out, no matter how inconsequential.

A few of the pedestals punch upward then lower back down, and her mind begins to pick out a faint pattern in their movements. A smile starts to play across her mouth.

"I get it," she says to herself. "It's a timing thing."

Taking closer note, she watches the pattern again, working out a path in her head. She lets the sequence go through once more, just to be sure, then she leaps for the first pedestal. Her shoes grip the surface well, and she stretches her leg out for the next one, careful not to linger too long. She picks her way from tile to tile, her landings quicker the closer she gets to the other side. The last five, she starts to fall behind. The pedestals are too quick to carry her downward, so she has to throw her weight upward to catch the next one. The last one is almost to its lowest point when she reaches it, but she hurdles her leg up over the ledge. Just as her toe leaves the bottom tile, a shock grips her right side, every muscle seizing at once.

Her shin gets a nasty whack on the edge, but she rolls over the floor until she's clear.

That was it. She'd done it. And completely by herself.

Lyra takes a moment on her back to catch her breath, grinning like a fool. If only someone had seen it.

She touches the cuff on her right wrist, the skin beneath it still warm. There's no doubt it was the source of the shock, so that just meant they'd invented yet another way to punish them if they didn't follow the rules.

When her shoulder starts to ache from the pressure, she sits up and starts back on the path. The corridor leads her along a curve, passing sealed entrances she can't see past. She tries calling names at them, but if there's someone inside they can't hear her.

Unease starts to curdle in her stomach, wondering how far this maze goes. How far is she from the others? Clearly they had intended to separate them, but how long is that meant to last?

The next entrance she's guided through takes her to a room of sorts: three walls and a low ceiling boxing off the space. Four pedestals line the corners, and as she walks into the heart of the room, she notices a spot of red light on the ceiling. Warmth touches the top of her head as she passes under it. She lays a palm over her scalp, feeling the heat on the back of her hand.

A heat lamp, she realizes, staring up at it. It starts to creep infinitesimally forward, or maybe it's been moving this whole time, making a slow path to the left side of the room.

She walks over to the closest pedestal, but nothing about it stands out. It's smooth and glossy, just like everything else, and sits about chest high. She brushes her hand over the top of it, and the flat surface flushes the same shade of red as the spot on the ceiling.

"Is it like a heat thing?" she asks aloud, laying her palm over the surface again and leaving it longer this time.

Motion at her knee catches her attention, and she glances down. A number has appeared on the face of the pedestal, and as she watches it flips from 97.7 to 97.8.

Temperature. It's measuring her body temperature.

Footsteps echo around the hall outside, and her heart leaps in excitement as a shape moves in the doorway.

Cygnus walks through, and her mood takes an immediate dive. He's rubbing a red spot on his elbow, a leftover from whatever challenge he's just finished, and he looks a little less than thrilled to have walked into the next one.

"Hey," she says, making him jump. "Put your hand on that pedestal."

Cygnus raises an eyebrow, but meanders over to lay his palm on the top of the column. The top blushes the same color as hers, and the base reads 98.1. The roving heat lamp on the ceiling changes direction, heading back toward her, and she swears she can feel the rise in temperature before it even gets close

"What is this?" Cygnus asks, peering at the spot.

"I think each pedestal needs to be heated," Lyra says. "If we heat three of them, the spot will travel over the empty one eventually and heat it too."

"So we just need one more person," he says, his voice climbing with excitement. "That's awesome, the weird kid was right behind me."

Lyra blinks at him, and a second later Pollux wanders in through the doorway.

"Hey! Speak of the devil," Cygnus says. "Go put your hand on that pedestal. Pocket-sized already figured this one out."

Lyra rolls her eyes just as Pollux looks over at her. He doesn't look entirely convinced, but he walks over to the far right column to rest his hand on the top.

His temperature reads out on the pedestal, and the red spot changes directions again.

"Well, that's not right, shouldn't it be going—"

Cygnus takes a step toward the center, but the moment he tries to take his hand away from the column an electrical snap rings out through the room. He jumps, a cry escaping him.

"Jeez, what was that?"

The sound cracks out again, and this time Pollux sucks in a breath.

"We're hit with electrical charges if we try to take our hands away," he says roughly, his eyes studying the ceiling.

"Is it hot in here?" Cygnus asks, and Lyra has to admit a film of sweat has broken out under her clothes.

"These are neural transmitters," Pollux says, bending at the waist to examine the pedestal. "They're raising our basal body temperatures and sending a message to the modes to shock us if we take our hand away."

Lyra glances at her own reading. It's gone up three decimals. "Why?"

He glances up at the ceiling, watching the spot move lazily toward Cygnus again, and frustration begins to flare in her stomach. She'd solved this already. Why wasn't it working like it always did for the others?

Pollux's eyes fall on her, the judgement in his expression stinging. "Did you notice the pattern?"

"Pattern?"

"It moves in a slow but repeating pattern, getting wider each loop. You're right that all the surfaces must be heated at once. You just chose the wrong position. It'll travel over the empty one last."

A floating sensation pulses through her brain, making her hazy for a moment. When she checks her read again, her temperature has broken 101.

"When is it going to stop over that one?" Cygnus nods to the far corner no one occupies.

Pollux studies the spot unblinkingly, seeming to count in his head. "An hour. Maybe less."

"And our temperatures are just going to get higher until then?" Cygnus demands, his voice getting louder.

Chills take root in her spine, shaking her whole body as her head grows heavier. Her mind starts to swim, her vision blurring like she's slipped into a dream.

The gravity of her mistake washes over her. Across the room, Cygnus is glaring at her, his steely blue eyes hard as chipped slate. He leans over his own pedestal, running his free hand over his reddening face.

"You stupid bitch," he breathes, hanging his head.

The oddest thing is that her feet give out long before any other part of her. Her arms still hold her sagging body up long after the spikes of pain in her heels became too much to bear.

The fever burning through her makes her whole body as sensitive as if she's just been skinned, even the touch of her clothes hard to bear.

She crouches on her toes, leaning her torso into the base of the pedestal while her shaking arms alleviate some of the weight from her feet. Cygnus has slumped over the top of his, one hand trapped beneath him, and Pollux is bracing his back against the wall to keep standing.

"I'm sorry," she says again, her voice rasping.

"Shut up," Cygnus growls.

She leans her head against the cool surface of the pedestal, taking a moment of comfort from its touch. Her skull begins to rattle with her chills, and she tenses, expecting the next wave of pain to hit. It's been impossible to remain still enough to not get shocked, and the anticipation of the next one has been the only thing keeping her upright.

When it doesn't come, she straightens, realizing the trembling in her feet isn't just her fatigued muscles.

Pollux has opened his bloodshot eyes, a puzzled look creeping over his face. Lyra opens her mouth to ask him if he feels it too. The room jolts beneath them, Lyra's stomach left behind for a moment, and everything blinks into pitch black. Red light floods the room, just like before, only this time it stays long enough for Lyra's brain to catch up enough to be afraid. A high-pitched alarm ripples through the air, piercing her eardrums, and she slaps her palms over her ears. Just when she realizes no shock has punished her, the pedestals begin to recede.

The wail of the alarm continues, and a voice begins to repeat a pattern of words she can't make out over the din. Pollux and Cygnus are in the middle of the room, and it's the first time she can remember an expression on Pollux's face that isn't his stable, non-reactive mask. His brow is clammy, his mouth slightly open, and she could almost swear it's fear that shines in his dark eyes.

Her head is pounding with her own pulse, and it takes her far too long to realize the walls have started to sink into the floor.

The maze is receding, laying the Tect open in its vacant state.

The others are spread to the far corners of the space, looking just as panicked and lost as she is.

The phantom voice keeps repeating the same three words, and for a moment she thinks it might be a glitch. Pollux shouts at her, but his voice is lost over the racket. He points to the center, where a bright grid of light has sprung up on the floor. Everyone is running toward it, and Lyra stumbles to her aching feet to join them. When she reaches it, everyone is fitting into an outlined square and kneeling. As she takes a spot she sees why; two handprints pulse in each quadrant, calling to be covered with their own palms.

Lyra gets to her knees, peeling her hands away from her ears and letting the sound flood in as her palms fit into the outlines. Her forehead presses to the ground, and she finds herself promising an unseen deity anything it wants to stop the noise.

Cass is running toward them, having been the farthest away, but before she can reach the grid her mode glows red and she collapses on her side, convulsions racking her body.

The voice keeps repeating, repeating, and finally Lyra's ears sort out the words.

Inmates access checkpoints. Inmates access checkpoints.

Then, all at once, the lights flip back to their clean white settings, and the alarms vanish. The grid beneath them has disappeared as if it never existed, though no one seems brave enough to stand up yet.

Finally, Aquila gets to her feet and runs to Cass, who's been motionless since she went down. Pollux straightens next, wandering to a pile of broken glass where an overhead light tube must have shattered. He picks through the shards as everyone else gets up uneasily, still expecting the ceiling to cave in.

Lyra sits back, feeling her heartbeat like a fist at the base of her throat. Words keep cycling through her mind like slippery eels, impossible to catch. She knows what she heard, but it's like trying to remember a dream after just waking up.

"What did it say?" Lacerta pivots on the spot, looking over the group with wide eyes. "What was that word it just said?"

"Inmates."

Pollux straightens, tossing a broken shard of glass onto the floor. "They called us inmates."

The grass in the courtyard reminds her so much of the turf inside the Eagle Convoys that it's a wonder she didn't notice it before. If she keeps her eyes closed, she could almost be back on one of her father's ships, the familiar tremble of the engines beneath her and the lingering scent of recycled air in her nose. The short, cropped blades press into her cheek, just on the verge of being painful but not quite there yet.

Her head is so heavy it feels like it could sink into the ground and keep dragging her down until she breached the wall of the ship and floated out into space. A longing begins to gnaw at her stomach to hear her father's voice again, to try one more time to be the child he'd wanted her to be.

The golf course on the Eagle crafts had grass trimmed just like this. He used to take her to play when he had a shift off. It always made her feel special to be the one he chose to spend his free time with instead of the other pilots. She'd only later wondered if it was because he didn't want them to notice the smell on his breath.

Once, on a particularly good day, he'd tried to help her with her short game for hours. She'd never excelled at hitting anything very hard, even with the child settings, but she loved spending time on the grass watching him concentrate. "Golf is a game of millimeters," her father had said, a deep line cutting across his brow as he focused. "Just like flying these big vessels. A ship like this is too big to move quickly, so you have to be able to see the trajectory and make tiny adjustments. Millimeters," he said again, then tapped the ball with the putter. It sailed past the hole, half an inch to the left of it.

Her father feigned clutching his heart in agony. "There goes the convoy, catapulting off into space."

"No!" Aquila had laughed.

She squeezes her eyelids tight, trying to trap the tears before they start. No matter how hard she tries, she can't think of the last time she saw her father's face, heard his perpetually hoarse voice.

"Okay, stand up."

Her eyes slit open enough to see Zeke's shoes even with her head. When she doesn't rally the energy to move, his hands scoop beneath her shoulders and he drags her to her feet. Her neck twinges a bit from being moved, but she's so focused on the warmth of his skin she can barely feel anything else.

He props her up against the base of the tree she'd collapsed next to after stumbling from the Tect, the Y-shaped branches curving along her back. Zeke leans back next to her, studying her with those sunlight hazel eyes.

"What can I do?"

Her heart wrings, seeing the worry on his face even though he must be feeling the same things.

"What *can* we do?" she says, peeling her voice from her throat. "We're stuck in here and we'll never know why. I've been trying to remember what I did, but th—" she just manages to stall her tongue before the word "alter" comes falling out of her mouth.

Memory loss is nothing new to her; she was usually left with a hazy imprint of what the alter had done, like the memory of a dream. The alter also liked to experiment with any substance that might cause a high, so often the hangover left Aquila with black holes across the previous night. She'd almost caused her father to lose his job once, when the alter led a group of kids down to the fuselage to get high on fumes and almost killed them all. Even then, though, when the story was recounted to her, there was a thread of memory through the event that she could grab onto. But when she tries to think of a crime, something that would land her in an orbital prison, there's not even a scrap of recollection that surfaces.

The frustration makes her want to tear her own hair out. She has never hated the split side of herself more than right now, knowing that it not only must be holding the memory hostage, but that it's also responsible for it. Aquila has spent years cleaning up after it, like it's a wily sibling that comes home at odd hours and wrecks her room, bullies her friends, and uses her things. Yet she's never resented it because for all its faults, it had all her missing parts. All of the confidence, the fierceness, all the bravery and loudness Aquila stuffed down inside her until it became its own identity. The alter did what she herself was scared to do. It didn't need anyone else, and it wasn't afraid to say exactly what it felt. Aquila admired it, and almost admired the tornado path of destruction it caused. At least it left a mark on the world, while she only passed through it like a ghost.

But this is different. It's walked Aquila into a trap she has no way out of and left her to answer for its crime.

The back of her nose stings, lifting tears into her eyes, and a scream of frustration rises into her throat that she can barely keep down. Her head swims again, too many feelings fighting for control, and she starts to list sideways, longing for the distraction of the grass again.

Zeke's hand closes around her arm, holding her firmly.

"Whoa, boss," he warns, concern sharpening his voice. "Just take deep breaths."

Aquila shakes her arm free, the pressure against her skin sending a shard of panic into her chest.

"How are you so calm?" she asks, hating the whine in her tone. "How can you not want to scream right now?"

"I like to bottle my crazy up and let it out in short bursts," he says, half of a smile crossing his mouth. When she doesn't respond, it drops away. "I guess I always knew I'd end up somewhere like this. Hospital or prison, there's not really a difference. Trapped is trapped."

She rubs her arms, trying to bring some warmth into her limbs. Zeke watches her for a beat, then spreads his arms.

"Could you use a hug?"

For a blessed moment, she's suspended in the surprise of the gesture. The day they had met, he'd been reluctant to even touch her. What a change has happened in the days since then. She's almost tempted to bury herself into his chest, let those arms cage her away from the world. The fantasy lasts a mere minute before her skin starts to crawl.

"I have . . ." She tucks her hair behind her ear, trying to puzzle together the best way to say it. "I can't, I don't like the feeling of being confined."

Zeke pauses, bouncing his heels up and down as he studies her.

"Okay. How about feeling supported?"

He reaches out a hand to her, and her brain scrambles, trying to verify what's happening. She lets him pull her toward him as her stomach leaps out of place. As soon as she gets close, he steers her around until her back is leaning against him, his chest cradling her like a chair. He lets his arms lay alongside hers, their legs propped out next to each other. His warmth seeps through the fabric of her jacket, and her frayed nerves begin to calm.

She faces out over the courtyard, looking back toward the lettered houses. The lights have started to dim again, feigning normality. She's wasted an entire day wallowing in self-pity.

The group has scattered, some of them sitting on the patios in silence, some just through the glass inside, but a bleakness has settled over all of them. Looking at them, she isn't filled with the warmth she was before, the feeling of trust they'd forged in the obstacle course and the days that followed. There's a shifting discomfort in her now, wondering what they're thinking. What lies in their pasts. What they really remember.

Even Zeke, as impossible as it seems, had done something to earn the name "inmate."

"What did you do?" she asks quietly, unable to shake the feeling that she's trespassing somewhere she shouldn't.

Zeke shifts a bit, and her back slips closer against him. His fingers brush the back of her neck, collecting her hair and laying it to one side. For a moment, Aquila is frozen by the intimacy of the gesture, unable to think of a single other time someone has touched her like that. But then the armor encases her, steeling her skin against him.

"I don't remember specifically," he says. "But I've done a lot of illegal things. My sister and I stole all the time. Sometimes we stole chemicals from the plants and sold it on the street to junkies. I used to get in a lot of fights. A few times we broke into our neighbors' houses. Almost everyone in Huygens is born a criminal, it's just a matter of time."

As he speaks, his breath carries over her shoulder, sending a shiver up her back. His thumb drags across her forearm, passing over her tattoos, and the touch is so tender and personal it almost feels like his fingers have traveled there before.

"What's happening?"

Her voice is as sharp as a slap, and he tenses against her. When he answers, his tone is tentative, as if he's waiting for a blow to land.

"What do you mean?"

"What is this?" she says, surprised at the bite in her own voice. But the world has broken into pieces beneath her feet and the only thing tethering her in the tumult of her emotions is the cold clarity of her mind.

She pushes off from him, needing to break away from the lulling warmth of his chest. When she turns back, he's suddenly bristled like a cat in a corner.

"It's like that now?" he asks, his brow quirking. "Do I need to remind you we're both in here for the same reason?"

"It's not about that," she snaps, heat buffeting through her. "I can't . . . There's no space for this right now. This is survival, I can't get distracted."

His stare refuses to let her go. "You seemed okay with it in the tent."

It takes her far too long to conjure a murky memory of what he's talking about, and her reaction doesn't get past him. She can see a flash of an image, Zeke helping her hang blankets on a line by the pond, of his face across from hers on the ground, those gold-ringed eyes glimmering in the dark. It's a memory that doesn't belong to her, of the night before she'd woken up alone in a too-small tent, her mode buzzing.

Zeke's eyes narrow, clearly suspicious of her blank face, and she tries her best to shake out a nonchalant answer.

"That was different."

Zeke exhales, surprised. "How?"

"I wasn't myself."

He straightens, his body language hardening over like ice on water. Blood storms beneath his cheeks, and he can't lift his eyes to hers.

"Who are you now, then?"

Aquila flushes cold. Her mouth opens, but no words come to her rescue.

"Who are you at all?" Zeke starts to turn away from her, but she catches the wound in his tone. "Which one is the real you?"

When he finally turns his back on her, she tries to say his name but her throat feels like it's been stuffed with cotton.

The question echoes around her head, the same thing she's always wondered. Was she the real Aquila? The one that was meant to exist? The weak one, the one who couldn't speak her mind or stand up for herself, or make someone laugh. The one who puts mind over emotion, every time.

Or was it always supposed to be the alter?

It's dark when she's finally too cold to stay at the tree, her circulation stymied. Lyra is still sitting out on her patio, staring into the faux-fire light feature. Zeke and Pollux are just behind her in the living room of C-House, the sliding door muffling their conversation as they walk around and around the furniture.

Lyra breaks from her trance as Aquila steps onto the patio, her eyes startled and wide.

"Hey," Aquila says, her voice dull from being silent so long. "Can I sit with you?"

"Yeah, of course," she says, dragging a chair closer into the fall of the light. "You are basically the only person I can tolerate right now."

Aquila hazards a glance at the living room one more time, but Zeke has his back to them, his arms moving sharply as Pollux nods. She bundles herself into the chair, pulling her legs into her chest.

Lyra sniffs, shaking her head.

"Did you see they gave us a completion ring for the maze?"

Aquila doesn't answer. Everything about this place has changed for her, like a veil has dropped away and beneath it everything is dark and honed to hurt them. The challenges had seemed like a way to pass the time, something to keep them occupied. Knowing what she knows now, the tests haunt her.

What were they, really? What happened when they finished? Her brain itches to pull it apart, to understand it, but her head is swimming with emotion to the point where she can't focus on anything.

She leans her head back, her gaze landing on the patch of window. Saturn is peeking into the edge of it, just a fingernail of golden-yellow glow beneath the overarching rings. It was always her favorite part of the convoy voyage, when Saturn appeared as a prick of light on the horizon and grew and grew, every day taking up more of the sky.

The thought of this being her only view of Saturn for the rest of her life starts her sinking into sticky, heavy despair.

"What are you looking at?" Lyra asks, breaking into her spiral.

"Just Saturn," she says. "Makes me think of the view back home."

Lyra sighs, the smallest hint of a smile touching her lips.

"My mom used to call it Mother Saturn. She basically worshipped it because she thought she was infertile until she and my dad moved to Titan."

Aquila winces, knowing the true myth of Saturn. It's too cruel to be funny, so she holds back, but Lyra can see the change in her face.

"What?" she pushes.

"What what, that's a nice story," Aquila answers breezily, hoping it's convincing.

"You made a face. I'm getting very good at reading faces, all this time I'm spending with that blockhead." Her eyes cut at Pollux inside.

Aquila swallows, regretting it before the words even leave her mouth.

"Saturn was named after a god," she says quietly. "The myth goes that he ate his own children so they wouldn't rebel against him."

For a moment, Lyra's eyes are wide, horrified. Then she starts to laugh. It isn't loud, but her whole body shakes with the ripples of it. Her head drops into her palms.

"That's so horrible," she giggles to herself.

Aquila watches her with a strange sickness twisting in her stomach. It isn't the infectious laughter she's heard out of Lyra before, and the sound is unnerving. There's a flash in the firelight, a bead of reflection falling from Lyra's hands to land on her thigh. She breathes in sharply, and Aquila finally realizes that it's no longer laughter racking her body.

In one stride, she crosses the gap between their chairs, slipping into the space next to Lyra. The movement draws the attention of Pollux, who looks quizzically at the pair of them but seems to think better of coming out. Aquila wraps her arm around Lyra, bracing her against her own body, and she doesn't even think twice about how spiky her bones must feel pressed up against Lyra's side.

One of Lyra's tears splashes onto her arm, but she doesn't move to wipe it away. Her body is shaking so violently that Aquila is afraid she might come apart entirely if she lets go.

"I don't know why I'm crying," Lyra gulps between breaths. "I think . . . I think something happened to my family. I keep trying to remember why I'm here, and there's nothing. I just want to know *something*."

The scrape of the door behind them startles Aquila. When she twists around, Zeke is hovering in the opening, shuffling his feet awkwardly.

"Hey," he says. "Is she okay?"

"I'm fine," Lyra says wetly, wiping her nose with her fist.

"She's fine, can we just get a minute?" Aquila seconds. Zeke still can't look at her, and every moment of it is like a knife in the ribs.

"Why are you crying?" Pollux says, appearing behind Zeke and pushing his head through the gap. "Have you been hurt?"

Lyra seizes the cushion from the chair next to them and hurls it at the door, sending them retreating back into the living room. Zeke slides the door shut, and Aquila slouches in relief.

"Are you guys okay?" Lyra asks, studying her from behind puffy eyelids. "You two seem weird now."

Aquila crosses her arms, hooking her thumbs in the creases of her elbows. "Now?"

"I mean the other day you two seemed . . . close."

"Well, we're not."

Lyra squints at her, confused. "But the other day you said—"

"Please stop talking about the other day," Aquila begs. It comes out harsher than she means it to, and Lyra blinks, taken aback.

"It's just, the other day things were different. Nothing is the same now."

Lyra looks at her for a long time, obviously piecing something together in her mind. Everything about her happens on the surface, open and apparent, and Aquila can't help but be slightly envious. Lyra is incapable of being anything other than herself, everything out on her sleeve at all times. Nothing is weighed or measured; she just lets it out as it comes.

"I know Pollux is a pain," she says eventually. "But here's the thing about him: he always tells the truth, no matter what. Even if it's something no one wants to hear. You could learn something from that, Aquila."

She stands up, padding softly across the patio and squeezing through the door, leaving Aquila alone once again. She watches Lyra join Zeke and Pollux through the glass, and her ribs start to close around her lungs.

She gets to her feet, stalking off the patio into the shadows. At first she's pointed toward A-House, but then her legs carry her past it. Instead, she takes the path between the houses, the gentle slope quickening her steps. Her muscles start to ache, acid running through them, but she keeps pushing until she reaches the pond. Her toes land just short of the edge, stopping her from diving into still water. She'd never been a swimmer, but now her body has a strange longing to be held by the water based on a day she can't even remember fully. The idea of floundering around in the pond makes her think of Fish, and she realizes he's been alone in the room she left him in all day.

Feeling stupid and irresponsible, she turns back toward the neighborhood and freezes.

Cygnus is walking toward her, following the same path she'd taken down from the houses. She can feel the hair on her arms rising with every step he takes, but she starts back toward the lights. Her jaw sets as they draw even, priming herself to walk straight past him, but he steps into her path.

She stops, huffing out an annoyed breath.

"What?"

"I just wanted to check on you," he says gently, holding his hands up in surrender. "I saw you go by the window."

"I'm fine, thanks," she says, stepping around him.

His hand closes around her arm, clamping it in a tight grip. She glares at him, locking onto his shadowed eyes.

"Ouch," she says through her teeth. "You always grab girls like that?"

He smirks, his smooth lips drawing up over his perfectly even teeth, and something spooks inside of Aquila. Her heart beats against her ribs like a trapped bird, and she's suddenly tempted to sprint for the nearest house.

"Guess I'm lucky you're not a girl," he says.

Something flashes across her vision and her skull rattles, pain exploding across her cheek. Her hands slam into the ground and she blinks, trying to clear her sight, but another blow jolts her head forward. The grass is touching her cheek again, and her muddled mind takes comfort in the feeling as it spins off into space.

Then she's being crushed into the ground, and her world dissolves into one singular, splintering pain.

ZEKE: 20

Pollux is going to drive him up the wall. He wanders in a circle around the furniture, taking the same path every time like a moon-locked star. What had started as a dialogue has dissolved into Pollux's continuous monologue, wearing Zeke down like a wave beating against a rock.

"People find comfort in merit-based systems," he says, focused on a level point in front of him. "Maybe it's an attempt to placate the participants."

Zeke doesn't even bother responding. He'd figured out early on that no matter what he said, Pollux just kept plowing right through. He glances at the patio door, watching the darkness beyond the fake fire for movement. Lyra had gone out after Aquila, and the thought of being around her again starts to gnaw at his stomach. Just having her in the same room would help, even if she wanted to pretend there was nothing between them.

Maybe he'd presumed too much. Maybe the connection he'd felt in the tent had just been a carry-over of emotion after she'd told him about her stints in rehab, or the way her father had manipulated her to cover his shifts on the convoys. But he'd felt the shimmer in the air between them, the pull of their bodies like they'd been paired in orbit.

He starts to let the memory play out behind his eyes while Pollux talks, picturing her hair falling over her face as she lay beside him, her laugh when he told her about his Mama Rie practicing her singing auditions in the shower. How it'd felt like time stalled when she moved closer, and how everything went quiet when her hand rested against his arm.

"I don't know if . . ." He'd started to say it, his hand drifting to rest at the curve of her hip. Her skin beneath his fingers was silken and chilled, reminding him of the feel of fresh sheets before they warmed.

"You don't know what?" she'd coaxed, her eyes heavy on his face. Her touch traveled up the slope of his arm, sending a warm wave over his torso.

"If I like you like that," he'd finished, his voice husky.

"I think you do," Aquila murmured, the edge of her bottom lip tugging up in a way that made him want to trap it between his teeth.

The patio door slams open, making him jump, and even Pollux looks startled. Lyra is hanging on the frame, panting to catch her breath, but it's her drained face that makes worry hit him like a punch in the gut. Pollux stands up, gazing at her with concern, but Zeke is already walking toward her across the living room.

"What's wrong?"

"I . . ." She gulps, sucking in air. "I don't know, I think I saw something."

She smears the hair out of her face, pressing her hand to her diaphragm.

"I went to find Aquila, and down by the pond I saw Cygnus. I don't know what I saw, but now I think . . ." She shakes her head, her brow knotted. "I don't know what I think."

Zeke pushes past her, panic boiling through him as he jogs into the shadows. He hears the footsteps behind him but he doesn't wait for them to catch up. The pond is a fair distance from the houses, and he's running when he reaches it.

The ground around it is empty, the water still. He's walked the whole diameter of it by the time Pollux and Lyra get there, red-faced and huffing.

"Where was it?" Zeke demands. "What exactly did you see?"

Lyra braces herself on her knees, pointing toward the spot where they'd pitched tents.

"I saw Cygnus there, and—I was up the hill, but it just—it seemed . . ."

He cuts her off, walking toward a patch of grass that looks out of place from the uniformly cropped lawn. The closer he gets, the more his veins race with panic.

Divots have been carved out of the turf, maybe by scuffling feet, and blades of grass lay scattered around like forgotten confetti. A few dark spots catch his eye in the silvery-blue tube light, and when he drags his shoe through them, they smear.

He stoops down to touch them, his fingertips coming up wet.

"Oh my god," Lyra says, her hands clasping over her mouth. "Is that blood? Is that her blood?"

She stumbles toward a patch of trees just beyond the pond, her voice tearing through the silence.

"Aquila! Aquila, where are you?"

Zeke can't stop staring at the tips of his fingers, certain in some deep part of him that the blood is hers. Seeing it outside of her body fills him with a cold weight that threatens to drag him to the ground.

Pollux appears to his right, looking over the scene.

"Well," he says, close to impassive. "We are criminals, after all."

For a moment, Zeke envisions hauling him into the pond and holding his head under water. But the thought dies out, washed over by the need to lay eyes on Aquila, to hear her voice, to know she's still breathing.

He and Lyra call her name for what seems like hours. They search the houses in the neighborhood, the trees, the lake. He tries to go back toward the strip where they found Lacerta, but Lyra throws such a fit that it summons Pollux, who manages to settle him slightly.

"Even prisons have to uphold health standards," he says, steering Zeke back indoors. "They'll have taken her to the hospital."

From the look Lyra gives him, she isn't so sure.

The three of them stay in the living room, each on their own piece of furniture. He and Lyra spend the whole night awake, watching the patio as if they expect Aquila to stagger in.

"I just left her," Lyra says softly, staring through the glass. "I didn't do anything."

"They would have stopped him, right?" he whispers, not wanting Pollux to overhear. "The people in charge? They wouldn't just let someone die in here."

Lyra doesn't answer, her eyes wide and unblinking as if she's replaying the scene in her own head. The house stays deadly quiet the whole night, and at some point he slips into a fitful sleep painted with violent dreams. He sees Dione, blood dripping like syrup from her nose. He sees his hands splayed over the face of a man underwater, bubbles of air streaming out of his mouth and nose as he claws at Zeke's arm. He sees Aquila being dragged backward into the pond as she reaches for him.

It's only in the morning, when the voices wake him up, that he realizes he's forgotten to take his pills. And it's only when he goes back to search B-House that he realizes they're gone.

Fish hops through the grass, stretching his tatty wings in half-hearted flaps. Once he gets to the edge of the pond, he stares into it for a moment before scurrying back to Zeke's lap.

He opens his fist, letting Fish peck a few crumbs from the lines of his palm.

That thing is never going to fly, Caelum says, his hoarse voice grating on Zeke's nerves. *You should toss it in the lake for the fish.*

"Shut up," Zeke growls aloud.

You can't take care of it, Volans seconds, so loud and deep Zeke swears he can feel the vibrations in his skull. *You can't even take care of yourself. You got killers all around you.*

It's a thought that had plagued him long before he'd made it to Carcer. Between the boys that followed Dione around like flies and the hardened plant workers who harassed Mama Beck for her foul mouth and Mama Rie for her spell-binding eyes, Zeke was always playing the shield. In his mind, he was all that stood between the people he loved and the corroded world they lived in. Love and protecting became the same thing to him, the only way he could provide anything to the ones he cared most about. But he was just as flawed and unstable as the cheap, eroding city they lived in. In the end, he'd failed them all.

And even now, he's still failing.

"No one said we were killers," he says, but it doesn't even sound convincing to his own ears. He'd felt it around Pollux, around Cygnus—like they had a damp gray ring around their bodies that sucked up light and warmth. The feel of someone who was missing some part of them, some humanity chip they were born without.

Fish turns in a circle and nestles his head in Zeke's elbow, settling into sleep. His thin eyelids close, his little ribcage moving up and down like an inflating balloon. Zeke touches the tip of his finger to Fish's head, stroking the wispy feathers that cover it. The black, reflective orb of the control center looms into his vision from above. It must be almost comical to anyone watching; a buzzed-cut, hundred-seventy-five pound criminal cradling a tiny bird in his tattooed arms.

When he looks back down, Aquila's freckled hand is cupping Fish's body, smoothing down his feathers.

He reels back, catching himself with his free arm, and the vision blinks out of existence like it was never there. Fish fluffs out his wings, clearly displeased about being woken up. Shock has stolen the air from his lungs, and he tries to stop himself from gulping in breaths.

"Easy, boss," Aquila's voice says, wiry and mocking in a way it had never sounded in real life, and he jumps to his feet.

Fish flaps a few times in protest, but Zeke holds him to his chest as he marches back toward B-House.

He throws aside the door, setting Fish on the couch before returning to the bathroom one more time. He tears through the cabinets, not bothering to put things back in place, and when he's done he sets in on the kitchen.

When still no rattling bottle of pills materializes, he slams his heel into the nearest wall. The house lets off a low, droning sound, like a warning buzzer or the start of a fire alarm. Heat boils up in Zeke's chest.

"Oh, you don't like that?" he says, reaching for a barstool to throw and finding it bolted to the ground. Instead, he grabs the cabinet door he left open and tries to tear it from the hinges.

The poly-welding stays strong, not even budging despite the pressure.

Nice and secure, Volans rumbles in his mind. *They care more about their facility than the people in it.*

They don't care about you or her, Caelum layers on. *They didn't care when she screamed for help. They watched her die screaming.*

You were the only one who could have stopped it.

A roar of frustration tears out of his mouth and he folds forward, pressing the heels of his hands into his eyes.

"You're not real," he tells the voices, forcing himself to erase their names from his mind. "Stop talking to me."

How do you know what's real?

Which one is the real you? His own voice repeats back to him. *Who are you now, then?*

"Stop!" he begs, sinking to his knees on the floor. "Just stop!"

A tiny, high-pitched beep pierces his mind, and his eyes pop open. His scattered thoughts collect in curiosity, focused on the sound. He stands up, looking to the living room, and spots Fish hopping from the couch to the chair, emitting a small peep with each jump. His attention is on Zeke, and he could almost swear there's concern reflected in the bird's glassy, yellow eyes.

In a few steps, Zeke reaches him and kneels down, holding out his hand so Fish can walk into it with his spindly legs.

"I'm alright, boss," he says, tucking him into the pocket of his jacket. "Sorry I lost it for a second."

A different sound fills his ears, familiar and deep, and his stomach sinks to his feet. He lifts his wrist, the light from the mode making his irises seize.

Another test. They expect them to report for another test as if nothing has changed. He sets his jaw, his fists balling, and strides out of the house.

Lyra and Pollux are waiting for him halfway across the court-yard. Lyra's face is mottled with pink, and her eyes are just as swollen as the day before. She picks at her shoulder as he nears, playing with the edge of her scab.

"Pollux made me come," she says when he's close enough to hear. "I think we should protest. No more Tect until Aquila comes back."

"I've pointed out that compliance has always meant rewards," Pollux says, his tone sour as if they've been having this same argument for hours. "It's entirely possible they're withholding her presence as incentive."

"I don't care," Zeke says, squinting against the splinters of light from the tubes around him. "Let's just get it over with."

The inside of his head has been thrashed and left in ruins in forty-eight hours, turned into a dreamscape he can't wake up from. If another challenge means a handful of Moxifarin at the end, it's enough to keep him fighting for one more hour, one more day.

He walks between them, forcing himself to keep heading toward the building. The doorway starts as a dark cave in his sight, shadows moving behind it in the depths, and he makes himself stare into it until the visions fade.

His resolve lasts all the way up to the landing. As soon as his foot touches the smooth platform of the building, his legs lock, feet adhering to the ground. He sways on the spot, trying to make out what the room holds for them in the shadows. A hand grabs his arm and he shrugs it off, thinking it's another hallucination.

"Zeke," Lyra's voice hisses, pulling his attention from the doorway.

She's looking back toward the neighborhood, her face pale and stricken. When he glances over his shoulder to see what has her so spooked, his blood freezes in his veins.

Cygnus is coming toward them across the grass, the smallest

limp in his step. The right side of his face is swollen, blood collected beneath his sharp cheekbone like the stained edge of a knife.

It's only when Pollux snags Zeke's elbow that he realizes he'd been moving toward him. The force of his motion swings him around, and Pollux leans in once he's stopped fully.

"We might need him," he says, quiet and firm. Just like the supervisor he'd always seemed to be. "Don't do anything stupid."

Very carefully, Zeke peels off his jacket and holds it out to Lyra, careful not to jostle Fish in the pocket.

"Hold the chick," he tells her. She nods, folding the jacket to her chest.

He turns, starting out across the lawn. As soon as Cygnus sees him coming, he stops, swaying back on his heels. He's exhausted, his eyes dull and mouth slightly open, but his muscles still tense the closer Zeke gets to him.

"Where is she?" he says, his voice ragged, and Cygnus flinches.

"Look, nothing happened," he starts, but Zeke stops whatever lie is coming next with his knuckles. The scabs from the last time his fist met Cygnus's face peel back, sending a flash of pain through his hand, but seeing Cygnus tumble back onto the ground, prone and scared, is worth it.

"I don't know where she is, I don't know where *I* was. I don't know what happened, I woke up back in A-House this morning, then the mode went off—"

Zeke takes a few steps toward him, and he twists and flaps on the ground like a landed fish.

"Okay, okay, back off," he says, holding his hands up. "Yes, okay, yes we hooked up."

Zeke brings his foot down into the soft part of his belly, enjoying the startled groan it gets out of him.

He watched her bleed out, Caelum mutters in his ear. *He watched her die and he loved every second of it.*

Zeke's hands bunch up the front of Cygnus's shirt, his knee driving up into the gap between his ribs. He can feel Cygnus's muscles fight the impact, tensing against him, and he brings his knee down again harder.

If it doesn't end here, he'll do it again, Volans roars, shaking his brain. *End this now. Do what you should have done all along.*

You could have saved Dione if you just had the guts to do it, Caelum scratches out.

Zeke freezes, his blood-streaked hands locked against Cygnus's chest, and for a moment the nightmare returns to him. He sees the face underwater, the whites of the man's eyes glinting like glass at the bottom of a river. The open mouth vomiting out bubbles of breath, the sound of his cry muffled beneath the choppy waves.

Zeke leaps back, colliding with Pollux, who's wandered closer. The world swirls around him, the edges blending together, and he shuts his eyes against it for a moment.

Aquila would want you to do it, Volans growls in his ear.

You failed Aquila and you failed Dione, Caelum snarls.

A pained cry bursts from his throat, and he presses his wet fingers into his eyes.

Kill him now, the voices repeat, layering over each other. *Do it for Aquila. Do it now.*

They drown out every other thought until there's nothing else. Zeke opens his eyes, red leaking into his vision to make a crimson film over Cygnus on the ground, curling around his own stomach.

Something squeezes his arms, bringing him back into his body, and Pollux looms into his view.

"Do you hear them now?" he asks.

Zeke's teeth chatter together, but he manages to get one word through them.

"Yes."

Pollux turns him sideways, steering him toward the door. Vaguely, he's aware of the countdown timer pinging off, but he can't stop seeing the face of the drowning man every time he blinks. Cool air dusts his face, and when he looks around, he's made it into the building. Lyra is next to him, her face lit with the outdoor tubelight as she stares out the doorway.

"Stay away from us, you psycho!" she yells back at Cygnus, clutching Zeke's jacket to her chest.

The countdown stops, and the door seals, just as the voices finally cease. It's like being cut free, and he folds forward, bracing himself on his knees. Shudders rack his body, tugging his spine apart.

Pollux grasps his shoulder, pulling him upright.

"Have they been giving you medication?"

Zeke wipes at his lip, finding it slick with sweat. "At the end of every challenge."

Pollux nods, turning to the room. "Better get through it, then."

POLLUX: 21

This is all very wrong.

Things have become a faulty system, glitches and bugs all around him, and no one is fixing them. The maze had been interrupted, yet they had still received credit for completing it. But because they hadn't, they had received no prizes for doing so. The established teams had been shot the first day, but he'd been confident in the substitutes that had formed in the wake of Orion leaving. At least there were enough people to complete whatever challenges the room presented. But now, they'd lost Aquila, Cygnus was ostracized, and Lacerta and Cass were nowhere to be found. Clearly pieces had been moved by the hand in charge, but what was the purpose? Why were they left?

More than that, the mood had been altered irrevocably by Aquila's absence. Both Zeke and Lyra had become emotionally unstable in their grief over the past day. Without medication Zeke's schizophrenia seems to have reached a peak, most likely due to his heightened stress levels, and unfortunately that made him an untrustworthy participant. They'll have reached the midway point with the completion of this challenge, and less than half the players remain. If the point *was* to weed them out, somebody was doing an excellent job.

His first thought when looking over the new challenge is that it's also a mistake. The room hadn't finished setting itself up for them before sending out the call, or maybe wasn't meant to call them at all. Instead of the elaborate barriers and structures the Tect usually holds, everything is retracted except for one, singular pedestal at the center of the room. It reminds him a bit of the ancient religious temples he'd seen pictures of, with all the architecture giving importance to a single point.

He moves toward it, sensing Lyra behind him. Zeke is the last to follow, his steps slow and dragging.

"Where's Cass?" he says, breaking the dense silence around them. "And Lacerta? They didn't make it inside."

"Oh my god, you're right," Lyra whimpers, worry wringing her voice.

"They were moved the same night Cygnus and Aquila were," Pollux tells them, glancing over his shoulder. It was surprising it took this long for them to notice their absence, given how comforted they were by the herd.

Lyra stops in her tracks. "What? Moved where?"

"Probably to one of the other sections," he says. "Like the one Orion came from."

"Wait, what?" Zeke asks distantly, his steps shuffling to a halt. "What does that mean?"

Pollux swallows down his annoyance, turning around.

"There are multiple sections in this station. Surely you noticed."

"I guess I figured there were, but why do you think the girls are there now?"

"I said probably, I didn't say I think," Pollux corrects, which gets an eye roll from Lyra. "It's the most probable thing."

"What if Orion got them, Pollux?" Lyra says, her tone stoked with anger. "Did you think of that? Or Cygnus? What if they needed our help?"

"Honestly, I think helping each other is counterproductive to the goal," he says, wincing when her eyes start to burn furiously.

"So you don't care about any of us?" she pushes, clearly willing him to disagree. "You'd be happy if we all disappeared."

The first words that come to him are "of course," but as he looks at her, her brow set, determined to ignore the tendrils of hair that have escaped from her braid as she glowers at him, he starts to imagine what it would be like for her presence to suddenly be gone. It would certainly mean a lack of something he can't put a name to, a kind of warmth she brought to every room she was in. Beyond that, though, there was a particular comfort in her sheer existence. She was like a tiny sun, her light reaching into even the farthest depths. The idea of her being removed altogether is . . . displeasing, to say the least. Perhaps that's why they were so upset at the disappearance of Aquila: she brought the same kind of light with her presence that couldn't be kindled now that she's gone.

Lyra shakes her head, looking away, and he realizes he's waited too long to respond. Instead, he turns his attention to the table in the center, trying to realign his thoughts.

It's rather small for the purpose of giving a clue, with a slightly curved surface like a dish, funneling downward. Eight partitions line the bowl, and his chest tightens at the sight of it. Whatever it is, it was intended for all eight of them to participate.

Zeke puts it together soon after he does, and turns to give him a narrow-eyed stare.

Pollux ignores him, his attention on the pillar beneath the dish. A thin rectangular outline is etched into each side, and he runs his fingers over the one facing him. It flips inward to reveal a pocket. His fingers dip into it, finding a pen-like tube rolling around on the shallow bottom. He pulls it out, holding it up for the others to see.

"A Lidopen," he says when they're silent.

"Great," Lyra sighs. "So whatever we're doing, it's going to hurt."

"Give it here," Zeke asks gruffly, holding out his palm for it. Once Pollux surrenders it, Zeke pops the top and presses the thin barb into the back of his mangled hand. Yet another reason Pollux avoided fights—no one made it out unscathed. After a blank moment, the smallest sigh of relief issues from Zeke's nose.

Pollux searches the next side, finding a screen that lights up when he touches it. After a moment, it goes back to sleep, and he moves on. The opposite face holds a similar hidden pocket, and out of this one he pulls a silver scalpel.

The blade is capped, but he knows the weight of it in his fingers without even taking it off. Holding it causes a memory to flit across his mind, of Castor twirling their uncle's scalpel between his thumb and pointer, the end of it making a lemniscate pattern in the air. He'd caught Pollux looking and grinned in that maniacal way he did when he was going to do something erratic.

Pollux drops the tool into the dish, wanting the vision to stop. The action causes the screen to light up again, this time displaying numbers. It counts up slowly, as if deciding what to display, then blips a red "x" accompanied by a lackluster buzz.

He reaches his hand into the dish, splaying his fingers over the bottom and pressing down. The screen lights up again, and the numbers climb for a moment before the blip and buzz repeat.

"It's a scale," he observes.

Lyra squints at it, then looks around.

"For what? There's nothing in here."

"There's always something," he tells her, backing away. "We just have to find it."

They sweep the building, turning up nothing. They walk the floor inch by inch, shoulder to shoulder so as not to miss a single trick tile. When that fails, they use their hands to test the walls. Zeke even lifts Lyra onto his shoulders to try the highest point they can reach, but nothing reacts.

Pollux eventually uses the scalpel to try and pry open the pedestal when he starts to suspect the room has denied them some integral clue. Lyra watches him from her seat on the ground but says nothing, though the wheels are clearly turning in her mind. After a while, her silent judgement starts to irk him.

"Feel free to offer ideas," he says bitterly, the scalpel slipping on the smooth surface of the pillar.

The edge of her mouth twitches just slightly. "So you can make fun of them?"

"Everyone makes incorrect assumptions, it's not something to degrade yourself about."

He would have thought that part would be obvious, seeing as how everyone but him had been wrong about something up until that point. The image of her triumphantly sliding the scissors across the kitchen counter flashes before him and he almost smiles. Guess he had been wrong about something after all.

"Is that your way of saying we're all equally stupid?" she says, bringing him out of his memory.

He jams the fine end of the blade in the seam of the pedestal, answering her honestly. "I don't think you're stupid."

"It's fine," she sniffs dismissively. "Everyone does. I'm used to it."

"You're not stupid," he says, frustration straining his tone. "But you rush into everything and that reads as stupid. You do things before you've finished thinking about them. You answer things before you understand the question. You trip yourself on your own feet," he adds, quoting the ridiculous saying his mother used to throw into conversations whenever she could. Colloquialisms like that tended to soften the message, he'd observed.

Lyra's expression changes, a storm clearing away from her face. He has little time to enjoy the change he's brought over her before Zeke storms up to the pedestal, forcing him to stand up or get stepped on.

"There's got to be something else in this," he says.

Pollux forces himself to keep a straight face. "My thoughts precisely."

He walks around the base, cutting through Pollux's space to study the bowl. He stretches a ragged hand into it, testing the bottom again and activating the scale. When he pulls back, his fingers have left a bloody smudge on the sides, and seeing it makes the space behind Pollux's ears twinge with annoyance. He waits for the buzzer to voice their failure, but it doesn't come.

Curious, he leans to the side to look at it. The numbers are still illuminated, reading a tiny fraction of weight. His stomach sinks, hunching his shoulders with the weight of it.

Organic matter. That's what it was meant to measure. And the only thing organic in the room is them.

"A test of will," he says out loud, glancing down at the scalpel in his hand. Or a test of character. Would you hurt yourself before hurting another person.

"Zeke," he says, inching closer to him. "Give me your hand."

He pulls farther away, eyeing the tool. "I don't think so."

"I'm just going to scrape some blood," he assures him. "You won't feel it, anyway."

Warily, Zeke extends his hand into Pollux's grasp. He uses the dull end to gingerly scrape around the largest wound, enjoying the jelly texture the clotting platelets have created. Once he has a decent amount, he taps it off into the dish, careful to hit a clean section.

The scale jumps a few numbers, and Pollux drops his arm, not sure whether he's relieved or disappointed.

"It wants our blood?" Lyra asks, clearly repulsed by the concept.

"Eight partitions," Pollux says. "Each player is meant to give equally."

"So we have to make up for *five* missing people?" she goes on, her voice rising. "That's not fair!"

He bites his tongue, but Zeke can't help himself.

"What about this has seemed fair to you, Lyra?" He fumes and she wilts slightly, tucking her hand under the opposite arm. "Do you think they care about making things fair? We're just rats in a maze to them. They don't care what happens to us in here."

"I don't believe that's true," Pollux starts, but one look at Zeke cuts him off. His hazel eyes burn like liquid gold, and Pollux isn't sure he can recognize friend from foe at the moment.

"Really? You think they're going to let us out if we do what they say?" he presses, stepping closer.

"If you don't think they will, why are you here?" Pollux asks evenly.

"For my *freaking* pills," he says, barely able to keep his voice in check. "Give me the thing."

He holds his hand out, and after a long moment Pollux hands over the scalpel. Zeke makes a fist and holds it over the dish, sucking in a breath to steady himself. He swipes the blade across the back of his hand, opening up a pink gash. It takes a moment for the blood to rush into it, but once it does, a steady stream drips into bottom. Lyra knits her brow, a delicate sheen of sweat breaking out over her forehead, and her gaze adheres to the ceiling.

The numbers climb on the scale as the bottom of the dish pools with ruby liquid, beautifully rich and vibrant. Pollux can't help but watch it with wonder. Blood newly parted from the source almost looks alive in its own right.

Eventually, Lyra caves, surging forward to wrap her hand around Zeke's bicep.

"Jesus, Zeke, enough," she says, pulling him back.

He pinches the skin together, trying to staunch the bleeding, but heavy drops hit the floor beneath him. The scale has moved up, but the pedestal is still quiet, expecting more.

"It can't need more than that," Lyra says, pointing to the shallow pool Zeke has left at the bottom. "He'll die."

"It's meant to be the combined weight of eight people," Pollux says, surprised at the regret in his own voice. "We'll each need to contribute more than that."

Lyra swallows so thickly he can hear it from three feet away. She steps up to the pedestal, holding out her left hand.

"My turn, then," she says, reaching for the scalpel.

"Wait."

Pollux sweeps the Lidopen off the floor, jabbing himself in the palm. After the initial sting, numbness begins to spread beneath his skin, making his hand feel stuffed with sand. He takes the scalpel from Zeke and makes a slit along the bottom of his hand, where he can easily control the flow simply my opening or closing his fist.

He lets his own blood mix with Zeke's, the colors marbling together. The scale climbs painfully slow, and after a while the cut clots up on its own and he has to reopen it. Eventually his feet begin to needle with cold, and when he tries to shake some life back into them he finds himself swaying.

"Okay, boss," Zeke says, cupping his elbow to guide him away. "Take a break."

The floor tilts beneath him, making him stumble a step before Zeke sets him on the ground. There's a tinkling sound of metal and he realizes he's dropped the scalpel when Lyra picks it up.

"Not her," Pollux says, his tongue sticking to the roof of his mouth. "Not you, Lyra."

"Shut up," she says, wrapping her fingers around the handle.

"She's too small," he goes on, but Zeke is already tossing her the Lidopen.

"I wouldn't tell her that," he mutters to Pollux, his hand squeezing his shoulder lightly.

As Zeke straightens, Pollux notices the lump in his jacket pocket where the heron chick has been sleeping. It moves slightly, rotating in its makeshift nest, and an idea begins to dawn on him.

Lyra is holding her arm over the basin, her hand shaking as she brings the blade to her skin. She raises her eyes to Pollux as if daring him to comment. When he doesn't, she drags the blade across her palm, making her pinkie finger twitch when she goes too deep. Pollux bites the inside of his cheek, restraining himself from pointing it out. His head is too heavy, sloshing like a water balloon with every motion.

Lyra's blood runs much faster than either his or Zeke's, alarming all of them with its tenacity. She only gets through a quarter of what they put in before her knees start to buckle and her skin washes gray, and Zeke forces her to sit down.

"This is impossible," she says, letting Zeke wrap the sleeve of her jacket around her palm. "There's no way we can make up for five people. Let's just bring Cygnus in here and take it all out of him."

Zeke chuckles half-heartedly, tucking in the sleeve tight.

"There's something else we can try."

They turn to look at Pollux, the color of their faces muted.

"We could use a different blood source," he explains slowly, attempting to walk them into it gently. "Something that's not human."

"Great, what can we use?" Lyra says, glancing around.

"The heron chick probably has a full portion's worth of blood."

Zeke's chin goes slack, his arm tightening against his side as if making a barrier around his pocket.

"Forget it."

"We can't keep giving blood like this," he goes on. "It's too dangerous."

"We don't even know if it would work. I'm not going to kill him for nothing."

"Look at us," Pollux pants, raising his hand to gesture at them. The motion takes almost all his energy. "If it saves us from bleeding out, it's worth it. We only have so much we can give."

Zeke shakes his head, taking a step back and stumbling onto his knee. He catches the lump in his pocket with his hand, cradling it into his lap as he sits back.

"I'm not doing that," he says.

"I'm with Pollux," Lyra seconds, regret softening her tone. "At least if it's Fish, none of us get hurt more."

"No one is touching Fish!" Zeke yells, his voice filling every corner of the space.

He rocks forward onto his feet, sweeping up the scalpel as he goes, and marches to the pedestal. His fist tightens around the instrument, and he braces his free hand against the flat surface around the basin.

"Zeke, no!" Lyra screams, trying to get her feet under her.

Before Pollux can determine what he means to do, Zeke sucks in a breath and forces the blade down against the pedestal, a hollow cracking sound following the motion. A mix between a growl and a cry issues through his clenched teeth, and a burst of blood smatters the floor. The scalpel tumbles out of his hand, and a moment later he reaches over the basin and drops something into it. He tucks his left hand into his chest, darkening the fabric of his jacket beneath it, and the shape of it strikes Pollux as odd until he notices the space where his pinkie finger should be.

The scale climbs quickly, chiming happily and flashing green. The fourth side of the pedestal opens, and Zeke's good hand grapples around in it, pulling out a packed first aid kit. He tears it open with his teeth, sending the contents rolling across the floor.

Lyra gathers them together, rushing over to jab his streaming hand with a new Lidopen. Her fingers are shaking so violently that she almost misses the mark, and Pollux stands up to help.

"I'm fine," Zeke snarls, grabbing for the coagulant spray. "Bring me my pills."

Pollux turns, noticing a door in the back wall has opened. He hurries to it, already able to see the familiar names illuminated beyond the doorway.

He finds Zeke's box, lifting out the bottle of Moxifarin and tucking it into his pocket. He debates going through the others' prizes, pausing to look at the bottle of orange hair tint in Lyra's box. It's only when he's halfway across the floor that he realizes he hadn't even thought to look in his own. Somehow, the importance of trinkets from the past is beyond him now. And he can't help but find it inequitable that they put Zeke's medication on the same level.

When he gets back to the others, Zeke is bandaged and relatively cleaned up, but the pinched look of pain still lingers on his face. He extends his healthy hand out when he spots Pollux, pressing the bottle against this forehead once he hands over the pills.

"Thank god," he sighs.

Their modes all ping simultaneously, and when Pollux lifts his, the new completion ring meets his eye.

"Only three more," he murmurs to himself.

Zeke hisses, seeming to stop himself from uttering some curse directed at Pollux. He mutters something under his breath, and the only word that makes it to Pollux's ear is "crazy."

A switch flips in him, every nerve lighting up in unison like a shield.

"I'm not crazy," he states, his voice prickling.

As if he can feel the intensity sparking, Zeke lifts his eyes to him. "What'd you say?"

"I'm not crazy," Pollux repeats, taking a step toward him.

"What do you think these are?" Zeke says, tugging the sleeve of his jacket up enough that his tattoo shows. "Huh? Smart guy? What do you think they mean?"

Pollux presses his teeth together, unwilling to admit he's wondered that himself. "They're classification of some kind."

"Wow," Zeke laughs, but there's no touch of humor in his eyes. "Something I know and you don't. These are diagnosis codes, genius. For mental illness. Every one of us is screwed in the head. Criminally insane."

Cold creeps over Pollux's limbs with sticky fingers, closing his airways as the knowledge sinks in. He lifts his own arm, staring down at the numbers with a new reverence. Without understanding it, he can feel what they mean. It's like looking at a word written in a different language, strange and familiar all at once. It's the same word he heard out of his parent's mouths, hushed and frightened as they whispered to each other in the kitchen when they thought he and Castor were asleep.

"But they called us inmates," Lyra says softly.

"Don't you get it yet?" Zeke seethes, curling his wounded hand against his chest. "We were criminals to them before we ever did anything wrong. To them, we're dangerous. We were always going to wind up in a place like this. These challenges don't mean anything. All of this, it's all for nothing. They are never letting us out of here."

He storms past them, his movements jerky and uneven. At the door he pauses, glancing down at the bulge in his jacket pocket where the chick is still nestled. When he speaks again, all the anger is gone. The fire inside him has been doused, and only a few wisps of steam linger.

"And no one gives a shit," he says. "No one gives a shit if they ever see us again."

LYRA: 22

The emptiness inside her is so dense and clawing that it steals her sleep. It's a void that keeps eating her alive, like the collapsing stars they'd learned about in C7. Lyra used to romanticize the image of light vanishing into the heart of them, like their deaths were so heavily felt that nothing around them escaped. It's something her mother would have said. Giving lives and emotions to the cold stars who felt nothing and never would.

Lyra flips onto her stomach, hoping to smother the ache in her chest with her own weight. The ear pressed into the pillow fills with her heartbeat, and her head starts to throb. Aquila's face blinks through her mind, and she grinds the heels of her hands into her eyes as if she can scrub Aquila from them. The guilt is too heavy to bear, knowing that she'd been the only one standing between her friend and the pain she'd suffered.

If she could read the code pressed into the skin of his forearm, would it have told her what Cygnus was? Did it even matter? Whoever put them all together clearly thought they were the same species of damaged.

For nothing, her brain repeats, though it isn't Zeke's voice any-more, but hers. *It's all for nothing.*

Was he right? She'd seen the shift in her mother after she tried to explain the music she heard in fire. How everything Lyra did following that day was viewed with guarded withdrawal, even from her sisters. They'd seen cracks in her she couldn't see herself, and everyone was waiting for her to erupt into pieces and slice them apart.

The void rises, pulling in her heart, her lungs, crushing them together inside her. She sits up suddenly, afraid the feeling might swallow her completely. Her feet touch the floor, and she tiptoes past sleeping Pollux into the kitchen. Without fully understanding why, she ducks beneath the kitchen counter and hooks the bottle of disinfectant powder with her index finger. She lifts it out quietly, her other hand searching out the glycerin soap bottle from the pantry.

A memory surfaces of this pair of chemicals on a black coun-tertop. It was her Chemics class, and Homer had been throwing half-sucked candy into her hair from the seat behind her, but she was locked onto what the instructor was saying. She remembers the codes he wrote out, like a secret language, chained together to make something important.

She'd remembered it the first time she'd been in this kitchen, when she'd seen half of the code on the disinfectant bottle and its counterpoint in the pantry. She just hadn't remembered the second half of the story.

How when these two came together, they made beautiful fire. How the little puff of it they'd made in Chemics class had stalled her heart, and she hadn't even noticed Homer. How she'd hidden the remainder of her experiment into her pockets and smuggled it home.

Lyra slips through the patio door, the Tect a shadow across the courtyard. The grass rustles against the soles of her feet as she walks toward it, every step bringing it closer. It had always looked out of place among the neighborhood, like the start of a virus no one had noticed yet.

The terror she'd learned to feel at approaching it is gone. Everything that happened to them inside the Tect was a result of the power it had over them, making them afraid to disobey or step out of line. But it was an imposter with no real power. It was Homer Oleyedo, looming and threatening to look at, but its true power was to make you hurt yourself from the inside out. And Lyra is done being hurt.

The entry door is still open, like the gaping mouth of a sleeping giant. Lyra stops in front of it, staring into the dark belly of the Tect as she sets the disinfectant on the ground in front of it. Cold from the floor bites into the soles of her bare feet but she ignores it, unscrewing the top of the bottle and pouring in the glycerin. She stands and hurls it into the monster's mouth, watching it sail down its throat.

The room erupts with light, flooding every corner with illumination. Once the flash passes, the bottle has turned into a glowing heart at the center, wreathed in flames that take root in the ceiling. The sound passes over her like a wave. The low beat vibrates in her ears, snaring her heart, and she stumbles onto her knees, closing her eyes as the warmth reaches her.

The music climbs, growing louder until it soars and swirls around her. She tilts her head back, letting it wash over her and fill every pore until she's floating in it. Tears push through her closed eyes, spilling down her cheeks as the music builds, twisting together into the most beautiful melody.

What are you doing? A voice cracks through her chest and her eyes fly open. But there's no one near her.

Get back from there! It comes again, distant but clear.

She can see it. She can see the remainder of her Chemics experiment on the floor of her living room, the mess the black powder had made across the carpet as it spilled out of her hands. She can feel the raw hurt inside her, alone with her sisters upstairs. She can hear her parents' last words to her as they left to meet with her instructors after her failed Primary Tests. How disappointed their faces had been, how her mother had not seemed to recognize her.

"Born too early," she had said as she shoved her arms into the sleeves of her coat. "Born with half of your brain still missing."

As the door had shut, the silence set in, the loudest silence of her life. Her blood had begged for the music. With no lighter, she'd stumbled to her bag to pull out the only tools she had, and they'd spilled onto the carpet as her hands shook.

She couldn't wait. She could have cleaned it, she could have taken it to her tub, but she couldn't live another second with the silence slowly killing her.

The fire had started so small, just a handful rooted in the carpet, and the thinnest, slightest song crept from it. It had hooked her, body and soul, and she could only close her eyes and listen as it grew. When the heat started to sting across her skin and her lungs itched from the smoke, she must have gotten up and gone outside, but all she can remember is the sound of the raging symphony in her ears that brought her to her knees while it consumed her house before her. It weaved a spell as it rose higher and higher, the sounds of a thousand songs intertwining. It paralyzed her limbs as her heart ached from the beauty of it.

"Get back from there!" the voice had shattered her bones, splintering the magic. There were two officers in her yard, shielding their faces against the heat from the inferno in front of them.

"What are you doing?" the nearest had yelled down at her,

seizing her elbow and hauling her away as the other broke down the front door.

"There was music," she said, choking on her own voice as it scraped her throat.

"Lyra, stand up!" the voice shouts, but it isn't part of her memory.

She's moving, someone's hands tight around her soot-covered arms dragging her away from the burning building. She gets her feet under her, stumbling a few steps until the hands drop her on the cool grass.

Pollux stands over her, his face lit with pale orange light from her fire. He works his fingers into his hair, his mouth slack as he stares at the blaze.

"What did you do?"

"I think . . ." she says, the words like knives in her chest. "I think I killed my sisters."

He's silent, unable to tear his eyes away as if hypnotized by the fire.

"Why did you do this? We can't finish. They're never going to let us out now."

"That's what you care about?" she spits. "Pollux, it doesn't matter!"

He finally looks at her, his eyebrows knit together. "It's the only thing that matters."

She fights to her feet, her fists clenching as rage catches inside her.

"If that's all that matters then finish it by yourself!" The last part comes out as a scream, and she sways a bit with the force of it. "It's not like we've ever been real partners anyway."

Pollux studies her, chewing his lip in the flickering light for a long while.

"Is that really how you feel?"

"I just," Lyra's throat constricts, trying to suffocate the sob threatening to burst out. "I just feel like I'm the only one who's never really had a partner in this. I'm the only one who's been alone."

Sharpness knifes through Pollux's eyes and the usually vacant black of his irises turns icy and hard. The look is so piercing that Lyra takes a step back, feeling like she's somehow stepped on a spring trap.

"You think you're alone?" Pollux says, his voice quiet. "Then be alone."

He turns, cutting the last cord between them. It's as if the tightrope she's been standing on has fallen out from under her, and Lyra fights the urge to stumble after him.

Distance unfolds between them, Pollux stalking off across the lawn. Once he's out of the glow from the fire, he could almost be a shadow, and the thought of this being the last image Lyra ever sees of him is somehow more haunting than the burning monster in front of her.

AQUILA: 23

Her nose itches.

It's so insistent and irritating that it bridges the deep, sticky black of sleep to tug at her consciousness. Distantly, she orders her fingers to scratch it, but her hand hits a hard stop. She tries again, a cold pressure around her wrist yanking her out of sleep.

Light floods into her eyes, and the world begins to sharpen into focus beyond them. She's on her back, surrounded by sterile white, and she squints against the harsh brightness of it. Her right hand tries to reach for her nose again and stalls, reaching the end of a tether, and she finally sees the binding around her wrist. Her left hand is the same: encased in a hard cuff attached to a cord that fastens her to the bed beneath. Panic starts to sweep through her and she sits up, instantly regretting the decision as pain clenches her lower back like a dog bite. Defeated, she flops back down, pivoting her head to get a better view of the room.

The wall in front of her is one expansive window, giving her the sensation of standing on a ledge. Beyond it, she can see the landscape of the station speckled with white buildings, and it strikes her that she must be in the eye of the giant. She'd been right after all; someone had been watching the whole time.

The room she's in is clearly a medical facility, with six other pristine, tightly tucked beds on either side of her. Fluids run through tubes into her left arm, disappearing under a gauze sleeve at her elbow. Over her head, a screen is awake and flashing silently, no doubt broadcasting her vitals to anyone who walks by.

The suction sound of a door opening hisses to her right, and she cranes her neck to see who's come in.

A plump, moon-faced woman with a tight bun shuffles in, heading straight for Aquila as if she knows what to expect.

"Good evening," she tells her curtly, reaching over Aquila's head to tap the screen purposefully. The rough navy fabric of her scrubs brushes Aquila's cheek, and a flurry of pain travels over her skull.

The memory of Cygnus's knuckles driving into her cheekbone returns to her, and with it the memory of everything else that happened right up until Cygnus landed beside her unconscious on the ground. She tries desperately to shove the images aside, forcing her eyes to follow the woman instead as she tests the tubes running alongside the bed.

"Bring your hands up, please," the physician asks, and Aquila dutifully lifts them as far as they'll go.

The woman disconnects one of the cords from the bed, looping it through a hook in the opposite cuff and cinching them together before releasing the other side. She feeds the free end into a hole at the bottom of the bed, getting a secure click.

"You can get up and walk around now, if you'd like," she says with a tight smile. "Short walks. An officer will be in to talk to you shortly."

"Thank you," Aquila says softly, her voice foreign in her own throat. It's hard to tell what startles her more, the fact that she can't remember the last time she spoke aloud or that she's about to come face to face with an officer. Her experience with officers was limited. Any trouble the alter had gotten her into on the convoy was swept over by her father, who preferred to handle it with long, sloppy lectures about his misspent youth. She'd always found the confrontation junkies that patrolled the Eagles unnecessarily intimidating, and that was enough to keep her on the straight and narrow. Unfortunately, her alter didn't share the sentiment.

The suction of the door comes again and her heart leaps, but the officer that comes in looks like a weary father of five. The neck that pokes out above his stiff collar is puffy and soft, blending into a pudgy, slightly shadowed face. Instead of the combat-level uniform the officers on the convoys had, he wears a simple charcoal work suit. The same letters they all sported on their shirts are emblazoned on his chest, though they somehow look higher quality on him.

He stops at the side of her bed, his fingers resting beside her elbow, and Aquila could swear there's genuine concern twisting the stranger's brow.

"How are you feeling?" he asks her, his voice slightly tinted with a familiar accent. It takes her a moment to place that he sounds like Pollux, which meant he had probably grown up on Earth as well.

"Any pain?" he goes on, his fingers hovering an inch above her arm before he pulls his hand back again.

"I'm okay," she says, forcing a little more effort into her vocal cords. "Thank you for . . ."

She hesitates, not sure who was responsible for finally putting Cygnus down. The whole episode is like smoke in her mind, hazy and incorporeal, but she doesn't want to try too hard to bring any of the details into sharp focus anyway.

The man motions to the phys in a sweeping gesture, and she brings him a chair before retreating to the far side of the room.

He taps a few places on the screen above Aquila's head, wafting the smell of something sweet and yeasty he'd just eaten, and a moment later her bed begins to lower. He settles into the chair beside her, bouncing his right knee as he pulls a mode screen from his pocket and holds it close to his mouth.

"Ptolemy Project manager Pavo Irez here, with inmate Aquila Navarro." He catches her watching and gives her a reassuring wink. "Classification A2-E, willing participant in the Ptolemy rehabilitation project. Inmate suffered a . . ." It takes him a moment to land on the right word. "Physical altercation with inmate Cygnus Beaumont, and was transferred to med bay for treatment. Inmate, do you agree that you are speaking with me of your own free will and no methods have been used to coerce you?"

He raises his eyebrows, indicating she should answer.

"Take back the altercation part and I'll say yes," she says gruffly.

A twitch of a smile plays at the corner of his mouth.

"Inmate Aquila Navarro was physically attacked by inmate Cygnus Beaumont, without provocation, as stated in the full report."

He moves the screen closer to her, and she relents.

"I'm not being coerced," she agrees.

The man pockets the mode, leaning forward and softening.

"Aquila, I'm so sorry," he says. "This shouldn't have happened. It was our negligence, and I . . .we can't make it up to you. I'm sorry."

His voice is kind, tumbling lightly over his words. But despite the warming she feels toward him, the apology causes a memory to drift to the surface of her mind. What her father had said when she'd been sitting in the cockpit, her bare legs stretching for the footrests while he tried to stay upright beside her.

"Why are you sorry?" she murmurs furiously, letting her father's words fill her mouth. "It happens to half of us. It was always just a coin flip whether it was going to be me or not."

She expects the uncomfortable fidget, the half-guilted throat clear that she usually gets from CisHets, but instead she's met with a stony, determined expression that doesn't match the man's gentle features.

"Are you trying to get me to say you earned it? That being the real you is a risk you shouldn't have been taking? Just because there was a mistake in your packaging doesn't give anyone permission to do what they please to it."

It's just the kind of thing she would say. The sudden familiarity of him bolts through her, like seeing a face from a dream, though she can't attach a single memory to him.

She watches his small movements, noticing how comfortable he is around her for being a stranger. He almost seems like a worried parent, the way his brow collects itself when his eyes pass over the marks on her arms.

"Do you understand where you are?" He scratches along his jawline, bothered by the new growth of hair there. It strikes her that he looks tired, frazzled even, as if he's gone days without his normal routine.

Aquila nods. "What did I do? Why can't I remember it?"

The man sits back, trying to affect what he clearly believes is a professional air.

"Unfortunately, due to the legitimacy of the project we cannot disclose that information at this time presently."

She blinks, attempting to keep her face devoid of judgement. He's at least making an attempt to be nice to her, that earns him some leeway.

"You can call me Irez," he says, placing his palm over his chest. "You won't remember it, but we worked closely before you were initiated into the program. As much as I hate that this happened, it's given us a good opportunity. I think, based on this and the testimony you gave to the other inmate, we have a good case to move you to a minimum security facility."

"You want me to leave here?" she asks, her heart pinching inexplicably at the idea.

"Trust me," he says, giving her a look heavy with sincerity. "Carcer was never the place you were supposed to be. I knew it when you were convicted. It's why I pushed the warden so hard to let you into the program. Everything that's happening, it seems to be working out for the best now."

"You want to explain that one to me?" she growls, her skin heating with a flush of anger.

He sighs a small breath through his nose, slouching back into his chair.

"We're evacuating this station. Most of the staff is already gone, almost all the surveillance crew, or someone would have stopped . . . " His gaze flits guiltily at her before diving to the floor. "The rest of us go at the end of the week. Since you're under medical care, you'll receive transport with us back to Edessa. Once we're there, I think we can petition them to review your case."

"Why can't I stay here?" she asks, almost unable to believe the words as they come out.

"Moon Rhea," Irez answers, smiling wryly as if speaking about an annoying relative. "She hit some debris on the far side of Titan and has been dragging it with her. Her orbit takes her right by us. The last time she passed, the debris almost took out the electrical system along with our comm satellites. Since then it's spread out even more, and Rhea will pass by us again in a few days. We just can't risk being here. We're short a power cell already."

Aquila struggles to sit up, adrenaline fighting through the surge of pain that accompanies the motion.

"So you're just abandoning everyone in here? You'd just let them die?"

"The priority is to save the workers," he says slowly. "There aren't enough shuttles to evacuate the entire station. We've got no long range comms to call Titan, but even if we did I can't imagine the DOT would risk damaging vessels to transport criminals."

"They're still humans," she says, setting her teeth. "Doesn't anyone care?"

The look he gives her is almost pitying, an adult trying to explain to a child why they threw away their art project.

"You gotta understand. Everyone in Carcer has killed someone. They've been convicted. It doesn't buy a whole lot of sympathy."

The reality of the statement hits her like a frigid wind, sending chills scuttling over her skin. She swallows, pulling her dry lips apart.

"Does that . . . include me?"

Irez passes a hand over the bottom half of his face, scooting his chair closer.

"Look. You're part of a very exclusive rehabilitation program. We have a very high success rate of reintegration. But it all hinges on you having limited knowledge of your . . . your conviction."

Aquila's eyes ache, and when she squeezes them closed tears empty onto her cheeks.

"I don't understand."

Irez rests a hand on the blanket near her arm.

"Which part?"

"Any of it. I can't . . ." She pulls in a shaky breath, her lungs trembling against her ribs. Another round of tears escapes, dripping off her chin.

Panic crosses Irez's round face.

"Hey, okay, okay," he says, trying to pacify her. "This is hard. But I think . . . I *know* you have a good shot at transferring to a minimum security facility on Titan for a few years and then being released on parole. Titan's growing, but it's still small. Lifetime facilities like this one are rare, and they don't want to waste a perfectly good young life if you can be rehabbed. This is all good stuff. But you don't have to think about any of that now. Right now we just need to get you well enough for transport. So I just need you to take it easy, okay?"

Aquila sniffs roughly, forcing her emotions to settle inside her.

"What about the others? Are any of them getting evacuated too?"

"All Russian and Chinese citizens are being evacuated to their embassies on Titan," he says, nodding along like it should mean something to her.

"What about the others in the program?" she presses. "Zeke and Lyra? Pollux?"

He scoffs and sits back, finding something funny in the question.

"I'll request an evaluation of Zeke and Lyra. They haven't shown any concerning behavior since the program started, so anything is possible. But Pollux is definitely a no."

"Why?"

"Pollux Crane is only in the program because he's more of a danger to the other inmates when he doesn't have a distraction," Irez says, standing to fish inside his pocket. "This is his fourth time through, and it took him this long to even participate with his partner."

He plucks out his mode screen, glancing at it offhandedly. His brow forms a hard ridge, reading something she can't see, and a moment later a distant alarm begins to blare.

"I don't believe it," he says tightly, his head whipping to the vast window. He closes the distance to it in three short strides.

"Son of a bitch," he hisses, his hands braced against the glass. "Son of a bitch. She really did it. That little pyro did it."

He pushes back, hurrying around Aquila's bed toward the door. Once it's open, she can hear his footsteps quicken into a sprint, slapping feverishly against the floor as they grow more distant. Outside the infirmary, the faint alarm continues to wail, rising and falling in waves.

Aquila rolls up, wincing at the streak of pain along her tailbone.

Her feet feel for the ground below, putting weight onto one and then the other. Shuffling in her disposable hospital socks, she makes it the distance to the curved window, the expanse of the station opening up below her.

In the dark, there's a fire raging like the hull has been ripped open.

POLLUX: 24

Pollux stumbles over the ground, reaching into the smoggy gray haze in front of his eyes. The station has turned into a smeared, colorless version of itself, the world around him blotted out by smoke.

The repeating howl of the alarm is almost ghoulish, like some creature is hunting in the murky air. The dark edge of a building comes into view and he catches himself against the corner. Walking his hands along the wall, he finds the door and slides it open, but a foul-smelling mist greets him inside. Flame retardants, meant to choke a fire without damaging the interior of the house. The smoke must have tripped them all.

He shuts the door, backing away. The hum of drones trails over his head, moving back toward the glow of light from the inferno behind him. Only a matter of time before it's under control and the air filters kick in, but the knowledge does nothing to calm his jumpy nerves. The memory of the voices rising out of the dark the last time the particle walls had come down loops through his mind, raising the hairs on his arms. As dark as it is, there's no way to tell if the barriers still stand.

A shadow moves across his path, and he reels back, tripping over his own foot. He lands hard on his knee, all his muscles bracing at once. The shadow continues over his head—just a heron flying low.

Pollux stands again, adrenaline shooting through his veins. It's irrational to fear something he can't remember, clearly, yet he finds himself wondering if he should go back to Lyra.

Steeling himself, he keeps walking, his spine crackling with unease. The ground evens out in front of him, turning into a flat, black expanse, and he realizes he's reached the lake. A disembodied voice floats to him across the water.

"Pollux?"

"Zeke?" he answers, willing it to be him, though he's not sure who else he would expect to call his name.

"Can you see me?"

Motion from the right draws his eye, and he's able to make out Zeke's arms waving to signal him. Pollux picks his way carefully along the bank. Zeke is perched on the rim, his feet dangling in the water.

After a moment, Pollux arranges himself alongside, careful not to sit too close to the edge. Folding his long legs always makes for a challenge when sitting on the ground, but the annoyance he usually feels when called to do it is absent.

Zeke's hand is still crudely bandaged with the self-adhesive gauze from the first aid kit, the ends sticking out and the fabric lumpy around his missing finger. The imperfectness of it starts to nettle him, so he takes Zeke's wrist gingerly and starts to unwind it. He doesn't fight, even when the blood-soaked pad peels away from the swollen, stumpy mess that's left of his last knuckle.

"The coagulant is still working," Pollux says aloud, turning Zeke's hand to see where the bruises are pooling. "Just keep it dry so it doesn't rash."

He flips the pad over, laying the clean side evenly against the wounds. As he winds the gauze around, layer over meticulous layer, the anxiousness in his stomach begins to ease. Zeke watches him with a tweak in the side of his mouth, like he's expecting Pollux to make a mistake. When he's done, he sits back to admire his work.

Zeke takes his hand back, looking over the bandage with just a shade of reverence.

"What's happening over there?" he asks, nodding to the eerie, watercolor glow of the fire through the smoke.

"You didn't see it?"

Zeke shakes his head. "When I smell smoke, I head for water, just like my mamas taught me. Everything is built so close in Huygens, if one of those houses goes up it'll take its neighbors too before the responders show up to put it out."

Pollux fastens his eyes on the smooth surface of the lake, anger stirring between his ribcage.

"Lyra set the Tect on fire."

Zeke is silent, a puzzled expression melting the hardness of his face.

"How?"

"I'm not sure."

"Is she okay?"

"She wasn't physically harmed the last time I saw her. But she's been . . . disturbed recently. I should have been watching her more closely."

A scoff comes from Zeke, and he shakes his head. "You seem like the only disturbed one to me, boss."

Pollux starts to feel his hackles raise, but he sets his jaw against it. Zeke had proved to be the only one as dedicated as he was to finishing the courses, even if it was for a different reason. Pollux doesn't want to alienate himself from a potentially valuable partner.

"It didn't do anything to you?" Zeke goes on. "Finding out what this place is? What happened to Aquila?"

There's no malice in his tone, but Pollux can't help detecting the thinly veiled judgement. Castor would have known how to steer Zeke's view, the perfect words and tone to diffuse someone's mistrust. It was something of a wonder to watch him at work, mimicking emotions and mirroring them back to whoever he was speaking to. He could pass for the most charming, empathic model citizen when he wanted to. It was the reason their parents had been so eager to believe in his innocence over Pollux's.

Castor had never worn the same tags that were applied to him. He was never the cold, heartless robot. It had fascinated Pollux, how two beings with identical cells could have been so completely different. He'd been sure there was something—some key hidden inside Castor that could have unraveled it all.

When the time had come, however, when Castor was open in front of him, he'd found nothing. There was nothing out of place, nothing to prove his theory. Nothing but the same blood that filled Pollux.

"I always knew where we were," Pollux answers finally. "Even if I couldn't remember it at first."

Now that the truth has been spilled, there's nothing he stands to gain from keeping it to himself. There is no game to defeat anymore, no playing pieces he needs to control. There's only the shared reality, and the bleakness of it. "And why would Aquila's situation have any effect on me? She wasn't my partner. She wasn't *your* partner."

"Jeez," Zeke breathes, running his hand over his eyes. The look Zeke gives him is perplexing, laden with sadness that borders on pity. He's still trying to decipher it when the heron chick stirs in Zeke's lap, rousing from sleep to turn around and resituate.

"I'm glad she did it," Zeke says, and Pollux's head snaps toward him.

"How? How can you be glad?" he demands. "We had one purpose

here, one way to change the circumstances, and she just destroyed it. Now we'll never know what would have happened. We could have gotten out."

"We're never getting out," Zeke responds easily.

Pollux shakes his head, propping his elbows on his knees to massage the tension in his forehead.

"Wanna know why I call everyone boss?" Zeke asks after a pause. "It's a Huygens Landing thing. We call everyone boss, because if you're from Huygens Landing you're always going to be working for somebody. This place is no different."

Pollux drops his hands, wanting this heartfelt monologue to stop. Zeke was strong, cold. He'd never bent to Pollux even slightly. This softened, grieving version of him is displeasing to witness.

"We belong to them," Zeke goes on. "They're always going to be the boss. At least she found a way to tell them to stick it."

"She gave into emotion and she took away the only important thing in this place."

A deep, low vibration shakes the ground beneath them, the air recycling kicking on at last, and the thick smoke begins to shift slowly.

"So you feel nothing when you think about her? She could just be some random stranger to you?"

Pollux rolls the question around his mind, trying to pick out any change in his body when he conjures an image of Lyra. Certainly his pulse quickens in his ears, but he'd grown used to that. It was a common enough hormonal response to being near someone with good genes and relative facial symmetry. It had always confused him, though, that it was present around Lyra and not with Aquila, or Cass, or Cygnus, all arguably more classically attractive. Lyra was short, her hair always tangled, her waist and arms oddly disproportionate to her breasts and buttocks, and her attitude was always touched with venom. And still, every day that he'd woken up to see her still sleeping across from him in the living room, it had given him a sense of calm. He'd even grown to like the surprise of whatever it was she was going to say next, having failed so many times to predict it. And whenever her skin had brushed his, no matter how briefly, it had caused a reaction in his body he still couldn't classify.

Having watched Zeke and Aquila, how they seemed to be drawn to each other like the hearts of two magnets, the warmth and solace they found in each other's company . . . that's what Zeke expected him to feel.

"Lyra's bright, and she doesn't take up much space," he answers honestly.

Zeke sniffs, shaking his head.

"I'm not buying it," he says. "You may not feel things the way I do, but the one person you've been concerned about since day one is Lyra. Like, maybe even in a creepy way. And she sure as shit is the only one who cares about your sorry ass."

Pollux runs his hands over his shorts, his fingertips searching out the scorched spots where floating embers had landed.

"She said she was alone," he says. Even as it leaves his mouth, he's not sure why he's telling Zeke, or why it struck him so deeply to hear it. "She said even when she was with me, she still felt alone."

Grass rustles next to him—Zeke moving in place—and for a moment Pollux is afraid he might try to touch him. But the hand never comes.

"She lost her family, and then you left her," Zeke's voice finally speaks out. "She kinda is alone."

LYRA: 25

By the next morning, the station has recycled out the smoke and the air is back to being clear, though maybe a little more chemical-scented.

The house Lyra had crawled into had been spraying extinguishers for the better part of the night, and she ended up locking herself in the bathroom and covering herself with towels.

She sits up, the towels falling off her into a sooty, ruined nest. Her skin is streaked with black, and the smell of singed hair greets her whenever she moves. The residue should make her happy; it's the last remaining part of her fire, maybe the last one she'll ever make. Yet somehow it just fills her with a weight that threatens to crush her into the floor.

She manages to climb into the shower, leaving what's left of her clothes in tatters across the floor. After she's scrubbed the last of the soot from her skin, she forces herself into a new uniform. When she walks through the living room, her eyes finally land on the charred, blackened hull of the Tect. The roof is gone, the rubble of it scattered across the foundation.

Is that what her house had looked like, after the fire had eaten through it?

Her arms tangle around her body, afraid if she lets go she might crumble like the wreckage itself. The house surrounding her is oppressively silent, reminding her with every passing second that there's no one left. It starts to press in on her, and she runs to the nearest room to rip the blankets off the bed.

The day at the pond had been the one day she'd felt hope. That maybe this wasn't some cruel test that could only end tragically. Zeke showing them how to swim while Cass complained about her wet hair, Aquila laughing and teasing Lyra about her strangely shaped feet, Pollux perched like a grumpy troll on the bank watching . . . It had all felt so normal. It felt like the life she was supposed to have, had she not been pegged as the dumb welfare girl whose only worth was to be talked about when she wasn't there.

As she throws her blanket over the line between the trees, she tries her hardest to rekindle the same feeling in her chest she'd had that day. The feeling of being surrounded, protected. But as the lights fade in the station, slipping from orange-gold to the dim, nightlight blue, silence follows her into the makeshift tent and it's clear that she's truly alone.

Lyra's calf is clamped in a tight, clammy grip. Her mind, still caught in a dream, tries to make sense of the sensation by conjuring a vision of her leg being swallowed by one of the tarpon Zeke had pulled out of the lake. She jigs her knee, feeling it happen in real life, but the grasp only tightens in response.

Her body whips over, landing on her back so quickly it feels like the ground has dropped away from under her. Her eyes fly open, trying to sharpen the edges of the dark around her, but there's only a dim shape hanging above her. Pressure grinds into the soft

spot below her elbow, pinning her arm over her head, and a blunt
weight kneads into the top of her thigh. There's a scent hanging in
the compressed air of the tent, something like sweat and the inside
of a mouth.

His teeth are the first thing she recognizes, gleaming and all
the same length, reflecting the faint glow from the tubelight outside.

Lyra grunts, trying to speak Cygnus's name, but is met only
with her breath pressed into the palm of his hand. His chin juts
forward, his jaw set against the sudden wave of motion as she
struggles. His long fingers spread over her face, and for a moment
Lyra is afraid they might swallow her head whole.

"Cygnus!" She tries again, thinking that hearing his own name
might have some power over him, or at least that the noise might
conjure someone. This time there's a little more power to it, enough
to at least get a strangled yelp past his palm.

The muscles in her stomach tense and ache, trying to pull her
out from under the pressure of Cygnus's hands and knees pinning
her. Her one free hand works its way between them, trying to
reach his throat, eyes, anything she can dig her nails into, but he
twists his face away.

He's so heavy, she thinks desperately, imagining Aquila's bone-
thin arms trying to lift the weight from her fragile frame. His body is
hot against hers, as if he's burning on the inside, and her skin retracts
under the touch of it. It's so different to feel fire inside of someone
else, not like her fire. Her fire is wild and powerful, free. This fire is
trapped, caustic.

Cygnus frees one of her legs, adjusting for a better grip, and Lyra
snags the moment to dig her heel into the ground, using the leverage
to throw her body sideways. She has to pry her other leg out from
under Cygnus's knee, and the motion makes him fumble. He seems

oddly smooth in the half-light, all the slopes of his body contoured in shadow, and she realizes with a sickening turn that he's naked.

He lunges for her just as she scrambles to her knees, reaching for the tent opening. Her fingers brush the fabric, then his weight throws her down to her elbows. This time a sound does leave her mouth, but it's far from being as coherent as a name.

Light floods over her, the tent flapping open in front of her nose. There's a flurry of thuds and the weight is blessedly hauled off her. Something hard like a kneecap catches the back of her head, but then she's free.

Lyra stumbles through the gaping tent door, slipping on the damp grass. In the clearing, Cygnus is on one knee, his other leg straight out to brace himself. Pollux stands over him, their arms locked together in a circular cage. A strangled growl issues out of Cygnus, but Pollux is silent. Cygnus's lean body arches backward, one of his hands losing its purchase, and Pollux wedges his elbow between them to grip the hair on the back of Cygnus's head. He shakes his other hand free, balling his fist and snapping it into Cygnus's windpipe.

Cygnus's hands fly to his throat, a sharp, dry cough rasping out of him. He stumbles back, long legs whipping out to balance himself. Pollux takes a step closer and hits him in the throat again, harder this time, and there's a sound like a cracking knuckle.

Cygnus falls back onto the grass, his fingers clawing at his neck as if he's trying to pull something away. His face darkens, blood collecting beneath the skin. Lyra's knees are locked, but she sways on the spot, feeling like the world is turning sideways.

Pollux walks to his head, lowering himself to hover just above the ground. He watches Cygnus's face, unblinking, as if he's an insect under a microscope. To Lyra, he seems to be fascinated by every tiny movement Cygnus makes, the faint quivers that grip his body, the sharp, quick rasps that come in and out of his dark blue lips.

Lyra feels like she should tell him to stop. Like something deeply private is taking place and Cygnus should be left to end this in peace. But the thought of his feverish skin pressing against hers keeps anything from surfacing aside from disgust. She wants him to hurt. She wants him to feel every touch of Pollux's gaze.

The time in the tent felt like it was over in milliseconds, but it takes Cygnus endless minutes to die. Pollux watches the entire time. Eventually the throaty, gargled chokes stop, and his body falls still. He's still handsome somehow, but in a vacant way, like a swan stuffed for display.

Pollux, losing interest now that Cygnus has quieted, stands and walks over to Lyra. Her hands press against the tops of her thighs, though she can't remember how she had gotten to the ground. He pauses, looking down at her with that unreadable blankness and his hands dangling at his sides. When it's clear he isn't going to offer, Lyra stretches out her hand to him.

"Help me up," she says, her voice scraping the sides of her throat.

Pollux obliges, leaning back to anchor her. She unfolds her legs, standing, and before she can understand what her body is doing she's circled her arms around his neck. He hunches forward under her weight, his hands hovering to either side of her waist but not quite touching.

The back of his neck is dry and cold, and somehow that seems just as bad as the heat trapped under Cygnus's skin. She drops her arms, becoming faintly aware of her knees stinging and a dull pounding at the base of her skull.

"Thank you," she says finally, but the words aren't quite right. There is no warm sense of gratitude inside her, not even a feeling of relief. There's nothing other than the humming of nerves incessantly reminding her she's still alive.

Pollux examines the tops of his knuckles. The skin is raw and pocked, but he doesn't seem to be bothered. More like he's trying to piece something together.

"You came back," Lyra says. Shivers rack her body, rattling her spine, and she wraps her arms around herself though she can't imagine why she'd be cold.

He bends down, and she almost steps back in surprise as he kneels in front of her. It takes a moment to realize he's inspecting her knees, which are splotched and scraped. When he stands again, Lyra nearly topples backward.

Something close to emotion is creasing Pollux's face, and the image makes her heart stall. He takes a breath in, then pauses, casting around in his own mind for the right words.

"You are not alone," he says at last. "You're not."

AQUILA: 26

It only takes a day of forced bed rest for her to start to lose her mind. The shackles let her walk between her bed and the wall but no further. The window lets her see over the starboard side of the station, up to the edge of the space allotted to the Ptolemy participants, which she'd heard referred to as H-Block. If she focuses through the blur in her vision, she can make out the backside of the pond, but the sight taps at a door she doesn't want to open.

She presses her shoulder into the glass, picking at the rough hem of her hospital garment. Something Irez said keeps circling back through her thoughts, about the testimony he'd heard. There was no memory of her crime, and she'd been careful not to share anything important from her life with the others. Which meant that the alter had been talking, and that she remembered something.

She had hoped that Irez would come back, now that her head wasn't spinning out in a thousand different directions, but since the fire the phys had been the only one to come in and out. And she was less than generous when it came to giving information.

Aquila quickly learned the only answers she was willing to give were medical ones. Still, Aquila had managed to use that format to learn that their selective amnesia was caused by targeted micro-traumas to the memory centers of their brains, which when she broke it down essentially meant jamming a vibrating needle into the corners of their eyes. It was far from a perfect process, and they usually needed multiple treatments since the memories often returned as the brain healed.

She'd learned that the mode on her wrist, which had been removed so she could get fluids through her hand when her arm became too bruised, was capable of a debilitating electric shock. She'd seen Cass hit with it firsthand when she didn't make it to the checkpoint in time. It was meant to be a hands-free way to keep the inmates of Carcer in line, though judging by the damage on some of the patients she'd seen come and go, Surveillance was using it sparingly. If there was even anyone left watching at all.

Rather less interesting, she'd also learned that Titan boys were chemically sterilized from ages thirteen to twenty-two, something she probably could have learned in Public Education if her father had let her go. He'd always kept her apart from the other kids on the convoys, always on call.

It's night outside the window in the Terrarium, as the phys called it, and from her perch it looks like the rounded bowl of the station beneath her is spider-webbed with pale blue light. Throughout the day, she could watch the inmates mill around in the other cell blocks, tending trees and feeding the herons in order to earn credits for the commissaries. Food and supplies were given less freely in the rest of the station, and most of the inmates seemed committed to the daily routines they'd developed to earn them. From what she's seen, her group is certainly the youngest in Carcer, though the phys swore there was a cell block for teenagers.

Aquila props her elbow on her knee, blocking her face in case anyone thinks to look up at her. The knowledge they can't see her gives little comfort while dangling over a station full of criminals like wounded bait on a hook.

Even though you should count yourself among them now, she chastises herself.

The air around her braces as the door opens, and she jumps from the thin ledge along the window. The phys ducks inside, casting a hurried look in her direction.

"Secure inmate," she says aloud, turning back to the doorway as the shackle cord begins to retract into the bed automatically, yanking Aquila with it. It leaves her with barely a foot of leash, and she crawls back onto the mattress with a sour belly.

The phys shuffles in backward, helping to maneuver a stretcher into the room. A navy-uniformed guard follows her in, but the insignia on his chest is different from the one Irez sported, and he doesn't look at Aquila with any recognition when he glances her way.

The pair of them stop beside a bed, lifting the new patient from the stretcher to lay him heavily on the nearest mattress.

The air deserts Aquila's lungs as her gaze falls on the pale, frozen face of Cygnus. His eyes are still open but hooded, his lips bluish and slightly parted. At first she imagines something is protruding from his mouth, but after a moment she realizes the dark object is his purple, swollen tongue.

The phys peels off a new heart monitor and slaps it roughly onto his chest, something about his body striking Aquila as odd until she realizes he isn't wearing clothes. The guard brings over a crash cart, the same kind they'd had on the convoys, and the phys preps two defibrillator wands.

"Clear," she says before touching them to Cygnus's chest.

His body seizes, and for a moment the movement convinces

Aquila he's alive. Then he flops back, a limp doll. The phys tries twice more, each attempt squeezing Aquila's stomach like a vice. When it's clear that no spark of life is left in him, a strange floating sensation washes over her. She's trapped in the harrowing moment between jumping and landing, her body weightless and longing for the touch of stability again.

Finally, the phys steps back, holstering the wands on the cart. Her eyes flick over Aquila and she hurriedly parachutes the sheet from the stretcher over Cygnus. Wearily, she draws the back of her hand over her forehead, propping the other on her hip.

"Inmate Cyndus Beaumont—"

"Cygnus," the guard corrects, getting a heavy sigh in response.

"Inmate Cygnus Beaumont, Ptolemy Project, declared dead by asphyxiation by Aster Jules, Onboard Physician," she rattles off, turning to the guard. "Can you take him down to cold storage?"

"I doubt I have time. I still need to load the *comrades*," he says the last part with an overly teasing, classic Russian accent.

Another look at Aquila and the phys leans in to the guard.

"When are they coming for her?" she asks, attempting to whisper. "I need to close down the infirmary so I can get loaded."

He seems to notice Aquila for the first time, his light eyes catching hers.

"I can take her down now," he tells the phys, shrugging good-naturedly.

She hesitates, shifting her weight onto her left foot.

"Are you briefed for Ptolemy inmates?"

"Yeah, just . . ." he leans in, lowering his voice. "Don't tell them anything, right?"

The phys seems less than convinced, drawing in a long, slow breath.

"Okay. Thank you."

The guard skirts around the bed, coming toward Aquila with his hands crossed in front of him.

"Hello," he says, leaning forward as if he's talking to a child. "You need to come with me now . . ."

He pauses, turning back to the phys, who's entering something on the screen above Cygnus's cloaked head. "Do they remember what their names are?"

She lets out a tight sigh. "They remember everything except their trials and crimes. This one is Aquila."

"Aquila," he repeats. "Hands up."

She complies, feeling the cuffs slip a bit down her wrists, and she silently wills him not to notice. The phys had been generous when she cuffed her, leaving significant slack that Aquila had been experimenting with all day.

The young guard adjusts the cord between her shackles so they touch in front of her then taps a fob to the edge of the bed, releasing the cord.

"Stand up," he orders, attaching the other end to his belt then turning sideways so she can walk in front of him.

Aquila stands up, shuffling down the aisle of beds toward the door. She can't help but look down at Cygnus as she passes, something in her not trusting the stillness around him. He looks so small now that she considers hovering for a moment to make sure it really is him, but the guard's presence urges her on. His boots clomp against the floor behind her, making the space between her shoulder blades tense. She tries to ignore it, dragging herself out of the infirmary at last.

As soon as she's in the hall, she considers trying to run. She could kick him, maybe elbow him in the gut. She could try to find the way into H-Block, now that Cygnus is gone, and gather her friends.

Even as she thinks it, her heart sinks with the hopelessness of the idea. The curved hallway in front of them almost looks like an illusion, stretching on infinitely with a hundred identical doors she has no way of opening.

"Move, inmate," the guard orders, though it's missing the hard edge she'd have expected from a prison guard.

They take an elevator, Aquila standing silently as his breath moves the hair on her neck.

After what seems like minutes on end, she hazards asking, "Do you have to walk this whole station every day?"

"Hmm," he says, adjusting his arms in a way that tugs on the cable connecting them. "Not usually. But it's been an unusual few days."

"With the station being evacuated?" she tosses out, hoping to ease him into conversation.

He doesn't answer her directly, but after a moment he lets out a slow breath.

"Almost makes you feel bad."

"Leaving everyone else behind?" she says, trying to hide the sharp tone of judgement from her voice.

The elevator comes to rest, pausing to reset the doors. As they wait for them to retract, he leans in.

"Guess that's what you get with a life sentence, inmate." The room beyond the doorway is bustling with commotion, guards and uniformed prisoners moving all along the rectangular space she recognizes as an interior dock. Doorways into the ships break up the far wall, and inside she can see rows of simple crash seats being filled. Aquila is struck with a strange sense of nostalgia, looking over the familiar structure of the docks. The ships are nothing fancy, just standard, auto-piloted lifeboats, but the excitement of flying starts to course through her veins. The memory of sneaking down the docks to joy-ride her father's Cessna during a quiet night lifts her spirit for a single, bright moment before the guard grips the back of her arms to halt her. "Hey, Irez," he calls, and Aquila is happy to see a familiar face moving toward them through the crowd. Irez stops just short of them, scratching a new beard which seems to have grown overnight.

"Oh, great. I was just going to grab her. Thanks."

He touches his fob to the guard's belt, releasing the tether and reattaching it to his own. Aquila tries not to brood too obviously. This business with the leash is starting to make her feel like a pet.

"Let's get you settled with the others," Irez says, looking over the heads of the other guards to pick a path.

"The others?" She repeats as he maneuvers her past a prisoner in a black uniform with scraggly hair who bares her teeth at Aquila like a tiger.

"The other Ptolemy participants. We have to separate you from GenPop to keep the results valid."

Her heart flies into her throat, her body floating with relief. All this time spent agonizing over her friends, and somehow it had worked out on its own. She lets Irez move her past a group of red-clad men who are each sporting some sort of muzzle, their arms locked behind them in shackles that go up to their elbows. Even as their eyes travel over her, she can't hide her smile. Her friends are just steps away, and this nightmare is about to draw to a close. Or at least change venues.

Irez guides her over the threshold of a ship, turning her onto a short row of crash seats. Lacerta and Cass raise their heads, their eyes widening as they recognize her.

"No way," Cass says excitedly. "No way! I didn't know you were Russian, too!"

"Hey," Irez warns, stopping Aquila in front of an empty crash seat welded into the wall. "You know the rules, Cass, no talking. I wasn't kidding about the muzzle."

He raises the solid harness from an empty seat across from the others, gesturing for Aquila to sit. She's happy for the excuse, the weight of her disappointment all but crippling her. She slouches heavily into the bucket seat, her stomach aching so painfully that if she'd had anything in it, it would have emptied itself.

"The others aren't coming too?" she asks Irez, barely audible over the hum of the engine starting up. She needs to hear it, to have the truth spoken out loud.

Irez separates her shackles, pulling down the harness over her chest and threading her arms through the holes. It cranks into place just above her thighs, and he secures the shackles together once more.

"You three are the only Ptolemy participants being evacuated. If Carcer makes it, we'll bring you back and start over. If not, we'll find a place on Titan to reinstate the project."

He leans in closer, his voice dropping to a whisper.

"Let's keep what we talked about between us, okay?"

He starts to pull away, but Aquila holds on to a fold of his uniform, pinching it between her fingers.

"Irez," she says, her eyes boring into his. "You said I gave information, while I was in the Terrarium. You meant the alter, didn't you?"

He pauses, his bottom lip trapped between his teeth as if he's trying to cage the words in his own mouth.

"What did she do?" Aquila presses, refusing to blink. "Who did she kill?"

Irez debates it in his head for a few more seconds before he steps back, turning to Lacerta and Cass.

"A rep from your embassy will be waiting when we land on Titan," he tells them. "They'll decide where you'll be held until we can restart the program."

"Irez, can I please just post one thing?" Cass says, kicking her ankles like a petulant child in a booster seat.

"How much would this twist blow people's minds? Fleeing for our lives?"

"We're taking off soon, just sit tight," he says, walking past them toward the front of the ship.

Aquila casts her gaze around the tight cabin bitterly, counting the number of empty seats that could be filled. The chatter outside their door starts to die down after a while, and it becomes clear that no one else is going to be placed in their ship. Irez seals off the front section, the face of another guard filling the comm screen as he chats with them, their conversation lost behind the glass.

"This is lame," Cass groans, rolling her almond eyes.

Ignoring her, Lacerta turns to Aquila. "Where's your bird?"

"I lost him when they pulled me out," Aquila answers, trying to hold her fist in the least suspicious way she can. The fob she'd unclipped from Irez's uniform pushes into her palm, already slick with sweat.

"That blows," Lacerta says, propping her feet out in front of her. "I heard they're trashing the whole breeding program. Irez said they were making bank off the EPA raising birds to habitate on Titan. Would have been cool," she finishes broodily. "I always wanted to see birds over the ocean."

"Maybe you should have just stolen one," Cass says tartly, raising her thin eyebrows. "Oh, by the way Aquila, if any of your stuff went missing, it was definitely this bitch."

Lacerta clucks her tongue, cutting her eyes at Cass. If it weren't for the harnesses, Aquila's pretty certain they'd be clawing each other's eyes out. Judging by the scratches along Lacerta's thighs and the little bruises tainting Cass's perfect skin, they might have tried already.

"Did you know that Cass is clinically obsessed with herself?" Lacerta drones, her glare locked.

"Yeah, what's your brand of crazy, Aquila?" Cass says, starting to kick her feet again, clearly unperturbed. "Are you a klepto like Lacerta?"

"What are you talking about?" Aquila asks, unable to focus on the sounds outside with their babble filling her ears.

"That everyone in Ptolemy Project is crazy somehow? Irez said we're all 'mentally unstable,' which sounds masterclass judgy to me."

Aquila blinks, looking at the serious faces across from her. "All of us?"

"Yeah, that's like, the point of the project," Lacerta says, using air quotes to punctuate the sentence. "The Tect was a way for them to see if our conditions made us predisposed to violence."

Aquila can almost hear Irez speaking through her as Lacerta parrots the words. Her blood runs icy inside her, thinking back over the challenges they'd been put through. How they'd pushed them, shaken their sensibilities and brought out the worst in all of them.

The whole time, each of them had been sick and struggling, thinking they were alone. She swallows, wondering just what the others had kept from her this whole time. What demons they were at war with inside their own heads.

A threatening beep starts to fill the cabin, accompanied by a flashing orange light over their heads. Aquila's pulse beats in her ears, adrenaline lighting up in her blood. The scrape of the doors rattles the ship, and every one of her muscles tenses in expectation.

Secondary doors always have about a minute of leeway before they close; she has to time it just right.

She counts down in her head, summoning every ounce of her resolve. Three, two . . . one.

Tossing the fob into her mouth, she pulls hard on the cuff as she tucks her thumb into her palm. She says a silent prayer of gratitude for the phys, gritting her teeth as the edge of the loose cuff scrapes her skin. When it reaches her knuckles, the skin catches but she forces it off, dragging it over her fingers and wincing at the sharp stab of pain.

With her hands free, she slips under the harness, working her hip bones out and then her ribs, her flat chest snaking through easily. For once, she thanks the stars for her bony, skeletal structure. She lands on her knees on the floor, looking up at Cass and Lacerta, who are both gaping at her, thankfully silent.

Aquila pops up to her feet, forcing herself to run as fast as her legs are capable. The door is already halfway down, the light of the dock spilling across the floor beneath it. With all the strength in her body, Aquila leaps for the space and dives, her elbows and knees hitting the ground hard. She twists, throwing her body across the rough floor and rolling until she's clear.

Raising to her hands and knees, she lifts her head just in time to see the primary doors shut on the lifeboats, the secondary doors lowering after them. The air in the docks compresses, re-pressurizing as the docks seal.

As the low, guttural sound of the ships detaching outside the hull creaks through the air, Aquila clambers to her feet again, whipping around to see where the guards will be coming from. But the dock is deserted, strewn with trash like a windswept street.

The lights are dimmed, some sort of power saving setting, but Aquila still steals across to the exit as fast as she can in case the cameras can see her. She spits the fob into her hand, pressing it to the keypad and yanking open the door when the lock retracts.

The hallway is deadly quiet, the sound of her own breathing echoing off the glossy floor. She presses herself into the wall, inching along hunched and slow, sure that someone is going to come bursting out of every door she passes.

It takes until her back is spasming and the arches of her feet ache to stop sneaking. If there are any guards left in Carcer, they certainly don't seem concerned about the wispy teenage girl creeping through the halls.

She starts to open doors, bolstered by the knowledge. The wing she'd come out in seems to be sleeping quarters, every room stripped and emptied in preparation for the evacuation.

She's halfway down the wing when the lights go out. It takes a moment for her brain to process the change, convinced for a second that she's blinking too long. The emergency lights kick on almost immediately, illuminating the hallway in the same red glow as before. Panic erupts through her, but she forces herself to breathe down the feeling, keeping her mind present.

One foot leads the other, walking her trembling body down the hall. When she reaches the end of the section, demarcated by a thick gate, her eyes lock onto a sign adhered to the far wall where the hallway splits. One arrow points to Surveillance, the other to Special Projects.

Aquila lets herself through, the dregs of an idea starting to swirl in her head.

"Hang tight, guys," she says aloud, hoping that somehow her friends can feel her presence.

That somehow they know she's coming for them.

ZEKE: 27

In the days after the fire, Zeke finds that a greasy film has covered everything, including Fish's feathers, and decides to inflict a bath on him. The bird struggles in the sink, flinging water across the kitchen floor as he slaps his wings around in protest.

"Come on, buddy," Zeke coos, trying to soothe him. The chick seems to have grown at least an inch in every direction almost overnight, barely fitting into his pocket nest anymore.

Pollux grunts in frustration from the living room, his head bent over the low table. He'd pulled a camera out from the wreckage of the Tect and spent all morning taking it apart, examining each piece for an hour at a time. Lyra spent most of the day sleeping with the streaming on, waking only when Pollux became bothered by her lack of hygiene and made her shower or brush her hair, at one point taking on the job of taming her tangles himself.

Every few minutes that go by, Zeke finds himself wishing he could say something to Aquila, make some joke about Lyra and Pollux, hear her defend them in response.

"Wonder what his parents did to mess him up that bad," she'd said to him when they were lying eye to eye under the tented blanket.

"I wouldn't jump to blaming his parents," Zeke told her. "I knew a guy like that back home. He was just born with something missing."

"I don't know if it's something missing or just too much brain," she'd said. "Sometimes it's your mind that ends up sabotaging you."

"Well, that's why I medicate," he half-joked.

Aquila's eyes had glazed, her mind rolling off in some distant direction.

"I can't do that," she'd said. "I have to keep her safe."

"Keep who safe?" he'd asked, moving a wayward strand of hair from her face.

She focused in on him as if remembering he was there, a tiny smirk touching her mouth. "Me. I'm the only one that can protect me."

There's an electrical pop and then a sharply descending humming sound, sending a jolt of shock through Zeke's body as the lights in the house shut off. A red glow seeps in through the windows, the same as when the power had blipped in the shrinking room. But this feels more permanent somehow.

Lyra's silhouette rises from the couch, black and solid against the wash of red light.

"What's going on?"

Pollux's long shadow joins hers, moving slowly as if he's afraid of tripping a wire.

"The station is on some kind of power saving mode," he says, his tone measured. "Or a partial shutdown."

"They wouldn't just shut down the station with us inside," Zeke says, though it doesn't sound convincing even to him.

"Is . . . is this because of the fire?" Lyra asks, fear shaking her voice. "Are they punishing us?"

"Doubtful," Pollux says, and Zeke's glad he didn't choose this moment to kick her when she's down.

"What is it, then?"

Pollux raises his arms to the sides. "I don't know anything you don't."

"You *always* know something I don't," she quips back saltily, but moves closer to him.

Zeke lifts Fish out of the sink, setting the bird on the counter to shake himself dry. Carefully, he picks his way around furniture to the living room, moving toward the patio door where Pollux and Lyra have lined up.

Outside, every light tube in the station has filled with a bloody tinge, making it seem like they've been swallowed by a living creature and are looking at it from the inside.

"Do you think the particle walls are still up?" Lyra whispers, the whites of her eyes flashing in the dim glow.

All three of them squint silently into the depths of the creature, trying to pick out the familiar lines of electrical-blue light slicing through the landscape. After a moment of trying, Zeke reaches out to lock the patio door.

"Just in case," he says.

Once the house is secured as much as it can be, Pollux goes to the kitchen to watch out the window, unable to relax. For Lyra's sake, Zeke takes the couch opposite her, but even as she starts to make sounds that border on snoring he's no closer to feeling tired. A wiry, uncertain energy has taken hold of every nerve in his body, and he thanks whatever gods are watching him that he hasn't run out of

Moxifarin just yet. Were he unstable at all, he might think the whole setup was a living nightmare he can't break out of, or maybe a test meant to finally drive him over the edge of insanity.

As he lies with his eyes wide open, he tries to count the beats of his heart. It was something he'd done in Huygens when the voices were at their worst, trying to convince him that every person on the street was out to hurt Dione, or Mama Rie, or Mama Buck. When they were too loud to hear his own thoughts, the only thing he could listen to was his pulse, steady and constant.

He starts to hallucinate that his wrist is being squeezed by a hand, and he shuts his eyes against it. The last thing he can take right now is another Aquila apparition. The feeling comes again, but this time something about it strikes him as odd.

Zeke opens his eyes, raising his wrist so the mode face lights up. Instead of the running time or the progress rings, there's a pulsing arrow, just like the first time they were summoned to the Tect. As he stares at it, the mode vibrates, making the skin beneath it tense.

Slowly, he sits up, trying not to wake Lyra with a sudden motion. The arrow shifts, moving like the hand of a compass to point out across the patio. Zeke stands up, gently lowering Fish onto the couch. Thankfully, the chick doesn't make his usual sound of protest and instead settles into the fold of a cushion, tucking his head under his wing.

The mode vibrates again, the arrow jabbing insistently. He hurries on the balls of his feet toward the patio, slipping by Lyra and catching himself on the handle of the door. His fingers pause on the lock. What if this is a trick? What if the house would be flooded with criminals as soon as he opened the door?

He raises the mode, something in him unwilling to think the

voice behind it is evil. They'd never tried to trick them into danger before. The rules have always been clear. And somehow, this didn't *feel* like a game. It felt personal, like it was meant only for him.

Ever so carefully, he slides the lock over, inching the door open. When the gap is large enough to slip through, he squeezes his body outside, closing it behind him.

The arrow glows vibrantly against the crimson air, pricking the backs of his irises. It rolls around the screen as he lowers his wrist, always pointing in the same direction: toward the pond. The station around him is like a dreamscape version of itself, all harsh shadows and silent, red-washed buildings. He keeps close to the walls, eyes peeled for any movement. When he breaks out into the open, his heart rate climbs, and the whole endeavor starts to seem like a huge mistake.

His feet come to a full stop, preparing to turn around. But the mode vibrates again, a gentle encouragement. Zeke blows out a breath, forcing his knees to carry him forward. He nears the bank, noticing the tatters of a blanket tent thrown across the ground, and the mode trembles again, this time in a different variation. When he looks down at it, it's simulating tiny fireworks on the screen, and he starts to consider hurling it into the pond, even if it means sacrificing an arm. Then his eyes move to the ground beneath him.

He's standing on Aquila's blood stains. He reels back, slipping on the grass and coming down hard. His lungs constrict, air coming in and out in gasps. His hand grasps his chest, trying to calm himself.

"Aquila," he breathes, launching himself onto his feet. "Aquila!"

His voice carries into the air, and he curses himself for drawing so much attention. If there is anyone in the area, they know exactly where he is now.

He spins in a circle, trying to spot her, but nothing moves in the space around him. An object pushes into his sight, looming above him. The giant's eye, as Aquila used to call it. At the center of the station, watching everything.

As much as he's known anything in his life, he knows she's there. He breaks into a run, his legs carrying him up the slope toward C-House as fast as he can. When he reaches the patio, he throws open the door, making Lyra leap to her feet, her hair sticking out in peaks.

Zeke slams the door, rounding on the living room just as Pollux appears in the hall, looking over the scene quizzically.

"It's her," he says, shaking the cuff at them. "Aquila, she's alive."

Shock slackens both of their faces, their eyes wide. Then, a slow-moving horror creeps over both of them, their gaze falling behind Zeke out the window. He turns, just in time to see the dark forms of three people move across the courtyard.

POLLUX: 28

It was Castor's fault.

Everything that had happened since the moment they'd been placed with their parents, Castor had designed the path and forced Pollux to walk it. There was a watery memory he'd always questioned from the foster center, right before their parents had come to take them home for the first time. When Castor had poked the tip of a needle into Pollux's leg and made him promise not to talk until they were home. Castor always told him he'd dreamed it, but it did seem like something he'd do. He liked to use needles; they caused the most pain while leaving the smallest mark.

His obsession with causing pain always puzzled Pollux. Pain was nothing more than the body's response to threat and could be caused just as easily by stubbing your toe or biting your tongue. Yet Castor had been fascinated by it to the point that it became a hindrance. He'd grown tired of hurting the animals on the farm, and after their parents had caught them it became too hard for him to do it at home. Once they'd relocated to Titan, he'd convinced his parents that he— he alone—needed to go to public school.

It was to give him access to more people, Pollux had known, but the purposeful exclusion had stung. Pollux understood it; people were put off by him, by his monotone voice and his inability to mimic emotions the way that Castor could. But he had always felt that they were joined in their strangeness. Whatever they experimented with, they did it together. They were two imperfect anomalies, two genetically identical copies who'd both been born flawed. But they'd been tied by that, and the duplicated face they shared. It had surprised him that Castor could so casually discard him.

While Pollux became more interested in discovering the workings of a living body, watching videos for the better part of the day while Castor was at school, Castor himself began to explore his ability to cause pain to his classmates. Usually they were girls, usually malnourished and from the lower income territories. He would take them to the fort they had built in the woods, and find the most effective ways to cause them pain. He had wanted Pollux to repair the first one as best he could, stitching her leg with their uncle's medical thread and reviving her from the sedation, which Pollux had enjoyed. It was satisfying, finding ways to jumpstart the miraculous healing properties of the human body. But every one he brought to the fort after that was damaged too extensively to repair. Though he had still tried.

Because of the restrictions on taking human life, they had buried the bodies in the woods around their house. Once he started, it had only taken a year for Castor to completely unravel. His school had been questioned, and he'd grown too afraid to continue his explorations. He'd become convinced that Pollux would turn on him, and with no other outlet he began to test how far he could push his own brother.

He started slipping Pollux sedatives and pushing needles

between Pollux's teeth as he slept, or using surgical knives on his scalp, each time denying it when Pollux questioned him. He'd had to retrain himself to sleep lightly, waking every few hours to make sure Castor hadn't stolen in.

One of the nights that they were cleaning the fort again his brother had snapped entirely, lunging at Pollux with the scalpel. Pollux had turned it against him and watched the life drain from Castor's body as he leaked to death, his blood seeping into the hard ground. It had seemed like such a waste. Even in death, he was so familiar, and it struck Pollux that it was his only opportunity to see what lay inside him—inside them. Was there something that could explain why Castor had grown up so differently? Why they had grown apart?

In the end, there wasn't. In the end, they were both killers.

After the property was searched, the bodies covered in his and Castor's DNA had been stacked against him, with no way to prove it hadn't been his own doing. He'd been most disappointed by his parents. Throughout the trial, he'd watched them grow even more distant and fearful when they alone should have felt the truth. If they'd known him at all, they should have known he wasn't capable of the same cruelty Castor was. They could have put aside their unease at his cold personality, or looked beyond the charming mask Castor had presented to the world. But it was a rock they hadn't wanted to turn over, lest they witness the true unpleasantness beneath.

In the end, Pollux had been tallied at four victims, three murders he hadn't committed.

The prisoners who had died since he got to Carcer station were all his, though. Memories had been returning since he'd seen Orion, memories of the inmates he'd harmed to survive.

It's some of those inmates that are circling C-House now. He feels it with a certainty he can't articulate.

Lyra and Zeke are frozen in the reality of it, afraid to move. The group outside wanders by the remains of the Tect, kicking through the charred piles. Their voices bark through the silence, but he can't make out what they're saying.

His gaze falls on Lyra, whose body is motionless in fear, and he finds himself picturing all the things that might happen to her if the other inmates got their hands on her. The scene of Cygnus in her tent had plagued him for days, and he'd found himself distressed at the idea of her coming to harm. She would not have fared well with the GenPop inmates, most likely why she'd been placed in this program she was so determined to rebel against. But now the threat has come to them, milling around their courtyard.

Lyra looks over at him, as if trying to verify that he sees what she does. Without speaking, he ticks his head at her, hoping she will connect the gesture. After a glance out the patio door, she starts to back away from the couch, her steps just inches at a time.

"Zeke," Pollux says, as quietly as he can. "Lock the door."

Zeke is still rigid at the door, but when he hears Pollux he reaches forward and flips the lock into place. The sound of it breaks the stark silence around them, and collectively they stop breathing for a moment.

Luckily, it seems the men are too far away to notice. They lose interest in the rubble, moving off in the direction of the lake until they disappear behind the line of trees.

Zeke pivots on the spot, looking up at them. Pollux has been so focused on the intruders that he hadn't noticed Lyra at his elbow, her hand clamped around his. She's touching him, yet his skin isn't resisting the sensation this time.

The tendons in his wrist seize, and at first he thinks his nervous system has finally decided to react to Lyra's grip. But she jumps as well, lifting her right hand. Pollux turns his mode face up, triggering it to wake.

A rolling compass arrow has appeared, the same as the first day they were called to the Tect. It pulses as he looks at it, locked on something to the port side of the station.

"This is her," Zeke says, his voice still low. "This is Aquila. She's in the control center."

"How do you know?" Lyra whispers, throwing her arms out to the sides. "This is probably them trying to lure us all out so we kill each other."

"It's not," he says.

"I don't believe it's a trick either," Pollux seconds. "Forcing conflict wouldn't serve a purpose. It's more likely they've abandoned the station and are no longer in control of it."

Both Lyra and Zeke stare at him as if he's just announced they have a terminal disease.

"You . . . you really think so?" Lyra asks. "You think they just left us here?"

Something in him shifts at the thought of making her unhappy. "It's the most likely explanation."

"It doesn't matter why," Zeke cuts in, spreading his arms. "This is Aquila, and she's trying to get us out."

"How do you know she's alive? You saw the blood," Lyra says.

"Cass and Lacerta went missing too. Are they dead?"

"I don't know, maybe! That's the point!"

"Be quiet, both of you," Pollux breaks in when their voices start to verge on loud. "Lyra, you're the one who claims to have metaphysical abilities."

Lyra narrows her eyes at him, trying to discern what he means.

"I said I had a feeling the dried peas were bad," she says finally. "The bag was busted, that's not clairvoyance."

"What is your feeling about this?"

She drops her arms, sighing out a short breath to showcase her frustration with them.

"I don't know. It doesn't feel like a trick somehow. Still doesn't mean those people out there aren't going to kill us."

"Let's just see where she's leading us," Zeke says gently, taking a few steps toward her. "Don't worry, we can keep you safe."

"I don't need you to keep me safe, I have all ten of my fingers," she snaps, turning anxiously on the spot.

A splinter of hurt crosses Zeke's face, and he closes his right hand over his left.

"She's lashing out as a show of strength," Pollux tells him, hoping to curtail the fight.

"Pollux!" she growls in response. She massages her eyelids, steadying her breathing. "Okay. Let's go."

When they both hesitate, she shakes her head. "It's either go, or wait here for mystery criminals to find us."

She walks down the stairs, going to the patio door to look out while Zeke corrals the heron chick from the couch. Pollux scans the courtyard again, raising his wrist to align the compass point with the direction it's indicating. It seems to be urging them to the far end of their cordoned section. At least, what had been cordoned before the particle walls shut off.

Seeing no one in the immediate vicinity, he unlocks the door and slides it sideways, pushing his head through to listen. Zeke and Lyra's presences hover behind him, waiting for the cue to follow. Holding his breath, he steps out into the courtyard.

The modes guide them straight through the short neighborhood. They cut between houses, hurrying past the pond to the clump of trees behind it. This had marked the edge of their territory before, the particle wall rising up just beyond it. But now there is only the open, sprawling expanse of the rest of the station. The true size of it finally sets in, seeing the curving structure without the hindrance of the particle walls, reaching high above their heads. He's so busy staring at it he doesn't notice the trio of inmates coming toward them.

"*Pollux*," Lyra hisses, just as the heron chick lets out a startled squawk, most likely from Zeke tightening his grip.

One of the men pauses, the sound clearly reaching him. He looks toward them in the trees, squinting.

"We gotta move, boss," Zeke whispers, panic shaking his breath.

The man has spotted them, his hands snagging his partners as he mutters something to them, never letting his gaze wander from their spot between the trunks.

Pollux checks the mode again, looking desperately in the direction it's indicating. There appears to be nothing but a grassy flat, and the chance of them getting across it undetected is nonexistent. Then he sees it.

The edge of a trapdoor rising up from the ground, square in the middle of the field.

"Hey!" the man in front yells, starting to move toward them from the right. "That's him."

Without speaking, Zeke shoves Pollux forward, sending him tripping out into the open. The three of them take off running, their legs beating against the ground.

"Pollux!" the inmate calls, nearer this time.

Zeke reaches the trapdoor first, sliding on his knees for the last foot to get his hands under it. He pulls upward, the process painfully slow, but soon there's a wedge of an opening spilling bright white light over the grass.

"Lyra!" he says, reaching a hand out to her.

She grabs it and he drags her forward, dropping her into the gap. She disappears below and he tosses the heron chick after her, looking up at Pollux.

"Come on!" he shouts, and Pollux realizes he's been frozen.

He drops to his knees, climbing through the gap just as the man's voice rings out again.

"I told you I'd pay you back, Pollux!"

His feet tangle beneath him and he tumbles down, his chin hitting the solid floor hard. Zeke pulls the trapdoor down over them, turning the lock over heavily. He hangs on the bar handle as if he's afraid it'll fly open, and over their heavy breathing Pollux can hear the muffled thud of footsteps above them.

All of a sudden, it's as if his lungs have collapsed inside his ribs. He tries to draw in a breath, but the muscles seize, blocking out all air. Tremors shake his heart, which is erratic and beating far too quickly, and he finds himself grasping at his own chest trying to alleviate the sudden pressure.

Memories of the prison flash through his mind, of all the pain he'd caused. Pain that even Castor would have been proud of. The enemies he'd electrocuted in the pool. The man whose eye he'd carved out for jumping him behind a building. The woman whose ear drum he'd ruptured with the tine of a fork. All the things he'd done that he would be made to answer for.

"Pollux," Lyra's voice floats over him, but she sounds miles away. Shapes move in front of his eyes, but he can't focus on any of them. The only thought in his mind is that he is about to die. Now. In this moment.

"Pollux," Zeke's low voice joins Lyra's. "You okay, boss?"

"No, don't touch him," she says quickly. "Just go sit behind him."

Pollux wraps his hands around his knees, trying to grasp something solid. A figure settles behind him, like a wall to lean on, and he's mildly aware of another sitting in front of him.

"Pollux, we're here," Lyra says. "You're safe. Stop freaking out."

He latches onto the sound of her voice in the mist, the warmth of her body in front of him, the support protecting his back. His heart starts to slow, his lungs beginning to relax a bit, but words remain too far away to reach. It's as if his brain has been cut free of his body, and there's nothing to do but wait for it to return.

We're here, Lyra's voice keeps repeating through the ether. *We're here. You're not alone.*

AQUILA: 29

Aquila sits back in the chair, relief folding over her body. She's exhausted, though the adrenaline has kept her from feeling it until the exact moment the danger had passed.

From her crow's nest view in the bottom of the eye, the Terrarium is laid out beneath her, a red bowl with no lines of light left to demarcate the cell blocks. No particle walls to separate anyone. The space is expansive enough that the inmates haven't spread much, yet. The three that had made it into H-Block were in the adjacent paddock, but that didn't mean there wouldn't be more. Luckily, for now, everyone that got left behind seemed to be too consumed with looting the commissaries to go exploring. The others in G-Block had headed east, and I-Block appeared to be vacant, which was saving her friends' lives at the moment.

The three inmates in the green uniforms hover over the spot where Zeke, Pollux and Lyra had disappeared, and she prays she hasn't just sent them into a furnace. The locking systems she's been playing with have little in the way of labeling, but she's triggered enough subterranean doors that she could at least get them to the closest one.

She pushes back from the switchboard, pulling the fob from its lock. Irez appeared to only have access to a little over half the controls, which blows considerably. But it's enough. It has to be.

The issue is that she can't open just any door—that would allow anyone to escape, and from what she can tell, they've been sealed beyond access anyway to avoid just that situation. Clearly the staff used a different method to get in and out of the Terrarium, but she can't waste time tracking it down before her friends are safe again.

The chair bumps into the side panel, causing a screen to illuminate. Aquila swoops over it, hoping to find anything that might help. The home screen is a mess of icons with zero organization, but buried beneath she spots one labeled "manuals." It takes her a few taps to get to it, but a two-hundred page document loads at last.

"Great," Aquila whispers to herself, flipping across the pages. On a lazy day on the convoys, this would have been right up her alley. Her brain loved to unspool information, find out how things worked. She had read the entire manual to the Eagle crafts, a feat even some of the co-pilots hadn't mastered. She could have rebuilt a disassembled cockpit and flown it to Celeste. One of the reasons she had hated settling on Titan was that there was nothing to decode in her life anymore. Her father had finally lost his license and wasn't allowed near ships, and everything in their house was too simple to be challenging. It was like being trapped in a white-walled box, with nothing to stimulate her.

She flicks through the table of contents, the names striking her as odd. Nothing seems to be appropriately labeled for a prison; there certainly isn't a "shopping district" anywhere in the Terrarium.

Zeke's words on the first day fade back to her. He'd mentioned the floating communities he was building in the Gekko manufacturing plant. Seems he'd been right after all. Carcer was meant for a much different demographic than it was currently holding. The age old saying "no waste in space" drifts through her mind, and she can't help a wry smile at the umbrage the company must feel, knowing their polished, floating pearl is being touched by the dirty hands of criminals.

Aquila scans the rows of images, looking for anything that might show her a way to get her friends out. The maps are useless, outdated, showing entries and exits that are clearly not there anymore, but she's at least able to glean that Zeke, Pollux and Lyra are in a subterranean plant nursery meant to grow edible crops.

Would have been nice to have that last week, she thinks grumpily, minimizing the map of the east quadrant. The word "Systems" grabs her attention and she hurriedly taps it. Finally, something useful.

Her eyes fly over the text, scanning through the information as quickly as she can. Her fingers begin to tap against the side of the table, itching to get to work. If she can't find a way to get them out immediately, she can at least reset the particle walls.

Aquila strides into the hall, her steps hard against the floor. Irez's fob lets her into the elevator, and she makes her way back down to the ground floor beneath the Terrarium. She has to steady her will as the doors open again onto the seemingly never-ending hallway, reminding herself that the staff walk this distance every day.

By the time she's halfway to the internal systems room, she has to stop to catch her breath. The sheer vastness of Carcer is astounding; it gives a few of Titan's moons a run for its money. Her eyes have almost gotten used to the crimson half-light, but she can't make out what the black mass blocking her path down the hallway is. She blinks a few times, trying to get her pupils to focus.

"Aquila," it says. "This is . . . interesting."

The panic that floods through her makes her feel as if she's been blown off her feet for a moment. She scrambles back, turning so sharply that she smacks her elbow into the wall. Her legs carry her as fast as they can, each stride longer than the last.

"Aquila, it's alright," the woman—she's sure it's a female voice—calls after her. Then she speaks softer, as if to herself. "Close ground floor section eight."

A particle wall springs up in front of Aquila, the light near blinding in the dim hallway. She stumbles to a stop, pulling up just short of it. Her bare feet squeak on the waxed floor, and she throws out her arms to steady herself, careful not to touch the gleaming force in front of her.

"Open ground floor section eight," she shouts.

The particle wall stays intact and shimmering.

"Well, it was worth a try," the stranger concedes, meandering slowly toward her with a choppy, uneven gait.

The closer the figure gets, the more the wrongness of it strikes her. Its legs are spindly and jointed, and its face is a flat, expressionless black. One cycloptic camera lens sits between the ridges of its eyebrows.

She remembers the humanoid proxy drones used to patrol Titan cities, but to see one this close and behaving so strangely deeply unsettles her.

Aquila throws herself on the nearest door, wheeling to face the drone when she finds it locked. It spreads its hands as if corralling a scared animal into a corner.

"Aquila," the drone repeats, its voice firm. "There's no need to be afraid."

"Stop saying my name," she demands, unnerved by the familiarity of it.

The figure drops its arms, the elastic cording inside it twanging. It's as tall as Aquila, with only the barest resemblance of features on its face. The drones used by the enforcers were always armed, but this one seems to be lacking any kind of weapon.

"Don't like being on a first name basis?" it says, and she picks up on the soft feedback from the speaker in its mouth. "Most of the inmates don't. Numerologists believe that first names hold a certain power over people. I assume that's why they do it here."

"How are you operating a drone?" Aquila demands, her curiosity getting the better of her. "I thought the satellites were knocked out."

"I don't need a satellite relay," the voice on the other end answers. "My ship is close by."

"If that's true, tell someone on Titan to come evacuate us."

"Let's get back to you," the voice says, directing the drone to move into the center of the hallway. "You are supposed to be on your way to Titan right now, and Irez certainly hasn't reported you missing. How is it that you're wandering the halls unsupervised?"

"Are you, like, the warden?" Aquila says acidly, eyeing the openings to either side of it. Without a weapon there's nothing stopping her from simply running away, but if the person on the other end has the kind of power to activate particle walls anywhere she might have the ability to stop anything Aquila needs to do.

"No," the voice states plainly, reminding her a bit of Pollux. "I am not."

"Just some guard too scared to be here in person? Sitting in their parents' basement walking a proxy drone around a prison?"

The drone is silent for a beat, and Aquila wonders if maybe the connection has been lost. Finally, it moves a step forward in its jerky, disconnected way.

"You're aware you're in a special program, aren't you?" it says.

"Yeah, Ptolemy project or something," Aquila answers. Ever so slowly, she bends her knees in preparation to run.

"Well," the drone says, its arms lifting slightly. "I suppose you could call me Dr. Ptolemy."

Disbelief paralyzes her for a moment. Part of her brain is expanding with the possibility of all her questions being answered, but she forces herself to focus. Answers mean nothing if her friends are dead.

Without letting another thought in, she springs off her back foot, slicing to the left of the drone and pelting a few feet down the hall until she skids to halt. She pivots, just as the lumbering drone starts to shuffle around to face her, and takes off toward it at full speed. Just as it reaches its last turn, Aquila plants her foot into its abdomen, sending it flying backward into the particle wall.

A white flash bursts across her vision as she lands hard on the ground, pain shooting through her back. Sparks erupt in a flurry around the drone, and it clatters to the ground, leaving singed black marks on the floor where it hits. The head pops free of the body, rolling over once before settling.

Aquila props herself up one elbow at a time, hissing when the movement brings on a new wave of splinters through her tailbone. Possibly the most athletic thing she's ever done and not a single person to witness it. What her physical activity instructor would think of her now.

The drone head is burbling, the speaker halfway out of the machine and hanging on by one spindly cord. She lifts it, tucking it against her side as she stands up.

"Nice to meet you, bitch," she mutters, then has to roll her eyes at herself. As good as it felt to win a battle, she hasn't actually accomplished anything yet.

"Let's find Systems," she says, heading away from the particle wall. Luckily it hadn't gotten in the way of where she was supposed to go.

The signs lead her past a few doors, and she takes the path a little more carefully now. If one superior had their own drone, who knows how many more are lurking around the station.

The Systems HQ is massive; almost half the floor is blocked off for the room. She swipes Irez's fob over the keypad, letting herself in.

"Lights on," she commands the room, then immediately amends, "lights half power," when the surge almost blinds her.

A crescent of long tables takes up the front of the room, with a screen station every few feet. Aquila walks to the nearest one, resting the proxy drone head on the tabletop with the shattered camera pointing down in case it's somehow still operating. She jabs the fob into the keyhole, waking up the screen in front of her.

Ticking off the list in her memory, she sifts through the programs until she finds the power settings for the station. The lowest power setting has been selected, most likely to try to minimize the damage should they be hit. The fuel stores were kept in airtight, essentially bomb-proof containers until called up for use; keeping the station at low power meant less in the pipes to potentially spread fire.

Aquila programs the power change, prompting a warning window asking if she's sure she wants to proceed. Without hesitating, she presses yes. She's just going to have to get them out of here before the real show hits.

A shudder ripples through the floor, followed by the electrical purr of the subterranean systems flooding with energy. Outside the room, the red glow is burned out by clear, blue-white light, and a weight lifts from Aquila's spine. At least it doesn't *look* like the world is about to end anymore.

She closes the program, scrolling through until she finds "Containment." A bird's eye view of the station opens up, each quadrant superimposed with labels. She expands Cell Block H, recognizing the charred Tect and the lettered houses facing it. Her heart hitches for a moment as her eyes fall on the pond, but she bites her cheek against the memories that threaten to push through.

"Okay," she breathes, tapping her thumb against the key bar. "Let's fix those walls."

ZEKE: 30

When the crick in his side starts to poke through the haze of sleep, Zeke lifts his head up. Fish is in front of him, stretching his neck as far as it will go to pick leaves off the lowest row of plants. The room is filled front to back and stacked floor to ceiling with rows of planters overflowing with vegetation. The growth cascades like a waterfall over each box until it reaches the ground. Thick humidity clings to everything, dampening his clothes and making his skin slick.

Lyra fell asleep in the corner, as far from the stairs and trapdoor as possible, somehow peacefully stretched out on her stomach.

Zeke pushes himself up to a seat, his bleary eyes searching the long rows of plants for Pollux. The growlights are so bright that he has to squint, but he makes out Pollux's long figure moving along the side wall.

"What are you doing?"

Pollux looks over at him, his hands braced against the sweaty wall.

"Something just happened," he says, pressing closer. "The power in the station came back on."

"How can you tell?" Zeke asks, peeling his cold shirt away from his stomach.

"You can't feel it?"

He sighs, focusing on the floor beneath him. The constant, miniscule tremble he's grown used to over the past weeks is there, humming through every fiber of the station.

"Does that mean they didn't leave us?"

"Doubtful," Pollux says. "But maybe it means Aquila figured out a system reset."

Zeke gets to his feet, his shoulder popping as he goes. "So you believe me. You think it's her."

Pollux steps back, gingerly getting to his knees and pressing his cheek against the floor.

"*What* are you *doing*?" Zeke asks, watching him inch along the ground.

He pauses, his ear glued to the gray floor. "This station is enormous. It needs at least three power cells to run it. Where are they?"

Zeke scratches his chest, the wet clinging to his skin like it used to in Huygens. There wasn't a surface in that city that wasn't covered in a coat of slime from the clouds of moisture that hung around it.

"Am I supposed to answer?" he asks after a moment.

"All the systems must be subterranean," Pollux says, sitting back on his heels. "There's an entire open layer beneath us. If we can get through the ground, we can break into it. We can get out."

Lyra sits up, her eyes pink and swollen. "What are you talking about?"

"Pollux says we can get out if we just phase shift through the ground," Zeke says, meandering over to the nearest row of plants and popping off a few mini tomatoes.

"Which is most likely just five to seven feet of reinforced metal sheeting, by the way."

He pops the tomatoes in his mouth, trying to keep the reaction from his face as the sweet, earthy juice bursts across his tongue. His first fresh-grown food, and he had to come to a maximum security prison to get it.

Missing the thick sarcasm in Zeke's voice, Lyra turns to Pollux. "Really?"

"Obviously we would need to find a weak spot," Pollux says, standing and shaking his legs out.

"And a jackhammer," Zeke throws in.

"Maybe," Pollux concedes. "Maybe not."

"There's got to be a door," Zeke says. "How do they bring prisoners in and out? What if they need to get in here for something?"

"They use hover drones."

Lyra looks at Pollux, mirroring Zeke's own suspicion.

"You know that how?"

"I've seen them."

"When?"

Pollux shrugs. "Before."

The cuff shivers against his skin, and when he glances at it, a new location beacon has taken over the screen. It seems to be pointing back the way they came, but the notion of going topside anytime soon is a bit too much to think about.

"Wait," Zeke says, crossing his arms over his chest to stifle the message. "Outside, I thought I was crazy. Those inmates knew you. They said your name."

"What?" Lyra storms to her feet, her hands clenching into fists. "I don't understand. Pollux, what do you mean *before*?"

"Before the program started," Pollux says. Maybe he's imagining it, but Zeke can almost see a trace of guilt crease his brow. "When I was in a different cell block."

Lyra crosses the space in four short steps, shoving Pollux hard.

"Are you kidding me? You knew where we were this whole time? How could you not tell us?"

"Not the whole time. I didn't think it would be beneficial to your well-being. I needed everyone cooperating in the Tect."

"We don't *work* for you," Lyra fumes. "We were supposed to be on a team."

"I know," Pollux says, his head slightly bent. "I made a mistake."

Lyra takes a step back, unsure of where to direct the fury that's clearly seething inside her.

"I underestimated the situation," he adds. "We stand a better chance if we work together now."

Lyra's chin pokes forward, and she grips her hips. "And you're sorry."

Pollux blinks at her. "I don't know if I need to be remorseful, given—okay!" He derails when she moves toward him suddenly. "I am sorry. To both of you. You've been . . . valuable."

"Jeez," Zeke whistles, knowing that's the best they're going to get from him. In his family, apologies were always long and heartfelt. His Mama Rie used to say the Bahari family were deep wells: their emotions flowed freely and fathomlessly. Pollux was like the cracked bottom of a dry puddle. Even if he'd wanted to show true remorse, there was little to pull from.

Zeke collects himself, trying to sidestep his own bad faith as he faces Pollux again. "Okay. How long have you been in Carcer?"

"I'm not sure," Pollux says, his voice heavy. "Our memory centers have clearly been tampered with. I'm not certain when things took place."

The muscles in Zeke's right arm seize, every nerve being split beneath his skin at once. A pained grunt escapes him as he drops to a knee, but the sensation is gone as quickly as it came. He looks up to find Lyra and Pollux in similar states, panting and shaking out their cuffs.

"Ouch," Lyra says sharply. "What the hell?"

"The mode shocked us," Pollux observes, and Zeke stifles the urge to elbow him in the mouth.

Zeke's cuff vibrates and he jumps, expecting another burst of electricity, but it doesn't come. He turns the mode face up, finding a message on the screen.

Oops.

"I think . . . I think that was Aquila," he says, dropping his arm heavily. "She must be doing something to the system."

Lyra moans, folded over her own knees.

"Tell her to do it without killing us."

Go home, the next message reads, followed by, *Walls reboot 5 min.*

"Shit," Zeke hisses to himself, dropping his arm and heading to the trapdoor. "I think it's time to go. Aquila's going to reset the particle walls in five minutes."

Lyra's eyes widen. "But we're on the wrong side."

"I know, Lyra. That's why I *just* said we need to go."

"You want us to go out there? With the criminals?" Lyra asks incredulously, pointing over her head.

He grabs the bar of the door, his hand on the lock.

"Did you forget you're a criminal?"

"Well, but they're . . . bigger," she says, trailing off at the end.

Zeke shifts the lock, the thick metal rolling back, and Pollux moves toward him across the room.

"We can't go out there," he whispers, his dark eyes slightly widened. *That must be what fear looks like on him,* Zeke can't help but ponder.

"We can't stay down here. You wanna get out, right?"

Zeke thrusts upward, unsealing the trapdoor, and Pollux grasps his wrist.

"Don't be scared," Zeke tells him quietly. "We just have to outrun them past the tree line. Then we'll be safe on our side."

"It's not that. We have to time it appropriately. If we go too soon, they'll be in H-Block with us. We—"

The door yanks upward out of Zeke's grasp, and he lunges for it just as it's thrown open above them. The bottom of a shoe emerges through the light, catching Zeke in the mouth and jolting him backward. He braces himself on the stair railing, stopping his backward motion before he topples to the floor. The next leg that comes through, he's ready. His hands grab it, yanking it toward him so the inmate tumbles down the short steps to the ground. It's the squatter of the three, a man with a scraggly beard and chipped teeth. He wallows on the floor for a moment after he lands, just enough time for Pollux to plant a knee in his throat. The man croaks a few times, his hands grasping at Pollux's thigh. He catches them both at the wrists and holds them until the man passes out.

Another assailant reaches down to rake his nails over Zeke's head. He catches the arm as it retreats, pulling the man through the hole. Weight topples down on top of Zeke, knocking him to the floor, and his skull takes a few knocks—though he can't say whether it's from a fist, foot, or elbow. What the man lacks in girth he makes up for with the length of his limbs, which he uses like whips, cracking all over Zeke's body.

At last the flailing man is hauled backward, Pollux's arms locked around the back of his neck and chest like some sort of harness. His hands flap back toward Pollux's face, who tries to turn away from the grotesquely long fingernails scraping at him. Zeke struggles to roll onto his knees, his mouth filling with a gagging, metallic scent.

Before he can come to Pollux's aid, Lyra leaps up to the prisoner, striking him across the cheek with a sheet of metal plating she must have pulled off the planters.

"Agh," the man yelps, his cheekbone flushing purple already. He starts on a string of insults that turns even Zeke's stomach.

"Hit him in the temple," Pollux says over the tirade, and Lyra swings the sheet again, putting a stop to his racket.

Pollux lets the man slump to the ground and leans back against the wall to slow his breathing.

"Let's go, come on," Zeke says, trying to get them moving. "Get Fish."

Lyra pivots, running to scoop the bird from the floor beneath a blackberry planter. She tucks him against her chest, jogging to join Zeke on the steps.

He peeks through the trapdoor, glancing around the flat lawn. The lights have come back on, making the station look almost cheery compared to the last view he'd had of it. The third man is nowhere to be seen, which seems a bit like a trap to him.

A voice creeps in through the back of his mind, whispers rising out of the garbled static so he can only make out the words "trick" and "die." The last dose of Moxifarin is on its way out of his system, and if nothing else he needs to get somewhere secure so he doesn't become a liability to the others.

He pounds up the steps into the open, wheeling around in a circle as he half-expects the missing inmate to drop out of the sky. When he doesn't, Zeke helps pull Lyra up by her elbow, pushing her in the direction of the tree line they'd come from.

She takes off running across the lawn, her arms wrapped tight around the squawking chick. Pollux emerges after her, seizing the trapdoor and shutting it over the hole. It sinks perfectly into place, hardly noticeable in the grass. How many holes were there like this all over this station, hidden unless you were looking for them?

Something tugs at Zeke's memory, scraps of an idea swirling in his mind. Pollux claps his arm, shaking him out of his daze.

"We need to hurry," he says, trotting off toward the spot in the trees where Lyra has just disappeared. Zeke follows, trying not to count seconds in his mind as they near the ridge. Relief sets in as they reach the tree line, gaps of their neighborhood showing through the trunks.

A shape leaps from the right, plowing into Pollux with a meaty thud. The pair hit the ground, Pollux landing on his back, and the figure kicks his leg over to straddle him. Zeke slides to a stop, catching himself on a tree to turn around.

The third inmate, the one whose face had struck him as off when he called to Pollux, has one hand splayed over the side of Pollux's head and the other clamped around his throat. Pollux thrashes, trying to loosen his hold. He gets a few fingers inside the man's mouth, pulling at the loose skin of his cheek and getting a shocked yelp of pain for his trouble. The man shakes him off, and Zeke can see what had looked so wrong from afar. The man is missing his right eye, the socket empty and concave beneath his eyelid.

"I said I'd get you," he laughs roughly. He pushes Pollux's head into the ground, his fingers tight against his neck. "I said I'd get you back."

Zeke slams himself into the inmate's side, knocking him off, then braces as the bruised spots on his torso make their presence known. The inmate rolls once and pops back up to his feet, clearly better at fighting than his two lackeys. His body is tight and lithe like a street dog, and the way his hands hover at his sides reminds Zeke of the boys he used to fight for tailing Dione home.

"I got no conflict with you," he says, his one good eye locked on Zeke and shining with adrenaline. "But this one owes me."

He nods at Pollux, who's sitting up to spit on the ground beside him.

"Just go," he wheezes without looking at Zeke. "The walls."

The whispering scratches behind Zeke's ears, trying to form words that he knows he can't hear right now. He shakes his head, just as the inmate lunges for Pollux again, grabbing him around the knee. Zeke pulls him off, careful to stay on the right side where he can't see him coming. Even without sight, the man is as slippery as an eel, ducking out of Zeke's grasp and spinning around to face him. He must have been a terror with both eyes.

"Get up, boss," Zeke tells Pollux, letting his annoyance and desperation come through.

It takes a second, but Pollux clambers to his feet. Before Zeke can gauge what his plan is, he's running for their block.

The man curses and takes off after him, tearing right by Zeke. Realization spreads through him in a rush, and he turns to sprint out of the trees. The one-eyed man has just caught up to Pollux, their arms locked around each other as they stagger around the grass. The inmate gets a knee up, catching Pollux in the top part of his thigh. He grunts, his eyes sliding to Zeke as he draws closer.

"Get him off," he groans.

Zeke claps his hands around the inmate's dense arms, wrenching backward and just managing to send him stumbling.

An ear-splitting hum slices through the air, moving the hairs on the back of his neck, and Pollux shoves the man backward right past Zeke. Across the paddock in the distance, a particle wall leaps up over the rooftops. He stutters a step, realizing how close he must have been to the boundary line.

Zeke turns slowly, warmth touching his cheek. The wall is so close to him that had he fallen backward he would have hit it. Shaken, he stumbles away from the buzzing glow. The inmate has vanished, but he can't tell whether he'd made it to the other side of the wall before it went up.

Pollux slumps down onto his knees, the tension releasing from his body.

"Cutting it a little close, weren't you?" Zeke demands. "If you'd miscalculated we all could have been fried."

Pollux shrugs, his mouth slightly parted. "I didn't."

Zeke sinks down next to him, his muscles so fatigued they feel as if they might fall out of his body. The swelling has already begun to set in on his face, his lip and cheek pulsing with every heartbeat.

"I think I caught a couple punches for you," he says, eyeing the lack of damage on Pollux. Besides the long red streaks across his throat, there doesn't seem to be a scratch on him. "You want them back?"

Pollux breathes a short gust from his nose, and Zeke swears the start of a smile twitches at the corner of his mouth.

"I thought you enjoyed physical altercations," he says. "You said so the first day."

Now it's Zeke's turn to snicker, and he shakes his head. "I think I'm a different person than I was then. That guy would never have saved your sorry ass from anything."

Movement draws his eye, and they both turn to see Lyra coming toward them from the pond. She's running as fast as her short legs will carry her, her hair barely being contained by the little bit of braid left intact.

"I think I am too," Pollux says quietly, watching her progress up the hill.

The mode vibrates on Zeke's wrist, and when he flips it upright a message illuminates, a single word from Aquila.

Safe.

"What happened?" Lyra pants when she's close enough for them to hear.

She drops down to a walk, huffing the last steps toward them. "Is he gone? I heard the walls go up and I thought . . ."

She kneels between them, putting a hand on each of their shoulders as if they might float away. Her head dips forward, and her fingers tighten.

"Are we good?" she asks softly, her eyes closing.

"Yeah, we're good," Zeke says, trying to sound sure for her sake. "For now, anyway."

A smile breaks across her mouth, and a burble of laughter escapes her. They sit together, too exhausted to get up, until the tubes start to display their golden-peach sunset settings. Zeke finally stands, pulling Lyra up with him and then Pollux.

"Let's go home and figure this shit out," he says.

AQUILA: 31

She tosses the drone head onto the wide table, waking up several screens as it rolls over them. Hooking the nearest chair with her foot, she pulls it closer and sinks into it, her body slouching. Her muscles feel like stretched out rags hanging off her bones, and there's a slight pulse of a migraine in her temples.

The walls are back in place and her friends are safe for now. That at least buys her some time to figure out what her next step is.

"Search live radar maps for Saturn," she says, her voice bouncing around the empty Control Center. It's a smaller circular room, meant for maybe four people, which feels a bit more manageable than the massive Systems chamber.

The seats in here are much more comfortable as well, which makes her think that higher salaried bodies were meant to fill them.

The holograph takes a second to load, but then the radar jumps into the air over the projection hub, floating orbs swirling around the rendering of Saturn.

"Zoom on Moon Rhea," she says, and the view narrows.

Aquila stands, leaning closer to see the smattering of spots trailing after the moon. They've fanned out, dragging behind in a slowly expanding net.

"Show future view, eighteen hours."

The net is even wider, some of the debris on track to reach Titan. If only they had a tenth of Titan's atmosphere; they might not even notice the cloud passing them.

Something pricks her attention as she watches the replay, the way the debris moves creating a pattern in front of her eyes. She scrabbles for the nearest screen, waking it up and opening a blank page. She casts around for a stencil, reaching across the table for the closest one and bumping the drone head with her elbow.

A bout of static coughs out of the microphone, and she freezes, afraid the phantom voice might speak another particle wall into being. It falls silent, and she closes her fingers around the stencil, starting to draw out the pattern in her head.

"Show previous radar, twenty-four hours," she says without looking up. Excitement is buffeting around inside her, pieces of a plan starting to slot into place.

The static burps out again, and this time she swears she can make out her name.

"What?" she demands, palming the head and turning the shattered camera toward her face. "Are things not going the way you planned, Warden? We didn't just sit here quietly after you abandoned us?"

The static sets in again, and Aquila drops it roughly on the tabletop, using it to prop up her right elbow as she writes. Her mind is exhausted, running like a clogged engine in fits and starts.

The faintest flickering starts at the corners of her eyes, the sensation of tipping backward into nothing creeping over her.

"Don't you dare," she warns, forcing her eyes to stay open. She can't afford to lose the next few hours, not when she can't predict what the alter will do. She may decide finding the nearest liquor cabinet and spending their last hours passed out on the floor might be more fun than saving all of their lives.

The rustling sounds start spewing from the microphone in an unyielding stream, grating on her frayed patience until she turns the head over. Gingerly, she threads the stray wire back into the microphone, pushing it into its mount.

"What do you want?" she asks tightly, her fingers still poised in case the phantom says anything close to "particle wall."

"What do *you* want?" the severed voice parrots. "Do you want to see your family again? Do you want to fly your Cessna? Do you want to pick out your own clothes every day?"

She doesn't respond, suspicion growing inside her like mold. Every time adults try to bargain with her it usually ends up with her giving away more freedom.

"I can have a ship there in an hour," the head goes on. "We can get you off Carcer and in a comfortable bed by this time tomorrow."

"Take all of us and that's a deal."

The head is silent for a stretch, and she wonders if it's finally dead for good.

"This program needs participants like you, Aquila. You can help prove the validity of our methods and give so many more the chance to change their lives. But we need to come to an agreement."

An idea creeps into her mind, and she straightens in her seat.

"Search news for Aquila Navarro," she says, each word trailing out slowly. There's a part of her that could stay in the dark forever, hiding under the ignorance of whatever it is she'd done. Yet she knows that every day she spends not knowing is corroding her from the inside out. That it's like a poison she has to draw out, no matter how painful.

The projection switches to a forming and reforming nucleus, the computer searching. In a matter of seconds the bile in her stomach starts to turn, her anxiety rising like a tide.

Finally, it flicks to the image of a stick figure face frowning over a few lines of text.

Darn! Satellite feed lost . . .

She slumps, whatever strings holding her up cut.

"Aquila," the head says, attempting to put on a comforting tone. "Not knowing is crucial to the program's integrity. Don't you want the chance to live a normal life?"

"I told you to stop using my name."

"I can help cure you," the head says, no hint of manipulation in her tone. "It doesn't have to end the same way for you as it did for your mother."

Hearing the words makes an image of her mother flash through her mind, and her chest suddenly becomes so heavy she has to lean forward, resting her head on the cool tabletop.

She used to think her mother was some sort of changeling. That she'd lived in her own world, one that existed in her head, where Aquila and her father were just side characters. Sometimes she would get high and tell Aquila stories of things she'd done that couldn't possibly be true. Stories about traveling to a different city with friends she'd met that night, about dancing on tables and convincing strangers to give her credits using nothing but her own wit. Then she would fall into a deep sleep that would sometimes keep her in bed for days. She would forget things—whole weeks—sometimes being confused by how Aquila looked or how old she'd grown.

Convoys were torture for her, like keeping a bird in a cage. There was nowhere for her energy to go when she was up, and the tight cabins were like a coffin when she was down. It used to drive Aquila insane, watching her blow through their lives, lifting everything into the air in a frenzy then letting it crash to the ground for them to pick up. She'd shown no remorse when her father had gotten addicted to the drugs she'd introduced him to, berating him for it when she was feeling low. She'd bought Aquila her first hair extensions and makeup only to cry the next week when she saw her wear them.

It had taken Aquila years to realize her mother was simply two very different people who shared the same body. Two warring factions that could never be reconciled, destined to fight until they destroyed each other. That was the fate that awaited her.

"See, that's how I know you're full of it," she says, a grim smile crossing her face. "There's no cure for Split."

"I can help you, Aquila," she says. "Just let me."

"I don't need your help!" she seethes, standing so quickly she sends the chair spinning behind her. "I don't need it! I don't need you, and I don't need her."

She is not the child she was on the convoy, with parents who were too self-absorbed to realize she existed. She is not the twelve-year-old left alone in the wreckage. She is not alone anymore.

"I never needed anyone."

She sweeps the head off the table, her fingers prying the microphone from its hole and pulling until the wires detach. Dropping it onto the floor, she picks up the screen from its port and tucks it under her arm.

"Bring up internal programs," she says, her voice jumpy with adrenaline. "Show me where the cockpit is."

LYRA: 32

Walking back toward C-House, Lyra is as happy as she can remember being since this nightmare started. Zeke branches off from them, heading to the pond to retrieve Fish from where Lyra left him, and she and Pollux continue on in silence for a bit.

"Never thought I'd be so happy to see that house again," she sighs when the front door comes into view. "I'd kiss you if it wouldn't be taking your virginity."

"Kissing someone wouldn't make me not a virgin," he responds, glancing up toward the eye. Maybe he's thinking about Aquila, just like she's been.

Lyra snorts to herself. "Now I know you're one."

He cuts across the lawn of the courtyard, his long stride covering ground quickly. "If you're implying that I haven't kissed anyone, you're correct."

Lyra pulls a face. "You're making it sound less appealing by the second."

Pollux stops mid-step, rounding on her, and she slides to a halt from the abruptness of it. He bends his long torso, his face drawing so close to hers she can feel the warmth of his skin across the bridge of her nose.

"If I did kiss you," he says, his breath touching her lips. "I'd be great at it."

Lyra pins her eyes to his, refusing to look down at his mouth. She can see the freckle over his top lip hovering in the bottom of her eyesight, like some kind of freaking beacon clawing at her attention.

"Why?"

She loads the word with every ounce of annoyance she can muster, determined not to give anything away to Pollux's dark eyes. They'll absorb the slightest wrinkle in her brow or twitch in her throat if she lets it show.

"Because I've thought about exactly how I would do it," Pollux says.

Lyra takes a step back, trying to make it casual. Her head feels cloudy standing so close to him. "And you just know I'd want that?"

Pollux straightens, his shoulders rolling back. "Fairly certain."

"Sounds like something Cygnus would have said."

As soon as the words leave her mouth she wishes she could seize them out of the air. Even though she wants to make a point, to show that he doesn't hold any kind of power over her, he's no Cygnus and could never be. For all his faults, Pollux takes no joy in the pain of someone else, though on the flip side she isn't sure he feels anything at all.

Pollux turns away from her, his long stride carrying him up the slope toward the house.

"I didn't mean that, I'm sorry," Lyra calls after him, but he doesn't stop. "Pollux!"

He reaches the sliding door on the patio and wedges through the opening, disappearing into the living room.

"Pollux, come back," she tries again, the effort of the statement dying out as she starts to jog toward the house. "Come on, I said sorry."

She hasn't seen him be *this* determined to ignore her since the first day they were partnered.

Lyra slips through the door, her eyes adjusting to the dark in the house. After a few steps, a hand catches her elbow and tugs her sideways into the kitchen. She stumbles at the sudden movement, but Pollux catches her under the arms and hoists her up, lifting her like she's weightless and pressing her back against the wall.

Before she can even gasp in surprise, he kisses her.

The world seems to fall out from under her. She grips his arms, afraid she might plummet through the floor beneath them, but Pollux holds her steady. Lyra's hands find the lip of a solid surface under her, and she realizes he's set her on the counter that borders the kitchen.

Pollux tilts his head back, pulling away from her enough to break them apart, and she stops herself from growling in protest.

"Was I right?" he murmurs, his eyes closed as if he's making a silent prayer. His hands are still hovering at her knees, paused in a way that almost infuriates her.

"Yes, you idiot," she snaps, hauling him back to her until they melt together again.

Pollux pushes closer, his hips fitting between her thighs, and Lyra tries not to gulp in breath. Every touch of his mouth on hers makes her blood race wildly. Very distantly, she feels his hands close around hers. She'd been clinging to him, the fabric of his shirt clenched in her fists, but he gently tugs them free and presses her palms against the countertop. Her fingers hook under the lip and her muddled mind makes the connection. Her touch had always been too much for him, overloading his brain, and this was something he wanted to focus on.

His hands spread over the tops of her thighs, and her skin burns beneath the touch so fiercely she wonders if he can feel it. Does she feel to him like fire feels to her? Tugging at him with the same insistency?

His fingers dip just beneath the waistband of her leggings, tracing heat across her stomach, and she starts to ache in a way she's never felt before. Like she isn't quite whole and Pollux has the missing puzzle piece hidden inside him. He urges her mouth open with his tongue, then presses her bottom lip between his teeth. Explosions are going off in her bloodstream, and even when he pulls away, her thoughts keep swimming in a thick smoke.

Pollux hovers, waiting, his fingers still tucked into the edge of her leggings.

"What?" Lyra eventually snaps, embarrassment starting to poison her perfect haze.

"I don't know what happens next," he says flatly.

It takes her a moment to process, and she has to keep a laugh from bubbling up in her throat.

"That's as far as you thought, huh?"

He nods. The thought of there being *anything* that confuses Pollux is oddly endearing, and the blank look on his face is so genuinely lost that she can't even tease him.

"Okay," she says, hopping down from the counter and lacing her fingers through his. "Come with me."

When she wakes up, the room is empty and a moment of panic washes over her. She pulls the cover off her legs, forcing herself to swallow the feeling, and stands up.

There's light beneath the door, and her pulse begins to slow. She pulls a jacket on, realizing it's Pollux's when it almost reaches her knees, but if he wants to fight her for it he can.

He's standing in the living room, his fingers fiddling over the strings of his violin, but he looks up when the door opens.

"It scares me a little, the amount of sleep you get," she says, walking out and wrapping the jacket around herself like a robe.

He takes a few steps away from the window, pausing in front of one of the chairs.

"At the fire," he says, taking a seat and arranging the angle of his long legs in front of him. "You said there was music."

Lyra chews the hem of her sleeve, reluctant to delve too deeply into the memory. "Yes."

"You hear music in the fire. But only in the fire."

"Sure," she agrees quickly, hoping he's not going to make her sit through another one of his solos. Everything about the scene tells her it's going to happen whether she wants it or not.

"I think I know how to make you hear it," he says, tucking the violin beneath his chin. The light bounces off its waxed surface, softening his sharp face. "Will you let me try?"

The way he looks at her, the hint of hopefulness in his voice, Lyra knows there's no way her conscience will let her say no. She leans sideways against the arm of the couch, trying to keep the annoyance from her voice.

"Okay."

Pollux raises the bow, drawing it across the strings so softly it's a wonder it can make any noise at all. The bow draws out a sad, long note, the song starting slow, which at least doesn't make her want to jump out a window yet.

He plays a melody, his thumb moving across the buttons on the underside of the neck, and the tune plays again on its own. Pollux starts another progression, layering it over the first, and she has to admit it's better than the other times he's played.

Listening to the two separate refrains weaving together, something begins to stoke Lyra's heart. The deep, sorrowful sound of the first punctuated by the sharp notes of the second reminds her of the beginning of the flames. How their voices joined, creating the base that stayed while the fire climbed. She takes a step closer, needing to hear the familiar beauty of it around her.

Pollux laces another melody into the song, then another, his thumb moving across the looping buttons as the bow moves faster each time. His eyes raise to hers, watching her face, and she sinks to her knees as the sound climbs, swirling around her and shaking the very air. It's as if her fire is there, filling the room with its song. As if the violin has snared her heart with a thousand strings and is trying to tug it from her body with each note.

She closes her eyes, and the music swallows her. In the dark, the fire dances against her skin, sending chills rippling through her. Tears slip down her cheeks, landing in her open palms, and she floats from the ground, held aloft by the sound.

When the music finally ends, it's as if the cords have been cut from her heart, and she falls forward. Her cheek brushes Pollux's knee, startling her. She hadn't realized how close she'd moved to him. Without the music, the room is cold and lifeless, and she finds herself shivering. She wraps her arms around his calf, her chin resting on his thigh, and after a minute she hears the violin touch the floor. Pollux's hand rests against her head, and in that moment she doesn't care if it's just a gesture he's mimicking or something real.

"Thank you," she says, her voice rasping.

For once, he voices no opinion, and she thanks her saints for that.

POLLUX: 33

There had been a weekend that their parents took him and Castor to Kraken Mare. They'd camped in tents on the shore, canvas stretched over the coarse sand. Pollux had been fascinated by the broken-down grains, struck by how ancient they must be. He'd sat and wondered what the pieces had come from, if they were tall mountains or fallen meteors.

Castor had been more interested in the creatures he found in the water, dragging jellyfish and bottom feeders onto the bank all day. He'd gotten tired of listening to Pollux's theorizing, and even their parents had been too busy battling the fierce wind across the water that wanted to make a mess of their campsite. So he'd sat in thought for hours, watching the golden light play across the waves, reflecting and refracting.

For some reason, watching Lyra weave her hair into an intricate pattern, he starts to imagine what it would have been like to have her there. Somehow, he thinks she would have listened to his theories. She would have sprawled out on the warm beach, maybe throwing in a jab about how much thought he was putting into a grain of sand.

If they ever set foot on Titan again, he'd like to find a way to take her to that same place.

"Do you enjoy the ocean?" he asks her, and she looks over from her spot in front of the couch.

She snorts, tying her hair off at the end. "I dunno. Never been."

The patio door slides open, and she jumps, still nervous at every sound. Zeke hurries through the gap, and the heron chick stands up on the couch arm to greet him.

"I was thinking about what you said," he starts. A shower of water drips from his elbows to hit the floor, and the faint musty smell of damp clothes trails off him.

"Jeez, are you wet?" Lyra says, scooting away from him.

"Yeah, I was in the pond. There's a drain at the bottom. I knew I'd seen one in the tarpon lake, but there's one in the pond too."

Pollux can sense there's a connection there, and his mind starts to fit it against possible ideas.

"A weak spot," he arrives at, and Zeke nods.

"I told you I used to build floating communities back on Titan for a while. They had water features too, and they always had a secondary use as emergency coolant if the systems overheated. I bet that drain empties out in the power centers."

"Yeah, but we'd have to like . . . blow it up, right?" Lyra asks. By her expression she's not completely perturbed by the idea, and that worries Pollux slightly.

"I don't know," Zeke shrugs. "Maybe we can get Aquila to trigger them somehow? She's figured everything else out."

"The modes don't allow for outgoing messages," Pollux points out.

Zeke gives them a lopsided smile, raising his hands as if making them an offering.

"We'll do it the old fashioned way, then. Lyra, can you make some more fire?"

Pollux looks between them, realizing he's been in the company of what his mother would have described as "dangerous street people." Yet he doesn't find them half as off-putting as she made them sound.

When he tells them this though, they don't seem to find it as sentimental as he does.

There are probably at least twelve other, less dangerous and destructive ways to contact Aquila than what Zeke and Lyra have chosen. Pollux can think of three just standing there.

He braces Lyra's thighs with his hands, balancing her weight across his shoulders. The heat of her body is making his skin creep with sweat, though the discomfort is almost minimal. His body recognizes the touch of hers, having been so immersed in it that not a piece of it was unfamiliar to him now.

He watches Zeke walk backward pouring glycerin, an unhappy pout compressing his features. The idea of giving Lyra access to more fire feels like taking an unnecessary risk, to both their immediate surroundings and her mental state. At the same time, it also feels like they are very high up, and his mind is preoccupied tallying the ways they might topple off the flat roof.

"Go higher," she says, raising her hand to point, and Pollux has to offset her weight shift.

Zeke does, lengthening the letter "a" to match the others. When he reaches the end, Pollux lowers Lyra back to the ground as slowly as he can, each wobble sending an image of her sailing off the roof through his mind.

"Okay," she says, reaching for the bottle of potassium permanganate, the last legs of sunset tubelight touching her face. "It's not going to burn long, so it has to be totally dark first."

They stand shoulder to shoulder, waiting for the lights to fade.

"I'm wondering if this is the right course of action," Pollux says, a knot forming in his stomach as he watches Lyra.

"We have the extinguisher, we'll be fine," Zeke brushes off, but Lyra tucks her lips together.

"Will you be okay?" he asks her quietly. "Lyra?"

She breaks her trance, raising her eyes to him.

"Just don't let me . . . don't let me get lost," she says. Somehow he knows what she's trying to communicate.

The station fades out of sunset, the dark growing around them until shadows cover their faces. Lyra unscrews the top, scattering the black powder over their message.

For a moment nothing happens, and Pollux wonders if they've applied the correct amount. Then, flames burst along the letters, traveling with aggressive speed. He takes a step back, the heat reaching him even feet away. His mind flashes back to the Tect with a shudder, recalling how helpless he'd felt when faced with so much uncontrollable energy.

Fire reaches the final letter, and their message glows so brightly in the dark the whole station must be able to see it. They all turn, looking up at the control hub, and he notices how the orange luminescence reflects off its surface. The streaky, mirrored letters appear backwards across it, but he can still make out "DRAINS." If Aquila is up there, she can see it.

When the ferocity of the flames starts to taper off, Zeke sprinkles the extinguisher over the remains. Sickly gray smoke rises up into the air, and Lyra grips her own arms, dipping her head. Maybe he's imagining the slump of relief in her shoulders.

"Now what?" she asks, her voice gravelly.

Zeke caps the extinguishing powder, casting one more glance at the hub. "Now we see what she says."

They settle inside, waiting quietly with their own thoughts for any sign that they've been heard. The longer the night stretches on with no message from Aquila, the damper his companions' spirits seem to get.

"It's entirely likely she simply doesn't know how to flush the coolant system," Pollux says, hoping to alleviate their moods. "This station was designed to be run by teams of people with specialties. If they're gone, it's improbable that one teenager could determine how to run everything. However exceptional she is," he adds, feeling he needs to give her credit for the work she's done already to save their lives.

Lyra rearranges her legs, crossing them the other way and tucking her feet beneath her.

"It isn't that," she says, leaning her head against her hand. "I was thinking about my mother. What can I possibly say to her?"

"We can't seek out our families," Pollux says, thinking it would have been obvious to them. "If we somehow manage to get off the station, we should attempt to find relatively undocumented communities that won't delve too deeply into our identities. Maybe something in habitation."

Lyra makes an unattractive scoff in the back of her throat. "Great. You want us to slog through marshes on the dark side? Sounds like my true calling."

"There are other positions you could fill. There's structure design."

She sits up a little straighter, the wrinkle in her brow receding a bit.

"I wonder what my family would do," Zeke says, his eyes focused on a spot in front of him. "If they saw me again. I wonder if it's been easier for them with me gone."

"You don't seem that bad to me," Lyra tells him warmly. "For what it's worth."

"I've had meds. You know what those cost a family like mine? At least when I got committed someone else got to pay for a bit. I'm not sure they'd even want me back at this point."

"You wouldn't want to see your parents, Pollux?" Lyra asks, turning to him. "You don't wonder what they'd say?"

A weight hooks his stomach unexpectedly at the thought of seeing his parents' faces again. He finds himself imagining their expressions. The last time he can remember speaking with them, there was a pane of clear glass between them and he was swathed in scratchy orange scrubs. They said goodbye to him through a speaker at mouth height, and neither of them met his eyes. He remembers how badly he wished that they had. He wanted to see that shine of affection one more time, see the paternal drive they felt to keep him safe as if it might provide some comfort. The statistical probability of seeing them again is next to nothing. Doing so would mean he had not only made it off of Carcer and back to Titan, but also managed to track them down without being caught, and all the steps in between that were equally ill-fated. And yet the unfounded notion of it is extremely comforting.

"I think I would like to see them again," he says, surprised at the grief in his own voice.

"I don't know about all that," Zeke says, leaning forward to toss a corn kernel to the heron chick. "But I took my last pill two days ago, so this situation is about to get a lot hairier if we don't get topside soon."

"What do we do if Aquila doesn't answer?" Lyra asks, pressing her index knuckle into her bottom lip. "How are we going to get through?"

"Maybe we could pull the drain off somehow," Zeke says. "Or maybe there's an exhaust pipe or something we haven't found yet."

"Maybe we could blow the cover off somehow," Lyra says with the slightest smirk. "I don't think we've fully explored that option."

Zeke narrows his eyes, clearly uncomfortable with her enthusiasm. Even Pollux has to admit the idea is sound . . . but it definitely should not be left up to Lyra's wild expertise.

"I could do it," he says. "I could build an incendiary device."

Silence hangs in the air as Lyra and Zeke watch him, gauging how serious he is, or perhaps fearing it. After a long moment, a scowl contorts Lyra's features.

"Just say bomb," she says sourly. "Why do you have to make us feel stupid?"

LYRA: 34

Pollux has disassembled bits of nearly every piece of technology in the house and spread them over the grass in the courtyard. If they weren't sorted into such meticulous piles, she would have sworn a storm had ripped through the neighborhood, dumping its spoils on their lawn. Pollux sprawls across the grass on his belly, propped up on his elbows as he works to attach the acrylic dome of a light covering to a tile he'd pulled from the floor of the bathroom.

Lyra lowers onto her stomach, trying to get more comfortable on the grass. Ever since they'd been back at the house, it's been hard for her not to cast glances around every time they're out in the open. In her mind, there's always at least four inmates hiding around every corner, up every tree—even though she knows if there were, Aquila would have warned them. If she's even still up there, that is.

She raises her head so that she can see the eye of the giant, trying to picture where Aquila might be inside it.

Pollux casts a quick glare over her, seemingly annoyed.

"Can you please stop that?" he asks, focusing intensely on the work of his fingers.

"What, breathing?" Lyra drawls, resting her chin on her forearm. "Living?"

"Distracting."

"How am I distracting you?"

Pollux huffs, letting the tool drop from his hand.

"With your body."

Lyra blinks, trying to work it out while heat starts to burn her cheeks.

"You're mad at *me* because *you* are checking me out?"

"You're purposefully trying to distract me by arranging yourself attractively."

"Well, I wasn't," Lyra says, propping herself up on one elbow and rolling onto her side. "But I am now."

Pollux fixes on her face, and she half expects him to say something sharp and dismissive. But the longer he stares at her, the more her limbs start to warm.

She traces the bottom of her lip with her thumb, remembering the feeling of Pollux's teeth gently nipping it, and watches his gaze follow the movement.

"Is it working?" she asks softly.

His long arm reaches out to grab her ankle and he pulls her across the ground. At some point she realizes she's flipped onto her back, but everything has dissolved into Pollux's mouth on hers, the weight of his chest on hers, the feel of his hip on the inside of her leg.

The first kiss had been a blind surprise, and her brain had spent most of the time trying to catch up to what was happening. But this feels familiar. Her lips know the shape of his now, like they somehow belong to her.

His hand grips the curve of her waist and he pushes deeper into the kiss, the arm under her head holding her closer.

"Jesus. Gross," Zeke's surprised voice cuts between them like a knife.

Pollux springs back onto his knees, and she can't remember ever seeing him this undone. His shirt is tousled and askew, and he seems to be fighting to recapture his breath.

Lyra sits up, spotting Zeke on the patio trying to look anywhere but at them.

"Y'all are nasty," he says, his eyes glued to the sky. "Have you actually gotten any work done? We're only trying to save our own lives."

Pollux rakes his hair back into a semblance of order and reaches for the creation he's been working on. He stands, extending it toward Zeke who eventually saunters over to take it.

"It's for the heron chick," he says. "So he won't drown in the water."

If she hadn't already been on the ground, she might have fallen over. Even Zeke seems to think he misheard, turning the odd instrument over in his hands.

"The tube will allow air in but not water," Pollux explains, pointing to a small fixture in the top. "We can seal it with conductor jelly and break it apart once we're through."

"Thank . . . you," Zeke says haltingly. "I didn't even think about it. Aquila would have killed me if we left him."

"You've just been building a pet carrier all morning?" Lyra asks, meaning to tease him. Pollux stuffs his hands in his pockets, his shoulders slouching forward.

"Yes. The bomb is inside. I built it while you were sleeping."

Watching ripples move choppily across the surface of the pond, all the confidence she'd had in their plan begins to flicker out. Zeke's head pops up again, shaking water from his ears as he stands up. The pond only comes to his chest, but Lyra couldn't touch the bottom the last time she'd been in, depending on Zeke to ferry her to and from shore. And now she's going to get sucked down a drain that might be too small, or blocked, or just too long to hold her breath through. So many things could go wrong, and even if they made it through, then what?

She holds the air in her lungs, realizing it's whistling in and out of her nose in a panicked wheeze. Zeke trudges out of the water, his clothes clinging to his skin.

"It's a valve, so we can just force it open on this end. But I don't know how far the hose goes."

"It doesn't matter," Pollux says, standing on the edge of the bank. "The pressure bomb will create enough compression in the tube that it'll blow through the other side. We'll get pulled through." He looks down, pushing one bare foot into the water regretfully, and then the other. "I'll need you to help prop the valve open."

"Whatever you say, boss," Zeke drawls, but there's less venom in it now.

Pollux wades out, Fish's carrier under one arm and the pressure-bomb under the other. It looks more like a failed robotics project than a dangerous device to Lyra, but she reminds herself that she'd flunked out before even getting to robotics so she can't rightfully judge.

He slips a few times, shaking off Zeke when he tries to offer a steadying hand. They tread water over the drain in the center of the pond, Pollux holding the device in front of him.

"Lyra, get in the water," he says. "Remember, arms tucked, feet together."

A slimy hand of fear wraps around her stomach. "I'll just wait. I don't really want my face getting blown off."

The boys glance at each other, making her prickle with annoyance at whatever private message they're sharing.

"It's going to happen very quickly once the pipe blows," Pollux explains slowly. "There will be emergency shutoff valves so the water won't flood. We'll have a very short amount of time before they kick in automatically. It's better for you to be close."

"As soon as it blows, I'll jump in," she says, crossing her arms.

Zeke shakes his head but leaves her alone, drawing in one deep breath before slipping underwater. Pollux does the same, and the silence closes around her like a fist. Her heart beats in her ears, gaining momentum the longer the time stretches. Then their heads pop back up, blowing out breath like breaching sea creatures, and she opens her mouth to call to them.

A screaming burst of water cuts off her words, surging up from the bottom of the pond and spraying in every direction. The boys barely have time to turn their faces away from the onslaught before a funnel takes its place, sucking water down in a whirling hole the size of a human. Zeke clutches Fish's container to his chest, gasping in one more breath before he slips into the flow, his head disappearing beneath the surface. Pollux is dragged in by the force, turning to look at her as he's spun around by the pull.

His eyes go wide, and he opens his mouth just before his head slips under.

"I know, I know," she mumbles, preparing to throw herself in.

Before her step can land, she's pulled backward. Her shoulders hit the ground, a startled grunt issuing from her throat at the force of it. A presence moves over her, and for a panicked moment she sees Cygnus's face backlit above her. But then her eyes recognize the rust-colored hair, the wide nose, the freckles, though the skin beneath is nearly drained of color.

Orion's fingers scrabble at her throat, and adrenaline finally kicks through her bloodstream. She twists on the ground, keeping his hands from landing a grip as she wriggles backward. His lips pull back over gray gums that are oddly slashed and gnawed, and he presses his knee into her gut, pinning her down with the pressure.

"Tell your boyfriend he should make sure I'm dead next time," he snarls.

He lunges forward and she just manages to turn her head to miss the fist aimed at her eye. His knuckles snag against her cheek, jolting her head sideways. Despite the panic searing her skin from the inside out, the pressure of his knee sinking into her organs feels like a trespass. The unfairness of Cygnus using his weight to keep her helpless was almost the most insulting part of her memory, the same way Homer Oleyedo's tailbone had dug into her sternum as he pinned her down to spit on her face.

Without meaning to, her fingers grasp his wrist, riding the motion as he tries to yank it back. The movement knocks him off balance, giving her a blessed moment of release from his knee. She wrenches her hips sideways, and Orion tips off of her, landing on his hands.

Lyra flips over, scrambling to get her feet under her. Her muscles tense as she launches off her back foot, but her leg snags as if reaching the end of a tether and she lands flat on her stomach. Orion's fingers weave into her braid, jerking her head back until her neck seizes. A sound she's never made before rips out of her throat, a scream caught between rage and terror. His foot lands beside her head, his heel knocking her collarbone, and she manages to turn just enough to set her teeth against the skin of his calf.

She bites down hard, her jaw aching with the effort. Hairs break beneath her teeth just as they sink into the flesh, then his leg rips out of her mouth. The sound of his howl rings in her ears but she's already fighting to her feet. This time he isn't quick enough to stop her.

A sharp, metallic taste lingers in her mouth, but she doesn't stop even to spit. Her feet hit the ground so hard her shoes fly off, tumbling across the grass behind her. Her thoughts are bouncing around the edges of her mind, and she tries to gather them together as the lake comes into view. The only clear need in her head is to get to her friends. Even if it means she has to smash through the ground herself.

A drift of conversation comes back to her, and her feet stall, bringing her to a stop. When Zeke had come in from the pond, he'd said there was a drain in the lake. And now they're on the other side, maybe even able to see her right now. Maybe able to trigger the drain like they'd been waiting on Aquila to do.

She takes off again, heading straight for the lake. It's only when she reaches the edge, when her body is airborne over the still surface, that her self-preservation kicks in and she remembers the feeling of water choking into her mouth.

Cold closes over her head, dark indigo flooding into her eyes. Bits and pieces of Zeke's swimming lesson blip through her mind as she surfaces, and she tries to pull her arms through the water the way he'd taught her. She's halfway across before she thinks to look for the drain.

Her legs tip downward, water sloshing into her nose as she tries to tread in place. Twisting over her shoulder, she can just make out Orion pacing the bank, but thankfully he seems perturbed at the thought of getting in.

Lyra tries to draw in a breath big enough to hold, but her lungs are spasming so frantically it takes multiple attempts to get one down. As soon as her head goes under, she forces her eyes open.

Dark shapes move beneath her; the huge fish seem even larger now that she's floating among them. She scans the bowl of the lake, trying to pick out anything glittering or even slightly abnormal. A glint catches her eye, about halfway between the surface and the bottom.

Her head pops back up, air sweeping into her lungs, and she pinpoints the spot on the shore that the drain lies beneath. Acid is pooling in her muscles, responding to the strange activity she's forcing her body to do, but she kicks hard enough to move through the water.

Orion watches her like a lion, prowling the edge and waiting to see where she goes. Lyra pauses, realizing that she'll have to swim right up against the bank to get to the drain, maybe even reachable to Orion if he follows her. If she can't find a way into the drain, she's basically throwing herself into his grasp.

The eye of the giant hangs low in her vision, and she wonders if Pollux is there right now, watching her and silently critiquing every decision she's making. Maybe he and Zeke found Aquila, and they're scanning the station right now, looking for her.

She raises her arm out of the water, waving it over her head and sending a shower of drops over the surface.

"Hey!" she shouts, summoning every decibel of sound she's capable of. "I'm here! I'm here!"

She blinks, clearing her eyes, but there's no reaction on the mirrored surface of the control center, no movement to tell her they've seen her. Her hand splashes back down beside her, and she inhales the deepest breath yet to stoke her will.

Kicking as hard as she can, she beats her arms through the water, heading for the drain. Orion follows, moving slowly along the bank until he matches her trajectory. A disbelieving smile tweaks his mouth, and his shoulders start to shake as he watches. He's laughing at her, thinking she's given up already and come back to die.

Lyra keeps going, her breathing ragged with the effort. Two feet out from the shore, she gulps in a breath and dives. Her body wants to float back to the surface but she fights it, kicking herself farther and farther down until she's even with the manhole.

It's covered by a retracting flap that moves up when she forces it, but beneath it is a mesh sheet screwed in place. With her elbow, she props the flap open and jams her fingernail in the crosshatch of a bolt, willing it to turn. When her index nail breaks, she moves to the next one, working her way down to her thumbnails which finally get some motion.

Her lungs are screaming at her, threatening to burst, and she kicks off the wall backward, riding the float to the surface to gasp a breath of air.

Orion shouts at her, but the water muffles his words. From the red boiling in his cheeks she can guess what he has to say. Her own fury rises to meet his, and she sets her jaw, raising her hand out of the water to give him the finger with all the hatred she can muster.

He narrows his eyes at her, but before he can retaliate she dives again, reaching the flap and raising it with one fluid motion. Her fingertips seize the loosened bolts and she twists them as fast as she can with the water slowing her down. They come out painfully slow, but finally the last one tumbles free, bouncing off the slick side of the lake to sink into the depths. She threads her fingers into the mesh and drags it out, staring down the hole behind it.

It could go on forever, she finds herself thinking. There could be no way out once she gets in, no opening at the end like they'd thought.

She shakes herself, pressing her feet against the wall one last time. Pollux is the smartest person she's ever known. If this is his plan, she would bet on him ten times out of ten for the win. She kicks off, surfacing for one more breath of air.

She comes up closer than she means to, and Orion's arm snakes out just in front of her face. He's on all fours, leaning out as far as he can to reach her. A startled yelp breaks from her mouth, but she sucks in one last breath and dives. Forcing the flap open, she stuffs her body into the hole, saying a silent prayer she hasn't just killed herself.

AQUILA: 35

Her hand is starting to cramp.

She's spread her work over three screens, trying to hold all of it in her mind at once without dropping a single piece of it. It's been so long since she had to write any kind of flight plan, and there seems to be no programs for it in the Carcer system. Her father used to tease her for writing out everything by hand. To him, it was a waste of time when there were applications to do it for you.

In reality, he probably needed the programs because he couldn't trust his own compromised mind, though the thought hadn't occurred to Aquila until this moment. Maybe he'd even envied her ability to chart free-hand. Maybe he'd been able to do it when he was younger too, before he'd burned holes in his brain with petrachemicals.

A clear drop of liquid hits the screen beneath her, and she realizes her brow is sweating. She drags the back of her hand over her forehead, looking up for the first time in what seems like hours.

It's sweltering. Maybe it's the lights in the room, or maybe she set the power in the station too high. She sits back, realizing how many programs she has open at once all around the room.

"Shut down screens six through ten," she says. Half the room dims, leaving a spotlight on the desk in front of her.

She rubs her jaw, the smooth skin almost disappointing her. At least when she had stubble it gave her something trivial to worry about. The stencil is slippery in her hand, and she sets it down to stretch her fingers.

"Show orbital radar," she says, bringing up the rotating image on the hologragh projector.

Her blood stills. Had so much time really passed already?

The debris cloud is advancing, already just hours away. She stands, pushing closer to the looping map. Even though they were moving fast, she'd still been able to predict which way they would spin. That had to count for something.

A weak bleeping starts to issue from one of the screens, and she jumps back. Working her way around the room, she taps each screen until she finds the alert.

"Coolant?" she says aloud, squinting at the blinking spot on the map. "What's backup coolant?"

The map indicates an area on the subterranean level of the station. Anxiety starts to rattle around in her chest at the idea of something stupid like a leak killing them before the oncoming debris got the chance.

She picks up the screen on her way to the elevator, silencing the alarm and holding it like a plate in front of her so the map aligns to her location. Once the doors open again, she steps out of the elevator and into the hallway.

Her foot lands in water, and she jumps back. A thin layer covers the entire floor of the hall, being pulled into a few small drains that line the walkway. There's a familiar smell to it, something dank and musty that she can't place, but reason tells her it isn't dangerous.

Maybe extra condensation on one of the power cells, even though the heat around her makes that hard to believe.

Aquila holds the screen out again, stepping into the lazy flow. The closer she gets to the source of the alarm, the more the water thickens under her feet, chilling her toes. By the time she reaches the door, it's flowing out from beneath so freely that she doesn't even need the map to know which room is the culprit. Tucking the screen flat against her side, she reaches for the handle.

The door rushes aside before she can touch it. The shock doesn't even have time to set in before her eyes process the sight of Zeke's face. His eyes widen, the golden color gleaming in the light, and his hand drops away from the frame.

"You're alive," he says, swaying a bit as he takes a step back.

"Of course I'm alive," she says, her heart hovering in her chest. "Who do you think saved your ass in G-Block?"

He lifts his hand, his index just brushing her chin as worry ridges his brow.

"Your face . . ."

"It used to be worse," she offers, unable to come up with anything else to diffuse him.

The statement has the opposite effect, a deep, furious light hardening behind his eyes.

There's a clash of metal behind him, and Pollux raises up from a soaking heap on the floor. Water is cascading at a steady flow from a valve in the top corner, steam hissing from the machinery in the room, and it occurs to Aquila that this is one of the power cells keeping the whole ship alive. All at once, the water cuts off, leaving only drips.

Pollux stumbles toward her, slinging water everywhere with his sharp motions.

"Surveillance?" he demands, ripping the screen out from under her arm.

"Nice to see you too, Pollux."

"Lyra didn't make it through," he says, growing more and more frustrated when the screen can't detect his sopping fingerprints. "Orion was there. He pulled her back."

"Orion?" Zeke says, turning toward him. "Why would he stop her?"

The screen finally pulls up a camera view and Pollux doesn't answer, his eyes intent on the image. The feed is divided into ten sections, one box for each cell block, and before Aquila can even explain it he's selected H-Block and zoomed in.

"Lyra's still in the Terrarium?" she presses, willing him to answer.

He's scrolling across the terrain, past the remains of the Tect and their neighborhood, until finally a blip of motion in the lake catches his eye. Lyra's head is bobbing at the surface like a tiny piece of lint, and as they watch she waves frantically as if feeling their gaze. Then she slips beneath the choppy water.

"She's looking for the drain," Pollux murmurs to himself.

His head whips up to Aquila, his dark eyes crackling with a manic energy she's never seen in him before. "We need to flush the emergency coolant system for the other power cell."

"Right, okay," she says, pressure pricking the sides of her eyes as she tries to focus. "They wouldn't keep them together, so the next cell must be down the hall. We can probably flush it manually from inside."

Before she's even done speaking, Pollux pushes past her and veers right, running down the hall. She takes off after him, Zeke following behind after slipping on the slick floor. Pollux is already trying to force the door open when she catches up to him, and she swipes Irez's fob over the keypad. The door retracts and he tosses the screen at her as he hurries inside. She only just manages to catch it before it hits the floor, and she stifles a hiss.

The display still shows the lake surface, but another figure is patrolling the bank just feet from where Lyra went under. Squinting, Aquila zooms in.

"That is Orion," she says softly just as Zeke jogs up behind her. "What's he doing?"

"Not the real Orion," Pollux says distractedly, running his hands over the wall next to the padded silo encasing the power cell.

"What do you mean?" Aquila asks just as Zeke pushes a silky bundle of feathers into her arms.

"Fish!" she exclaims, his head cocking at the sound of her voice. He looks over her with his amber eye, the fluff on his head more ruffled than usual.

"Would have been a waste to leave him," Zeke says, the smallest hint of a smirk playing across his mouth. "He's almost fat enough to eat."

Movement on the screen draws her eye, and she lifts it just in time to see Orion swiping at Lyra's face. She screams silently, her eyes wide and terrified just before she goes under again.

"Oh my god," Aquila breathes. "I think he's trying to hurt her."

"He's trying to kill her," Pollux says, snatching the screen from her. The color drains from his face, the tension in his brow releasing to shock. "She's in the pipe."

He flings the screen at her again as he turns back to the tower of machinery in the room, throwing himself into it.

"Where has he been this whole time?" Aquila turns to Zeke. "Orion? I didn't even see him from the Surveillance room."

Zeke shrugs, opening his mouth, but a frustrated growl flies out of Pollux and they both freeze.

"Lyra is going to drown. So can you two *please* . . ." he stops, trying to catch his breath. When he raises his eyes, it's the closest thing to a normal human emotion she's seen on him. "*Please.* Help me save her."

Cold lucidity gathers around her body, and Aquila sets Fish down alongside the screen. Without another word, she and Zeke spread out, searching the room.

"The controls will look like a keypad," Aquila tells them.

"I've got it," Zeke's voice rings out, and she hurries to his side as Pollux jumps down from the machinery.

A small square box juts out from the wall, and he pulls the silicone cover from it. Beneath, a screen shows the manual controls, and Zeke's fingers hover over it, uncertain.

"Here," she says, pushing around him to select the systems program. Her hand moves deftly across the screen until she's found the right command. Without hesitating, she orders the system flush.

A valve in the ceiling clanks open, and a flood of water rains down from it in a torrent. Aquila hurries to scoop Fish up not a moment too soon, but the screen disappears under the rush. The force of it against her calves pushes her into the wall, and she steadies herself with her free hand.

"There's a grate," she hears Pollux call over the noise of the water rushing across the pipes and the steam that rises after it. He's balancing on one of the pipes closest to the flow, trying to reach into it.

Zeke pushes himself up from the ground where he slipped, climbing up alongside Pollux in the smoky haze of humidity that fills the room. The two of them reach into the downpour, their faces contorting with the effort of holding on.

Then the grate gives, flying out of the ceiling and bouncing off the floor to career out of the open doorway. Aquila turns away just in time to miss the bullets of spray shooting off it.

There's a monstrous thud in the center of the room, and three figures tumble to the ground, their forms blurred by the punishing flow of water beating down on them.

Aquila pushes off from the wall, starting to head for the control box to stop the downpour when the valve shuts itself off, cutting the flow midstream. The water level falls, rushing out through the door, and three forms are left on the ground once it recedes.

Pollux and Zeke sit up, slowly and painfully, but Lyra's small body is motionless. Pollux grasps her arm and turns her over. Her hair is pasted to her pale face, and her jaw is slack.

Zeke runs his hand over his mouth, his brows drawing together as he looks at her. Aquila takes a shaky step toward them, her knees threatening to buckle. Pollux leans over Lyra, his ear close to her blue-stained lips. He draws in a sharp breath, looking at Zeke.

"In Huygens," he says, his voice low. "Did you ever perform mouth-to-mouth resuscitation?"

"I . . . I did once, yeah," Zeke says, raising up to his knees.

Pollux tips Lyra's chin up, then measures three fingers under her ribcage, pinpointing her diaphragm with his index.

"I know the theory. Will you help me?"

Zeke nods, leaning over Lyra's face to pinch her nose shut. She looks so delicate and finely featured, almost like a doll, that Aquila starts to worry they'll break her as they take turns palpitating her chest and breathing down her throat. Her little body shakes with the force of it, and Aquila finds herself clutching Fish closer as she watches.

Lyra's foot twitches first. It looks like the kind of motion that comes right before sleep, a body trying to wake itself before it tumbles over the cliff of consciousness. A motion to bring herself back.

Her stomach tenses, and Zeke reels back as she starts to choke. Pollux pulls her to a seat and she hangs over her own legs, water spurting from her nose and mouth. Once it's all up, she coughs so hard that Pollux starts to slap her between the shoulder blades. After a few moments, her hand swipes out to smack his arm, startling him.

"Stop hitting me," she rasps, then lets her head fall into her hands. "Oh my god, my head."

"You have oxygen depletion in your brain," he says, rubbing the red mark on his skin.

"Don't call me stupid," she moans softly. Her head lifts, her bloodshot eyes landing on Aquila.

"Is that really you?" she says, her voice straining. "You're okay?"

"Yeah," Aquila says, kneeling in front of her and resting a hand on her bare foot. "I'm okay."

Lyra throws herself forward, wrapping her arms around Aquila heavily. She loses her balance and they fall sideways into Zeke, who locks them both in his grasp. It's as if they're back in the obstacle course, arms weaving together until it's impossible to tell who's touching whom. The bundle of bodies rocks sideways, and Aquila realizes Lyra has pulled Pollux in by the shirt front. He holds his elbows awkwardly out to the sides, patting them both on the tops of the heads.

When her biceps start to ache, Aquila pulls back and they break apart.

"We should take her to the infirmary," Pollux says, getting to his feet and scooping Lyra up under the arms. He sets her on her feet, waiting a moment longer when she wobbles on the spot.

"Right," Aquila says, straightening as well. "It's in the eye. We need to get to the elevator."

Pollux helps Lyra hobble out of the room, their footsteps splashing in the dregs of water. They turn the corner and Aquila starts after them. She only lands one step before fingers close around her arm and pull her back.

Zeke turns her to face him, his hand slipping around her waist to pull her into him. His arms wrap her close, her face fitting into the curve of his neck, and he takes a deep, shuddering breath.

Shock swallows her body, but then a floating sensation erupts through her, spilling along her limbs like she could lift off the ground itself. Her fingers dig into his shoulders, afraid if he lets go she might topple backward. Never has she felt comfort from being embraced like this, but in this moment, it's everything she needs.

"I thought I lost you," he murmurs, the tenderness in his voice making her pause. Guilt starts to poison her haze, and she draws back from the embrace.

"I don't remember . . . what we did," she says. "I don't remember what happened between us. I have this . . . split, in my personality. Sometimes I'm me, but sometimes I'm not me, and I think maybe . . . she's the one you actually want."

Zeke doesn't blink for a bit, trying to follow what she's saying. "Which . . . which one threw herself in the lake to save Fish?"

"That was me, but—"

"Which one helped Lyra in the obstacle course?"

She shifts her weight, crossing her arms over her stomach. "Also me."

"Which one stopped the fight between me and Cygnus on the first day? Who shared B-House with me and used to tease me about wearing my shirts a size too small?"

"Those were me," she concedes. "But—"

"So all the best parts were you. The other you was just the loud-mouth version who almost got me into a fight a few times."

Despite the ache in her chest, she fights off a snort. It's the first time she's ever heard anyone speak badly of the alter. Usually she's the one who's depressed, or weird and withdrawn compared to the more lively version.

"We didn't do anything in the tent," Zeke says, surprising her back into herself. "You . . . *she* wanted to, but it felt . . ."

"Oh."

He takes her arm in his left hand, turning the tattoos to face the light, and she notices a thick bandage wrapped expertly around his knuckles. She draws in a breath to ask what happened, but his thumb tracing her numbers sends a shiver deep through her bones.

"It's called Dissociative Identity," she says, guessing his question. "Or Split."

"That's not what I was gonna ask," he says, letting her arm slip from his fingers. "I was going to ask which version was it that wanted me?"

She opens her mouth but before a word can leave her lips, her body is thrown sideways. She and Zeke collide with the wall, their sides slamming against the unforgiving metal, then she's on her hands and knees in the dark. Almost instantly, the lights flicker back on, the power cell emitting an enthusiastic hum at the surge.

"Shit," she hisses, righting herself.

"What was that?" Zeke groans, pushing himself up to his feet.

Aquila is already out of the door, catching herself on the wall of the hallway and turning to run for the elevator. Pollux and Lyra are waiting outside the doors, Lyra leaning her weight against the wall and looking a little worse for wear.

"What just happened?" she wheezes, out of breath.

Aquila swipes the fob over the keypad and the doors pull back just as Zeke catches up to them, carrying Fish in his arms. Pollux maneuvers Lyra inside, looking over the floor selection. Just as he reaches out to touch the infirmary icon, Aquila pushes his hand aside.

"There's no time," she says. "We need to get to Control."

"Why?" Pollux asks dryly as Zeke just manages to wedge Fish and himself between the closing doors.

"There's a debris cloud off Rhea that's heading for us," she explains. "All the staff evacuated because there's a risk of us getting critically hit."

Stunned silence stretches across them, except for Lyra's labored breathing in the corner.

"The blackouts," Pollux guesses, and she nods.

"The blackouts have been small hits," she goes on, trying not to sound so sharp. "But this time around it's going to be severe."

"They evacuated and left us all here to die, probably?" Lyra demands, her voice scratching out of her throat.

"What did they use?" Pollux presses, cold-minded as ever. "Did they have emergency pods?"

"There's none left," she answers solemnly. "They took the last one two days ago."

"Can we use their communications system? Call a passing ship? Or someone on Titan?"

"Irez, the guy that was in charge of me, he said the last time the debris passed it took out their satellites. They haven't been able to comm for weeks."

Pollux lets a breath hiss between his teeth, turning away from them to tug his fingers through his short hair.

"So, that's it?" Zeke says, letting Fish hop from his hands onto the floor. "We just sit here and hope we don't get hit?"

Zeke massages the corners of his eyes, and Aquila wonders if he's having the same twinge of phantom pain she's been having.

"Why are we going to Control?" Pollux asks suddenly. His eyes are fixed on her, and her nerves begin to stir at the expectation in his gaze.

"I'm . . ." she starts, trying not to question her own sanity when hearing the plan out loud. "I'm going to try to move the station."

The elevator cab descends into a crushing silence, every face turned to her in slack disbelief. It's only punctuated by the doors finally drawing back and a triumphant bell ringing out to signal that they've arrived on their floor.

For a long time no one moves. They all seem to be contemplating just how crazy she's become, and she can feel her defenses start to rise inside her like a swirling wind. Then Zeke holds his arm out, gesturing for her to go first. "Lead on, then, boss."

ZEKE: 36

In the production plant, he'd always tried to imagine what the pieces they made would look like joined together and whole. Nothing was assembled in any large part on Titan. Everything was moved past the atmosphere in bits and pieces to be assembled by crews in the orbital stations. There was a side of him that always thought he'd try to get one of those jobs someday, just to have the satisfaction of sitting back witnessing the result of his work.

Looking out at the station from inside the eye, he can almost imagine that feeling. The greenery shocks his pupils, it's so vivid from above, but it's the architecture that strikes a deep chord in him. The way the whole aesthetic flows together, each cluster of buildings giving way to an open space, almost like a breath.

What a waste this place is. A feat of design that they've filled with people deemed too poisonous to share the ground below.

Aquila shuffles around behind him, moving screens across the table like she's piecing together a puzzle. Zeke turns away from the wall of glass, noticing a round, black ball resting on the floor. As he gets closer to it, he starts to recognize the shape of a head cast in matte black carbon fiber. Proxy drones were used all over Huygens in place of real law enforcement, and even in its disassembled state it strikes a nerve to see one.

Zeke fits his palm against the synthetic skull, lifting it off the ground and turning it face up. The center camera has been fractured, and there's a sizable knock in the smooth, black brow, but the eerie semblance of a human face is still recognizable.

"Who's this?"

Aquila looks up from her work, her gaze sweeping over the head before returning to the screen.

"That," she says. "Is the Master Chief herself. Dr. Ptolemy, maybe, if that's her real name."

She raises her brow, craning her neck up to look at him, and gestures to her chest where the letters "Pt" used to lie. Her uniform has been swapped out for a white shirt stamped with a red "I"—perhaps for infirmary—but Zeke still makes the connection.

"We are the lucky subjects of the Ptolemy Project, folks."

He sets the head down gingerly, his fingers leaving humid smudges on the matte surface.

"Do we get a prize?" Lyra says, wringing the residual water out of her braid.

Aquila grows a little more somber, plucking up her stencil to start writing.

"We maybe could have been rehabbed back into society. One day. Maybe not," she adds, looking up when a stunned silence meets her. "Basically they wanted to see if we are truly damaged goods or just . . . partially."

"The Tect," Pollux says tightly, his knuckles going white. "It was the only way out."

"The Tect was just a tool to see if we'd turn on each other," Aquila corrects. "To see if our . . . mental illnesses get in the way of us being decent humans."

An uncomfortable ripple moves through the group, a collective shame at having their secret spoken aloud. She goes back to searching her notes, Pollux hovering over her shoulder to peer at her scribbles.

"What?" she eventually snaps after bumping into him a second time.

"I'm reading," he says quietly, as if she's the one interrupting.

"You're second guessing," she quips back, stretching across the table to the holograph hub. After a few taps, a map of rotating moons around Saturn leaps into the air.

"I'm just going over your work. Don't react so emotionally."

Aquila's cheeks flush red beneath her dark freckles, and the muscles tense along her jawline. But her eyes are locked on the radar image, and the anger slowly drains away from her face.

"Goddamnit," she mumbles.

"What?" Lyra asks from her spot curled up on the floor. "What's wrong?"

"The cloud is just moving faster than I thought," she says, pulling back from the table. She glances around for a particular screen, pulling it out of Pollux's hands when she finds it.

"Where are you getting this thrust?" he asks, letting her take it.

Aquila chews the corner of her bottom lip, and a faint unease starts to slosh in the bottom of Zeke's stomach watching her expression. She pulls up a station map, though it takes him a moment to realize that's what it is. From the outside Carcer is shaped like diamond, wider in the middle then tapered to two points with a ring centrifuge around the center that is probably responsible for the sense of gravity they feel. From a mechanical standpoint, it's one of the most imposingly perfect things Zeke's ever seen.

Aquila points vaguely to a few circular divots on the sloping sides of the hull.

"There. There's always built-in thrusters somewhere for exactly this kind of situation. You can't get operational clearance if there aren't. Otherwise people would just be parking them in front of moons and raking in the insurance."

Doubt hooks into his heart, dragging it down as he looks at Aquila's face set in determination.

"I dunno," he says. "I don't think these stations are meant to move once they're in orbit. It might come apart."

"I'm not saying it's going to be pleasant," she says. "But we only need to adjust its orbit by feet. Maybe even inches."

"You're leaving very little margin for error," Pollux says, and for once Zeke welcomes his freakishly cerebral input. "Can you accurately predict how the scatter will move?"

"I don't have to predict it. It's happening now." She draws in a steadying breath, smoothing the hair from her forehead. "I've been watching it for hours. I've been able to factor in all the orbital pulls so far. I just need to put us in the right spot."

Although none of it makes sense to Zeke, Pollux doesn't offer any objections, which seems like a good sign.

"How do you know all this stuff?" Lyra says, her voice ragged and shaken by her shivering. She's looking warmer and more colorful with every passing minute, but Zeke has seen the effects of chemically treated water in the lungs come back to wreak havoc even weeks later. The way her breath is rattling gives him a skulking sense of foreboding he doesn't want to look in the eye quite yet.

"My dad flew Eagle Convoys," Aquila says. "We used to have to do course corrections like this all the time."

"If you push us too far we could start spinning," Pollux finally weighs in.

She crosses her arms, her eyes icy. "I won't push us too far."

"Why didn't the people who work here move it, if they could," Zeke asks, the question nagging at him. "Seems a lot less expensive than leaving a whole station to explode."

"Because they're wardens, they're not pilots," Aquila says, frustration mounting in her tone. "They're scared as balls and they aren't trained to do any of this. I am trained. And I can do this."

A soft rustling sound, like the start of a rain shower, fills the space around them. Zeke is trying to hone in on the source when the screens all start to chime in unison, an identical pop-up alert displaying across them.

Aquila lifts the closest one, and Zeke reaches for a screen himself, wedging it from its stand. The sound stops, but the alert continues to flash in threatening orange tones.

Hull pressure under stress.

"Under stress?" Aquila huffs, her jaw tight. "Thanks for summing that up."

"What's that noise?" Lyra says, bracing one hand on the wall behind her, her body going rigid like a frightened rabbit.

"It's the dust field preceding the debris," Pollux says, bending forward to study the moving radar map. It only shows a few seconds of motion at a time, then resets, and every time the scattered spots of color move closer to the dot on the map that represents Carcer.

"I need to do this now," Aquila says, the stencil falling from her hand. "Everyone strap in because this is going to suck."

When no one moves, she lifts her arms to the sides, looking around the cabin.

"I wasn't joking. Everyone get in a crash seat, it's very dangerous."

The three of them break into motion, Pollux pulling Lyra to her feet as Zeke searches the wall for an emergency icon. He finds one in between screen stations on the wall and pulls down a folding crash seat. It's little more than a stiff board with a harness at the back and an oxygen hood, but after the few times he's been tossed around by the smaller bumps, there's no reason to risk it. He settles in, strapping the harness over his chest.

Aquila lines up her screens with the complicated algorithm continued across them. She perches at the head of the table, her fingers moving fast over the keyboard as she inputs her code. When she reaches the end, her hand stalls over the enter key. Her dark brows pull together, her eyes clouded with doubt.

"Hey," Zeke calls out. It may be his imagination, but it seems as if the sound around them has risen to a steady storm.

Aquila looks up at him just as the sound of alarms start to chime again, filling the small space.

"Save our sorry asses, rich girl," he says.

For a moment, she almost laughs. Then her face settles, and she brings her finger down. It takes a few rounds of confirmations and inserting the fob she's been carrying around into the keypad, but the system accepts it. She turns and rushes for her own crash seat, barely getting her arms through the harness before the station shudders all around them, a giant taking a waking breath. Pressure crushes Zeke into his seat, and a collective groan escapes each of them.

"It's okay, it's just the station moving," Aquila growls, her hands tangled in the harness she didn't quite get on.

A metallic howl picks up around them, Carcer itself screeching and rattling as its mass is displaced. An unseen weight flattens him, and it feels like his very bones are being forced together. His lungs struggle to inflate, every organ compacted inside him. He can only imagine what's happening to the others down below with nothing holding them in place.

Then the worst of the pressure lifts, his stomach jolting back into place. The screens are all erupting in alerts, and Aquila struggles out of her seat to reach the table. Her legs buckle under the remaining force of motion, making her path jagged as if she's walking on a boat.

She catches herself against the lip of the table, her face reflected with the orange light of the alert in front of her. The holograph flushes orange as well, an image of the station appearing in place of the radar.

"Shit," she says roughly, reaching out for the keyboard. "The counter thrusters aren't priming."

Zeke works the harness over his head, slowed by the fact that his arms feel twice as heavy as they should.

"Which means?" He presses.

"We'll spin," Pollux says loudly, watching Aquila frantically page through her notes. "We'll lose control of the trajectory."

"Only if we tilt over fifteen degrees," she responds coolly, but the hard collection of her voice doesn't fool Zeke. "They're just rusty. It's not like they've been used since they put the station in place."

Lyra coughs once, rolling her head toward Zeke and fixing him with a pointed stare.

"Isn't that what you do?" she asks dryly. "Like, for a living?"

It takes Zeke a moment to catch her drift, but then the reality of the situation forms in his mind. He's a mechanic, and right now the station is one big, injured machine. He steps out of the crash seat, shifting his weight heavily onto his feet.

"I can go look at them," he says. "Where are they?"

Aquila shakes her head, panic swelling in her eyes like a storm cell. "If we start to spin you can't be moving around the station."

"I'll go with him."

Pollux is peeling off his harness as well.

"Pollux, be careful," Lyra orders, but he's already staggering toward the center console.

He picks up a screen, prying it from its holder.

"You'll have to write a new protocol for the adjusted tilt," he says to Aquila, who waves him off like a bad smell.

"I'm already starting. Use their messenger system if you need to comm me. It's internal."

"Or you can text us on the modes," Zeke says, dragging his feet under the weight.

Confusion wrinkles her forehead, but she stays bent over the new notes she's drawing out.

"I don't know how to do that. I only figured out how to send locations."

Even with the pressure pinning him to the spot, surprise drops through his body. He stumbles back a step, his heartbeat quickening. Aquila is busy scrawling, stopping every few seconds to scrub a number away with the edge of her hand. Pollux trudges heavily up to him, gesturing with the screen.

"Let's go, we have to hurry."

They make their way out into the hallway, heading for the elevator at their painfully lagging pace. The further they get from Control, the quieter the alerts fade, leaving them in an eerie, static silence filled with the slight rushing sound of dust enveloping the station outside.

The elevator doors close, and Pollux selects the base level. It sounds like the cables work a little harder than usual, a sharp twang in the normal rumble.

"The messages didn't come from Aquila," Zeke says aloud, slouching against the wall in an attempt to lessen the load on his spine.

Pollux sinks to the floor, his face twisting with discomfort.

"Don't worry about that now," he groans.

He knows something you don't.

The deep voice rises in the back of his mind, making him wonder if he's been imagining the static the whole time.

He's working with the prison. Has been this whole time.

"That's not true," Zeke says aloud, heat boiling up in his blood.

Pollux's dark eyes lock onto him, maybe trying to pry meaning from his face. The constant pressure on his body is doing nothing to calm the cortisol coursing through him, and the lid on his mind is loosening. He can feel the dark fingers of other presences unfurling inside him.

Pollux's discomfort is clear, wanting to pretend Zeke isn't unravelling right in front of his eyes. Just like his mothers had always pretended. They'd kept brushing over it, too dependent on using him as the foundation of the family to admit he was crumbling. And then, when he'd truly gone too far to return, they'd abandoned him, convinced he was too broken to fix.

Any second now, Pollux will do the same.

He's going to push you out of a trash shoot the first chance he gets, the deep voice whispers. *The only reason he wanted to come was to get you alone.*

The doors open, and he rolls up to his feet, thankful for any distraction. Pollux follows a few feet behind, watching him with that unwavering gaze.

Don't turn your back on him.

"Can you walk up front?" Zeke says loudly over the rattling of the outer hull. They're closer to it here, and he can almost feel the void of space beyond like a prickly energy. The whole time they've been in Carcer he's managed to avoid thinking about the black, deadly expanse surrounding them. His mind pastes an image over reality of a gaping hole opening up in the sidewall, blinking in and out of existence as he stares at it.

He's gonna push you out, the raspy voice says.

What's your brain going to taste like when it leaks out of your nose?

His left knee buckles under the stress of walking, and his shoulder knocks into the wall. The floor beneath him turns into a single pane of cracked glass, the dark maw of space waiting outside it. He squeezes his eyes shut, cutting the vision short.

You're going to die here.

Die here, the raspy voice seconds.

They've been waiting for the chance to take you out since you got here.

"Zeke," Pollux's voice states, though he can't tell if it's outside or inside his head.

"We have to keep moving. It'll only get harder," he goes on. "Stand up."

Stand up so he can kick you out of the station like he kicked the prisoner into the wall.

"Shut up!" Zeke bellows, his voice shaking in his throat.

"Zeke," Pollux says again, his voice steady above the rest. "If you know anything about me, it's that I don't care about providing you comfort. I wouldn't lie to you. So believe me when I tell you there is nothing in this hallway."

His veins flush with adrenaline, his heart squeezed between swelling muscles.

"I don't think I can do this," he says, though his own voice is unfamiliar in his ears.

"You're the only one of us with mechanical experience. You're the *only* one who is equipped to do this."

Zeke curls his fingers around the pipe he's landed on, his breath fast. The chatter in his head is overlapping, making it impossible to pick out one voice.

"Okay, let's switch tactics," Pollux says. "If we don't correct, the station will spin until it falls apart. That is the very real situation we are in. Is that decent incentive to address the imaginary issues later?"

Zeke forces his eyes open, pushing himself to his feet. "Just show me where it is."

Pollux, who had sunken to a knee in front of him, stands and turns back toward the unfurling hallway. They pass a pair of field boxes adhered to the wall and Zeke stops to read them. The top is the emergency kit, labeled with a glowing red cross, and the bottom shows two green hammers forming an X. He pulls the second one free with his good hand, tucking the patch kit under his arm. Every hazardous facility had some version of the same kit, meant to repair holes or leaks quickly. Hopefully there's something useful in this one.

Pollux stops, checking the map on the screen, then touches the wall to his right.

"It's here, on the other side."

He squats, running his fingers over the paneling. A few toggle switches line the aisle runner, and he flips the first. A pressurized puff of air hisses out, and a square of wall retracts to show the opening of a duct. Zeke tries to shake the vision of a tongue lolling out of it, like they've opened the mouth of some tunnel creature.

"There's a conduit behind this."

Zeke kneels beside him, dropping the kit to the ground and opening it. A hood with a clear face mask sits on top, and Pollux lifts it out curiously. Beneath it a few tools are lined up, bookended by two tubes with snap-off tops. A pair of electrical gloves are rolled in the corner, and he works them onto his hands. The nub on his left hand leaves the finger floppy, but he can still make a weak fist.

The mask in Pollux's hands comes to life, lighting up blue and emitting a high-pitched frequency. He peeks inside, his fingers spreading the stretchy fabric at the neck.

"Oh," he says, something clicking in his brain. "It protects from embolisms, in case the hull is breached while you're inside. For a short time, at least."

He holds it out to Zeke, who works it over his head. The skin-tight fabric squeezing his throat sends another round of panic flooding through his body, but he busies himself with loading the tools into his good hand. The blue light inside the mask casts a cool glow over everything, almost like being underwater, and he lets the notion calm him slightly. Two sets of numbers in the right side of the mask tick up and down with each breath, measuring the oxygen he's getting. At least he'll have full warning before his lungs explode inside him.

He peers down the duct, which is little more than a crawl space. It only goes a few feet before it dead ends.

"Once the door seals behind you, my guess is that these toggles will open and close the lock doors in the tunnel," Pollux says, flipping the other switches back and forth with no reaction.

"You're gonna seal me up in a mystery tunnel," Zeke says, sitting back. His voice is muffled inside the mask. "What if it just blows me out into space?"

Pollux reacts like it's the dumbest question he's ever heard, his eyes narrowing and his hands coming up.

"Why would that exist? What would be the purpose of having something so dangerous?"

Zeke grinds his back teeth together, unwilling to let it go. "Trash ejection."

"This is a maintenance tunnel. There just may be less oxygen because it's in the outer shell of the station," Pollux says firmly, locking him with his gaze. "I wouldn't send you into danger."

"I'm not doing it for you, boss," he drawls, leaning forward to lower onto his elbows. "All the same, I'd appreciate it if you don't let me die."

Pushing off his toes, he starts to shuffle into the tube. The top of his head touches the wall blocking the end, and he notices the groove around it where it's meant to retract.

"Okay," he says, his breath filling the mask for a moment.

There's a shudder by his feet, and he cranes his neck to watch Pollux disappear on the other side of the closing wall. Air floods the duct, re-pressurizing the space, the only light a dim blue glow from his mask. A long moment stretches out, and he starts to run through every curse word he knows as the whispering swirls around the tight space. Then the door in front of him shoots aside, opening the conduit ahead. From his restricted view, he can just see a drop-off at the end and strings of tubelights running vertically through the wall beyond.

Crawling through the tunnel with the added pressure of the station moving is like dragging himself through the thickest mud. When he finally reaches the edge, his head pokes out into the outer shell. Cold grips his skull, and his fingers ache as he grabs the grip bar over the opening.

He pulls himself free, his foot finding the rung below. The space between the hull and the inner shell is an arm's length, and the noise here is almost deafening. He glances up, taking in the curve of the hull that goes on for miles above him.

Just a thin sheet of metal and your death on the other side, the deep voice coos in his ear.

His breath is steaming up the inside of the mask, the defogger unable to keep up with his hyperventilating. He pivots, looking around until he sees the thick cylindrical tube that reads "secondary thruster" in luminescent letters beneath him.

He climbs a few rungs down, his movements choppy in the freezing air. Throwing his leg over, he winces at the icy sting on his bare skin, but shifts his weight onto the dense structure. The panel on the top opens easily, and he pulls out the wires inside.

The bundle is covered with sticky gray clumps, maybe a chemical buildup from the casings freezing and melting several times over. It smears off under his thumb, revealing frayed wires beneath. A sloppy connection job that left a strand out.

The mechanics probably never thought they'd be using thrusters on a stationary object. Why take the time to connect them meticulously?

"Now I know it's a Gekko," he allows himself to chuckle.

He unscrews the connector caps, moving to pop them between his lips for safekeeping before realizing he can't. Instead, he tucks them into the rim of his shoe, trying not to look down at the drop below.

You should have a safety line, the raspy voice caws. *Why would he send you in here without one?*

"He didn't send me. I volunteered," Zeke responds aloud, trying to distract himself from the sound of moon rocks hitting the hull behind him.

He strips the rest of the gunk from the wires, using the clippers to cut the damaged heads. Peeling back the rubber casing exposes new strands on each end, and he starts twisting them into the home connectors.

A particularly loud thud makes him jump, and he hazards a glance over his shoulder. It may be another hallucination—the dim lighting playing tricks on him—but he could swear there's a new bump in the metal far above him.

His fingers are moving too slowly, each motion taking an age. Pain chews at the end of his amputated knuckle, making it hard to hold the wires together while he screws the caps back on. Finally they snap into place, and he hurriedly stuffs the bundle into its box.

As he reaches for the cover, the culvert beneath him lurches, the station giving one massive shudder. His legs slide out from under him, and his weight drags him over the side.

His wounded hand catches the lip of the panel opening, a shard of lightning shooting up what's left of his finger. The panel cover clatters into the depths below him, his dangling feet swinging over the fall.

Shakily, he hooks his ankle onto the ladder rung, wrapping his arms around it as he shifts over. His heart pulses in his chest, spreading his ribs with each beat, and he races up the rungs back to the opening of the tunnel. Threading his legs into the hole, he scoots backwards as fast as he can in the restricted space. When his heel hits the far wall, he stomps against it, tucking his head into his chest as the door ahead of him starts to close.

Then the hallucinations envelop him and he's in the throat of a monster, its steamy breath all around him, about to swallow him down. He claws the sides, his knees knocking its flesh, and he struggles.

He starts to slide, and it's only when he pops out in the hallway that his vision clears and he realizes Pollux has pulled him out by the feet. He hits the toggle over Zeke's head, sealing the door in place.

Zeke wrestles the mask over his head, the sweat on his face cooling instantly as he gasps in a breath. Beside him, Pollux types furiously on the screen, signaling Aquila to restart the program she's designed.

He drops the screen sharply, hooking his elbow through the nearest banister and grabbing a handful of Zeke's shirt.

"This is going to be unpleasant," he says, just as the station begins to howl around them.

The weight that's been holding Zeke down doubles, squeezing the air from his lungs like a foot pushing him down. The aisle starts to tilt beneath them and he feels himself slide, his shirt going taut in Pollux's hand. Before it can rip under his weight, he reaches above his head for the bar, and not a moment too soon.

The station lurches downward, dropping the ground out from under them, and they both land heavily after a moment of unnatural hovering. Metallic thuds clap the walls around them, smaller debris dinging off the hull outside, and it occurs to him that this might actually be the final moment of his life. And for once, his mind is oddly clear. It's almost as if the voices and the corrupted parts of his mind sense the end is near and have abandoned ship in the last few remaining seconds. All he can think about is the pump of his lungs filling and emptying from one breath to the next.

They roll into the near side of the wall, and almost immediately the pressure begins to lift from his body. He's been pressed down for so many minutes that the release makes him feel like he might float off of the floor. He grips the banister, too disoriented to stand.

Pollux stretches for the screen, which came to rest in the center of the hallway. When he pins it with a finger, he hauls it toward him, typing in something Zeke can't see. His head rolls back in relief against the wall.

"She did it," he says, letting the screen fall off his thigh.

The station radar is pulled up again, and Zeke watches the scatter-shot debris slice all around the mass of Carcer.

He can't pry his eyes away until the last trailing bits have moved on, and the rustling of the dust across the hull has faded. By that time his back is aching and Pollux has fallen asleep with his head tipped back. Zeke rolls onto his shins, reaching out to give Pollux a shake.

"Hey," he says when Pollux's eyes open. "It's over."

Pollux presses his fingertips into his tired eye sockets.

"Excellent. Now we have to decide how we're getting off this death trap."

POLLUX: 37

In true Lyra fashion, she doesn't want to stay in the infirmary a moment longer than necessary.

Pollux could have lingered for at least an hour, taking inventory of all the equipment in the med bay. It's one of the few rooms in this station that's actually serving the purpose it was designed for, and the life monitoring instruments built into the very beds themselves are a fascinating novelty.

Zeke calms a bit after a shot of Lidocaine and a dose of Moxifarin, though Pollux can't help but notice the sudden twitch in his neck at a voice none of them can hear. Watching Zeke stuff his pockets with Moxifarin, Pollux finally feels they've put off the obvious question long enough.

"Does anyone have a useful idea about how to get off the station?"

It's almost humorous the way all three of them tense in unison, wanting to put off the inevitable.

"Well," Aquila sighs, leaning back against the counter between the medicine storage cabinets. "I had one. The Ptolemy director's floating head said she was close enough that she didn't need a satellite relay. It made me think maybe there's another station nearby that we could hop to."

"With what, though? Didn't they take all the pods?" Lyra says, resituating herself on the bed beside Pollux. She hasn't been able to sit still since getting into the infirmary, which at least is a positive sign that she's feeling more like herself.

"When we were still in H-Block, someone was sending us messages on the mode cuffs," Zeke says. "You think that could have been her?"

The news surprises Aquila, making her bony frame go rigid. "What kind of messages?"

"Just . . . nudges to get back to our cellblock when you were rebooting the fences. We might not have made it in time without them."

"I don't know. It could have been her," Aquila admits, shaking her head. "Regardless, she might be the only one with something we can use. I think we should check out the Special Projects wing and see if we can find anything of hers. If she has her own proxy drone, she may have all kinds of fancy crap. Maybe even a private transport somewhere close."

It's a thin hope, but Pollux has nothing better to offer. Based on the trajectory of the debris storm, it'll pass Titan within a day, which means they have hours to come up with something that will get them off Carcer before the staff start returning. It's a problem Aquila had already identified; when he'd looked through her notes she had an entire screen dedicated to predicting how long the storm would be over Titan, grounding any aircrafts that might come their way.

Aquila and Zeke stalk out of the infirmary, and Pollux starts after them before realizing Lyra is lagging behind. When he turns back to her, she's squinting at him, a look he's learned means she's working through a problem in her head.

"You forgot your violin," she says, sadness slowing her words. "I just realized."

He pushes his hands into his pockets, letting his shoulders relax. "I only had time to make the carrier for the heron chick."

Her head tilts, a smile warming her mouth. "You saved a life instead of saving something of value to you. That's disturbingly close to compassion."

"Well. Value is a relative term," he says, flustered at the idea of making a decision based on emotion.

"Be careful," she says, hopping onto her feet and striding past him. "Hanging out with dangerous street people is changing you."

There's a hint of amusement in her tone that makes his lips tug upward, and he follows her into the hall. Her presence near him is such a balm to his ragged nerves that he finds himself plagued by the thought of its absence. Her pale, bloodless face after she came out of the pipe had sent a splinter deep into the heart of him, and he can still feel traces of the wound.

His hand snags her wrist, swinging her around, and she blinks in surprise.

"I . . ." he starts, suddenly unsure of what he wants to express. The brown of her eyes is so warm and alive with the flicker of fire she carries around inside her that he's nearly crippled by the idea of it being doused forever.

"I'm glad you didn't die," he finishes.

Lyra makes a face like she's suppressing a laugh, but to her credit she keeps it down.

"Well," she says, touching the back of his hand. "Back at ya."

The four of them take the elevator down, Aquila unlocking the gate to the Special Projects wing. They pass rooms heralding the names of rehabilitation for addiction, anger management, and even a program dedicated solely to inmates born on the dark side of Titan.

When they reach the door marked the "Ptolemy Project," he's almost underwhelmed. While the other programs had expansive rooms, meant to hold teams of people, the space dedicated to their project is little more than a repurposed office.

Aquila uses her fob to open the door, and the room automatically floods with soapy tubelight. It's small, less than half the size of the Control room, and meant to be occupied by one person. One extremely disorganized person.

A single screen station is set up in the corner, and the remnants of compostable food containers in various states of decay are scattered across the desk. A slightly more comfortable office chair faces the back wall, and notebooks of handwritten lines are strewn around it. Picking one up, he's struck by how much the project manager must have spent to get real paper, and how slow and methodical their writing would have to be to write so many volumes by hand.

Aquila has been studying the back wall, the only one not obscured by cabinets or furniture, and the more he looks at it the more he begins to think it's deliberately been left clear. Aquila has locked onto the same observation, and finally she spots a projection hub on the floor. At her touch, the back wall fills with images of H-Block: their houses, inside and out; the courtyard; the lake. Half the squares toward the bottom are filled with blackened rubble, their screens greasy, and it strikes him that they must be the cameras from the Tect.

"Gross," Aquila says, narrowing her eyes at the images. "I knew they were watching us, but this is so much more . . ."

"Creepy and personal?" Lyra finishes for her, raising her hand to swipe some hair away from her eye.

The video images minimize, shrinking into the far left corner to reveal a desktop beneath.

"Oh whoa, it's one of those fancy interactive ones," Lyra says, waving her arms above her head and making a selection light dance around the files.

Aquila steps in front of her, pointing to one of the folders. It opens, unfurling a litany of titles all starting with "Pt Batch." Aquila rolls her wrist, scrolling down to the bottom before her elbows drop slightly.

"And there we are," she says, selecting the final file. "Pt Batch 17."

Tiles with moving images of their faces spread across the screen, though they're hardly recognizable. Each one is a mugshot, taken against a plain gray backdrop, each of them looking straight ahead with vacant, defeated expressions. Their eyes dart around like startled fish, unsure of where to focus. It takes a moment for Pollux to remember there had once been eight of them, at the start.

"Wait," Aquila says, getting closer to the screen. The projector follows her intent, zooming in on the unfamiliar pale face of a boy with black hair. "The name says Orion, but that's not him."

"No," Pollux agrees, sinking into the chair and breaking open the notebook in his hands. It's filled with tightly written script he can barely read. "The real Orion either died or was killed the first day. Another prisoner crossed into H-Block when the walls were down and hid the body. Most likely he attempted to kill the girl with vitiligo to cover his tracks. That's when we found them."

"Lacerta," Zeke inserts, checking the empty minifridge on the far side of the room.

"Great," Aquila says, dropping her arms. He can sense her attitude toward him turning prickly, her eyes cutting. "How long have you known that little nugget?"

"It's not just his fault," Lyra says guiltily. "We found the real

Orion's body and we didn't tell anyone. I didn't want anyone to try to confront him and get hurt."

"I had the same thought," Pollux says, flipping through the pages aimlessly. "That's why I went back after the fire and bound him with ropes made from sheets."

The room around him is quiet, and eventually he lifts his head to see all of them watching him.

"Clearly he escaped," he says, assuming they're waiting for an ending to the story.

"You were just going to leave him tied up somewhere?" Aquila says, shrugging sharply. "Forever?"

"I assumed starving to death would be an ironic end for a cannibal."

"I think you mean fitting," Lyra says quietly, climbing into the observation chair next to the projection hub.

Aquila turns to face the screen, pointing to open the file with Pollux's face. Zeke straightens, taking a step closer.

"What are you doing?"

"Irez told me Pollux is the only one of us who'd been in the system before. He called him a danger to the other inmates. I just want to see how accurate that is."

Lyra's mouth draws into a line, but she doesn't protest. Unease sparks in his stomach as Aquila flicks through the files. She lands on a video, spreading it to fill the wall.

Pollux, his hair long and curling over his face, stands behind a pane of clear glass. His hands are locked into the stand at his waist, and two guards flank him. It's his court hearing, though he can't remember this moment. Off screen, a judge with a shrill, irritating tone questions Pollux about the night Castor had attacked him. Pollux gives the account, his voice tired and rehearsed as if he's already told the story a hundred times. The assessors mount their own questions, each one already framed to condemn him no matter how he answers.

Aquila crosses behind them, going to stand with Zeke in the back of the room. Lyra watches unblinkingly, her first knuckle pressing into her lips.

The footage skips sections, always remaining trained on Pollux, and the idea takes root in his mind that it isn't official footage. This was one of the observers in the courtroom, though for the life of him he can't remember a detail about the day. Not a face in the crowd, or wisp of the emotion he'd felt.

"Pollux Dimitri Crane," the judge states at last. "We, the Court of Titan, United States Outer Colonies, based on the evidence provided by the prosecution and the defendant's own account, accuse you of the murder of Wallerie McNeal, Tabitha Real, Regina Booth, and Castor Crane. How do you plead?"

"I plead not guilty," he says, his voice shallow in the recording.

"Pollux," Lyra says, drawing his attention from the video. Her eyes narrow like she's struggling to see him clearly. "Did you really kill all those girls?"

It would have been understandable had she looked at him with the same fear and horror his mother had, or the lawyer who had pretended not to have an opinion of the crimes leveled against him. But she doesn't. Her expression seems to be one of confusion more than anything else. As if the information doesn't stick when she tries to pin it to him.

"I did not," he says.

"Yeah, but he definitely killed his brother," Aquila grumbles in the back of the room, dipping closer to Zeke who's watching with his typical stoic expression.

"In self-defense," Lyra says, twisting to glare at her.

"Lyra," she sighs, as if Lyra's marked the wrong answer on a test when she should know better. "He definitely enjoyed hurting other inmates once he got here. The project manager told me the only reason they had him in Ptolemy is because he needed to have a distraction."

"You think you know him so well?" Lyra says, lifting slightly off her chair on the balls of her feet. "Do you want to see a real monster?"

She pivots back to the screen, minimizing the video and sorting through the files to find her own.

When the footage loads, Pollux is surprised to see her in the trial stand, looking almost childlike in stature compared to the guards flanking her. Her hair is loose, short bangs growing into long waves, the color fading to an umber orange at the ends. She probably found comfort in the color, like her hair was being slowly consumed by an ever-burning fire, and he thinks back to the box of dye that had been her reward at the last Tect challenge.

As the judge speaks, her frame is taut, but he can see a tremble in her interlaced fingers. He rattles off the court speech meant to be recorded for their own records, and when he pauses before the charges, Pollux looks over at the real Lyra beside him.

Her hands cover her face, fingers resting across her eyes, but he can see the tension in her body as she listens to what she already knows.

"We, the Court of Titan, United States Outer Colonies, based on the evidence and accounts provided by the first responders and witnesses, find Lyra Marina Mullen guilty of the murders of Vesta Mullen, Auriga Mullen, Ursa Mullen, Sagitta Mullen, Norma Mullen and Sao Mullen."

Each of the names seems to wound Lyra further, and she curls forward in her seat to rest her forearms across her knees, head hanging.

On the screen, the fiery-haired Lyra draws in a breath. "I didn't mean to."

Somewhere unseen in the crowd, a woman gives a strangled cry, and by the reaction it gets from both Lyras, Pollux guesses it's her mother. He stands, using his hands to stop and clear the video.

"Have you made your point?" he says, turning to Aquila. "We're all criminals here."

She stays silent, her thin arms folded across her chest. Pollux turns back to the screen, searching out Aquila's face in the lineup.

"Do you remember who you killed?" he asks, watching her eyes widen in dread. "Has it come back to you yet?"

"Hey, back off," Zeke says, taking a few steps forward. "If she doesn't want to see it, you can't make her watch it."

All the softness in him is gone in an instant, and he's just a ball of tense muscles ready to fight.

"Guys," Lyra says, standing slowly and raising her arms. The screen they'd taken from Control is balanced across them, and an orange alert is throbbing in the bottom corner.

"What is it?" Aquila says, walking forward to take it from her. She taps the alert, and the station map springs up under her fingers. The tension drains from her face, her throat contracting in a strained swallow.

"Someone just entered the dock."

Pollux grabs the screen from her, looking over the message.

"Is it the Carcer people?" Zeke asks, moving closer.

"It shouldn't be," Aquila says, running her thumb along her jaw nervously. "The debris cloud is between Titan and us for the next thirty some-odd hours. No one would try to fly through that."

"Maybe they didn't go back to Titan?" Lyra says, creeping closer to the circle. "Maybe there's another station, like you said?"

Pollux manages to find the video feed from the docks, opening the image of an empty loading harbor.

"There's no one there," he says, holding it out to them.

Aquila leans closer, peering at the screen.

"No, look," she says, pointing to the third berth. "That door is open. There's a ship docked."

"Could it be one of the pods?" Lyra asks, hope lining her voice. "Could you fly it back to Titan, Aquila?"

"If it's a pod, I wouldn't have to," she answers. "They're pre-programmed. But maybe . . . maybe I can manually land it somewhere else."

"There's probably a thousand protocols for landing on Titan that we can't fake, boss," Zeke says. "Especially when we're taking a prison transport pod. They'll know we're prisoners before we even get close."

"One thing at a time," Lyra says. "If there's a chance to get off of Carcer, we have to take it. Right?"

She looks at Pollux, her shoulders lifting. Misgivings immediately line up in his mind, too many unknown variables to even organize.

"The chances of this working are really low," he says, getting a frustrated huff from Lyra in response.

"If these *are* Carcer people, they're going to know we're missing the second they check Surveillance," Zeke puts in. "They'll lock down the station, if they haven't started already. If we're going to try this, we need to do it now."

Aquila's jaw tightens, and her eyes slip to Pollux. As much as they disagree, there's a similarity between them that he can't deny, especially in the presence of Zeke and Lyra. Two cold, calculating minds against two warm-hearted people who make decisions based on incomprehensible "gut feelings."

"Maybe we should try," he offers, noticing how Lyra's eyes gleam from just the smallest scrap of hope. Every step of the way so far has been chance tied to luck, their group simply swinging from one opportunity to the next with minimal planning. Why should this be any different?

"If we're going, let's make moves," Zeke says, snatching the heron chick from the floor where he'd gotten into an old container of rice.

He and Aquila turn for the door, and Pollux glances at Lyra. She seems to be in a trance, her gaze locked ahead. He reaches out to wave a hand in front of her face, and she pins him with a glare.

"What?" she snaps.

"Are you having second thoughts?"

She breathes out, diffusing a little. "No. I just . . . whatever happens, I want to stay together. All of us."

Her face is bunched up in that determined look, and in that moment he almost believes she could change their future by sheer force of will.

"Let's go," he says, reaching for the door.

They meet the others in front of the elevators, and Aquila swipes her fob to call the cab to their floor.

"When we get to the docks, let's go left," she says, turning to face them. "There's a sort of alcove we can hide in until we know for sure the docks are empty. The cameras can't see into it."

Lyra nods, and Pollux keeps silent, which he's sure Aquila will appreciate more than an answer. Zeke is gazing at her with a softness in his face, and it's a wonder to Pollux how disarmed the hardened convict became in her presence. As if he's forgotten that Pollux and Lyra are there, he reaches out to move the hair from Aquila's neck, and she turns to look at him. The doors pull open, and for a moment, none of them move.

Three men in ragged, mismatched clothes fill the elevator. Each holds a handle to the largest weapons Pollux has ever seen. From the look of them, they're Army grade, yet the weathered, grimy men wielding them are the farthest they could get from Army.

They seem to be just as surprised to see four beaten, uniformed teenagers standing in front of them. But their surprise only lasts seconds.

They snap into motion, each changing the grip on their weapon to aim at them, and they erupt in garbled, guttural shouts. Pollux snaps into action, grabbing Lyra by the back of the shirt and shoving her down the hall just as Zeke and Aquila break in the opposite direction. Pollux lifts his hands in surrender, hoping being the largest of the four of them will assign him the most attention.

The men stream out of the elevator. Two of them circle Pollux with their barrels trained on him, but the third turns to aim at the retreating backs of Zeke and Aquila.

"No!" Pollux shouts just as the man fires off a round. The sound bursts in his ears, and Zeke tumbles forward onto the ground, the heron chick flying a few feet in the air to flap down. Aquila slides to a stop, hurrying to his fallen form just as he rolls onto his back, grimacing in pain.

The air vacates Pollux's lungs, and he doubles over as the man in front of him plants a knee in his stomach.

"Hey!" Lyra's furious voice barks out, and she appears beside him. Her foot whips out, kicking the man hard in the shin and getting a sharp grunt out of him. Then he straightens, his fist popping forward to catch Lyra across the mouth. She disappears from view so quickly Pollux barely has time to blink, then they're dragging him backward into the elevator.

Lyra is on the floor, struggling to sit up as blood splashes onto the tiles beneath her. The man closest to her grabs her arm and pulls her to standing, tossing her into the elevator. The assailant behind Pollux kicks the back of his knees, bringing him to a kneel.

The smaller man with a tight black beard walks to the front of the cab to block the door, spreading his legs wide. The one who'd hit Lyra skirts around him, rubbing his shin once before stalking off in the direction Zeke and Aquila had run.

Anger crackles in Pollux's chest as he turns to Lyra. "Why didn't you run?"

She raises to her elbow, blood from her broken lip streaming over her chin. She scowls at him with the most fury he's ever seen from her.

"What did I *just* freaking say to you?" she seethes. "We stay together. No matter what happens."

The other two men return, one nearly lifting Aquila off her feet with his grip on her arm, the other with Zeke slung over his shoulder and the heron chick flapping frantically in his grasp. Zeke gets lowered far more gently than Aquila, though even the smallest movement makes him groan through his teeth.

After studying the bird for moment, the man tosses it into the air to land next to Zeke's pained form.

"They shot him," Aquila says, her eyes never leaving the strangers. Even though her face is set in a frigid glare, there's the smallest tremble in her bottom lip. "He can't move his leg."

Zeke's forehead is shining, his mouth twisted in silent agony. Pollux yearns to turn him over, get a look at the wound and what damage it's done.

The men mutter to each other, and he recognizes enough words to know they're speaking Russian. One of them appears to be the leader, the thickest of the three who'd shot Zeke, and he listens to his partners argue without looking away from his victim. Eventually, he nods, and the compact blonde man reaches for a bundle of wires where the button panel used to be. It's been torn off, a small mode screen attached by wires fed into the cables. As he works, Pollux notices his left eye is covered with a contoured patch, and he can't help wondering what hides beneath it. The blonde taps a few times and the doors close too quickly, reacting to the hotwiring, and the cab starts to drop to the floors below.

"Who are these people?" Lyra spits, clearing the blood from her mouth. "Are they guards?"

"I don't think so," Pollux says slowly, taking in the mishmash of gear they have strapped to them. They don't seem to belong to any official organization, no insignias or brands anywhere on their clothing. Even their weapons aren't the same manufacturing, each one different from the other.

If anything, they're looters. Following the wake of the debris storm now that it's spread enough to cause damage. They probably have no idea they've stumbled into a prison full of deadly criminals.

The doors open on the docks, and the black-bearded man waves the gun over them, bellowing commands they can't understand.

The leader stoops to lift Zeke, slinging him over his shoulder again, and Aquila jumps to her feet.

"Where are you taking him?" she demands, following as he steps out of the elevator and tucking the heron chick inside her jacket.

Pollux stands, Lyra climbing to her feet beside him, and he holds his arm out to shield her.

"Stay behind me," he says quietly, and she scoffs.

"Says the guy I just saved from a beating."

The bearded man shouts something Pollux takes to mean "stop talking," and gestures for them to walk forward. They shuffle out of the cab, moving across the stained dock floor. The leader walks through the third door onto the ship that lays beyond it, and Aquila turns over her shoulder to look at them before the blonde closes his hand around her elbow to pull her forward.

"Shit," Lyra whispers, her breath shaky. "They are fully kidnapping us."

"Most likely for ransom," Pollux adds.

"What are they going to do when they find out we're criminals and no one wants to pay for us?"

Pollux doesn't answer, forcing one foot in front of the other all the way across the platform. He steps over the door jamb, Lyra following close behind.

Through the door, the ship opens up to a massive, circular flight deck. Seats line the wall, though they're little more than tricked-out crash seats. A few others dressed in the same inconsistent civilian clothes are propping Zeke up in one of the chairs, Aquila settling next to him. A woman with a braid long enough to rival Lyra's gives him a Lidoshot in the thigh, and his contorted brow relaxes slightly.

They put Lyra and Pollux next to Aquila, motioning for them to strap in. After they've pulled on the harnesses, the blonde with the patch motions for them to hold their hands out, and he starts to bind their wrists together with thin cables. Noticing their mode cuffs, he fishes in his pocket presumably for something to cut them with, moving off to the higher deck when he doesn't find it.

Another pair of bulky, ill-assorted Russians drag a body through the doors, dumping it onto a seat on the other side of the room. The smaller of the two works cables around its limp wrists while the other reaches out to tap its face, and Pollux's stomach seizes as he recognizes the dark smattering of freckles.

Orion. Somehow, he'd followed Lyra through the pipes, though from the look of it, the journey had taken its toll. He'd heard stories about how long Huygen's Landers could hold their breath, but even by those standards, Orion had completed a feat.

The pair of Russians move away, leaving Orion slumped and harnessed in the crash seat. As he watches, Pollux notices the smallest flicker of movement behind Orion's pale eyelids.

There's a flurry of activity through the deck, the crew calling to each other as the doors start to close. A few minutes later, a metallic groan vibrates through the walls, and the thrum of the engine shakes their feet.

Pollux looks over at Zeke, whose head is lolling back against the seat; at Aquila trying to steady him as she surveys the crew; and Lyra, who keeps wiping roughly at her split lip and lifting her chin like it's a badge of honor.

"Well," he says, drawing their attention. "I think that worked perfectly."

The girls peer at him for a long moment before looking at each other.

"At least he's mastered sarcasm," Lyra says.

"Yes," Aquila agrees. "Thank the stars for small favors."

Turn the page for a sneak peek of

THE
PROMETHEUS
PROGRAM

DIONE: 1

The sky over Huygens Landing is on fire.

At first, Dione thinks one of the chemical plants has gone up. The light that pulses through her window is sickly and red, and her eyes pick up the difference before she's even sat up. She pushes to her elbow, fear battering against the inside of her ribs as her brain is ripped from sleep.

She pushes open the small window of her room, bracing for her nose to fill with the acrid smell of smoke, but nothing reaches her. The sky is a bleeding shade of red, the clouds so thick they almost seem to beat like a heart.

Debris from something is falling on them, something big. The atmosphere is making quick work of turning it to dust, but there's enough of it that it's poisoning the atmosphere above them. She'd seen it once before, when a project at the Gekko station had been demolished.

"Remember that?" she almost says aloud to her brother, who should be in the bed across from her. "Remember when they just dumped their trash on us and thought no one would notice?"

He'd loved to talk about Gekko. He liked to pretend it was a single entity with a mind and will, like an annoying local at the bar he could badmouth. But he couldn't answer now.

Dione rams the window back in place, taking a few tries to get it all the way down. When she turns back around, the room is hazy with a fine mist of airborne dust, and she growls quietly.

She marches through the cloud to the closet alcove, sifting through the hanging drawers until she comes out with the least crusty shirt.

Her mothers are both jammed in the small breakfast nook downstairs, their legs tangled together beneath the table. It would be romantic had Dione not just heard them arguing the night before, meaning it's less of a game of footsie and more a silent turf war.

"Did you see the starfall?" she asks, grabbing a bottled coffee from the fridge. "I think something big is coming down."

Mama Beck makes a half-interested grunt as she chews, nodding. Mama Rie's radiant blue eyes flick over Dione curiously, as if she's trying to work out a hidden meaning. Dione can't blame her; she's been feeling particularly prickly these days, starting fights whenever she sees the opportunity.

Her long hair catches in the fridge door as she closes it, further stoking the fire in her belly as she pulls it free.

"You're going to get that stuck in a wheel one day," Mama Buck says, raising an eyebrow at her. "Take your scalp clean off."

"I like her hair," Mama Rie tosses back without looking at either of them. "Makes her stand out."

Dione fights an eyeroll, wishing again that she could look across the kitchen to exchange mutual exasperation with her brother. Their parents would bicker all day long if they could— it made for more passionate make ups. Dione can't decide which she hates more.

There's a thump against the opaque window over their sink, making her jump.

She sets down her bottle, walking sharply to the glass to see if she can catch a silhouette of the culprit. "Is there a riot?"

"I think I heard the anti-Earth people were in a fuss over something yesterday in the plants," Mama Buck grumbles, leveling her gaze at her partner as if trying to tease out a response. Mama Rie doesn't disappoint.

"Anti-subligation," she pouts.

"It's 'subjugation,' Mama," Dione says wearily. Her mother's heart is in the right place, even if she's borderline illiterate.

"Who's being subjugated?" Mama Buck pushes. Clearly her morning caffeine is late kicking in, leaving her in just a foul-enough mood to want to goad Dione. "I don't see anyone in this room without food, a job, or a roof over their head. There's a hefty few on Earth that would kill for that."

"I would argue they subjugated you when they kicked you off for petty crime," Dione drawls, pivoting to face the table. "But that's just me."

"Nobody got kicked off of anything," Mama Buck says, her deep eyes unblinking. "You're starting to sound like the Colony of Criminals guy."

Dione inhales deeply, preparing to launch into yet another lecture, but a pulsing gleam of light on the wall stops her in her tracks. She surges toward the home screen next to their kitchen table, leaning over Mama Buck as she goes and getting a scoff of annoyance.

"You didn't tell me we got a message!" she barks, fingers jabbing the screen until it comes up.

"Dione, it's nothing," Mama Rie says, her voice pained.

Ignoring her, Dione scans the top line, feeling her heartbeat in the base of her throat. "It's from Community Authority."

Before she's even reading properly, her eyes are searching out any mention of the name she so desperately wants to see and landing on nothing. It's not a response. It's merely a Community announcement that a shipment of new clothes will be arriving later that day.

Disappointment threads through her like lead in her veins, weighing every part of her down. She steps back, determined not to cry from frustration.

"I told you . . ." Mama Rie says gently. Even without looking, Dione can feel the charged blue of her mother's eyes on her face.

In the moment when she's expecting fury to flood through her, to be saved by the distraction of her own acidic rage, the only thing inside her is a cold stone of loneliness between her ribs. The vacancy her brother left is a constant presence, even now in this kitchen — in the space on the counter he'd usually occupy, in the balance of power between her mother and her, in the mesh of their voices that bounces off the walls. The emptiness is so vicious that she has to force herself to move rather than be swallowed whole by it, and she whips across the room to where her Mode is resting on the counter.

"Tell them I'm sick," she says over her shoulder to her mothers. "I'm going to the Consulate."

Behind her, Mama Rie makes a sharp, pained sigh.

"Dione, let it go."

Dione rounds on them, graciously letting the fury take the place of her sadness as it rises inside her.

"You can give up, that's fine," she snarls at Mama Rie, who wilts a bit, but Mama Beck has perfected the ability to act like she doesn't hear things she doesn't like. "You can say he was a lost cause because that makes you feel better. I know you can't look at yourself and admit that all he needed was a hug and instead you gave him a knife."

"Your brother was sick, and he needed help we couldn't give him," Mama Rie tries, her musical voice dampened with guilt. "It was better for him to not be here."

"Better for you," Dione spits, wrestling her stiff canvas jacket off the back of the chair. "Easier to pretend like you couldn't help him when you didn't even try."

Mama Beck snaps finally, pushing back from the table. "Di, quit."

"Nope, won't do that," Dione says, lifting her chin as she shrugs on her uniform jacket. She's going to look ridiculous where she's going, but she can't help being a Lander, and she will not be brushed off this time. "I will get him back though. I will bring Zeke home."

POLLUX: 2

The irony is that Castor spoke Russian.

As Pollux listens to the mismatched scrappers warble and cackle to each other, he can't help but wonder again if it was always meant to be Castor in his place. If he had been the one meant to die that night in their fort.

But when his gaze falls on Lyra, the thought blinks out of existence. If it were Castor here, Lyra would most likely have been one of his victims. And even in his most self-punishing fantasies, Pollux can't allow her to come to harm.

The cut on her lip, the bruising on her cheek, weigh on him like an imbalance he has to set right.

And he will set it right, he decides as his glare turns to the man who'd inflicted the wounds on her.

After the initial jolts of movement from detachment, the ship settles into a smooth coast and the crew unbuckles from their crash seats. Something inside Pollux stretches, as if a part of him is still attached to Carcer behind them. He rolls the feeling around his head, trying to find a definition for it. Carcer was a prison, but a prison he had inhabited for years. It was the place he had met Lyra and the others, where he had started to change. Maybe leaving it at last is creating some form of nostalgia he hadn't anticipated. Or perhaps it's the complete incomprehensibleness of it. As soon as he'd realized what Carcer was and the memories began to trickle back in, he'd accepted the glaring truth that there would be no escape. No return to normal life. And yet here they are, being carted away from the most secure prison that may have ever existed.

This group—Lyra, Zeke, Aquila, himself—something about them together was a special set of variables that could shift the unshiftable. And that terrified him. Perhaps Carcer had been the last stable, predictable thing in his life, and his rational mind felt him slipping into chaos the further he got from it.

Eventually, the sound of the engine shudders to a faint hum, the ship slowing until the motion is nearly undetectable. The crew all unbuckles, going back their business. Pollux watches the woman with a braid who'd dosed Zeke with painkillers hurry to the chair where Orion is slumped. Somehow the cannibal had managed to swim through the pipes to escape the Terrarium in Carcer, the same way they had.

Pollux had always heard people from Huygens Landing were born swimmers, trained to hold their breath underwater for logic-defying amounts of time. But from Orion's state, even that may not have been enough.

The woman—the on-board physician by his guess — checks Orion's vitals, lifting one of his eyelids to test his pupil reaction. From the narrow hallway beside her, another crew member rolls out a medical stretcher. The two of them load Orion's sagging body onto the board, carting him back down the corridor.

The large man he takes to be the leader steps into Pollux's sight-line, propping his fists on his hips.

"I think it is time for a small talk, o-kei?" he says, his English thickly coated in a Russian accent.

"Our friend needs treatment for his gunshot wound," Aquila says, her eyes boring into him. She still has one hand on the back of Zeke's head, holding it up as if he might slump over when she lets him go.

The man twists, shouting in Russian over his shoulder, and a moment later the pair return with the stretcher. Aquila unbuckles herself, standing to help them move Zeke, and Lyra and Pollux follow suit.

Once Zeke is horizontal and strapped in, they start to cart him off in the same direction as Orion. The man ticks his head at them, indicating they follow.

Pollux obliges first, feeling Lyra follow, and Aquila eventually starts to move when two more scrappers crowd her from behind. The man leads them across the flight deck, pushing his mass through the narrow hallway until they descend a small, twisting staircase.

"There's a saying for this," Pollux says to Lyra, sifting through his mind for it. "Moving from one dilemma to another."

"Is it 'out of the frying pan and into the fire'?" Lyra grumbles miserably.

"That's exactly it."

She deflates a bit, her shoulders slouching. "My mother used to say that."

Seeing her spirit dragging so violently is rather upsetting. For better or worse, her emotions are always explosive in one direction or another. She is capable of holding an inferno inside her at all times, but it's as if she's been doused and is smoldering in a dying breath.

"Don't be sad," he tells her, then wonders if it's a good time to reach for her hand the way she occasionally does for his.

Her eyes lift, pink-rimmed and full of tears.

"Pollux," she whispers, her forehead furrowed as if she's in physical pain. "They're going to separate us. Don't you get it?"

Before he can tell her that it would simply be a strategy if they did, nothing to be upset over, the stairs bottom out and a large room opens up before them. The large man rounds on them, halting their motions, and the two other scrappers fan out to block their exit. They don't need to bother, and the fact that they are so desperate to show their control irks Pollux. Three untrained, fatigued teenagers would have no chance overthrowing a whole ship, and even if they did, what would the outcome be?

"O-kei, let's talk," the large man says.

He crosses his arms, his mouth soft as if he might be coaxed into a smile at any moment. Pollux can't tell whether he likes this man or whether he's the kind of dog that bites without warning, and he's pretty sure the ambiguity is intended.

"My name is Kresnik, it is my ship, and you now belong to me. O-kei?"

No one answers, which he takes as agreement, and Pollux is thankful Zeke at least is unconscious. He would most certainly have found an issue with that.

"You are crew now. We saved you, so now you owe me debt of life. I will allow you to work it off."

Lyra scoffs softly, and Pollux winces. Of course she isn't going to let that go without a fight.

"We already survived the debris," she spits. "You didn't save us from anything."

"So you know everything, huh?" Kresnik snaps, widening his

stance. Pollux has to smirk internally at that. A man of his size reduced to posturing by one tiny girl.

"You know what's outside this ship, then?" he goes on, directed at Lyra. "You know what happens if we decide you're not worth the food to keep you alive and we toss you out?"

Lyra chews her bottom lip, her eyes blazing as she stares at him, but she thankfully keeps silent.

"To be clear, I am your friend," Kresnik starts again, back to his smooth tone. "I want to get you home safely. We just need to make a few stops. So you will help us by earning your keep. Then, we will take you to Titan."

"Where you'll ransom us," Aquila says quietly, and he turns, noticing her to his left. She lifts her chin a bit as his gaze falls on her. "To be clear."

He looks at her for a long moment, seeming to be tallying up something in his mind. Finally, he twists back to the group.

"Yes."

He strides to the stretcher where Zeke is laying, issuing a stream of orders in Russian to the phys standing beside it. Pollux notices the faint lines that form between his eyebrows as he looks at Zeke, the way his mouth pulls into a line. Was that guilt?

The phys nods and starts to push Zeke off down the hall. Instantly, all three of them tense, their eyes snapping to each other's. It doesn't go unnoticed by Kresnik.

"We help your friend," he says, raking his fingers over the back of his neck. "He stays in our Med Bay until he can walk."

So it is guilt. Maybe not quite the hardened criminal he's portraying himself to be. He turns back to Pollux, Aquila, Lyra and the thug holding her.

"Your friend with the green shirt is already there."

"He's not our friend," Lyra fumes, realizing he's talking about Orion. "He's —"

"Lyra," Aquila cuts her off, her eyes severe. It saves Pollux the effort of trying to tell her to stop talking, which she'd like a lot less coming from him.

Clearly, this crew wasn't aware Carcer was full of criminals no one would pay ransom for. Keeping them in the dark about that fact might be the difference between life and death.

"Thank you for helping our friends," Aquila hedges, looking over Kresnik. "How can we repay you?"

"You three, you will work until we take you home," he says, getting back on track. "Earn your place. What can you do?"

Silence stretches across the hall. Eventually Kresnik loses patience and flaps his arms as if to stir responses out of them.

"Surely you're not all completely useless."

"I can help in the Med Bay," Pollux volunteers. "Our friend who was shot is trained in mechanics. The girls can cook and clean," he finishes, gesturing to Lyra and Aquila.

Both of them glare furiously at him, and he wonders how he could possibly have offended them. They're much less likely to be supervised in menial jobs, giving them more opportunity to come up with a plan. It especially behooves them to hide Aquila's intelligence for now, lest she become a person of interest.

He's also not too keen on them doing jobs that expose Lyra to the crew. He's already seen a few pairs of eyes wander over her, though he's not sure if they aren't in worse danger of her retribution should they try to touch her. A smile stirs at the edge of his mouth as he remembers how hard she'd kicked him when he'd try to grab the skinplant on her collarbone the first day they'd been paired. It seems so long ago now.

"O-kei," Kresnik says, clapping his hands together and turning to the two scrappers flanking Aquila. "Put the boys in 4B and the girl can sleep in the kitchen,"

Realizing what he's insinuating, Aquila's face grows stormy. "I'm not a boy."

"Down there, you are," he shoots back, waving a hand at her lower half.

"No, I'm not," Aquila growls, and Kresnik suddenly becomes very still.

His hand shoots out, grabbing Aquila's thin arm in his vice of a grip and hauling her toward him. His other hand fumbles with the bottom of her shirt, yanking it up, and she catches on to what he's trying to do.

Aquila sets back, digging her heels into the ground and pulling away with all her strength, but Lyra is already flinging herself on Kresnik in a screaming, furious fit.

"Get off her!" she screeches, kicking him hard in the kneecap before the blonde man seizes her from behind, gathering her up in one swoop. Her feet continue to strike out at Kresnik as she's hauled away, and she gets in one more satisfying hit to his tight torso.

He grunts, letting Aquila's arm slip from his grasp.

"'Tchyo za ga`lima . . ." he mutters to himself, running a hand over his stomach. "Put them all in 4B, I don't care. You," he says, taking a step closer to point at Lyra, who's still fuming in the blonde's arms. "You make trouble, you get a muzzle."

Kresnik turns sharply, heading down the tight hallway past Aquila. He pauses to study her as he passes, as if he's just noticed something.

"This one," he says, turning back to the blonde. "Watch her. Ona umna v glazakh."

And just like that, Pollux's plan to give Aquila freedom is shot. He catches her eye, hoping his disappointment in her behavior is apparent, but she shrugs aggressively as if daring him to speak.

Kresnik's footsteps clamp up the stairs as his form disappears, and the blonde drops Lyra heavily on her feet.

"Come," he says roughly, weaving through them to lead them down an offshoot hall.

Pollux goes first, the girls following, and the other two Russians bring up the rear. The hall dips down to another staircase, and they curve down the steps to the floor below.

It's a storage floor, freezing cold and lit by dingy, brown overhead tubelights. The ceiling is so low that Pollux has to duck under the doorways as they're led to the last door on the right. The blonde hits a pad on the outside of the frame and the covering retracts, making a terrible metallic screech as it goes.

He steps back, nodding for them to go in.

The room is sparse and small, with a bunk on the far wall and another cot running along the side. A sink and a shower and carved into the adjacent wall, and the entire space smells like wet clay. The three of them trail in hesitantly, spreading out to form a triangle. The blonde is resting his arm on the massive weapon hanging off his shoulder, and the nonchalant way he handles makes Pollux think it might not be loaded. Only Kresnik had fired his gun in Carcer, perhaps it was because he was the only one with live ammunition.

The man is letting his gaze flit over Aquila with a mixture of shyness and curiosity, trying to steal glances when he thinks she isn't looking. He catches Pollux staring at him and clears his throat in a forced show of indifference.

One of the women who'd been trailing after them pushes through the door with a bundle of clothes in her arms. She drops them in the center of the room and a few tumble off the top. Pollux recognizes the logo of a popular MobileDevice manufacturer on one, and briefly wonders where the clothes came from. As soon as the thought drifts in, he shakes it away. He knows the answer, and it would certainly upset the girls if they haven't already figured it out.

"Yours," the woman says, gesturing to the pile before squeezing back out through the narrow doorway. The blonde follows her after a moment, moving slow as if to communicate he doesn't trust them alone.

But they are. Alone. And away from Carcer.

Aquila folds forward until she's squatting on the ground, resting her elbows on her knees as she cradles her head. Lyra lets out a short breath of release, tipping her chin up as her eyes start to well.

"What the hell is happening?" she whispers, her voice coarse.

"We've been taken hostage," Pollux starts to explain, but she slants her furious glare at him and he halts.

"I think Zeke might be paralyzed," Aquila says without looking at them. "But even if he's not, how can we do anything while he's hurt like that?"

"We can't," Pollux levels. "We'll have to see the extent of his injuries before we can make a plan."

Lyra kicks at the pile of second-hand clothes. "So we're just a different kind of prisoner? We're trapped here?"

Pollux bends to pick up one of the clean T-shirts in the pile: plain white fabric with an unknown insignia on the chest. Something in him hesitates when he goes to tug off the Carcer uniform shirt. It's filthy, caked in sweat and grime and musty from the water in the pipes, but there is a familiarity to it.

"It would appear so," he answers Lyra finally, though minutes have gone by since she asked the question and he's not sure she wanted an answer in the first place.

He sinks onto the bed, looking at her in all her fearsomeness. She's dirty and blood-stained and unapologetic, but she's alive and she's here, and that's the most hopeful notion he's had since this whole ordeal started. "Welcome to our new home."

ACKNOWLEDGMENTS

I am so lucky to have incredible sisters, two of which created Wyrd Sisters Editing. I'm eternally thankful for Aubrey's many brainstorming sessions, for Shea's meticulous and tireless proofing, and for Kelsi's encouragement and inspiring creativity.

I'm beyond humbled to have had the advice of the great Fairy Queen, author Francesca Lia Block, and my cousin, Autism Education specialist Whitney Davidson.

Thank you to my guides who were with me every step of the way, and to Gala Darling for showing me how to use magic every step of the creative journey. The road was not easy, but if you are magically minded, you know that rejection is really just redirection.

I am forever in debt to the brave souls who leant me their stories to create this book. Thank you to Chuck, Katie and Annapurna, for being so open and honest with me about your internal worlds. You have my eternal admiration for what you go through, and I hope that by sharing your struggles in some small way, other's might realize they're not alone and change the very fabric of society around mental illness.

ABOUT THE AUTHOR

Kate St.Clair (or K-Saint) is a writer in Austin, Texas. Her books *Spelled* and *Cursed* both received *Moonbeam Children's Book Awards*, and she was named *Best Young Author* in the *IPPY Awards 2014*. She now breeds Black Swallowtail butterflies and runs barefoot through the woods on full moons.

katestclair.com
Instagram: @kate_st_clair
Twitter: @kate_st_clair

To inquire about booking Kate St.Clair for a speaking engagement, contact Amber at Ozwin + West, amber@ozwinwest.com.